UNQUIET

A NOVEL

LINN ULLMANN

TRANSLATED FROM THE NORWEGIAN BY
THILO REINHARD

HAMISH HAMILTON
an imprint of
PENGUIN BOOKS

HAMISH HAMILTON

UK | USA | Canada | Ireland | Australia
India | New Zealand | South Africa

Hamish Hamilton is part of the Penguin Random House group of companies
whose addresses can be found at global.penguinrandomhouse.com.

First published in Norwegian as *De Urolige* by Forlaget Oktober 2015
First published in English as *Unquiet* in the United States of America by W. W. Norton & Company 2020
First published in Great Britain by Hamish Hamilton 2020

001

This translation has been published with the financial support of NORLA
Translated by Thilo Reinhard

Printed and bound in Great Britain by Clays Ltd, Elcograf S.p.A.

A CIP catalogue record for this book is available from the British Library

ISBN: 978-0-241-46461-8

www.greenpenguin.co.uk

For Hanna

I

HAMMARS PRELUDE

A map of the island

. . .

The only maps and charts
he had to go by
were remembered or imaginary
but these were clear enough.

—JOHN CHEEVER, *"The Swimmer"*

To SEE, TO REMEMBER, TO COMPREHEND. It all depends on where you stand. The first time I came to Hammars I was barely a year old and knew nothing of the great and upheaving love that had brought me there.

Actually, there were three loves.

If there were such a thing as a telescope that could be trained on the past, I could have said: Look, that's us, let's find out what really happened. And every time we began to doubt whether what I remember is true or what you remember is true or whether what happened really happened, or whether we even existed, we could have stood side by side and looked into the telescope together.

I organize, catalogue, and number. I say: There were three loves. I am the same age now that my father was when I was born. Forty-eight. My mother was twenty-seven, she looked both much younger and much older than her years back then.

I don't know which of the three loves came first. But I'll begin with the one that arose between my mother and father in 1965 and ended before I was old enough to remember anything about it.

I have seen pictures and read letters and heard them talk about their time together and heard other people talk about it, but the truth is you can never know much about other people's lives, least of all your parents', and certainly not if your parents have made a point of turning their lives into stories that they then go on to tell with a God-given ability for not caring the least about what's true and what's not.

The second love is an extension of the first and concerns the lovers who became parents and the girl who was their daughter. I loved my mother and father unconditionally, I took them for granted in the same way that, for a while, one takes the seasons for granted, or the months or the hours, one was night and the other was day, one ended where the other began, I was her child and his child, but considering that they, too, wanted to be children, things sometimes got a little difficult. And then there's this: I was his child and her child, but not *their* child, it was never us three; when I browse through the pictures lying spread out on my desk, there isn't a single photograph of the three of us together. She and he and I.

That constellation doesn't exist.

I wanted to grow up as quickly as possible, I didn't like being a child, I was afraid of other children, their inventiveness, their unpredictability, their games, and to make up for my own childishness, I used to imagine that I could split myself and become many, turn myself into a Lilliputian army, and that there was strength in *us*—we were small, but we were many. I split myself and marched from one to the other, from father to mother and from mother to father, I had many eyes and many ears, many skinny bodies, many high-pitched voices and several choreographies.

The third love. *A place*. Hammars, or Djaupadal as it was
known in the old days. Hammars was his place, not hers, not
the other women's, not the children's, not the grandchildren's.
For a time it felt as if we belonged there, as if it were our place.
If it's true that everyone has *one* place, although I suppose it
isn't, but if it *were* true, then this was my place, or at least more
mine than the name I was given; it didn't feel uncomfortable
to wander around Hammars the way it feels uncomfortable to
wander around inside my own name. I recognized the smell of
the air and the sea and the stones and the way the pine trees
hunched in the wind.

To name. To give and take and have and live and die with a
name. One day I would like to write a book without names. Or a
book with lots of names. Or a book in which all the names are so
ordinary that they are immediately forgotten, or sound so alike
that it's impossible to tell them apart. My parents (after much
back and forth) gave me a name, but I never liked that name.
I don't recognize myself in it. When someone calls my name, I
duck as if I've forgotten to put on clothes and only realize it once
I'm outside with people all around me.

In the autumn of 2006 something happened that I've since come
to think of as a darkening, an eclipse.

The astronomer Aglaonike, or Aganice of Thessaly as she
is also known, lived long before the age of the telescope, but
could, with her naked eye, predict the precise time and place of
lunar eclipses.

I can draw down the moon, she said.

She knew where to go and where to stand, she knew what would happen and when. She reached for the sky and the sky turned black.

In "Advice to Bride and Groom," Plutarch cautions his readers against women like Aglaonike, calling them sorceresses, and instructs new brides to read, learn, and keep abreast. A woman who masters geometry, he argues, will not be tempted to dance. A well-read woman will not be lured into folly. A sensible woman schooled in astronomy will laugh out loud if another woman tries telling her it's possible to *draw down* the moon.

No one knows exactly when Aglaonike lived. What we *do* know, and what even Plutarch acknowledged, never mind the condescending comments he made about her, was that she was able to predict the exact time and place of lunar eclipses.

I remember exactly where I stood, but lacked the ability to predict anything at all. My father was a punctual man. When I was a child, he opened the case of the grandfather clock in the living room and showed me its mechanics. The pendulum. The brass weights. He expected punctuality of himself and of everyone else.

In the autumn of 2006 he had less than a year left to live, but I didn't know that then. Nor did he. I stood outside the white limestone barn with the rust-red door and waited for him. The barn had been converted into a cinema and was surrounded by fields, stone walls, and a few scattered houses. A bit farther off lay Dämba Marsh with its abundant birdlife—great bitterns, cranes, herons, sandpipers.

We were going to see a film. Every day with my father, except Sunday, was a day with film. I've been over and over it, trying to remember which film we were seeing that day. Maybe Cocteau's *Orphée* with its leaden dream images? I don't know.

"When I make a film," Jean Cocteau wrote, "it is a sleep in which I am dreaming. Only the people and places of the dream matter."

I have thought about it again and again, but can't remember. It takes several minutes for the eyes to adjust to the dark, he used to say. Several minutes. Which is why we always arranged to meet at ten to three.

That day my father didn't show up until seven minutes *past* three—that is, seventeen minutes late.

There were no signs. The sky didn't darken. The wind didn't tug at the trees and shake them. No storm was brewing and the leaves didn't swirl in the breeze. A nuthatch flew over the gray fields and off toward the marsh, other than that it was quiet and overcast. Not too far off, the sheep—referred to on the island as *lambs*, regardless of their age—were grazing as they always did. When I turn and look around, everything is the same as usual.

Pappa was so punctual that his punctuality lived inside me. If you grow up in a house near the railway tracks and you are awakened every morning by the train roaring past your window, by the trembling of walls, bedposts, and windowsills, then, even when you no longer live in the house by the tracks, you will be awakened every morning by the train hurtling through you.

It wasn't Cocteau's *Orphée*. Maybe a silent film. We used to sit in green armchairs and let the images, unaccompanied by piano tinkling, flicker across the screen. He said that when silent films disappeared, a whole language was lost. Could it have been Victor Sjöström's *The Phantom Carriage*? It was his favorite. *For him, a single night is as long as 100 years on Earth. Night and day he must carry out his master's business.* I would have remembered if it had been *The Phantom Carriage*. The only thing I remember about that day at Dämba, apart from the nuthatch over the field, is that my father was late. This was as impossible for me to comprehend as it was for Aglaonike's followers to comprehend why the moon should so unexpectedly vanish. The women who, according to Plutarch, were unschooled in astronomy and allowed themselves to be fooled. Aglaonike said: *I draw down the moon and the heavens turn dark.* My father came seventeen minutes late and nothing was out of the ordinary and everything had changed. He drew down the moon and time went out of joint. We had arranged to meet at ten to three, it was seven minutes past three when he pulled up in front of the barn. He had a red jeep. He liked to drive fast and make lots of noise. He had big black bat-eye sunglasses. He offered no explanation. He had no idea that he was late. We sat through the film as if nothing had happened. It was the last time we would see a film together.

———

He came to Hammars in 1965, forty-seven years old, and decided to build a house there. The place he fell in love with was a deserted stony beach, some gnarled pine trees. He was overcome by an immediate sense of familiarity, he knew this was his place, it echoed his innermost ideas of form, proportion, color, light, and horizon. And then there was something about the sounds. "Many a man erroneously thinks he sees a picture whereas he really hears it," Albert Schweitzer wrote in his two-volume work on Bach. Of course, there is no way of knowing what my father saw and heard that day on the beach, but this is when it all began, that is to say, this is not really when it began, he had been to the island five years earlier, maybe that is when it began, who knows when something begins and ends, but for the sake of order I will say: this is where it all began.

They were shooting a film on the island, it was his second shoot there, and she who will be my mother played one of the two female leads. In the film, her name is Elisabet Vogler. Over the course of the ten films they make together, he gives her many names. Elisabet. Eva, Alma, Anna, Maria, Marianne, Jenny, Manuela (*Manuela*—that's when they made a film together in Germany), and then Eva again, and then Marianne again.

But this is the first film my parents make together, and they fall in love almost immediately.

Elisabet, unlike my mother, is a woman who stops talking. Twelve minutes into the film she lies in bed, entrusted in her inexplicable silence to the care of Nurse Alma. Her bed stands in the middle of a hospital room. The room is sparsely furnished. A window, a bed, a nightstand. It is late evening and Nurse Alma, having introduced herself to her patient, turns on the radio, switches between stations, settles on Bach's violin concerto in E major. She exits and Elisabet is left lying alone.

In the middle of the violin concerto's second movement the camera finds Elisabet's face and stays on it for almost one and a half minutes. The image grows darker and darker, but it darkens so slowly that you hardly notice it, or at least not until it is so dark that her face is barely visible on the screen, but by then you have been looking at it for so long that it has become imprinted on your retina. It is your face. Only then, after one and a half minutes, does she turn away from you, exhale, and cover her face with her hands.

First, my eye is drawn to her mouth, all the nerves in and around her lips, and then, because she is lying down, I tilt my head so that I can look at her face directly. And when I tilt my head, it feels as though I am lying down beside her on the pillow. She is very young and very beautiful. I imagine I am my father looking at her. I imagine I am my mother being looked at. And even though it's growing darker, her face seems to light up, to burn, to dissolve right before my eyes. It's a relief when she eventually turns away, covering her face with her hands.

Mamma's hands are slender and cool.

———

One evening, my father took his cinematographer to a place he had spied out. Maybe I could build a house here, he said, or words to that effect. Yes, but wait, said the cinematographer, come with me a little bit farther and I'll show you an even nicer spot. When you walk along the beach, the way they did that day in 1965, you won't reach the end of the road, there is no headland, hill, clearing, or precipice, no geographic or geologic formation to indicate a change in the landscape; there is stony beach as far as the eye can see, nothing begins or ends. It just continues. If this spot lay in the woods and not on a beach you could have said that my father had been taken to a place in the middle of the woods and that it was here, right here, that he decided to build a house. The two men stood there for a little while. How long? Long enough, or so the story goes, for my father to have *made up his mind*.

If one were being pompous, one might say that I had finally come home, he said, *and if one were joking one might talk about love at first sight.*

I have lived with this account of home and love all my life.

He came to a place and claimed it, called it his own.

But language got in the way every time he tried to explain why things had turned out the way they did, and he always ended up with: *If one were being pompous, one might say that I had finally come home, and if one were joking one might talk about love at first sight.* But what if one were to use one's regular voice? Not too loud, not too soft, not to convince, not to seduce, not to make fun, not to move? Which words would he have chosen then?

So, how long did he stand there? Between pomposity and jest, between home and love? Had he remained standing there for too long and thereby noticed his own awe, noticed that he was giving it a name—home, love—the urge to shake his head and keep walking would surely have made itself felt. *I detest emotional sloppiness and bad theatre.* Had he remained standing there too briefly, chances are he would not have let the place *get to him* and consequently decided to devote his life to it. A few minutes,

maybe. Long enough to hear the wind in the already wind-bent
pines, the wind in his ears, the wind in his trouser legs, the peb-
bles under the soles of his shoes, his hand fiddling with coins in
the pocket of his leather jacket, the oystercatcher's shrill, Morse-
like *biik-biik-biik-biik*. I picture my father turning to the cinematographer and saying: Listen to how quiet this place is.

First, love. An intuitive certainty. Then a plan. There will be
no improvising. No. Never improvise. Everything has to be
planned down to the last detail. She who will be my mother
is part of the plan. He will build a house, and she will live in
the house together with him. He takes her there, shows her the
spot and points and explains. They sit on a rock. Actually, I
think she's the one who says, *Listen to how quiet this place is*. He
wouldn't have said it, not to her, not to the cinematographer.
There were a thousand sounds on the island. Instead, he turns
to the woman who will be my mother and says: *We are painfully
connected*. She thinks it sounds nice. And a little unpleasant. And
confusing. And true. And maybe a little bit corny. He was forty-
seven, she was more than twenty years younger. In due course,
she gets pregnant. The film shoot has long since ended. The
house is being built. In the letters he writes to her, he worries
about the great age difference between them.

I was born out of wedlock, and in 1966 this was still frowned
upon. Illegitimate. Bastard. Brat. By-blow. None of that mattered. Not to me. I was a bundle in Mamma's arms. It didn't
matter to my father either. One child more or less. He had eight
already and was known as the demon director (whatever that

means) and a womanizer (pretty obvious, that one). I was the ninth. We were nine. My oldest brother died many years later of leukemia, but back then we were nine.

Mamma got pregnant and it was frowned upon. *She* was frowned upon. Because she was a girl. She cared a lot about what other people said and thought. She loved her baby. That is what mothers do. She swelled up and bore a daughter. *Illegitimate*. But she was also ashamed. She got letters from strangers. *May your child burn in hell.*

Mamma's first husband was present at my birth. He was a doctor who, according to his colleagues, had a *lively, infectious, and cheerful nature*. My mother has told me that giving birth didn't really hurt that much, but that she screamed for the sake of appearances, and that he, the doctor, leaned over, stroked her hair and said, *There, there.* He knew the baby wasn't his, both he and my mother had taken their affections elsewhere, but they hadn't yet gotten around to getting a divorce. So according to Norwegian law, I was *his* daughter. I—2.8 kilos, 50 centimeters long, and born on a Tuesday—was a doctor's daughter, and for several months I—or she—carried his surname. In photographs she has round, chubby cheeks. I don't know that much about her. She looks content in her mother's arms. A first name had not yet been given her. She lived in Oslo with the mother, in the little flat at 91 Drammensveien that the mother had shared with her husband and that the grandmother, *Nanna*, would take over some years later. Many of the father's letters are addressed to 91 Drammensveien. In one of them, scribbled on yellow stationery from the Stadshotell in the small Swedish town of Växjö, he writes:

TUESDAY EVENING

A gray-black letter
The hotel is fine and everyone is kind and I am filled with
cosmic loneliness . . .

WEDNESDAY MORNING

Now it is morning, and there's an autumnal tree outside
my window and everything is better today . . . The sense
of paralysis has eased off. If we are to write down all our
thoughts, I must tell you about a very black thought I had
last night. It mainly concerns my physical person. In some
way or another, the very core of my being is rather worn
down. I have worked so hard throughout my career that the
consequences are beginning to show. There aren't many days
in a row when I feel really well. What frightens and worries
me the most are the dizzy spells, the signs of weakness, a
circle of unquiet that culminates in fever and depression. My
hysteria most likely plays a part in all this . . . in some ludi-
crous way I feel deeply self-conscious and ashamed of these
ailments that I scarcely can do anything about. I believe it
has to do with the older man–young woman conundrum.

One day, the mother, the father, and the doctor had to appear
before a Norwegian judge to sort out the issue of paternity.
They all got along famously. The mood was so upbeat that the
courtroom proceedings could almost have been mistaken for a
little party. The only obstinate person, according to the father,
was the judge—long-faced and thin-lipped—who required

the matter to be explained over and over again. Who, in truth, had had sexual intercourse with the child's mother, and *when*? And after a long day in court, the mother felt that a glass of Champagne would be in order. But no such luck. The child's father had to get straight back to the theater in Stockholm and husband number one was on late shift at the hospital. A quick glass of wine, then? Surely they had earned it? *She* certainly had. Waiting for evening to come, hoping that the child will sleep through the night. Lying in bed next to the girl in the flat at 91 Drammensveien, hoping she won't wake up and start screaming. Sometimes the child cries all night and then she doesn't know what to do, what's wrong. Is the baby in pain? Is she sick? Is she going to die? Who can she call? Who will get up in the middle of the night and venture out into the snow and the dark and come to her aid? In the morning the nanny arrives. She is wearing an apron and a kind of nurse's cap and a somewhat judgmental expression, thinks the mother, who is afraid of being late for work and also of offending the nanny, who has things she'd like to discuss. *I'm so tired*, the mother wants to say, but doesn't. *I'm going to be late. Can't you just be quiet and let me go.* It will be another two years before the child is christened, but on that day in court, by ruling of the judge, she is given the mother's surname, and when the mother and the father meet or speak on the phone, they call her *the baby* and *our love child* and Swedish and Norwegian words for soft things—*nap, maple leaf, linen, lull.*

The mother and the father were lovers for five years and spent much of that time at Hammars. The house was finished now. Their daughter was looked after by two women, one called

Rosa, the other called Siri. The one plump, the other willowy. One had an apple orchard, the other a husband who would get down on his hands and knees and let the girl ride around on his back while she hollered *Fifteen men on a dead man's chest, yo-ho-ho and a bottle of rum, HOPPLA!* In 1969, the mother left Hammars, taking her daughter with her. Four years later, one summer day in late June, the girl came back to visit the father. She didn't like leaving the mother, but the mother promised to call every day.

Nothing had changed, except that now it was Ingrid who lived there. Everything stood exactly where it had stood when the mother and the girl left, the grandfather clock ticked and struck on the hour and the half hour, the linen cupboard creaked, a golden light shone in on the pine-clad walls and fell in bands across the floor. The father crouched down in front of the girl and said gently: *I suppose Mamma is the only one allowed to touch you.*

She was small and skinny and came to Hammars every summer with two big suitcases that were left sitting in the yard until someone carried them into the house. She raced out of the car and round the yard and into her room and out into the yard again. She wore a blue summer dress that skimmed the tops of her thighs. The father asks: What have you got in your suitcases? How is it possible for such a little girl to have two such big suitcases?

His house was fifty meters long and kept getting longer, it took forever to walk from one end to the other. Running indoors was strictly forbidden. He furnished it and extended it, a little more each year, the house grew in length, never in height. No basement, no attic, no stairs. She would stay there for all of July.

He is dreading her arrival, *hello and how do you do*, there's a girl running around the yard, a little girl with legs like pipe cleaners and knobbly knees, or she's dancing, this girl is almost always in the middle of some complicated choreography, you can be having a conversation with her and instead of answering whatever question she has been asked, she'll begin to dance, or else she plants herself in front of him, a challenge of sorts, and then he'll smile, *What now? What to say? What to do?* The girl dreads being away from the mother, but looks forward to visiting the father, everything that is this place, the house, the island, her room with its flowery wallpaper, Ingrid's cooking, the moors and the stony beach and the ocean stretching green and gray between her father's island and the Soviet Union (if you lose your way and end up there, they'll never let you out), and the fact that everything is exactly as it has always been and always will be. The father has rules. She understands them. The rules are an alphabet that she learns even before she learns the real alphabet. A is A and B is B, she doesn't have to ask, Z is where Z has always been, she knows where Z is, her father is rarely angry with her. But he can get very angry, *He has a bloody temper*, the mother says, he can fly into a rage and shout, but the girl knows where the anger is and dodges it. She is skinny. Skinny like a filmstrip, the father says.

One day, the mother calls the father on the telephone, she's upset because he won't let their daughter drink milk. He believes that milk is bad for the stomach. The father believes that a lot of things are bad for the stomach. But especially milk.

The mother believes that milk and children go together. Everybody knows that. What the father says about milk goes against the most basic knowledge of what a growing child needs. And anyway, says the mother, he doesn't usually take much interest in the girl's upbringing, but this, *this*, he has opinions on. The mother's voice grows shrill, all children must drink milk, especially the girl who is so skinny . . . This, as far as I know, is the only quarrel the mother and the father have about the girl's upbringing.

Change. Disturbance. *Hello and how do you do. Let me look at you. You've grown. You've become pretty.* And then, perhaps, he puts his thumbs and forefingers together to form a square so that he can look at her through the square. He'll shut one eye and peer at her with the other. Take a picture. Frame her with his fingers. She stands perfectly still and gazes solemnly at the square. It is not a real camera—if it had been a real camera she would have wriggled and squirmed and wondered how she would look in the picture.

To be hauled away from what you're doing, by a child. Not to be left in peace with your work, your writing. But it's only now, at the moment when she arrives with her suitcases and it's been a year since they saw each other last, only then is he hauled away from his work. She dances around the yard. He forms his hands into a camera and looks at her through it with the one open eye. I don't know who carries the suitcases inside. Or unpacks them. Or hangs the dresses and shorts and T-shirts in the small closet in her room. Most likely it's Ingrid. Soon he'll be able to go back to his study (which lies at one end of the house, her room lies at the other) and continue working.

The girl's mother, she who is responsible for the girl every month of the year except July and who believes that milk is good for children, would also like to shut herself away in a room and be left in peace, she too wants to write, she wants rules and an alphabet just like the girl's father. But she can't figure out how. The mother's alphabet keeps changing, it's impossible for the girl to keep up, no matter how hard she tries. All of a sudden, A is L. It's baffling. A was A, but then it turned into L or X or U. The mother has tried installing herself in every room of the house in order to write, but all in vain. Disturbances wherever she goes.

My nerves are frayed, she says.

When the mother's nerves are frayed, it is a good idea to be very, very quiet.

The mother and the girl live in a big house in Strømmen, outside of Oslo. They live in lots of other places too. But first, after they leave Hammars, they live in a big house in Strømmen. There's a playhouse in the garden. On the wall inside the playhouse the girl has carved her name. No matter which room the mother chooses, the girl comes in and wants something. She wants to draw. She wants to ask a question. She wants to say: *Look at this!* She wants to ride her bike. She wants to brush her hair. She wants to dance. She wants to sit perfectly still and say nothing, *promise, promise, not a word*. She wants to dance again. In the end there isn't a single room left in the house where the mother can work in peace, so she renovates the basement and turns a small part of it into a study. (The house in Strømmen, unlike the house at Hammars, grew in depth and not in length.) But the girl finds her there too. Basement Mamma. Underground Mamma. The mother is trying to write a book, but it's not going that well. The girl finds her wherever she goes and then, when she does, the mother loses her concentration. And when you lose your concentration, the mother explains, it's *almost totally impossible* to get it back.

Life with the mother was so much more unpredictable than life with the father. This had to do with the circumstances of life. The father would die first, it would probably be very sad, but not altogether unexpected considering how old he was. The father's death was under way, the girl and the father were well aware of this, and that's why they exchanged sad goodbyes every summer. They were good at it. Saying goodbye to the mother was a very different story. The girl would scream and the mother would hold her close, *Don't cry now, be a big girl and don't cry*, hugging her tightly, glancing around, trying to stave off the girl's hands, which clung to various parts of her body. *Is anyone looking?* The mother is always conscious of who is looking and what they might be thinking. This screaming child. This ribcage-skinny girl so bristling with dissonance.

The father often told the mother that she was his Stradivarius. That is: an instrument of the finest quality with a rich, full-bodied sound. The mother took these words to heart and repeated them, *He said I was his Stradivarius*.

She is my violin.

I am his violin.

This is an example of how both the mother and the father allowed themselves to be seduced by metaphors. Neither of them knew or even cared about the numerous studies proving that a Stradivarius does not, in fact, sound better than other comparable violins.

On the other hand: what is the point of studies like these?

There is always a smartass in the audience mumbling, *I know how he does it, it's just a bluff, that's not a real magician up there on the stage.*

But what have the mother and the father made here? Listen! It's the girl! Well, one thing's for sure, it's not a Stradivarius. A small out-of-tune organ, perhaps, howling because the mother was leaving. And all this clinging—what's that about? Is the child not quite right in the head? And what sort of mother goes off and leaves her daughter again and again? (It was the mother they looked at accusingly, never the father.) The mother cared about what other people saw and thought, but the girl didn't care. She didn't notice the looks. She clung to the mother. The thought of never seeing her again was unbearable. She fantasized about different ways of dying. The mother's death, above all. And her own death as a natural consequence of the mother's. It could happen anytime—the mother might die from an illness, in a car or a plane crash, or she might be murdered. She, who traveled all over the world, might accidentally lose her way in some country at war and be shot and killed. The girl could not cut a hole in herself big enough to disappear into if the mother died. She loved the mother most of all. Not that she thought about love—about the word itself and what it meant. If anyone had asked her about love, she might have said that she loved the mother, the grandmother (Nanna) and Jesus (because the mother and the grandmother had told her that Jesus loved her), and the cats, but that she loved the mother most of all. She missed the mother all the time, even when the mother was right there, in the same room. The girl's love was more than the mother could bear. Having a child was harder than she had imagined. Arms and legs and big teeth and *dissonance*. She liked it best when the girl was asleep. My darling little girl. But when everyone was awake, it was just too much. Clingy girl. Clingy love. It felt as if the girl wanted to crawl back inside her. The mother would never have admitted that the clinginess got on her nerves, she was too full of desperate longing herself, of questions about who she wanted to be and who she was and what love was and ought to be. Her deepest longing, perhaps, was to be loved unconditionally, and at the same time be left in peace. But she never told anyone. It is shameful and egotistical to hope for unconditional love and at the same time want to be left in peace. The mother's inner worlds were neatly sealed—dark, gilded worlds.

———

At Hammars nothing changed. Or rather, the changes occurred so gradually that you didn't notice them, and for a very long time—until the father came seventeen minutes late without even being aware of it himself and thereby announcing that it was all over—the girl lived with the sense that the way things are *right now* is the way they have always been. Order and punctuality. The chairs stood where they had always stood. The pictures hung where they had always hung. The pine trees outside the windows were just as gnarly. Ingrid had a long, brown braid that flipped back and forth as she made her way through the house, dusting or fluffing up cushions.

Eventually, Daniel and Maria began coming to Hammars at the same time as the girl. They were older than her, but children nevertheless. And that was how it was: days and nights

in the long, narrow house surrounded by sea, stones, thistles, poppies, and barren moors reminiscent of West African
savannas. One summer was the same as the next. Every evening at six o'clock the girl and the Hammars family had dinner in the kitchen. Ingrid did the cooking and the food was
always good. After dinner everyone would sit for a while on
the brown-stained bench looking onto the gravel yard, on
which first one car stood parked, later two cars and eventually
a red jeep. Beyond the bike shed lay a forest with three trails
running through it. And while the father and the children sat
on the bench, Ingrid would stand—slightly leaning against
the brown-stained post that held up the little pent roof—and
smoke her daily cigarette.

The brown-stained bench was warm and slightly rough—if
you rubbed your hand against it, you'd get splinters. The house
was made of wood and stone and surrounded by a stone wall.
In the evening, when the grown-ups were reading their newspapers, the girl would walk down to the sea on her own. The
wave-sculpted stony beach sloped, and when she had walked far
enough to be able to wade in the water, she would turn around
and look up at the house and the stone wall. And then it was
almost gone, vanished, all of it, lost in a haze of light and gray,
gravel and sky, bleached by the summer sun, the years, the days,
as if someone had thrown an invisibility cloak over it, although
not completely invisible, the windows and the doorframes were
cornflower blue, and these you could see, there *was* a house
there, it couldn't hide itself completely.

Every once in a while, someone would say: Why don't we sit on the pretty side of the house, the side with the beautiful view of the sea and the shifting light on the horizon? But still they went on sitting at the front of the house, on the brown-stained bench, while Ingrid leaned against the post and smoked. It was as if everyone took part in the smoking of that one cigarette.

The father had a study in which he sat and wrote every day, *The only thing I can brag about is that I've been diligent*, he would say. The girl called his study *the office*, and every evening the office was transformed into a cinema. The father would pull a white canvas screen out of a black case, the lights were switched off, and the film could begin. The black case was so long and narrow that, when it was closed, it looked like a coffin—a coffin for a very thin person, a stickman. The case had snap locks and a handle like a suitcase or a ladies' handbag, and during the day sat on top of a silvery rack leaning against the back wall.

And then, at eight o'clock, the father opened the case, whereupon what during the daytime looked like a coffin would turn into a milky-white movie screen of such impressive dimensions that it covered the wall like a taut sail.

In a little room separated from the office by a wall with a glass partition stood the projectors. During her first years at Hammars, the father ran the films himself, but later he taught his son Daniel to do it. Daniel was paid ten kroner per screening. The girl mustn't touch the projectors. Touching the projectors was even more strictly forbidden than making noise during the grown-ups' afternoon nap, more strictly forbidden than leaving the doors at Hammars open or sitting in a draft, about as strictly forbidden as being late. No one was ever late at Hammars. But no matter how punctual you were—you had an appointment and you arrived perfectly on time—you would still say: *I'm sorry I'm late*. This was the Hammars greeting, as familiar as gulls' cries in summer. *I'm sorry I'm late*. And if, contrary to expectation, you happened to be running a few seconds behind, you would say: *Forgive me for being late. Can you please forgive me? I have no excuse!* That hardly ever happened though.

For the first few years, the girl is allowed her very own screening at six thirty in the evening. She sits in the big, battered armchair with her feet on a footrest. The black case has been opened and the projection screen unfurled. She is as skinny as a twig. She has long straggly hair and buckteeth. The father has switched off the light, closed the door, and stationed himself on the other side of the partition.

"Okay?" he calls out.

"Okay," the girl replies.

The office windows are shuttered, dark, quiet.

"Do you feel a draft?"

"No."

"Okay then, let's watch the movie!"

Later though, long after the girl had started seeing films along with the grown-ups, the father decided to renovate the old barn beyond the lilac hedge at Dämba. The cinematograph was finished the summer the girl turned nine, although nobody called it *the cinematograph*, they called it *bion*, Swedish for cinema, and it had a heavy, rust-red door and a huge keyhole with light streaming through it. The cinema had fifteen seats—soft moss-green armchairs—and two cutting-edge sea-green projectors that whirred softly in the darkness behind a glass panel.

To get from Hammars to Dämba, the girl and her two half siblings would squeeze into the backseat of the father's car at exactly 7:40 p.m., twenty minutes before the movie started. It was a short drive, ten minutes at the most, but once you had arrived you needed an additional ten minutes *to adjust*. No rushing in and out. Same thing in the afternoon. The afternoon screening started at three, but you arrived at ten to. The girl had a knack for drawing maps, many of them of Fårö using her blue marker to accentuate the places she knew best: First, there was Hammars, where she stayed every summer together with her father, Ingrid, her half brother Daniel and half sister Maria. Then there was Dämba, built in 1854, consisting of a main house and an annex, a lilac hedge, a ghost deemed to be friendly, a windmill, and a barn-turned-cinema. There was a new two-story limestone house called Ängen, meaning *meadow*, built to withstand winter weather and, also, a little cabin by the sea, called the Writing Lodge, although nobody ever did much writing there. There was even a place called Karlberga, on the southern tip of the island, near the beaches of Sudersand, which was later sold.

———

The house at Hammars had a small foyer with three doors, one door formed the main entrance and led straight out to the brown-stained bench, the second door opened up into the house itself, and the third led out into the garden, which was enclosed by a stone wall. The garden boasted a guest annex, a wash house, a rose bush, and a swimming pool.

During her first summers at Hammars, the girl's favorite place was the electrically heated narrow closet in the wash house, where clothes were hung to dry. The drying closet was hot and sultry, and on the bottom beneath the hanging rods there was just enough space for her to curl up. Ingrid's and her father's newly washed clothes hung in the closet, either dripping or damp, the father had striped pajamas, flannel shirts, and brown corduroy trousers. His clothes took up most of the space. Ingrid was small and delicate and stuck to a few sensible pieces: mostly skirts and blouses. Occasionally, the girl's blue dress would hang at the very tip of one rod.

She was a good swimmer and could stay in the pool for *hours*, said the father, he always exaggerated, not *hours*, said the girl. Sometimes he came out into the garden and said: Now your lips have turned completely blue, get out of the water immediately, he worried that the girl might catch a cold and that he might catch it too, so occasionally he interrupted his workday in order to get her out of the water.

All the windows in the house had to be kept shut, even on beautiful summer days. The father was afraid of flies and drafts. Conversations with the father usually began like this:

"Do you feel a draft?"

"No."

"Are you sure?"

"Yes."

"I don't want you to catch a cold."

"I don't have a cold."

"I know that, but I don't want you to catch a cold."

But for the most part, the girl was allowed to stay in the pool for as long as she liked. The father worked in his office and Ingrid did housework while Daniel did whatever it is that older boys do—the girl wasn't all that interested. And when she was done swimming she curled up inside the drying closet. She liked it best when it wasn't full of clothes, because when there were clothes hanging from all the rods there was hardly any room for the girl, and the more clothes there were, the hotter it was, and not just hot but humid like in a jungle; when the closet was full, she had to crawl, yes practically battle her way inside, and when the clothes were still wet, she'd get slapped in the face and on her body by shirt sleeves, pant legs, dress hems, like being licked all over by big animal tongues.

One day Ingrid opened the door and pulled her out. She said it was dangerous to sit inside the drying closet. Ingrid had pretty hair. She nearly always kept it in a braid, but for parties she would put it in rollers in the morning and wear it down in the evening. Then it would ripple down her back.

Lots of things were dangerous. All the usual things, of course, like putting a plastic bag over your head (death by suffocation), walking around in wet underpants, swimsuits, or bikini bottoms (death by bladder infection), twisting a tick the wrong way when detaching it from the skin (death by blood poisoning), going swimming less than an hour after eating (death by cramps), accepting rides from strangers (death by kidnapping, rape, murder), taking candy from strangers (death by poisoning, possibly kidnapping, rape, murder)—but there were also other dangers specific to Hammars: Never touch the flotsam that washed up on the beach below the house, liquor bottles, packs of cigarettes, shampoo bottles, tin cans with labels in foreign languages, foreign lettering, don't touch, don't sniff, and for God's sake don't drink (death by poisoning), don't sit in a draft (death by catching a cold), don't catch a cold (death by expulsion from Hammars), don't sit in the drying closet (death by suffocation, possibly electrocution), don't be late (if you showed up late, death would be a consolation, death was, if anything, the only valid excuse for a lack of punctuality). Give this girl a map and she'll follow it—she doesn't break a single rule, except the one about not sitting in the closet. Ingrid had told her over and over again, but still the girl snuck in to be enveloped by the warmth. Until the day she found a sheet of yellow notebook paper taped to the closet-door on which the father had written in big block capitals:

WARNING! IT IS STRICTLY FORBIDDEN
FOR SWIMMING CHILDREN TO FREQUENT
THE DRYING CLOSET!

The father spoke beautiful Swedish and often resorted to the old-fashioned custom of addressing the girl in the third person singular. *How is my daughter today?* He never used English words in conversation except when referring to his swimming pool, of which he was extremely proud. It lay stretched out in the middle of the lawn like a magnanimous, bejeweled old lady in a long turquoise gown; six meters long and three meters deep at one end, rectangular and, yes, turquoise, and smelling of chlorine. At night the wasps fell into it—either sinking to the bottom or staying on the surface and crawling about—as did spiders and beetles and ladybirds and cones from the trees and the occasional sparrow. Every morning, all the things that had fallen into the pool had to be fished out with a landing net. For this job too Daniel was paid ten kroner. Early, early in the morning the old lady would lie there sparkling with things creeping and crawling all over her, on her surface and on her bottom, surrounded by tall grass and lofty pine trees—a glittering turquoise spot on the map.

I have heard recordings of my father speaking English to British and American journalists and film students. He spoke it with a heavy accent, part Swedish, part German, part American, a jazzy sound unlike anything else I've ever heard and not like him at all—*yes, yes,* he'd rattle on, *as Faulkner once said, the stories you tell, you never write.* He thought Norwegian was a beautiful language and was fond of repeating the nonexistent word *buskedrasse,* which he mistook for the Norwegian word *buksedrakt,* meaning a woman's pantsuit.

Every day, he—the girl's father—went for a morning swim in the pool. And the girl would hide behind the rosebush and watch him. The father, she thought, was actually much too old to go swimming without any clothes on, too old to go swimming at all. Honestly! Splashing around in the water like a great big beetle! He always swam alone. First thing in the morning. Before breakfast. Before disappearing into his study. The girl didn't know much about the work he did in there. He wrote, this much she knew, on lined sheets of yellow notebook paper.

He wrote in the summer, the rest of the year he made films or worked at the theater.

Sometimes he and his editor, a friendly woman whose name the girl never remembered, withdrew to the guesthouse *to cut film*, this was in the days when strips of celluloid were actually cut and spliced together. He spent an entire summer cutting *The Magic Flute*, and then Schikaneder's libretto and Mozart's music would flow from the windows of the guesthouse—this was the only summer the windows were left wide open—and everyone at Hammars pricked up their ears. Tamino pleaded desperately: *O endless night! When will you vanish? When shall my eyes see light?* And the chorus replied: *Soon, youth, or never more.*

But when the father wasn't busy cutting, he was busy writing, and in the afternoon he would hand the sheets of yellow notepad paper to Ingrid. She had no difficulty reading his handwriting, hardly anyone else knew how, and she would type up a fair copy. When the father was writing, he was on no account to be disturbed, the girl knew this very well, *He has a temper*, said the mother before sending her daughter off to the house that had once been built for her to live in, What is a temper, said the girl, He can get angry, said the mother, Is it dangerous, said the girl, No, said the mother and hesitated, Or yes, if you hurt other people, but if you never show that you are angry or sad or scared, you can get a big knot in your stomach and that can be dangerous too, Does Pappa have a knot in his stomach, said the girl, No, said the mother, he doesn't have a knot in his stomach, but sometimes he can get angry and say things he doesn't mean . . .

and thunder and yell . . . and then other people get knots in *their* stomachs . . . that's what I mean when I say he has a temper . . . he's a hothead . . . he's got a short fuse . . . A short fuse, asked the girl, what's that? The mother sighed, Well, it means that you . . . that . . . that if you light a match and suddenly the whole house goes up in flames . . . Oh, right, said the girl, who knew very well that she mustn't disturb the father, but sometimes she disturbed him anyway. She knocked on the door to his study and told him to come—there was a spider in her room that he had to get rid of. She didn't dare spend another minute in there if he didn't come right away and get rid of it. Or a beetle. Or a wasp. He didn't start yelling. He didn't catch fire. He only sighed a little, got up, and followed her through the living room and the kitchen to her room. She was so thin. As though the insects were her kinfolk. And he liked the Norwegian words she kept piping. *Øyenstikker.* The girl liked the Swedish words. *Trollslända.* Two such different words for dragonfly. And she wasn't afraid of him. She was afraid of horseflies. *Broms.* And harvestmen. *Harkrank.*

When she had become an adult and spoke fluent Swedish, he told her to speak Norwegian instead. At least when speaking to him. He said that when she spoke Swedish, her voice went up several notches and sounded like it did when she was a little girl and now that she was a grown woman, she ought to stick to a lower key, it was more agreeable, more becoming, he preferred the sound of her voice, he said, when she spoke her mother tongue.

But there was a time when she was 113 centimeters tall and could hide behind a rosebush without being seen and could dis-

turb the father if there was a millipede in her room to be dealt
with. Or an ant, or a bumblebee, or a beetle.

Maybe I ought to call her something. The girl. I can also let it
be. When the father turned sixty, he invited all his nine children to Hammars to celebrate his birthday. It was the summer
of 1978—the summer the girl turned twelve. I don't remember
how the idea of a big party—the first of many—was presented
to her, she probably wasn't even aware that she had so many siblings, or maybe she was aware of it in the same way that she was
aware that Norway was made up of many different counties. She
had just finished fifth grade and would soon be moving to the
United States with her mother and go to an American school.
Her Norwegian geography teacher's name was Jørgensen, she
would miss him. She was good at geography. Maps were her spe-
cialty. And yes, she knew that she was one of nine siblings, just
as she knew that nine of the highest waterfalls in the world were
in Norway. She had written down their names: *Mardalsfossen*,
Mongefossen, *Vedalsfossen*, *Opo*, *Langfossen*, *Skykkjedalsfossen*,
Ramnefjellsfossen, *Ormalifossen*, *Sundifoss*. Apart from Daniel
and Maria, whom she already knew, she had only seen her siblings in photographs. A lot of people think that *Vøringsfossen* is
the highest waterfall in Norway, but it isn't. Far from it. Goes to
show how wrong you can be, Jørgensen would say. It was the
day before the big party. The father's birthday was on the four-
teenth of July, France's National Day, and she was finally going
to meet everybody. All eight of them at the same time. She
sat on the brown-stained bench outside the house and waited.
Every now and again she would get up and wander toward the
forest where she picked wild strawberries and threaded them

onto blades of grass. Then she would sit down again. She meant
to save the wild-strawberry necklaces and give them to her
sisters, she had four, but time passed and no one came, so she
ate them all herself. Her faded blue dress only just covered her
bottom. She had mosquito bites on her thigh and on her hand.
There was no place as quiet as Hammars as she sat there alone
on the bench watching the grasshopper wake up on the stone
wall. When a car came driving along, you could hear it from far
away. Usually, when she heard a car, she would run up to the
road and over to the first cattle guard, which according to the
father marked the boundary between private and public property, and wave her arms so the car would turn around and drive
away. They didn't want people here. But today she stayed where
she was, not running up to the road and chasing people away.
The father was probably regretting this whole bloody party. It
had seemed like such a good idea—a *delightful* idea!—when he
first thought of it. All of his children gathered at a party. But one
should beware of one's own good ideas, Aksel Sandemose—a
writer whom the father occasionally quoted—once wrote. You
can become so smitten with the *idea* that you forget everything
else. Sandemose was talking about writing, but the same can
no doubt be said of throwing parties. And besides: the girl sus-
pected that the party wasn't entirely the father's idea, it was also
Ingrid's. If all of *his* children were invited to Hammars, then all
of *her* children would also get to come. Not only Maria, Ingrid's
youngest, but her three other children as well. Ingrid had left
her children when she went off to marry the girl's father, and
now she missed them all the time, but her new husband insisted
it should be just the two of them. No children. They had waited
so long for each other, through all of his numerous marriages
and affairs and her marriage to the baron. Or was it the count.

Such is love. Sitting on the brown-stained bench, and someone once said *such is love*. The girl's mother would shake her head at any talk about the father's women, she didn't want to hear about wife number five, she didn't want to hear about wife number four, *I don't want to hear about them*, one tends not to want to hear about the one who came right before and the one who came right after. The mother didn't like being between number four and number five. What does that make you? Four and a half?

The father used to say that for his seventieth birthday he would invite all the wives too, and the mothers and the women who were neither wives nor mothers, but who had nevertheless played a part one way or another. What do you call them? But now he's sixty, not seventy, and the girl is sitting on the brown-stained bench waiting for her siblings, most of whom she had never met before, and tomorrow, on the big day, the father would be photographed with a wreath of flowers in his hair, surrounded by Ingrid and the children on the steps at Dämba. The girl turned, looked toward the road, and scratched her thigh. The first mosquito bite is the sweetest, the father used to say. It pops up somewhere on your body and it's white and new and slightly pink, shouting, *Scratch me, scratch me*. When you have lots of mosquito bites, it's not so sweet anymore, your skin hurts, the bites don't shout, there's no sound in them, and the itching keeps you awake at night. When she heard the first car, she stood up and immediately sat down again. *They're here!* They had arrived. She looked around. Where was everybody? *Pappa! Ingrid! Daniel! Maria! Come! They're here!* And then the first car turned into the gravel yard, and then another and then one more, and out of the cars tumbled young women and men, the girl's siblings, and their boyfriends and girlfriends and suitcases and silk scarves and red lips and laughter and

flared trousers and hair and voices. Where was the father? Was
he even there when they all arrived, or had he sought refuge
in his study? It didn't really matter. He was an old man with
stomachaches who hated visitors. *Look!* Here comes my little
family! More and more people filled the yard. The girl began
to laugh. This wasn't a *little* family. It was a *big* family. Look—
there's Jan. He is the oldest and the wisest with a wife and children. And there—there's the sister who lives in London, who
smiles like a movie star. And there's the airline pilot. The girl
knew that one of her brothers was an airline pilot who flew back
and forth across the Atlantic every week. He was the tallest of
them all, she knew it was him the minute she laid eyes on him,
he turned round in the yard and when he caught sight of her, he
set down his suitcase and opened his arms, he was treetop tall
and slim and the best-looking man she had ever seen, and she
had, despite her tender years, seen *lots*, and she ran toward him
and he swept her so high off the ground and swung her round
so fast that she nearly lost her breath, but instead of losing her
breath she opened her eyes, slowly, as if she were underwater, and from up there in his arms she saw not only Hammars,
with its flat moors, its lambs, as the islanders called the sheep,
whether they were newborn or fully grown, and its old limestone farmhouses, but the whole of Fårö, from the limestone
quarry up at Norsholmen and the English cemetery south of
Dämba, to the sand dunes at Ullahau where the girl had heard
that you could go sledding in the winter, to the old grocery
store down by the church and the beaches at Sudersand, Eke-
viken, and Norsta Aurar, and all the way out to the stacks at
Langhammars and Digerhuvud, and just when she thought he
was going to set her down on the ground again, his arms grew
even longer and she rose even higher in the air and now she

could see the ocean and the horizon and the Iron Curtain there in the distance, where, if you lose your way and end up there, they'll never let you out.

Half sister and half brother—as if they weren't real. Half-born, half-alive, half-remembered, half-forgotten—shadow children who vanished into the lilac hedge or slipped between the bars of the cattle guards. In the evening, there was a party at Dämba, and the girl danced a dance at full speed round and round and round until she hardly had any clothes left on her body.

The father gave her a green lined notebook and told her to remember to write in it every day. Her big sister, Maria, wrote in *her* diary every day and had done so ever since she was younger than the girl was now. If the girl didn't write things down, the father said, she would likely forget. But the girl didn't want to keep a diary. Instead she invented a secret language and filled the green notebook with secret tables and words: *Ivoefo qqjttfsS j tåmb*. She drew maps too. Hundreds of maps. The measurements didn't need to be too exact, what mattered were the borders. Beyond the brown-stained bench lay the bike shed and beyond the bike shed lay the forest with its three trails. One trail led to the sea, another trail led to a little shack, and a third led to a clearing or a meadow where the father would later build a new house.

The father's plan for the new house—all his houses had names and this one was called Ängen, meaning *meadow*—was for him and Ingrid to live there in their old age. He had it all figured out. They would stay at Hammars in the summer and at Ängen in the winter. Sometimes, he said, the winds from the sea were so violent that it was impossible to sleep at Hammars.

At such times he would rather sleep somewhere else. As would Ingrid. But then Ingrid died and left him grief-stricken.

Some summers were cold, and everyone said it was the coldest summer ever. The father liked it best when it rained. He said that all his worst nightmares played out in deafening sunlight. When the girl was little she wasn't allowed to go into the father and Ingrid's room until the man on the radio had finished reading the weather forecast with temperatures for all of Sweden. Once the man had announced the temperatures for Visby, *Visby, seventeen*, meaning that it was 62.6 degrees Fahrenheit, the coast was clear and the girl could go into the grown-ups' bedroom and wake them. Her adult siblings took turns staying at Ängen together with their lovers, spouses, and children. The girl was no longer the family's youngest. There was a house over at Sudersand, called Karlberga, which later was sold, and then there was the little cottage down by the sea, the Writing Lodge, where her older brothers would stay with their girlfriends.

The girl, like most children, enjoyed making lists and keeping count, and if anyone asked her about her father she could have said: My father has four houses, two cars, five wives, one swimming pool, nine children, and one cinema.

Pappa and Ingrid never lived at Ängen, the house on the meadow, but before she died, Ingrid decorated it exactly as she wanted it. Jan spent several summers there with his children. He started out as a locomotive engineer, but ended up in the theatre, working as a director. *King Lear* is not about a man who wants to be king, but about a king who wants to be a man. And *that*, Jan said, raising his hand, is the most difficult thing of all. Anyone can be king! Jan was the head of the sibling flock. One summer he suggested hoisting a big tent on the stretch of moor between Hammars and Ängen to make room for the steadily growing family who came to Fårö every year in July to celebrate the father's birthday. The father balked at the idea and roared at Jan that no fucking way am I having a bloody tent on my property, no bloody fucking way, that's going too damn far, I will not have people coming here thinking they can do whatever the fuck they want.

The girl lived in the United States for some time before returning home to Norway. She married and had a son. He was named after his father's father, Olav, but everyone called him Ola. She was no longer a girl, but she still had her maps. Every summer she stayed at Ängen. In the evenings Ola played soccer on the grass outside.

The art of telling a story without words—whatever happened to that, the father asked, and showed silent films at the cinema in the afternoons. *This is your education*, he said to the girl when she was still a girl. *Pay attention*. Back then, Åke operated the film projectors. Later came Cecilia: Tall, dark, beautiful, and barefoot behind the glass panel, waiting for the signal from the father: Right arm up in the air. A little wave. Lights out. The film starts. *Love in the Afternoon*. Jan was there. Several of the father's daughters were there. One summer Käbi moved into the main house at Dämba and after that she returned every summer. Years before, she and the father had been married, they had a son, Daniel, now they were friends and had dinner together every Sunday, and after dinner she would play him something on the piano. When Käbi came to see a film, she would stroll across the moor wearing a large hat and a long summer frock, like in that photograph of Françoise Gilot on the beach, the one where Picasso is running after her with a parasol. The father didn't exactly run after Käbi with a parasol, but he waited for her and called her *madame* and pretended not to notice when she, in the middle of the movie, made rustling noises with the water bottle and nuts that she had brought with her in a large wicker basket. No one else brought wicker baskets with water bottles and nuts, no one else made rustling noises. That would never have gone unremarked. Others came and went, such were the summer afternoons, and some were always there. Before going inside to take their seats, they would sit for a few minutes on a bench outside. You must give your ears time to adjust, the father said. And your eyes. Not just rush in and out. And in the middle of July, on the fifteenth precisely, the day after his birthday, the curlews migrated across Dämba in a low-flying flock.

"Look!" the father said, pointing to the black carpet of beaks and feathers weaving their way overhead.

"There they go, leaving Dämba to begin their journey south."

He grinned.

"Isn't it incredible? On *precisely* the same day every year!"

He was a punctual man who valued punctuality in others, birds included, and had a unique talent for partings.

———

The girl eventually divorced her son's father, and after a year she met a new man. He will make you very unhappy, said the father. A bit dramatic. The man was good-looking and she was in love.

One winter evening she spoke to her brother Jan on the phone. He asked how things were going with the new man and she told him that he had left her, and then Jan told her that there was a high survival rate for the type of leukemia he had, possibly as much as 80 percent, but that the last few nights had been a nightmare; strange to think that maybe I only got fifty-four years on my ticket, he added.

———

The new man came back to the girl and they were a couple once again. At their wedding they were both very out of breath, as if they had run all the way to church. In due course they had a daughter. They called her Eva. In the summer they would go down to Hammars and stay at Ängen. The lamp above the kitchen table had a yellow shade with a broad band of pleated trim that became a little more threadbare every year.

———

Every day the father drove his red jeep back and forth between Hammars and Dämba. The drive took ten minutes. The afternoon screening started at three. But you had to be there at ten to three. He once said he wanted to build a railroad track between Hammars and Dämba and ride back and forth to his cinema in a steam locomotive.

He also drove to Fårösund to buy the morning papers. This he did in the late afternoon, after the movie. To get from Fårö to Fårösund, you have to take one of the two yellow ferries. It takes five minutes to cross the strait. During the summer months, the ferries shuttle back and forth, but in the autumn and winter, there's only one leaving every hour. The ferry is always on time. Imagine you are the only one going across the strait. It's late October. Imagine you come driving at breakneck speed. The road to the ferry landing is long and straight and the ferrymen can see you from a distance. You drive past the church, the moors, the lambs, the pine trees, and an old wind-mill. The ferrymen see you, but you're too late and they will not wait for you. They lower the barrier, you can hear the boom even though your car windows are closed, they raise the bow ramp and set out for Fårösund.

———

He grew older, old, he said that things went missing.
    "What sorts of things?"
    "Words. Memories."

She didn't give it much thought at the time. His memory was better than hers. Nothing had changed in that respect. He remembered names, dates, historical events, films, stage sets, pieces of music. He told the same stories over and over again, but he'd always done that, it was part of the summer repertoire. Maybe the time between each telling of the same story had nar-rowed, but other than that there weren't any noticeable signs.

A yellow piece of paper on the kitchen table at Ängen, undated:

Dearly Beloved

Youngest Daughter!
You who come with summer (whatever the weather).
The warmest of possible welcomes
to you and young Ola (Olav?)
and dear friends.

> *Big hug*
> *Father.*

He liked to make the red jeep roar. He wanted to be heard, he wanted people to hear that he was coming. The girl, who is no longer a girl but a grown woman and mother of two, pictures a flash of red and whirling dust through the forest. Hear how much noise I'm making! See how high above the ground I'm soaring! Now he rounds the bend, he's going fast, very fast, brakes screeching, a final rev of the engine just for the fun of it, and then he turns off the engine. He opens the door, grabs his cane, and makes a brave attempt to jump out.

It is exactly ten minutes to three.

"What are the words that go missing?"

"Oh, I don't know . . . I'm in the jeep. I have turned off the engine, there are hardly any other cars on the ferry, I wave to the ferryman and he waves back. I believe he's been a ferryman here for forty years. Summer is finally over. The gray light has returned. There is a girl standing at the railing, face averted, in her twenties. I'm on my way to Fårösund to buy the morning papers. Suddenly the sky opens and the rain starts pouring down. The girl looks up at the sky but doesn't move. The ferry throbs. The rain pours down and I switch on . . . you see? Everything comes to a halt. It starts to rain, the girl looks up at the sky and I switch on . . . oh, for heaven's sake, what do you call them . . . ? The things you switch on in the car when it rains and then they move back and forth and go swish-swish-swish?"

"Windshield wipers?"

"Exactly! Windshield wipers!"

"You'd forgotten that they're called windshield wipers?"

"Like a white spot in the brain, forgotten, gone. It happens all the time. I forget things."

It takes several minutes for the eyes to adjust to the dark. You can't just rush in and out. He repeats the same thing year after year. Some summers he lets his hair and beard grow, other summers he shaves everything off. He has a mole on his right cheek, it gets bigger every year, and he wears huge sepia-tinted sunglasses. He is a little thinner now. And I'm taller than him.

"Ah, good afternoon," he says, climbing out of the jeep with difficulty. "Let's sit on the bench for a while before we go inside."

━━━━━

In autumn 2006, we went to Hammars by car. My husband drove. We took our daughter with us. I hadn't seen my father since the beginning of August. We had agreed to meet outside the cinema.

A few days earlier we had spoken on the phone. It wasn't a long conversation.

"What are we seeing?"

"Oh, you'll find out when you get here."

"I'm looking forward to it."

"Me too! I wish you a warm welcome."

"See you there at the usual time?"

"At the usual time."

I'm standing next to Cecilia, waiting, in the autumn gray. She has long, dark hair and wears a bulky parka. I was used to seeing her barefoot, but now she has on thick boots. After Ingrid died, she handled everything having to do with the houses, in addition to being the appointed projectionist. She was the only one allowed to touch the projectors, which he loved more than anything else in the world. *They're gorgeous old broads*, he said. *And wearing very well, I might add. To hell with all that goddamn digital crap.*

Sometimes he has visitors in autumn and winter, but for the most part he is alone.

I check my watch and glance up. It is eight minutes to three. The road is quiet.

I turn to Cecilia.

"He's late."

"Yeah, it happens."

"Pardon?"

She stuffs her hands in her pockets.

"It happens sometimes . . . it's not uncommon."

"Not uncommon . . . what are you talking about?"

I look at my watch.

"It's five to three."

"So what? We don't start until three."

She doesn't look at me.

"Cecilia, he is *late* . . . my father is late. He should have been here at ten to. That doesn't worry you? It worries me."

She sighs, looks at me.

"The first time it happened I was worried—that was last winter. I waited for six or seven minutes, and when he didn't show up I went looking for him. That time, he had driven off the road, opened the door, tried to get out of the jeep, tripped, and fallen. I found him lying in the ditch."

"But . . . we have to go look for him!"

"Go ahead if you like, but he's often been late since then and not because he's lying in a ditch. He'll be here soon, you'll see. If he's very late, I'll take the car and go find him."

We stand there in silence. I check my watch again. Five past three. A nuthatch flies over the fields and off toward the marsh. And then nothing. I want everything to be the way it was before, and everything around me is the way it was before. This landscape never changes. But no matter where I stand or walk, no matter what I say or think, no matter where I look, the time agreed upon, *ten to three*, has long since passed. And then I hear the jeep. It's coming now. Tearing down the road. Faint bird-song is drowned out by the drone of the engine. His sunglasses are so big they cover his whole face—he looks like a nocturnal animal. He slams on the brakes, opens the door, gropes for his cane. It is seven minutes past three. Seventeen minutes late. He takes off his sunglasses and stretches his arms out to me.

———

He does not say: *I'm sorry I'm late.* Or: *Forgive me for being late.*

Pappa puts his arm around my shoulders and we walk toward the door. I nestle up to him.

"Ah! There you are!" he says. "Welcome! Oh dear! Did you have a comfortable trip? Come, come, let's sit down here on the bench for a moment before we go inside and see the film."

II

SPOOLS

...

Have you been getting on with your memoirs?
Did you try the tape-recorder?

—SAMUEL BECKETT *in a letter
to Thomas MacGreevy*

HAVE A KINK IN the line running from my hip bone to my neck. It isn't noticeable to anyone but me. I think it's because of my purse. I stuff things into it and forget to take them out. I hang it over my shoulder and walk around lopsided all day. Often, when I reach in to get something, I prick myself on some object or other, a broken safety pin, for example, or a sewing needle. I have no idea why there are sewing needles in my purse. I can't sew and haven't sewn anything since I was a little girl in fifth grade and had to make a felt cushion. It took me a very long time to finish that cushion, I dreaded sewing classes, I made no progress, I would never be finished, it would never be pretty, all the other students were done with their cushions and I was still plodding away at mine. Winter came and it snowed for days in a row, it was dark when the school day began and dark when it ended. And so the weeks went by. When the cushion was finally finished, I thought it looked like a red cloud, with its coarse stitching and stuffing poking out through all the gaps, but the teacher, who suffered from migraines, did *not* think it looked like a red cloud. You haven't managed to sew it up properly! she shouted, and her voice resounded down the granite steps and out into the schoolyard, where the filthy mounds of snow in the corners were starting to melt. Her breath had an odd milky smell to it that stuck to her, despite the ammonia-strength lozenges she was constantly sucking on, something seeped from her pores, tiredness, I think, and perhaps I sensed, although I wouldn't have put it that way at the time, that she saw something of herself in that cushion—that no matter how long she worked on stitching herself together, she'd never be properly sewn up.

I have never pricked my finger on a spindle, never fallen asleep for a hundred years, fallen yes, but not slept for a hundred years, I rarely sleep for more than four hours at a stretch, five if I'm lucky, I once pricked my finger on a sprig of spruce, it was summer and I was carrying the remains of last year's Christmas tree around in my purse, I don't know how it ended up there, underneath my cell phone and my wallet and my mirror. I've pricked myself on twigs, stalks, a fragment of a pinecone—a forest grows inside my purse, autumn leaves, dandelions, yarrow, and grass.

My daughter gives me flowers, lip gloss, elastic hairbands, leaves she wants me to hold on to, once she gave me a drawing of a tree. It was tall and green with a thick brown trunk and two large branches reaching for the sky. This was when I still picked her up from school. Now she walks to and from school with her friends.

I had meant to unfold the drawing and hang it on the refrigerator door, but it got tossed into my purse and forgotten. *But it was for you. Didn't you want it?* Sometimes my daughter and I use the same hairbrush, also in my purse, often she brushes her hair so hard that strands of it tear out and get caught in the bristles.

For many years I carried my father, or what I had left of him, around with me in my purse. He died in the summer of 2007, and for several years he rattled about in there along with all the other stuff.

What I had left of him were six tape recordings from the last spring he was alive. His voice. And the silence. And my voice.

And all the sounds I can't quite identify that the microphone had picked up and which imprecisely could be labeled noise. The recordings were made with a small gray tape recorder the size of a thick finger. I knew I would have to deal with them somehow, the recordings, I mean. I would have to listen to them. This was my father. He was in my purse. There were probably more suitable places to keep him. In a safe-deposit box, for example, or a filing cabinet, or a small chest.

HE SAID THAT THINGS went missing. He said that *the words* disappeared. If he were younger he would have written a book about growing old. But now that he was old, he wasn't up to it. He no longer had the vigor of a younger man. This line of thinking prompted one of us, I don't remember who, to come up with the idea of writing a book together. I would ask the questions, he would answer them, I would transcribe the conversations, and finally we would sit down together and edit the material. Once the book was out, we could take the jeep and go on a book tour.

He was eighty-seven when the idea of a book first came up. He sometimes forgot words, or mixed them up, but his memory was better than mine. To have a plan. This is the family creed. I have a big family. One family on my mother's side and one on my father's. My father had nine children with six different women—I really ought to talk to him about that, I remember thinking. If we are going to write a book. Because I don't believe he *planned* to have nine children with six different women. I was *not* a planned child. My mother has told me that she carried birth-control pills around with her in her purse, but she either forgot or neglected to take them, I'm not sure which, the story is different each time she tells it. My father has told me that the discussion of an abortion was brief and undramatic, and that it ended with them agreeing she should have the baby. Happiness is finding yourself in the middle of the planning phase, when everything is possible and nothing is final. A plan is more tangi-

ble than hope, there is time to spare. "We may, indeed, say that
the hour of death is uncertain," Proust writes when depicting
his beloved grandmother's last days (although he was actually
writing about his mother), "but when we say so we represent
that hour to ourselves as situated in a vague and remote expanse
of time, it never occurs to us that it can have any connexion with
the day that has already dawned, or may signify that death—or
its first assault and partial possession of us, after which it will
never leave hold of us again—may occur this very afternoon,
so far from uncertain, this afternoon every hour of which has
already been allotted to some occupation." My father and I
made a plan without considering that death had already begun
to take possession of us. For two years, with time to spare, we
made plans for a book about growing old.

The readiness is all:

What to call it?

How to structure it?

What to ask him?

He said I could ask him whatever I wanted, but I doubted
whether that was true. I said: I don't believe you, and he said: No,
really, *whatever you want*, and I said: Okay, we'll see how it goes.

FOR TWO YEARS WE planned the book. We discussed it when we spoke on the phone, my father liked to talk on the phone and had opinions about my answering-machine message, his own message was short and brusque. We talked about the book whenever we met in person. I went to see him at Hammars, mostly in summer, but sometimes in spring and autumn. We talked about other things too, but when we weren't talking about other things, we talked about the book.

Now and then he would say something that made me think: I have to ask him about this. I should be taking notes. I didn't take notes. I remember him saying that growing old was work and that every morning he made a list of all his ailments (stiff hip, bad night, stomachache, inconsolable and filled with longing for Ingrid, leaden body, anxious when thinking about the day that lay ahead, toothache, et cetera), and if the list amounted to eight or fewer, he would get out of bed. If it came to more than eight, he would stay in bed. But that almost never happened.

"Why eight?"

"Well, because I'm over eighty. I allow myself one ailment per decade."

We spent a lot of time discussing schedules. My father was a punctual man.

So: at what time of the day should these recordings take place?

Eleven to one?

Ten to one?

Ten thirty to one?

Every other day?

Every day?

I voted for the shorter sessions, he voted for the longer ones. It wasn't always that way. As a child, I was occasionally allowed to visit him in his study and sit in the big battered armchair in order for us to *converse*. He called it *a sitting*. I remember wishing the sittings would never end.

"Shall we have a sitting tomorrow, you and I," he'd say when I was a child, "around eleven if that suits you?"

"Okay."

Ingrid in the kitchen.

"He's waiting for you, just go on in."

Pappa in the office.

"Well! How's my youngest daughter today?"

"Fine."

"Fine? What does that mean, *fine?* I don't want a communiqué."

"What's a communiqué?"

"I don't want empty words. *Fine, fine.* I want to know *exactly* how you are!"

We would sit facing each other. I took up only a tiny portion of the chair in which I sat. We shared a footrest for our feet. He wore thin, brown woolen socks, I had maybe a blue sock on one foot and a white sock on the other, neither very clean, I would have liked to have found a clean matching pair, but then I would have been late. He spread a blanket over both our feet.

"Do you feel a draft? Are you cold?"

One time I sneezed. It wasn't a big sneeze, just a little one caused by dust in the air.

My father went quiet.

"Do you have a cold?"

"No, no."

"You've spent too much time in the swimming pool. I knew it. You stayed in the water too long."

"No, Pappa. I promise. I don't have a cold."

"Well! It's time we finished anyway. I don't think you should swim any more today. Maybe you should lie down? I'll tell Ingrid you're not feeling well and that you need to lie down and rest."

Summer 2006. We continue planning our book and all that lies ahead. The book will emerge through many phases. Interviewing, transcribing, compiling, writing, editing. A great deal of work.

A woman in a red dress moves into the guesthouse at Hammars. She is a journalist, working in radio and television. I will call her Ana, after the Hungarian brothel madam Ana Cumpănaş. One day she appears in Ingrid's kitchen. She's making meatballs. I come riding down on my bike and catch a glimpse of her red dress through the window. Another day she's sitting with my father on the brown-stained bench. They're giggling. Yet another day they make plans to go to the local church to listen to chamber music, the musicians have come all the way from Stockholm. I insist on going with them. We squeeze into the jeep. My father drives fast. When we reach the church, Ana and I take hold of the gangly old man's arms as if he needs support on each side, which he does not. He goes for long walks every day supported only by his cane, but today he strides up the aisle with Ana on one side and me on the other, smiling broadly.

Late summer 2006. The phone rings. I'm up at Ängen. He's down at Hammars. Although we're only a few minutes' walk from each other, we speak on the phone more often than face to face.

"Guess what?" he says.

"What?"

"I'm engaged!"

"Okay."

"You think I'm making it up?"

"Yes."

He pauses for effect.

"I've heard that you're jealous."

"I'm not jealous. I'm your daughter."

"You're jealous!"

"I'm not jealous. I'm not one of your women. I'm your daughter. You're welcome to get engaged anytime."

Autumn 2006. The phone rings. I'm in Oslo. He's at Hammars.

"I've been thinking about our book."

"Okay?"

"I've been thinking about the . . . technicalities."

"Pappa, don't worry about it."

"No, listen. I've got an idea. How about Ana?"

"No."

"She's a radio journalist, you know that, right? She has access to first-class technical equipment."

"I don't doubt it."

"I thought it might be a good idea if she brought her equipment to Hammars . . . I mean, if we put her in charge of the actual taping of the interviews."

"You don't think a simple tape recorder will do?"

"I'm concerned about the sound quality."

"I'm literally on my way out to buy a tape recorder."

"What? Now?"

"No, not right this minute. But soon."

"Hmm."

"Pappa, this is *our* book!"

"Okay, okay, don't get mad."

"I'm not mad."

"Yes, you are, I can tell by your voice that you're mad."

Spring 2007. A series of minor strokes, says the doctor. I Google "minor stroke." *Temporary disruption of blood flow to the brain.* The medical term for this is *transient ischemic attack*. The change is gradual, but something is happening to his memory and his ability to distinguish between what is real and what is not real. By real and not real I mean: he no longer distinguishes between dreams (I don't know whether dreams is the right word here) and reality (I don't know whether that's the right word either).

All the windows of his brain have been thrown wide open.

————

Beckett wrote: "Such the confusion now between real and—how say its contrary? No matter. That old tandem."

He says: "Let me tell you a little about the order of my day. Every afternoon at precisely one o'clock I am wheeled to the kitchen and served an omelet."

He laughs with his mouth closed.

He used to laugh with his mouth open, but after developing an abscess on the inside of his cheek that makes it harder for him to speak, he laughs with his mouth closed. And then he says: "*Omelet at one*. That's a pretty good title for our book, don't you think?"

WE CALLED IT *the work*. Or *the project*. Or *the book*. It is difficult to know what to call things. On an undated yellow paper note, he writes:

> *My Dearest Daughter!*
>
> *I've tried in vain to call you to say that I'm at your disposal and prepared to work on "our project" whenever you want.*
>
> > *Hugs,*
> > *Your Old Father*

There is a stain on the note. The stain is big and round with a smaller teardrop stain jutting out of it. If it were a child's drawing and not a stain, I would have taken it to depict a hot-air balloon with a small basket for passengers. I must have left something on top of the note, a cup of coffee or a glass of wine.

The stain highlights some of the words: *Daughter, in vain, prepared.*

L ATELY, THIS SEEMS TO keep happening: I see one face and think of another. I don't know what to call it. Disappearing contours.

For a while I remembered nothing about my father, I read the notes he wrote to me, looked at pictures of him, but remembered nothing, and by the word "remember" I mean that I couldn't conjure him up, picture him, imagine what he would have said or done in a given situation, recall his voice. To mourn someone is to remember them, I couldn't do either, neither mourn nor remember. I walked around blindly, saw neither the dead nor the living, my husband wrote in one of his poems: *You have vanished into your father's house.*

When he was still alive my father had an archive and a foundation named after him. Eventually there would be three foundations, one dedicated to his manuscripts, notebooks, letters, and photographs, one dedicated to his houses, and one dedicated to the island he called home. After his death, his face graced a postage stamp and a banknote, he even had a street stub named after him. I walk up and down in the rain, the street lies in the middle of Stockholm, near the Royal Dramatic Theatre. It's really more of a stub than a street, I count my steps, up and down, but arrive at a different number every time. At the end of the street, which opens up onto a square also bearing his name, a heap of bikes are parked. The bike locks—black and silver—coil round the wheels. One of the bikes has toppled over and is gradually dragging the other bikes down with it.

Tell us about your father.

I shake my head.

I can't very well say that I don't remember anything.

One day I leaf through a book about the American artist Georgia O'Keeffe. When she grew old, she lived in New Mexico and painted the things she saw around her. Her mountains are rust-red, terra-cotta, yellow, like massive membranes, the plains and the sky barely visible. She combined perspectives, the book says, in such a way that when you look at her paintings you seem to be both very close and very far away from what you're looking at. O'Keeffe is famously associated with the expression *faraway nearby.*

In the early '80s, the photographer Ansel Adams took a picture of her. Adams and O'Keeffe were friends and drawn to the same landscapes. She was older than he was, but still outlived him by several years. In the photograph she's over ninety, ninety-two. She's wearing a white shirt, a white scarf in her hair, and a black jacket. Around her neck hangs a piece of jewelry that looks as though it's been forged from earth and light and sand. Her face is austere, her skin past wrinkled and aging, like a rocky outcrop, a lunar crater, or a sun-bleached bone. Her forehead is broad, her gaze determined, the nose long and thick like a naked branch, the lips firm and taut. My father looked exactly like that in the years before he died. The forehead, the nose, the mouth. For a long time I had felt as though I had forgotten everything, I couldn't even remember his face, but now here was Ansel Adams's photograph of Georgia O'Keeffe. I looked at her face and thought of his.

"Let's go to New Mexico," I said to my husband.

"Can't we just stay here for a while?" he said, and laid his hand on top of mine.

THE BOY WHO HELPED me was around eighteen years old, tall, skinny, with long hair and a pale, pimply face. He picked his way slowly through the store. It was a huge store, with cell phones and GPS systems in one department, TV and audio in another, small electronic items in a third, household goods and appliances in a fourth, computers in a fifth, cameras and video equipment in a sixth. I noticed his fingers, long, slender, as if he were using them to feel his way around. Occasionally, for no apparent reason, I start talking to strangers. Explaining myself. I told the boy that I needed a tape recorder because I was going to interview my father, that my father was eighty-eight years old, almost eighty-nine, that I needed the best tape recorder on the market, that I didn't want to be sitting there on some remote island with the old man and worry about faulty equipment.

"They're not really called tape recorders anymore," the boy said, and looked down at the floor, "there's no *tape*, just a digital recorder."

I tried to catch his eye.

"Well, yes, I realize that, but you know what I mean, right, what I need? Can you help me find a good one . . . you know, that's not technically complicated?"

He was spindly like an insect, his name tag said Sander, I couldn't decide whether he was clumsy or graceful, he constantly seemed on the verge of bumping into things. It had the quality of a carefully choreographed dance, this *almost* bumping into things, and yet avoiding it every time.

———

In the spring of 2007 we drove to Hammars. The new tape recorder was in my purse. My husband was driving. Our daughter Eva sat in the backseat, watching cartoons on a laptop. She had new pale-blue headphones. Now and again my husband would stop the car and rest his head on the steering wheel. I asked him what was wrong and he said that nothing was wrong. Eva's headphones were the size of jellyfish.

I hadn't seen my father for several months and had only spoken to him a few times on the phone. He was sitting at the kitchen table, eating an omelet and drinking a glass of wine. He looked up as I walked in, eyes flickering. He had aged a hundred years since I last saw him. Didn't he recognize me? He asked if I had come from the Royal Palace.

With a little wave of his hand, he invited me to sit down.

"Do you want an omelet?"

I shook my head, sat down, trying to catch his eye, but he didn't want to look at me. He said he was ready to resume his duties as royal coachman and that we could be on our way as soon as he had finished his lunch.

"Pappa. It's me."

He continued to eat, his eyes on his plate.

"Pappa?"

Women took turns caring for him. They came and went. First there was Cecilia and later also Maja. Cecilia supervised everything, Maja took care of the household. Eventually, there were others. That last summer I counted six women at Hammars. That's how he wanted it. *Be careful what you wish for*, he used to say.

To mourn another person is not necessarily the same as to despair. When Ingrid died, my father was grief-stricken. He despaired. He said he wanted to die but was too much of a coward to kill himself. *I am a seventy-four-year-old man and only now does God decide to kick me out of the nursery*, he said. My father lost a son as well. Jan, his oldest. If I lost a child, *despair* would be too feeble a word. As would *grief-stricken*. I wouldn't have known how to go on. But he did. Jan died, and he went on. Children were not what mattered most to him. I still busy myself with maps, lists, charts—important, unimportant, most loved, least loved—even though I know it gets me nowhere. To be honest, I think I have mourned my parents all my life. They changed before my eyes the way my children change before my eyes and I don't really know who I was to them.

Can I mourn people who are still alive?

Every evening, I follow the map and walk down to the sea, I'm in a new place and don't know my way around yet, it is very beautiful here, the towns have strange names like *Brantevik* and *Skillinge* and *Simrishamn*, it is winter and the sea is covered by a thin sheet of ice.

I remember my father-in-law used to say: *I don't ride the same day I saddle*.

My grandmother used to say: *Men—over and out!*

My mother also used to say: *Men—over and out!*

And my father used to say: *Be careful what you wish for*.

He also said: *Words that have flown the nest cannot be caught by the wing*. He was a minister's son, so quoting Luther (by way

of Strindberg) came naturally to him. Not to forget cleanliness,
self-control, order, and punctuality.

He was talking about anger. Were his children angry? Had
they inherited this from him?

"Are you angry, my heart?"

He never saw me angry.

"There's nothing unresolved between us, is there?"

"No, Pappa."

"Nothing eating you?"

"No, nothing at all."

"Good, nor did I think there was."

The kind of anger he called murderous rage. Or, what to
call it? A short fuse? Feeling like you can't breathe? Having a
bad temper? Scorn, contempt, resentment, self-pity? *I am grieving and no one will save me.* Rage as a form of gluttony: First the
anger devours you and then you devour the anger, it never stops.

If you are unfortunate enough to be saddled with such rage,
he said, you have to learn to control it. This was advice he had
learned early in life from older and wiser men than he, and he was
only too happy to pass it on. He said: Some people have perfect
pitch, they can hear the buzzing of a bee and say, *You hear that?
That's a G sharp!* Some people are stingy. Some people can dance.
Some are angry. The body consists mostly of water, the heart of
rage. The kind of rage that cramps up your jaw and makes you
grind your teeth and tends to land you in situations in which you
end up making a complete fool of yourself. Professionally, it can
be disastrous. There's no room for emotional sloppiness in the
workplace; if you let your rage get the better of you and lash out
like a poisonous liver sausage, you'll only waste valuable time
and ruin things for yourself and whatever you hope to achieve,
not to mention the fact that you'll have to call everybody the

next day and apologize. Which is both embarrassing and time-consuming. You may, in the course of your temper tantrum, have said something to another person that cannot be explained away or retracted. It has been said. Which is the opposite of unsaid. For *words that have flown the nest cannot be caught by the wing*. Remember that, my heart. This applies not only to professional life, but also to your romantic relationships. You think you're rich, that your reserves of love will last forever, but if you don't pay attention, you'll find yourself broke in no time. Bankrupt. You have to play your parts with care. One—*one*—pedagogical fit of rage per play or film can be effective, but it has to be professionally, and not emotionally, motivated.

"No, Pappa, I have not come from the Royal Palace. I've come from Oslo. I've come to interview you, remember? We have work to do."

I don't say *We agreed to meet*, or *we're going to sit and talk for a while*, I say *We have work to do* because *work* is a magic word, because nothing will get in the way of work. We do not call in sick. We do not malinger. We may lie, betray, wake up in the middle of the night frightened and crying and looking at the clock. Morning is not far off and the nightstand is covered in writing. But at six o'clock, we get up and go to work.

Pappa and I are writing a book. We start tomorrow.

Maja wipes the kitchen counter. She speaks to my father in the third person. Would he like some more wine? Would he like some more bread with his omelet? Speaking slowly and a little too loud. She wrings the cloth out over the sink, gray trickles dripping down, and hangs it on a little hook on the wall.

"Isn't it nice for him to have a visit from his youngest daughter?"

She nods enthusiastically, the way you do when you expect the person you're nodding at to nod back.

"Oh, yes," my father says, not nodding back. "Oh, yes, indeed."

He looks at me and winks.

It was no longer just the odd word that had gone missing. Maybe half of them. The forgotten words formed a long, sinuous trail that stretched from the stony beach, through the forest, and all the way into the rooms at Hammars. When the moon rose and he went out to look for them, the birds had gotten there first. Noises and images helter-skelter. I said to myself: But he has lost his senses, we can't do the interviews now, it's too late, but looking back, I wonder whether the expression *lost his senses* is misleading. From behind his thick spectacles my father could see a little bit with one eye and just about nothing with the other, in the diary that lay on his desk, someone had written the words "laser surgery." An appointment had been made at Visby Infirmary on the eighteenth of June. The surgery was supposed to restore some of his eyesight. One ear was in good working order, I had to shout sometimes, but only if I forgot to pay attention and stood or sat on the wrong side and talked to his deaf ear. It was up to me to remember which ear to speak to. His sense of touch must have been magnified sevenfold. He would flinch if I so much as brushed against him, as though his skin had been torn off. I didn't touch his cheek or hand as often as I used to. He opened and closed himself, continuously. It is hard work to get yourself going every morning, especially at the age of eighty-nine, and sometimes the most obvious choice is to go back to sleep, or not to wake up at all. What is it Pessoa writes in *The Book of Disquiet?* "I'd woken up early, and I took a long time getting ready to exist." Occasionally, *before*, Pessoa had come up in conversation when we talked about our book. Perhaps we could steal, or allude, to Pessoa's title, or would that just be putting on airs, we don't want to be putting on airs, there's an art to knowing exactly how much of that one can allow oneself, but as a working title it was good, maybe we'd come up with another title once we had finished writing and were ready to publish, but time passed and then he forgot all about Pessoa.

The boy in the store had suggested a tiny silver-gray electronic device from Sony. It was oblong and fit neatly into my hand. A book about growing old.

Growing old is work. Getting out of bed is work. Taking a bath is work, putting on your clothes is work, getting your daily dose of fresh air is work, meeting other people is work. Nobody talks about the work.

"It feels like this is the epilogue," he said.

We were sitting in the jeep on our way to the cinema. It was a year earlier, maybe even two, we had just started planning the book. Without warning, my father stepped on the accelerator and shot forward so fast I had to grab the edges of my seat. He swung off the road and into the forest, sped down the trail toward the sea, and slammed on the brakes right at the edge of a high cliff. He turned and looked at me, grinning from ear to ear.

"I scared you!"

"Yes."

"Hahaha."

"I don't think you should be driving like that."

"But I'm having fun! You should lighten up and allow the old man some fun now that he's a hundred and losing his memory."

"You're not a hundred and your memory's better than mine."

"So, are we going to write this book?"

"Okay. But you have to drive properly. I don't want to die yet."

"We can call it *The Epilogue*," he said.

"Maybe."

"Maybe? Well, I think it's a damn good title."

WE MADE THE RECORDINGS in May, he died at the end of July at four o'clock in the morning. That same evening, after a long day, I got out the tape recorder. It was in my purse. I sat on the edge of the bed, having sought refuge in one of the two upstairs bedrooms at Ängen. The family was still gathered downstairs. My husband had made soup for everyone. Occasionally he had taken my hand in his as if he wanted to tell me something, but there wasn't much to say. Everyone praised the soup. Carrot and ginger. Warm. Soothing. The perfect soup for the occasion, said one of my sisters, I think it was Ingmarie, my sisters noticed everything, even such a minute detail (considering the circumstances) as the soup. Earlier that day we had agreed that everybody would meet at Ängen to eat a meal together and maybe talk about what to do next. The obituary, the funeral, that sort of thing.

I looked at the tape recorder. It fit into the palm of my hand. When we did the recordings, I told him the technical equipment worked as it should, I told him I had listened to the interviews and had already begun transcribing. That was a lie. Every time I had been down at Hammars, taping a conversation, I returned to Ängen almost as worn out as he was. There was no way on earth I could sit down and listen to a day of us talking, or start transcribing. Leave me alone, I said to my husband and Eva. I couldn't deal with them. My father left no room for anyone else. So they went off to Norsholmen at the northern end of the island to gather reeds and shells.

———

I looked at my watch and calculated that he had been dead for sixteen hours. I pressed Play.

Was this it? Was this all I'd accomplished? The sound quality was awful. The tape crackled and sputtered—it sounded as if I had lit a fire and set us down in the middle of the blaze. Our voices were drowned out, his faltering, mine shrill, I couldn't tell one word from the next. After five minutes I pressed Stop and put the tape recorder back in my purse. An utter fiasco. I should probably have used an external microphone, a mic attached to his shirt collar, although there's no way you could have attached a mic or anything like a mic to his shirt collar. He wouldn't have liked me fiddling. He would have winced at that. He always wore faded checked flannel shirts. Thick flannel. Pale-green, gray, red, brown, autumnal orange. He decided on a style as a very young man and never changed it. During his last summer he needed help to get dressed. If my father were a tree, the faded flannel shirt would be the bark. I didn't want to poke and prod at him with gadgets. His top button would be undone and I remember noticing a fine, loose fold of skin above his Adam's apple, fragile as eggshell. So no, I couldn't have attached a mic to his shirt collar.

What I'm trying to say is that when I presented myself at Hammars to interview him, I had neither the technical know-how nor the equipment one might want to have in such situations, and that my obvious shortcomings had resulted in six acoustically disastrous recordings.

Even though I didn't listen to the recordings—yes, and even though the tape recorder disappeared and I was sure it was lost and gone forever—I thought about them often. In my mind, the five minutes I *had* listened to on the evening of the day he died grew large and dismally long. The tape recorder microphone had picked up all the sounds in the room, including our voices, and composed its own hissing, throbbing, crackling, murmuring, sputtering cacophony. And why hadn't I taken notes? I should have realized that these were the last conversations we would ever have. I should have registered everything that happened. Not just what we said, but everything else as well. The weather, for example. And what we were wearing. Which dresses I had chosen. Out of old habit I never wore jeans when I visited my father in his study. Things were happening all the time. The pine tree outside his window swayed ever so gently in the wind. None of this can be heard on tape. It can only be seen. The house at Hammars is built in such a way that when you're inside, you can't hear the outside. The pine tree swayed ever so—why didn't I write about that? Or about his hands? Or the light?

My father was dead. I sat on the edge of the bed in one of the upstairs rooms in the house at Ängen, the evening sun lighting up everything. I looked at the tape recorder. Small, rectangular, closed.

Down there in the house at Hammars he lay lifelike, waiting to be picked up. We had decided to let him lie for twenty-four hours so that children and grandchildren, those who wished, could come to Hammars and say their goodbyes. Not everyone wished to or was able to. One of my sisters slept in the house that night, in the room next to his, he shouldn't be alone, she said, not on the first full night of his death.

In the end, what I was left with were recordings of all the sounds in the room and, not least, the unbearable sound of my own voice.

What would *he* have said if he had been sitting there beside me on the edge of the bed, listening? *The ear is all-important.* He would have complained about the sound quality. The equipment. The workmanship. *These spools are crap!* And then he would have said: *Your voice, my heart, so silvery and thin and eager to please, like a maiden in her tower. I've told you to speak Norwegian when you speak to me,* and then he would have said: *We have to do it all over again.*

WHO IS THAT WOMAN shouting at the old man?
HOW IS LITTLE PAPPA DOING TODAY?
I pressed Stop.
Then I pressed Play again. Maybe it wasn't as bad as I thought.
HOW IS LITTLE PAPPA DOING TODAY?
I pressed Stop and slipped the tape recorder into my purse. I got up from the bed and drew up a new plan.
Go down and join the others.
Have soup.
Go to bed and get up and go to bed and get up and go to bed and get up.
Take one day at a time.
First bury him, then mourn him, and then—when some time has passed—listen to the tapes.

AFTER THE TAPE RECORDER had bounced around in my purse for three years, I took it out and placed it in a desk drawer—and this is where everything becomes a blur. My husband lost his father the year after I lost mine. Now we both had a dead father. Every night a mangy cat came to relieve itself in our daughter's sandbox, the house and the garden smelled of cat pee, no matter how much we cleaned. My husband fell for a woman with long, dark hair and slender wrists. We moved to Fårö and stayed there for a year. He sent her emails with links to songs. When I asked him why, he said it was because she wasn't me. We moved again. For many years I had no idea where the tape recorder was.

SEVEN YEARS AFTER MY father's death the tape recorder resurfaces in a box in the attic. It is my husband who finds it. I call my son, Ola. He is twenty-four.

"The sound quality is awful," I say. "I don't know why. The boy who sold it to me said it was the best on the market."

"Yes, well, that was a long time ago."

"Seven years."

"That's a long time in the life of a digital tape recorder."

"I know, but when you listen to the recordings they sound like they're a hundred years old."

"Have you actually listened to them?"

"Well, no, not exactly. Not now. It was bad enough the last time I tried. I couldn't listen to more than five or ten minutes."

I take a deep breath.

"So I was wondering if you could help me? I was thinking there might be a way of transferring the recordings to a laptop or a phone . . . maybe there's a tool or an app or something that could clean up the sound . . . don't you know a good sound technician?"

Ola is up to his knees in cardboard boxes. He is moving in with his girlfriend and doesn't really have time to talk to me now. I ask if I can send him a picture of the tape recorder. If he *saw* what kind of tape recorder it was, he might be able to suggest what I can do to salvage the sound.

"How about just trying to listen to it?" he says.

"It's impossible! It crackles!"

"Maybe it's just a lousy speaker. I mean, the tape recorder is tiny and it's been lying around for seven years."

He is infinitely patient now. When did he get that voice? A
grown man speaking to a young girl who's at the end of her tether.

"I don't know," I say.

"Mamma, listen to me. I think you should hook it up to a pair
of good headphones and see if the sound gets any better."

"Okay."

"And if the sound isn't any better, if you still can't hear what
you're saying to each other, send me a text. Okay?"

"Okay."

"I have to go now, okay?"

"Okay."

I dig out a big pair of headphones and settle on the sofa in
the living room. It is night, early morning. My husband and
our daughter are asleep upstairs. I press Play. It's like diving
underwater.

There's noise. Fumbling pauses, searching for words. My
hands are fiddling with something, causing even more noise.
The fiddling sounds are loud, occasionally drowning out our
voices. I remember that the tape recorder was lying on a little
wooden table between his wheelchair and my chair and that I
kept picking it up to make sure it was working, moving it closer
toward him whenever he lowered his voice, constantly worrying that I wouldn't catch what he was saying. And every time
my hands touch the microphone, it translates into a thundering
noise in my ear.

I want to say to her—she who sits there fiddling with the
tape recorder: Stop that fiddling! Put your hands in your lap!

Concentrate on the old man, he'll be dead in a few weeks. It's embarrassing. But I don't switch it off. I don't press Stop. He is more lucid than I remembered, and my voice is less shrill. We're doing the best we can. But the fiddling drives me crazy. I've never thought of my hands as a source of sound, obviously I can snap my fingers, clap, applaud, but hands are usually quiet, gestures are inaudible, fiddling too—or so I thought. "It is confusing and embarrassing to have two mouths," writes Anne Carson, describing a group of terra-cotta statuettes from the fourth century BC, each of which consists of "almost nothing but her two mouths," how much more confusing and embarrassing to have mouths in places where you didn't know you had them, to discover that even parts of your body you thought of as soundless are actually fraught with sound. The microphone picked up everything, making no distinction between the important and the unimportant. On the other hand, it's pointless to think in terms of categories such as important and unimportant. Pointless to think in terms of categories at all. I spend too much time distinguishing between the one and the other. "But the living all make the mistake of distinguishing too sharply," wrote Rilke. "Angels (it is said) often know not whether they walk among the living or the dead."

Later it occurs to me that the fiddling sounds are embarrassing in the same way that it's embarrassing to see yourself in photographs. When someone takes my picture, I squeeze my eyes together, I frown, I duck into my own neck, as if it were a tube into which I could disappear. My neck is long and slender, but new creases continue to appear as I get older. When I look at myself in photographs, I see two slits where the eyes should have been, in a face that hasn't made up its mind about what sort of face it ought to be.

Six recordings. Had my father been alive, I would have asked him about the pauses. The silence. The blank spaces. How to render them? How would he have done it?

SHE   So, we've been planning this for a long time.

HE   We've been planning this for a long time.

SHE   Yes.

HE   But last night I felt so incredibly unsure.

SHE   You did?

HE   Yes, I was lying awake, feeling unsure.

SHE   Why?

HE   Pardon?

SHE   Why were you unsure?

Long silence.

HE   I've been trying out a new sleeping pill.

SHE   Oh?

HE   I have been a dedicated sleeping-pill addict my whole life . . . Rohypnol, great stuff, two a day, plus two Valium, a couple of Valium in the evening and a couple in the morning.

SHE   In the morning?

HE   Yes.

SHE   Early morning? To help you sleep a little more?

HE   Yes.

SHE   Which means you slept quite well last night?

HE   I did sleep well last night, yes. I didn't sleep *quite well*, I slept exceptionally well all night.

SHE   But in that case . . . I mean, that's good, right?

HE   Yes . . . and so here we are . . . here we are in my study . . . designed by an architect specializing in acoustics, everything in here is set up for the sole purpose of listening to music . . . This is my room.

SHE   Yes.

HE   Yes.

SHE   But you started by saying that you were lying awake last night feeling very unsure about the whole project, so do you think maybe you woke up now and again and thought "no" . . . ?

HE   Yes.

SHE   Thought "no". . . and felt unsure about the whole thing?

HE   Yes.

SHE   So, what were you thinking about when you lay awake?

HE   (*clears his throat*) I was thinking that I should have been better prepared. I was thinking that we should have had a preparatory conversation and then proceeded from there.

SHE   Hmm.

HE   Or something like that. It was vague.

Pause. He clears his throat.

HE   Because the closer it got to morning, the more anxious I became.

THERE ARE SIX RECORDINGS in all. Each one a little over two hours long. By the time we got to the point of sitting down in his study with the tape recorder between us, we were both feeling very unsure. I remember it, and you can tell from our voices. Shy. As if we were in a strange city and had to speak a foreign language. On tape, the silence is not silent but sputtering, crackling, fiddling, fumbling. At times he sounds clearer than at others. At times I sound clearer than at others. I don't know whether the word "clear" is right here—as if it were a question of light and air.

SHE   You've had this study for many years.
HE   For many years.
SHE   Since 1967?
HE   Really? . . . Oh, I don't know.
SHE   It must have been 1967. You built this house when you and my mother were together.
HE   Was that in '67?
SHE   Yes, I was born in '66, the house was finished in the summer of '67.
HE   Hmm, yes . . .

Long pause.

HE   Were you born in '67?
SHE   No, '66.
HE   Sixty-six?
SHE   Yes.

HE   Dear me!

SHE   Anyway . . .

HE   (*interrupting*) It's good to see you!

SHE   It's good to see you too!

HE   (*hesitating*) How old are you now?

SHE   Forty.

HE   Forty? Good God! Are you that old?

I TRY TO PICTURE HIM, but can't quite manage it. Or, maybe. If I stand on the narrow forest road, the one with all the cattle guards, I see an old man on a big red ladies' bicycle. The bicycle is clearer than the man. A burst of red in an otherwise gray-green landscape. Nothing (apart from the red of the red bicycle) stands out. That's how it was. Strict. Austere. The man on the bicycle has no face.

I have a picture of him sitting hunched over his desk, peering at photographs through a magnifying glass. In the picture he is wearing a thin brown wool cardigan over a checkered flannel shirt. He looks thin.

He sits tall on the bicycle seat, pedaling without hurry, the forest on one side, the sea on the other, the bicycle has a luggage rack, big wheels, and a slender frame, he himself is tall and thin, his corduroy trousers are brown, his cardigan is green, his wooly hat is also green, he wears sensible shoes and elegant brown wool socks from Munich.

Ingrid was the one who mended his socks. Her spools of yarn are neatly piled on top of one another in her sewing box in her study.

Pappa and Ingrid each had their own study separated by a

narrow hallway and a small archive. Ingrid used her study to type up his manuscripts, balance accounts, answer letters, write in her diary.

The yarn was the same color as the socks, or possibly a paler shade, as if the sun had etched a little light in all the places she had mended. When he was at his desk, Ingrid would walk back and forth through the house. Only occasionally did she sit in silence, head bent over her needlework (socks, shirts, bed linens). I slept in sheets with tiny coarse patches darned by Ingrid. I was twenty-six when she fell ill, cancer of the stomach. When she died, I was afraid that grief would break his heart.

The old man on the bicycle resembles a thistle. Tall and thin and green. He blends so perfectly into the landscape that you almost can't make him out. You only see the bicycle. Thistles grow along the road to Hammars, around the cattle guards and out on the moors.

When I was a little girl, he used to read to me in bed. When he got to the end of the chapter—the chapter we had agreed to read before the light was turned off and it was time to sleep— he would glance up from the book and say: "One more? Shall we read one more?" He read Astrid Lindgren, Maria Gripe, Tove Jansson. Sometimes he would read a poem or part of a poem. He said he didn't like poetry, but in his trouser pocket he occasionally carried a folded yellow piece of notebook paper with some lines or verses he had come across in a book and copied down.

I was tucked up in bed, he sat on its edge, we looked at the sheet of paper being unfolded. Unfolding a piece of paper takes time. We didn't speak while he was busy doing this. A lamp burned on the bedside table. I had long, fine hair. I wished that it were even longer and that it shone. Nanna said it would shine if I brushed it a hundred times every morning and every evening. Over the chair hung a faded blue sundress that I had outgrown over the summer.

"Are you ready?" says Pappa, now finished unfolding the piece of paper.

"Okay," I say.

"Are you quite sure that you're ready?"

"Yes."

"Absolutely sure?"

"Pappa! Yes!"

> *I listen my heart*
> *my heart is*
> *I listen my heart*
> *when I know that my heart*
> *that stars tore themselves asunder*
> *I listen my heart*
> *my heart is.*

"That's it."

"Hmm."

"You want me to read it again?"

"No, it's okay, you don't have to."

"What do you think, was it any good?"

"I'm not sure."

The landscape is flat. The trees are gnarled. The road winds gently. The sea is cobweb gray, pale, green, still. The sea is dying from lack of oxygen. Sometimes the surface is covered with toxic algae, the algae are spongy like old wall-to-wall carpeting. The bicycle is red, the gravel crunches under its wheels. The bicycle is so red that no matter what I try to compare it to—poppies, for example, that also grow by the roadside at Hammars—it falls short. The bicycle is redder than any other red I can think of. I make a list of reds, but nothing is red enough. Even after Pappa is dead and buried, crumbled to earth and gone—I'm no longer able to describe his face—even then, the redness of the bicycle stands out in memory.

WE HAD ALWAYS BEEN better at departures than arrivals. Pappa was old when I was born, forty-eight years old, the same age I am now, always forty-eight years older than me. Every time we had to say goodbye I would think to myself that this was probably the last time.

I don't remember how old I am when I begin dressing up for him, a tiny bracelet around my wrist that slips off and vanishes because my wrist is tinier still (I spend a lot of time hunting for trinkets that have slipped off or come undone and gone lost), hair brushed away from my face and drawn into a tight ponytail. *You mustn't hide your face.* Seven years old, maybe. We will not say goodbye, he says, goodbyes give him sleepless nights, goodbyes cause anxiety and stomachaches, his runways for landing and takeoff are long, arrivals and departures aren't done in a blink, we'll just act like it's nothing, talk about ordinary things in our everyday voices. We're sitting side by side on the brown-stained bench outside the house. The car is waiting, it's time to go. He kisses me on the forehead, hugs me and says: Let's not say goodbye.

He stays at Hammars for as long as he can, but eventually he and Ingrid will also have to get in the car and drive away. When the snow comes, the house is empty. Ingrid will have cleaned and vacuumed every nook and cranny, but after a few weeks' time it is quite clear that no one lives there anymore, the dust gathers in the corners and under the beds, dead flies litter the windowsills, the flies got inside despite the rule about keeping all the doors and windows closed in summer. The house is what it is, immersed in gray and unaffected by all who came and went and filled it with sound, the house has waited for winter and opens up to it in the still, shimmering half-light. This is the place, this is the house he longs for when he's in Stockholm, in the flat at Karlaplan; winter on Fårö doesn't put on airs, it is what it is, summer caters to the whims of others, demanding and insistent, bright and coquettish: *Look how beautiful I am, look at my red poppies and the tall blue sky and the moors like West African savannas.*

So once more we sit on the bench, saying goodbye. Or rather: we *don't* say goodbye. The bench lies in the shade, sheltered from the wind. The other side of the house is prettier, with a view of the sea. But we hardly ever sit there.

THINK ABOUT THE WOMEN in my family and about their purses and the things they carried around with them. Nanna, for instance, carried my grandfather's ashes around with her in her purse. Nanna was rosy-cheeked and plump, sporadically sassy in high-heeled shoes. During the war, she and my grandfather and their two young daughters lived in Toronto. My grandfather was an instructor at the Royal Norwegian Air Force base, also known as Little Norway, on Centre Island south of Toronto Harbor. The purpose of the camp was to train young airmen for combat in Northern Norway. One day out on the airfield, my grandfather was struck in the head by a propeller. He died some years later in a hospital in New York. Brain tumor. I've never been able to work out whether there was a direct connection between the propeller and the brain tumor, or whether these were two unrelated events. His daughters were fair-haired, pale, gangly. I remember reading that all little girls look alike—fair-haired little girls look like other fair-haired little girls, dark-haired little girls look like other dark-haired little girls—it's next to impossible to tell one from the other. I learned this from an American police detective involved in a missing-persons case. In the autumn of 2007, not long after the death of my father, the body of a little girl was found in the waters of Galveston Bay in Texas. She was in a blue plastic box, she'd been lying there for at least two weeks. At the time no one knew who she was or how she ended up in the box. "Our life was to give name," wrote the poet Gunnar Björling. I remember that the detective in charge of the investigation gave the little girl the name *Baby Grace* and that he said the investigation was made more difficult by the fact that all little girls look alike.

But little girls don't look at other little girls and think: she looks like me. What they think is: nobody looks like me, I'm the only one like me.

It was quite a bundle Nanna brought with her when the war was finally over and she and her daughters boarded the first boat home to Norway. She brought her grief and a crate of oranges and her girls and her suitcases and her purse—black lacquer with an arched handle and a clasp that produced a little click each time she opened or closed it—and the urn with her husband's ashes. When they docked at the wharf in Bergen, the two little girls, one of whom would one day be my mother, tossed oranges to everyone who had come to greet the boat from America.

HE   I only have the one eye and I don't even see very well with *that*. In a few months I'm going to Visby Infirmary to be operated on. They tell me I'll get my eyesight back. In the meantime there's not much else for me to do than to sit here and listen to music. It's fantastic, you know, that over the years I've built up such a collection . . . all these books . . . music . . . all these *records* on my shelves.

With great difficulty he reaches out of his wheelchair—positioned an arm's length away from the shelves holding the turntable and his record collection—and with trembling hand he raises the stylus and lowers it onto the record. I picture him doing this. I have no memory of this moment. I didn't take notes. I only have the recording. Hissing, sighing, crackling, and a faint grunt from him, and then my voice asking: Can I help you with that, and his: *No! . . . No! . . . I said No!*

HE   It all began when I was a little boy and was allowed to go to the opera.

SHE   Who took you to the opera?

HE   Pardon?

SHE   Who took you to the opera?

HE   My aunt Anna von Sydow, she had a gigantic hat and was very rich.

Silence.

HE   I remember . . . I was ten or twelve, and the first one was *Tannhäuser* . . . Wagner's *Tannhäuser* . . . and I experienced it with a kind of fever . . . I came down with a fever that night . . . it was such fun, you see . . . I don't know what year that was.

SHE   Well, it must have been 1928, perhaps, if you were ten years old, in Stockholm?

HE   Yes, perhaps.

SHE   Tell me more about the night you came home from
        the opera.

HE   I got very sick, I came down with a fever.

SHE   Were you frightened?

HE   No.

SHE   Can you still be shaken, the way you were then?

HE   Yes.

SHE   Just as much?

HE   Oh, yes . . . but Wagner, of course, has taken a back-
        seat . . . I'd like you to hear . . . Let me see how this
        works.

*He fumbles, struggles to put on a record, the radio comes on at
full volume, a female voice says something about Vivaldi.*

HE   But this is all wrong.

SHE   That was the radio, you switched on the radio.

*He turns everything off, fumbles some more, she tries to help but
is told to get out of the way, he puts on the record. It is Beethoven's
Piano Concerto no. 4 in G major.*

HE   There is nothing greater than this, apart from Bach,
        perhaps.

For a long time there is just the music.
    *She says something on the tape, but it's hard to make out. He
interrupts her.*

HE   (*loudly*) I don't want to talk. I'd rather not talk over
        Beethoven. I won't talk at the same time as Beethoven.

SHE   I'm sorry. I won't say a word. We can just listen.

The music stops abruptly.

HE   We can listen to it some other time (*impatiently*) then
      we can listen to all of it . . . It takes about thirty-five
      minutes.

SHE   Yes, I think we should do that . . . listen to all of it . . .
      without saying a word.

HE   Yes, or you could just go out and buy the record
      yourself.

She doesn't reply.

HE   Now then, where were we?

THINK OF ALL THE shades of blue that spread across his hands and feet and parts of his face when there were only days or hours left of life. The common term for this is mottling of the skin, *blue marbling* in Norwegian. He became, even as he ceased to be. Marbling involves the mixing of two or more colors to create a marble-like pattern and transforming a surface—stone, paper, wood, skin—into something other than it is or was. I'm not sure whether to use present or past tense here. The tenth-century collection of writings by Su Yijian, *The Four Treasures of the Scholar's Study*, contains what is possibly the first reference to paper marbling: a type of decorative paper described as "flowing sand." When I rearranged his blanket and caught a glimpse of his blue-marbled feet, I didn't think of any of this, not of the color blue, not of paper, not even of flowing sand, of which there is so much on Fårö. I thought of what my mother used to say to my father: *If you're ever in doubt that she's actually yours, take a look at her feet. They're yours to a tee. Her legs too. Long and skinny.*

HE   I am taking a walk outside the house, and walking there right next to me is a person I don't know. An anonymous person. After a little while I say to this person: This is, after all, a fabulous house. And the person replies: Yes, you must be exceedingly proud.

He leans forward as though to confide in her.

HE   (*murmuring*) But I'm not the one who built this house. (*Sits back, raises his voice.*) I say to the person: But I'm not the one who built this house! And do you know what happens then?

SHE   No.

HE   The stranger looks at me, astonished, and says: But of course it was you who built this house!

Silence.

HE   And in so many situations . . . dreams . . . the stranger turns to me and says: Yes, you did all this. This is your house.

Long pause.

HE   It terrifies me.

The abscess in his mouth makes it hard for him to pronounce certain words, particularly multisyllable words or compound words, such as "sexuality," "contractor," or "Stockholm Opera," the words get stuck between tongue, abscess, and lips.

SHE Why does it terrify you?

HE It's a big nothing. A nonsense. The person says, you did all this. And I say: It was the architect . . . and . . . and . . . the con . . . the contractor who did it all.

SHE But what do you mean by *nonsense*?

HE What's nonsense is that they say things that are . . . *utterly misleading*! I haven't had anything whatsoever to do with the building of this house.

SHE But surely the house is an expression of who you are? You've lived here for over forty years and you've made decisions about how it should look?

HE Yes, I have. I have decided how it should look. I furnished the rooms and hung pictures on the walls . . . that I've done . . . but that's not exactly architecture. I've been indescribably passive as far as this house is concerned. You can't imagine. It frightens and astonishes me.

———

HE The onset of my illness goes back to the twelfth of August last year. One morning my nose started to bleed. I was bleeding like a hippopotamus. I stood over the sink and the blood poured down.

Long silence.

HE   I called the doctor and he said: No harm done, these things happen to old men, but you're fine now. But then, a few days later, after the hem . . . the hemorrhage . . . I think it was on the twentieth of August, I jumped into the swimming pool and to my astonishment I sank to the bottom.

SHE   You sank?

HE   I sank and couldn't come up for air, I pushed and kicked but couldn't.

Silence.

HE   Eventually I managed to cling to the wall . . . to the edge . . . and . . . and . . . and finally I was able to crawl back on land. For the very first time in my life I was able to experience how unpleasant death is, I had never experienced that before.

SHE   You were afraid you were going to die?

HE   Yes. But eventually it eased up.

SHE   Ah.

HE   But then, a couple of days later, I fell into the swimming pool again and sank like a stone.

He looks at her with his one good eye.

HE   I managed to . . . Oh yes! . . . I managed to maneuver myself over to the steps, but I thought it was odd . . . I thought it was strange that I sank to the bottom and was unable to surface again, so I called the doctor, the same doctor I had called about the nosebleed . . . and this time his tone was very different: You must come in right away so we can have a look at you! The way you're carrying on now could be fatal! Please come immediately! . . . Well, there you go . . . So I went to Stockholm and he examined me and ran every conceivable sort of test and it turned out that my illness was both peculiar and banal.

Silence.

SHE   So what was it?
HE   What?
SHE   What was wrong with you?
HE   What?
SHE   What was the doctor's diagnosis?

Silence.

HE   I had lots of dreams, uninteresting ones, like flopticon pictures . . .

He says *flopticon*, but means *balopticon*. Slides.

HE   . . . like old balopticon pictures that I have to look at.
SHE   At night, when you were asleep?
HE   The pictures were there during the day too. When I was awake. At night and during the day.

Silence

HE   Then I caught pneumonia. And when I recovered
          from the pneumonia, I began losing my balance. I
          walked and I fell, it could happen anytime, in all
          tracks, I'd walk and I'd fall. My whole damn body
          was black and blue . . . I found it quite comical . . .
          I've wondered about that . . . why I found it com-
          ical . . . It was fun going to the circus when I was
          little, I went with my aunt, Anna von Sydow, the
          one with the big hat . . . and . . . and . . . the clowns
          came in and fell on their backs and did somersaults
          and rolled about and bumped into each other, and I
          thought it was hilarious. When I fall over it feels a
          little bit like . . . well . . . it makes me think of that.
          When I fall—you must understand this—when a
          man who is five feet, ten inches tall falls and hurts
          himself, or does a kind of a somersault and lands
          on a piece of furniture . . . or whatever the hell it
          might be . . . there is something comical about it.
          People have always found it funny, throughout the
          ages . . . I fall . . . fall . . . and now it hurts more
          than it used to.

SHE   Poor Pappa.

HE   And then there are all the dreams.

SHE   The dreams?

HE   I dream that this anonymous person turns to me and
          says: What a fabulous house you've built here. And I
          say: But I didn't build this house, I don't know who
          lives in this house, and then he says: But it's *you*.
          You're the one who lives in this house.

SHE   And that is terrifying?

HE   I think it's terrifying, yes.

SHE   But why is it terrifying?

HE   I have a feeling that it's all an uncanny hoax ... a silent agreement involving a lot of people.

Silence.

This is where I think he raises his head and looks at her.

HE   Well! There you have it! This has been my entertainment for the past year ... Are you cold?

SHE   No.

Silence.

HE   I was still writing in my calendar back then. I don't anymore ...

She interrupts him.

SHE   Every day, you and I write in your calendar that we'll meet right here, in your study, the following day at eleven a.m.

HE   Yes, I know. But that's different.

SHE   I'm sorry. I interrupted you. You were about to say something.

HE   I was going to say that I wrote in my diary that I'd had a nosebleed. I wrote: This is where my confusion begins, this is where my dreams and hallucinations start to intrude on reality in a terrifying way.

What he actually said was: This is where my confusion *ends*, but I think he meant: this is where my confusion *begins*. That spring he tended to get words mixed up and often said the opposite of what he was trying to say. *Ends* presumably means *begins*, but I could be wrong.

WHEN MAMMA AND PAPPA were an item in the '60s, Mamma's face was so naked as to almost not be a face. It was constantly falling apart and putting itself back together again. Much has been said and written about Mamma's face, her eyes, her lips, her hair, her unsettling vulnerability and the way in which all great actresses channel every emotion to the area in and around the mouth, but no one has said anything about her ears. When I was little, I liked lying close to her and stroking her hair, I didn't yet have words for beauty, or for love; like most children I was more concerned with the size of things, whether they were big or small, and Mamma had big feet and big ears. We would lie in her double bed with its golden bedposts and pink flowery sheets, and she would let me stroke her hair while she read a book or spoke on the telephone. She often ended a phone conversation with the words *Men—over and out*. She said it with her face averted, as if addressing the walls. *Men—over and out*. Nanna also said *Men—over and out*. Once I heard Aunt Billy say *Men—over and out*, and I always paid attention to what Aunt Billy said. Aunt Billy had red curls, a floor-length fur coat (which hung at the back of the hall closet in the house in Trondheim and was hardly ever worn), five children, and a husband and a full-time job as store manager, she smoked two packs of cigarettes a day and read a new book every week. Mamma had many suitors, but I don't think she liked any of them. Like Penelope, she waited for the right one to come home. There was a white Cobra telephone on her bedside table. This was the one she always used. She liked spending time in her bedroom, lounging about in various stages of silk negligee. When I lay close to her and stroked all the hair away from her face, her ears came into their own. Mamma's ears were big like conch shells, and if I had put my ear to her ear I would have heard the ocean. We had a telephone in the living room as well. A red Cobra. It rang incessantly. When Mamma could no longer stand all the ringing, she would pull out both plugs and stick the telephones, the red and the white, in the freezer.

SHE   Can you tell me about Mamma?

HE   I have been thinking about Beethoven and how he goes right at you. Right at your feelings . . . feelings . . .

SHE   Okay?

HE   There was an orchestra rehearsal in Malmö, and Käbi was the soloist . . . it was the G major Concerto. I had never met Käbi before.

SHE   But I was asking about my . . .

He interrupts her.

HE   What you may not know about dress rehearsals is that in many cases it is the first time that the soloist and the orchestra actually play together with the conductor . . . we're talking a hundred and forty musicians . . . it's a big orchestra . . . the Malmö City Theatre is a big venue . . . I sat alone in the middle of the big auditorium and Käbi walked out onstage, she was wearing a red dress, and I thought, a more beautiful . . . that I'd never seen a more beautiful woman in my life. I was sitting in the tenth or fifteenth row, I don't know where I was sitting, and then the rehearsal began. Käbi sat down at the piano in her red dress, and her dedication, her passion, lit up this whole big orchestra, this gigantic concert hall.

Silence.

HE   Yes, and then they broke for lunch and the conductor
        came over to me and said: Would you like to meet the
        girl ... *the girl* wasn't much older than twenty ... and
        I had already fallen in love with her though she didn't
        know it, and I didn't know it. All of a sudden I was
        shy as a country bumpkin and said, no, no, I couldn't,
        and then the conductor said: all right, suit yourself,
        but we'll be having lunch in the cafeteria, just a sim-
        ple lunch, and then I said: Oh, well, I suppose I could
        come along ... And so we talked ... and we drank
        coffee ... the sandwiches were good, they had very
        good sandwiches in that cafeteria ... and then we fell
        in love for the whole world to see. It didn't take long.
        Yes, that's how it came about, my dance with Käbi.

SHE   And what about Mamma?

HE   What?

SHE   I asked you if you could tell me something about
        Mamma. Käbi is Daniel's mother.

HE   What?

SHE   Käbi is Daniel's mother. I was wondering if you
        could tell me about *my* mother.

Long silence.

HE   She traveled around and I followed her career, or
        rather, her travels. After some time we began writing
        letters to each other. We wrote so many letters ...
        there must be an unbelievable amount of letters lying
        around somewhere. Then one day ... you may not
        know this, but I had a one-room apartment in Grev
        Turegatan in Stockholm.

SHE   Yes, I know about it.

HE   Ah, you do, do you?

SHE   Mamma told me that I was conceived in that apartment.

HE   What?

SHE   My mother.

HE   Yes . . . ?

SHE   She claims I was conceived in the apartment on Grev Turegatan.

HE   Really? . . . Is that so? Well . . . Be that as it may, we met at that apartment, again and again . . . and then, bang . . . It was a wonderful little apartment, kitchen, bathroom, cupboard, bed . . . Yes, that's how things can go. And it all started with Beethoven's Concerto in G major.

He looks at her.

HE   Questions, questions, questions—what's with all the questions about music?

SHE   Well, you see, I also had some questions about my mother . . . about you and my mother and about love.

He looks at her for a long time.

HE   Love is an entirely different matter. I don't think I want to go mixing love into it. It's clear that love has played a part, for example right here. Listen to this.

———

He lifts the Beethoven record off the turntable and slips it into its cover. Each time he reaches out of the wheelchair to select another record or to replace the previous one, I'm reminded of how drivers reach out of their car windows to drop coins into the basket at a toll station.

He puts on Schubert's *Winterreise*. We listen to the last of the twenty-four songs. Then he reaches out of his chair again, lifts the stylus, and the room falls silent.

HE   The voice is perfectly clear—*that's* what I'm talking about. From the first chords . . .

He pauses. Looks at the record player.

SHE   (*tentatively*) Could you expand on that a little?
HE   It's alive. Listening to that music, it's as if you were injected with life. In certain situations, when I'm alone here in my study, I start to cry. And I'm not a teary-eyed lad. You know that. I'm not. But when I'm sitting here alone, listening to my records, the tears start coming. I get this heightened sense of being alive. Do you understand what I'm saying?

MAMMA WAS MUCH YOUNGER than Pappa when they met. She was twenty-seven and very beautiful.

She has told me that when I was born, Pappa came by plane from Stockholm and brought with him a green ring—an emerald—which he presented to her at her bedside. Once he had presented her with the ring and taken a brief look at his newborn daughter—yellow, scrawny—he caught the next plane back to Stockholm.

After one night in hospital, Mamma had to move to a private room because the other mothers in the maternity ward were giving her dirty looks, and every time she had the tiny baby in the room with her, she didn't dare to read or sleep or stare at the ceiling or look out the window. Nothing except stare at this thing she had given birth to. It was boring to lie in bed and just stare, but she would rather die than give the nurses (who came and went and came and went) reason to believe that she thought of anything except loving her child, no one should be allowed to think that *here lies a bad mother who shouldn't have gone and gotten herself pregnant with someone other than her husband.*

I don't know whether anyone spoke to her about the tears that come with the milk, I think maybe she was ashamed of crying. She who was supposed to be happy. Ashamed of the restlessness that haunted her and that she wanted no part of, the stray suspicion that nothing was as it should be, or as she had imagined it would be.

THE MOTHER AND THE father could not decide what to call her. Time passed. Other decisions were made. When the girl was a few weeks old, the father decided that the mother should stop nursing, tuck the breast back into the blouse, give it back to him so the two of them could go away to Rome together.

The mother wanted to name her after a doll she had had as a child. Her favorite doll, Beate. I know nothing about the doll. Was it fair or dark-haired? When the mother was a little girl, she played tirelessly and earnestly with her dolls, dressing and undressing them, singing them to sleep in the evening and waking them in the morning, and when, one by one, she had declared them dead, she would slip out at night to bury them at the cemetery and cry.

The father wanted to name her after his mother, the girl's paternal grandmother, dark-eyed, dark-haired Karin. A trained nurse, Karin took on the all-consuming role of minister's wife and (eventually) mother of three while still a young woman. She wrote in her diary every day for thirty years, wrote about her children, her household, her acquaintances, her husband, the congregation, the changing seasons, holidays and ordinary days, sickness and death.

After she too had died, the father discovered that alongside her regular diary she had also kept a secret journal. In the secret journal she wrote:

More and more it seems that my own story is the story of the whole family.

The girl was nearly two years old when she was christened, and walked up the aisle by herself. In a letter to the girl, addressed to *3 Svingen, Strømmen, Norway,* the father writes:

THE DAY OF MY DAUGHTER'S CHRISTENING

WEDNESDAY, JUNE 5, 1968

This is a letter.
Dearest little daughter of mine. Since I am thinking of you more today, the day of your christening, than I usually do, and worry that you might become frightened and impatient during the actual ceremony, I am writing to you. For the time being I suppose you are entwined with your mother in such a way that everything else, while interesting, is none of your concern. But I can tell you that a few months ago you planted yourself, small and sniffling, between my legs, having decided that I was, after all, Pappa . . . In photographs you look very strong and full of life and at times like a little general who has just issued an order. I like the way you look because you already seem to me like a little person and not just a blur of a baby. I have the feeling that one day you and I will understand each other. We will have something in common that is not so easily defined. I believe you will meet the world with considerable resistance, and that is a good thing, surely.

———————

The girl wasn't interested in listening to the mother's stories about how difficult it had been to find a minister willing to officiate. She was even less interested in the stories about how good and kind the minister had been—the one who said yes, when all the others said no.

The girl only listened with half an ear, but I imagine the whole thing went something like this: The mother was there, Nanna was there, rosy-cheeked and sassy in high heels. The minister was there—the one who said yes when all the others said no, and who was so kind. The girl walks up the aisle by herself. She is wearing the traditional Norwegian *bunad*.

The name they gave her was Karin Beate. Two girls' names. The father chose one, the mother chose the other. But the names were not for everyday use, no one called her Karin, no one called her Beate, and no one called her Karin Beate. Once she's an adult, the double name is used only on special occasions such as marriage or divorce, as if it were elegant tableware. All other days she is called something else entirely.

HE	Is the tape recorder working?
SHE	It's working.
HE	(*skeptical*) Are you sure?
SHE	I'm sure.
HE	Okay, If you say so . . .
SHE	Well, It's supposed to be the best on the market, according to the guy who sold it to me, and perfect for our purposes.
HE	Perfect . . . really?
SHE	Yes, and the sound quality is very good.
HE	Ah.
SHE	A highly sophisticated piece of equipment.
HE	Indeed.
SHE	But everything we've done so far is on tape, I've checked (*this is a lie*), and soon I'm going to transcribe everything. And then we should probably discuss how to proceed.
HE	What was that?
SHE	How to proceed.
HE	Exactly.
SHE	How are you today?
HE	I've just woken up from a delightful sleep . . . I was in my study, listening to music, and when I began to feel tired, I asked the girls . . . the ones who work here . . . they come and go, you see . . . I asked them if they knew of a place where I could lie down, and they said I could lie down in my bed. They took off

my shoes and put a blanket over me and drew the
curtains. I fell asleep at once. And now I'm here.

SHE   You look rested.

HE   Pardon?

SHE   You look rested.

HE   Yes, I feel rested . . .

SHE   Ready to party?

They both laugh.

HE   No, but so far I think these conversations have been
        delightful . . . would you like a cough drop?

He rattles a pack of lozenges.

HE   (*hesitantly*) Is it appropriate for us to sit here and, you
        know . . . ?

SHE   Sit here and what?

HE   Sit here sucking on a cough drop?

SHE   We can do whatever we like, can't we?

HE   No, we can't.

SHE   You don't think we can do whatever we like?

HE   Well . . . you can do whatever you like, but I can't.

SHE   You can't do whatever you like?

HE   No, I'm supposed to . . . I have to *behave* myself. I'm
        the subject . . . the target of these interviews.

SHE   Yes, that's true. You'd better behave yourself, then.

HE   (*taking her hand*) Your hand is cold.

SHE   Yes, my hand is cold.

HE   You're not coming down with something, are you?

SHE   Absolutely not! I just washed my hands and the water from the tap was cold.

Silence.

SHE   And besides, when you're coming down with something, your hands are *warm*—I mean, if you're sick.

HE   But your hands can be cold too—if you're sick.

SHE   Well, yes, I suppose.

HE   Hmm.

SHE   But I'm *not* sick!

He leans forward and rests his forehead against hers.

HE   Your nose is warm.

SHE   Yesterday your nose was cold.

HE   What were we talking about?

SHE   About growing old. I wanted to ask you if there were any advantages to growing . . .

HE   . . . old?

SHE   Yes, old.

He laughs.

SHE   Anything to look forward to?

HE   No, I can't say there is. I don't know what that would be.

SHE   Are you cold . . . do you want your cardigan?

HE   Not at all, the temperature in here is perfect. No, I think that certain parts of life have been unbear-

able, and when you get old, some of all this
unbearableness—or what one previously would have
defined as unbearable—loosens its grip and sinks like
sodden rags, down, down, and dissolves, and in some
way you're free of those bits of life that tormented you
before, but then, of course, there's so much you miss
out on, there's no doubt about that. I thought I might
lament those things more than I do. But no, I don't
lament the things I now miss out on and that I used
to think were important. Sex . . . sexu . . . (*he makes a
trumpeting sound*) sexuality, for example. It disappears.
Completely, I mean. And this . . . it . . . doesn't even
hurt. It just dissolves. Sometimes girls, certain girls,
beautiful girls, attractive girls, will show an interest
in one, and one can't help thinking, *Oh, now wouldn't
that be snazzy-pazzy* . . . but then one thinks, I mean,
when you get right down to it, well, then one thinks,
*Oh, for goodness' sake, what am I doing . . . no, no, no,
no* . . . although it's a lovely thought . . . so, yes, sex is a
whole separate department, actually. Different colors,
different forms. And the girls, the women have been
attractive. How can I put it? There is this whole part
that vanishes when you get old, it just quietly fades
away and you don't even lament its passing. You don't,
or at least I don't . . . and I've been tremendously fond
of women. I don't mean to boast, but . . . oh, I'm not
wearing a cardigan. Where is my cardigan?

SHE   Would you like to wear it?

HE   No, I want it here, over my shoulders.

SHE   Like this?

HE   Like that, yes. Please, continue. What were we talking about?

SHE   We were talking about girls.

HE   Pardon?

SHE   We were talking about girls, about your tremendous fondness for women.

HE   I believe that much of my professional life has revolved around my tremendous fondness for women.

SHE   In what way have women influenced your . . .

He interrupts her, leans forward.

HE   In every conceivable way, my heart.

My GRANDMOTHER KARIN had been worried for quite some time that her son's marriage to Käbi, his fourth, was in trouble. The stories of his extramarital affairs were never-ending, and one evening her darkest suspicions were confirmed. There *was* another woman, and *yet* another child on the way, his ninth.

In reading my grandmother's diary, I come upon the first sign of my existence:

March 8th 1966

Then Ingmar called in the evening, he was working late at the theater and asked me to come over, and now we've spent a good two hours talking and all, all I had sensed is true. May they get through these difficult times! God willing!

The new woman is almost four months pregnant. This is not good news. Karin has a weak heart, often she's in pain, sharp stabs. She dies five days later of a heart attack. Erik, her husband, is lying in hospital, and even though his tumor proves to be benign, everyone assumes he will be the first to go. So she has a lot on her mind during those last days of her life. She knows her heart is weak, but reckons she will live for a while longer. She's worn out, but too many things remain unresolved. And then, on top of everything else, her youngest son comes and tells her that he's got yet another woman pregnant.

Reading the entry in Karin's diary on March 8, 1966, it seems reasonable to assume that she learns about my existence that evening Pappa asks her to come to the theater. That I'm on the way. A four-month-old fetus. The heartbeat is clearly audible by then. Pappa and Karin talked for a few hours, and *all, all I had sensed is true* she writes in her diary.

I find a certain solace in this. *All, all. Sensed. True.* I am someone or something in the process of becoming, that is real. *True.*

But the news that I am on my way does not appease her heart. For Karin there is no solace in what her son tells her that evening. Consider the eight children and four wives he already has. Not to mention alimony and child support.

The financial aspect of all this is a story in itself, and not an insignificant one.

I would like to believe that my mother and I are included in the pronoun *they* when Karin writes: *May they get through these difficult times!*

The following day, March 9, four days before she dies, she writes:

> *This evening I received a wonderful big azalea from Ingmar, Lenn brought it up to me. And then Ingmar called himself to thank me for yesterday. Was I right to sit there quietly, listening to all he had to say? But I knew, of course, that at the first hint of preaching on my part I would put up a barrier between us. And he knows that my prayers and my heart are with him in his struggle, willing him to do the right thing.*

———

The azalea (*Rhododendron simsii*) is a perennial, evergreen shrub
that can grow up to 1.5 meters in height. Its leaves are dark green.
The blossoms can be large or small, simple or layered. The color is
red, pink, salmon, purple, white, some have two colors. It thrives
best in the shade. It is poisonous. Like the pine tree, the azalea has
been immortalized in the writings of Chinese poet Du Fu.

Karin writes: *He knows that my prayers and my heart are with him
in his struggle, willing him to do the right thing.* Her heart would
beat for four more days after writing this. My grandmother
believed in God, so I choose to believe that her prayers lasted
longer than her heart.

The art of doing the right thing: What did she mean? What
does it mean to do the right thing? Did she mean that my father
should stay with Käbi and Daniel? Probably. But at the same
time she must have believed that doing the right thing also meant
taking responsibility for the new woman and the unborn child.
Her son found himself (or so his mother thought) in an impossible predicament. Käbi and Daniel on the one side, Mamma and
the unborn child on the other. Not to mention all the other wives,
children, financial obligations. Could she bear to consider all the
variables? Daniel was only three when the father met the mother
and the girl was conceived. When Karin visited her son and
daughter-in-law, Käbi played the piano and spoke passionately
about the pieces she played. Karin admired her son's and Käbi's
beautiful home, the big garden, the bright rooms.

———

On December 16, 1962, a few years before the girl was conceived, my grandmother writes:

Today we have been to Ingmar's to christen his little Dan-
iel Sebastian. The music room was so beautifully arranged
with a tall, candlelit Christmas tree and the christening
table right next to it. As we raised our Champagne glasses,
Erik said a few words to little Daniel, who lay there gazing
at him intently with his big eyes. It was all so beautifully
arranged, and we so much liked Käbi's parents, her sister
and her brother-in-law, so everything was just perfect. Käbi
looks much more robust now, and they are both so happy
with their lovely home. Everything was white with snow.

SHE   Are there other things that go missing when you grow old?

HE   When you grow old?

SHE   Yes, you once said that words and memories go missing when you grow old. I was wondering if there are other things that disappear, things that you regret or don't regret having lost?

HE   That I regret or don't regret? I don't know. There are ordinary, everyday things that used to matter but that don't matter any longer.

Long silence. The tape hisses.

HE   (*agitated*) But now I feel that I'm sitting here improvising. That I have to perform an improvisation over your question. It has a false ring to it.

SHE   Do you want to skip the question?

HE   Yes.

SHE   Then we'll move on. You once said that growing old is work. Do you remember saying that?

HE   No.

SHE   Well, anyway, that's what you said, you said: growing old is work.

HE   It's what?

SHE   Work.

HE   Did I say that?

SHE   Yes, you did. And now that you're even older, do you still think that growing old is work?

HE   I think that growing old is hard, grueling, unglamor-
            ous work with very long hours.

SHE   Yes.

HE   But what's essential . . . what's essential! . . . Some
            things are important, others are unimportant. Music,
            for instance, has become essential for me. There was
            a time when I didn't give a damn about music, but
            now it's become essential . . . I want this cardigan off!
            I'm getting myself all worked up!

SHE   Are you hot?

HE   Yes, I'm hot.

SHE   Are you angry?

HE   No, not angry, but I'm sitting here with the feeling
            that my answers are lousy.

SHE   I don't think . . . I think it's going well.

HE   Well, that's wonderful. I'm glad you think so. I am
            making a considerable effort not to show off or pre-
            tend I'm something I'm not.

Believing in god was easier for the mother than for the father. The mother had her childhood faith. Evening prayer. *Our Father which art in heaven, hallowed be thy name.* God was quiet, but things were rarely quiet around the mother, and this quietness was possibly an indication that God was listening, not only with half an ear, but with an ear as big as the universe, and in this quiet the mother could become whoever she wanted to be, and love without being ashamed.

The mother grew up in Trondheim and lived in a small apartment together with Nanna and Aunt Billy. On the wall above the blue Biedermeier sofa hung a blue portrait of a dashing figure in an officer's cap who gazed down at the girl's mother with a somewhat indeterminable smile.

The girl should have listened more carefully when the mother spoke, for example when she spoke about her own father. Was he really struck in the head by a propeller?

But already at a very young age, the girl balked at the mother's stories.

The girl wasn't beautiful like the mother, her face never settled. She doesn't look like a single picture of herself, and every picture of her is different from every other. In this way, the story of her name fits with the story of her face. In photographs she does an odd thing with her mouth, she did it as a little girl and she still does it—she purses her lips and squinches her eyes.

The other day I came across a light-brown imitation-leather album filled with photographs from when I was little. I've taken many of the pictures myself. Like the two almost identical photographs of a pair of rag dolls sitting next to each other on a blue folding chair. These photos were taken at Hammars. It might have been Pappa who gave me the camera. I don't know. Another photograph is from the flat in Erling Skjalgsson Street. Mamma and I are sitting in the big bed with the golden bedposts, she's wearing a red nightgown and her hair spills over both of us. I think she must have given her hair a quick brush before we took the picture—we used a self-timer. I'm wearing a retainer over my braces. I sleep with the retainer at night. There's lots of fiddling inside my mouth every evening to get the retainer in place. Mini rubber bands and hooks and fingers all the way in the back. We're sitting in the golden bedpost bed and Mamma has put her arm around me.

I'm wearing a white top and a red corduroy skirt. Mamma has just woken up, you can tell because even though her hair has just been brushed, she still has traces of sleep in her eyes.

WHEN PAPPA WAS A boy, he rode his bicycle through the rolling countryside of his childhood summers in Dalarna. The family had a house there, in Duvnäs, called Våroms. My father's father was a minister, and his name was Erik. Pappa was known as Pu. They ride their bicycles up and down the hills, Erik in front, Pu a little way behind. They are on their way to church, where Erik will deliver his sermon.

"This is how we'll roam the world, Father and I," says Pu.

I have five blue notebooks belonging to Pappa. The books are filled with notes and old family photographs. Pappa was forever sitting hunched over photographs, studying them through a magnifying glass. He cut photos out of albums, stuck them into his notebooks (he had hundreds of notebooks, he called them his workbooks), and wrote alongside them wherever there was room left on the page. Sometimes he would even scribble something directly on the photo.

One of the notebooks contains a photograph of Pappa's paternal grandmother, her broad face jutting out of a sensible, buttoned-up blouse. She has a large bosom, a white cardigan over her shoulders, and on her head a broad-brimmed spring hat trimmed with an elegant and very elaborate arrangement of fruit and flowers. I try to picture her in the hours before the photograph was taken, one early morning almost a century ago. She's on her way out. Clothes freshly pressed, buttoned up, smart, neat, proper. I imagine how, almost by chance, her eye falls on the extravagant hat wreathed with fruit and flowers. It sits on the hat shelf, presiding over all the other hats. It is a little too big, a little too girly, a little too fruity, in short, a little too much of everything, the other hats pale in comparison. In the twinkling of an eye she decides to change her plan. *The hat plan.* Presumably, when you wear a hat, you are bound to have a hat plan. What happens is that she changes her mind. She stands on tiptoe like a little girl (the hat shelf hovers high above the other shelves) and seizes the one she wants. With a little *ahhh* she places the fruit-and-flower hat on her head and with a flick of the wrist relegates the neat little hat number she had originally chosen back to the shelf.

In the picture, Grandmother is flanked by little Pu on one side and Pu's older brother, Dag, on the other. Both boys lean devotedly against her, Pu is staring straight at the camera with a suspicious look in his eyes.

He is probably around four years old.

Under the photo, Pappa has written: GRANDMA'S HAT.

Here are two photographs of a twilit city, rooftops, shadowy streets, a church spire, a few frail, naked trees—ghostlike. Looking at the cityscapes in his notebook is like reading a novel by Sebald. I think of my father as someone who belonged. He had Hammars. He had the theater. He had the film studio. I was the fidgety one who could never settle. But the cityscapes in his notebook convey so much loneliness. In the margin he has written in large capital letters: TO DWELL IN THE INNERMOST REACHES OF SAFETY. I wonder what he meant by that. It doesn't sound like a very safe place—the innermost reaches of safety. It sounds like a place one would be forbidden to enter. And if one ever did get in, one would probably be kicked straight back out. There are border patrols everywhere, and tall fences, and the familiar sense that I don't belong here with the others.

Here is a picture of Pappa as a young man. No one calls him Pu now. He's far too grown-up to be called Pu. He has slicked-back hair and is wearing his Sunday best, your eyes fall on the white shirt collar, the black knot of his tie and the somewhat ill-fitting suit jacket. What year is it? Perhaps 1935, or 1936, I'm not sure. I don't think he likes having his picture taken. His mouth is closed, he doesn't smile, his lips are well shaped and sensitive, as if they were borrowed from his mother for the occasion. His ears are big and stick out, there is a sly glint in his eye, he looks at you with a combination of feigned indifference, suspicion (I recognize that look from the eyes of the twelve-years-younger Pu), and ingratiating devotion—there's no telling what he might do if you turn your back on him. Does he spit on your food? Does he ask for a kiss? Does he get up and bail, never to return?

Now I sit hunched over the same pictures that Pappa sat hunched over.

In my mind's eye I see him, the old man of over eighty, studying the young man of seventeen, he who is no longer called Pu, the youth with the sly glint in his eye. The eighty-year-old has written something in the margin. Just two words. But in order for all the letters to fit on the page—without having to write

across the youngster's face—he has written from top to bottom
rather than from left to right, as always with a black felt-tip pen
and in his big, childish capitals:

THE
MA-
STUR-
BA-
TOR

For a long time, the only image of my father I could picture was
of him lying dead. This picture doesn't exist, but for a while it
obscured all the other pictures.

He is lying with his head on a white pillow, in his own bed
in the house at Hammars. Outside it is overcast, I don't know
whether morning had broken when he took his last breath, and
whether he saw a streak of light between the curtains—the curtains were closed when he died—he died at the end of July, at
around four in the morning, the hour he himself called *the hour
of the wolf*, without knowing the slightest thing about wolves
and their habits. Someone had tied a checkered kerchief around
his face and made a bow at the top of his head, presumably one
of the six women who cared for him during his final days, someone who knew what to do with the dead: a scarf tied around
the face prevents the mouth from falling open and staying open
once rigor mortis sets in. Someone had also closed his eyes. We
will not go to heaven with open mouth or open eyes. I think he
looks cranky there on the pillow.

I picture the movement of *loosening and untying*, all of the
times I have loosened and untied my children's hats, scarves,

shoelaces, I sit on the edge of the bed, stretch out my hand, deliberating whether to loosen and untie the stupid bow, Pappa shouldn't die all tied up in a bow, but then I lose my nerve, there will be many of us coming to say goodbye today. We used to get together every summer for his birthday, his children would have a lavish meal, paid for by him, he didn't eat with us, but dropped by afterward; a frantic cleanup before he appears, no glasses or bottles on the table no dishes in the sink, everything has to look spic-and-span. Now that he was dead, we had agreed to go in one at a time, this was the first of many processions, when it's my turn, I walk in, sit down on the edge of his bed, place my hands in my lap, do not *loosen and untie*, the bow stays, like a joke, like a sneer, I don't know when rigor mortis sets in, I don't know whether his mouth will fall open if I remove the kerchief.

HE   I believe in God in every respect, but I don't expect to understand His will. God is in music. I believe that the great composers speak to us about their experience of God. This is not nonsense. For me, Bach is a constant.

SHE   But you used to have doubts?

HE   Not about Bach.

SHE   No, but about God.

HE   All that nonsense, it's over with now, it's gone, I don't have any energy left to babble on about lack of faith, lack of trust, and all that.

SHE   Did anything particular happen to put an end to your doubts?

HE   It has happened gradually, *peu á peu*, I suppose it's fair to say that since Ingrid's death I have had an acute sense of God's will . . . I can be outside, here at Hammars, surrounded by the sea and the sky, and I'll sense a presence.

OCCASIONALLY, THE GIRL WAS allowed to borrow one of his brown or green cardigans, the ones with the leather elbow patches and bits of stitching and darning. The cardigans were much too big, nearly trailing along the ground. Every day he rode up and down the shore on his big red ladies' bicycle. The girl stood at the door, swathed in one of his cardigans, and watched him disappear down the narrow path. There are stones everywhere on Fårö. On the beach. Along the gravel roads. Around the houses—stone walls. The largest and oldest rocks, the limestone stacks, are called *rauks*. One summer, the girl took her bike to the other end of the island to explore the stacks together with her brother Daniel, who believed his little sister was such a skinny, shivery, teetering slip of a thing that he was afraid she might fall between the bars of the cattle guards.

The four-hundred-million-year-old stacks force their way up and out of the sea, reaching for the sky. They look like heads, huge, weird old men's heads, and in the summer, flowers and grass grow on them and children climb all over them.

Daniel and the girl each had their own little room, wall-to-wall, at one end of the house. Their father let them draw and write on the doors. They shared a shower and a toilet. Because of the water shortage, no more than one shower a week was permitted and you were not allowed to flush if all you'd done was pee, but the girl flushed anyway so Daniel wouldn't see that she had been to the bathroom. Daniel was four years older than the girl and had written *fuck!* on his door. Ingrid made it clear that things now had gone too far. It was one thing to let the children draw and write on the doors, quite another to allow the word "fuck," but Pappa didn't mind, so that was the end of that. They could also make as much of a mess as they liked. Not in the rest of the house, which was always kept in perfect order, Ingrid saw to that, there was a time and a place for everything, but in their own rooms the children could make a mess. No one told them to go clean their rooms. It was a house rule of sorts. When the children visited their father, no adult would ever say: *Go clean your room.* The girl's room was small, with flowery wallpaper. She had her own radio on her bedside table and a box full of old magazines (that she read every summer) on top of her closet. On the floor, halfway under the bed, lay the two empty suitcases.

When the father's office door was closed you were not allowed to knock. Usually because he was at his desk, writing. Or giving Daniel a German lesson. The girl wondered whether Daniel would have done *absolutely anything* to get out of his German lessons with the father. *Ich bin der Geist, der stets verneint! Und das mit Recht; denn alles, was entsteht, ist wert, daß es zugrunde geht*, the father said, and laughed out loud. And now it's almost time for the lesson to begin. Daniel is sitting in the chair in the office, the same chair she sits in when she visits the father's study. She has wandered this way by mistake, she's not sure how, she's supposed to be somewhere else entirely: in the garage, which doubles as a ballet studio, in her room, out picking wild strawberries for dessert, but she has wandered this way and she can see her big brother through the crack in the door—head in his hands, the long, dark hair falling over his brow and eyes. *Ich bin der Geist, der stets verneint.* German grammar is beyond what any child should be expected to understand. And in the middle of summer vacation—that's probably the worst part. The girl is convinced that Daniel's mother is behind this, that she's the one who's insisting that the father tutor his son in German. Their mothers do sometimes get such ideas into their heads— *it's only right that the father should take some responsibility.* And now here's the girl peeping through the crack in the door at her brother, who is sitting in the chair with his head in his hands, but she must have made a sound, maybe she scratched one of her hundred mosquito bites, because the father turns and looks straight at her. Her brother raises his head and he too looks at her. She stands by the crack in the door, a thin strip of skin and blue, peeping and scratching and making sounds, she is about to say something but decides not to—short dress, tight ponytail, pipe-cleaner legs. No one says a word, it's not her turn to be at this end of the house, and she's not the one who has to learn German. The father gets up, walks across the room and closes the door without so much as a glance at her.

Pappa and the girl had an appointment. It was written down in his diary. Or his calendar, as it was also called. The calendar was kept on his desk. Everything had a place and a time. Time had been set aside for the girl and the father to *have a conversation.*

She tugged at her dress, it was blue and had grown too small for her over the summer. She sat in one chair, he sat in the other.

And after a long time he gave her an almost desperate look and said: "The problem is that there is such a big age difference between us. We simply don't have all that much to talk about."

The girl didn't know what to say to that, she squirmed a little in her chair, she had noticed that in the course of their conversation her father had started to look a little desperate, but had no idea what to do about it, there were forty-eight years between them and forty-eight years is a long time and it wasn't as if she could put on seven-league boots and try to catch up with him, and frankly, it wasn't a very insightful remark on the father's part, of course there was a big age-difference, neither of them could help that or do anything about it. The girl had told him about a chair she wished she had, a chair that was nicer than any other chair in the whole world.

"Is it a metaphor?" he asked.

"Huh?"

"Sometimes a thing is not actually that thing, but something else. This is called a metaphor. What I mean is: Does the chair symbolize something inside you? Something you're thinking about? Something you dream about?"

"No, I don't think so."

"Is it, perhaps, a magical chair?"

"No!" the girl sighed. "It's just a chair."

WHEN THE GIRL TURNED nine, she got her own record player. It would have its place in the old garage up by the forest. The garage had been turned into a ballet studio. She had been taking ballet lessons for several years, and the father and the mother were both very happy about this. The father said that if she wanted to be a ballet dancer she would have to practice every day for two hours in the garage, he had a new pine floor laid for her to dance on and a barre mounted to the wall. He had also ordered a box of rosin for her ballet shoes, all proper ballet studios have a box of rosin to prevent the dancers from slipping and falling. When it was windy outside, pinecones would drop onto the garage roof, first you would hear the thud of the pinecone hitting the roof, followed by the rumble as it rolled down the roof and landed in the gutter.

PAPPA SAID: "MAYBE YOU could write it?"

"The book?"

"Yes."

"About growing old?"

"Yes."

"Are you thinking it should be a kind of . . . interview book?"

"If you absolutely have to call it something, then yes."

"We don't have to call it anything."

"But maybe we should call it something."

"Well, we can always come back to that."

"I have a good title."

"What's that?"

"*Laid & Slayed in Eldorado Valley.*"

"Hmm?"

"I always wanted to call one of my films *Laid & Slayed in Eldorado Valley* but never made one that quite fit the bill."

E VERYTHING HAS A NAME. Every day, at five o'clock, Pappa takes the Volvo, also known as the Red Menace, and drives to the kiosk at the other end of the island to buy the evening papers.

Daniel always gets to go to the kiosk with the father. Sometimes the girl gets to go too. Usually, though, she will stay at the house with Ingrid and Maria and help set the dinner table, or she is sent out to pick flowers for the table, or wild strawberries for dessert. But sometimes she gets to go with Pappa and Daniel to buy the evening papers. She sits in the back. Daniel sits in front. She's nine, perhaps, and Daniel is twelve. The father drives fast. Much faster than what is legal or safe on these narrow roads, but every time a pretty girl or woman comes walking or cycling toward them, he slows down so that he and Daniel can have a good look at her.

The girl sits in the backseat. The backseat is much bigger than her, she can stretch out her arms and flap them, like a bird flapping its wings, but nobody pays her any attention, maybe they've forgotten she's there. Girls are different from boys.

"She's lovely!" the father says, shifting into first gear and smiling at the woman who walks or cycles past. The woman smiles back.

"Yes!" Daniel agrees, waving.

Then the father speeds up again, going fast, fast, so fast that dust and grit swirl and spatter around them and the girl cries *caw-caw-caw* because when they drive this fast it almost feels like they're about to fly, the forest whizzes past on one side, the sea on the other, fast along the road, past the moors spreading before them, until another girl or woman comes into sight, walking or cycling toward them. The father slows down.

"She's lovely too!" Daniel says.

"Yes, she is!" says the father.

Every Thursday, Ingrid served fresh cod. If there was one thing the girl hated, it was fish. There are hardly any cod left in the Baltic now, but women and girls still walk and cycle along the road.

SHE   Would you like to sit up a bit? Shall I lift you up so
        you can sit?
HE   What?
SHE   Would you like to sit up, or would you rather lie
        down?
HE   I want to be just the way you want me to be.

One of the recordings took place in his bedroom. He felt ill and
was unable to get out of bed, but didn't want to cancel their
work session.

*She gets up and walks to the window, pulls back the curtains. He
covers his eyes with one hand. She turns and looks at him.*

SHE   Is it too bright?
HE   Maybe a little bright.

She closes the curtains. Walks back to his bedside.

SHE   Would you like to lie down or sit up?
HE   I want to lie . . .
SHE   Is that all right?
HE   I don't know . . . I've had three dreadful days.
SHE   Have you?
HE   Three dreadful days and three dreadful nights.
SHE   Tell me.
HE   Could you open the curtains?

She gets up and crosses over to the window. Opens the curtains, turns to him.

SHE   Do you want to see the ocean?

HE   No.

SHE   Would you rather have it dark?

HE   Yes.

SHE   Completely dark?

She closes the curtains and walks back to the bed, sits down.

HE   (*faintly*) But we can still see each other, can't we, even though it's dark?

III

TO MUNICH

...

... in search of emotions, not landscapes.

—GUSTAVE FLAUBERT, Madame Bovary

NANNA'S TWO ROOMS AND kitchen in Oslo are furnished as if she were actually living in a much bigger flat, the walls covered with large and small paintings and reproductions. The eye catcher is the blue portrait of my grandfather in his officer's uniform displayed on the wall above the blue Biedermeier sofa, but the one that I find most interesting is the small reproduction tucked away almost out of sight behind the carmine Chinese cabinet. The woman in the painting is standing on a blue shore, looking out across a blue ocean. You can't see her face, only her long, white dress, her long, fair hair, so long that she has strapped the belt of her dress around its ends to hold it in place. Year after year, the woman with the fair hair hangs on Nanna's wall and gazes out across the ocean without turning even once to show her face, gazing and longing and waiting. I know that the woman in the painting is my mother.

"No, it's not her," says Nanna. "Your Mamma was just a little girl when Munch died."

I shrug my shoulders, I know what I know.

The coffee table is covered with books, mostly novels, and over by the window overlooking the tracks and the Skarpsno tram stop are two prim little armchairs upholstered in a vivid red-and-black rose-patterned fabric. This is the brightest spot in the flat and where I like to sit. There are potted plants on the windowsill, some of them send green tendrils twining up the frames and across the windowpanes, and arranged between the pots are Nanna's prettiest and most expensive music boxes. When you wind them up, it's important to wind slowly, and in the proper direction, to the right, as if you were winding up a clock; if you're impatient and wind too quickly, or in the wrong direction, you'll ruin the mechanism and the music box will stop playing. Several music boxes double as jewelry boxes, the most precious are made of mahogany and their lids are engraved. Nanna's favorite is a little case in blonde wood with a red velvet lining. Two tiny porcelain figurines live inside its crimson depths, she in a pink dress and he in a light-blue prince's costume, and every time you open the case, they dance the same little dance to the tune of "Edelweiss." Nanna knows all the words to "Edelweiss" and sings with such an insistent voice and mournful vibrato that she drowns out the faint tinkling of the music box.

To the left of one of the armchairs by the window, Nanna's sewing box teeters on long, slender, pale-brown wooden legs, Nanna has twenty-three thimbles in her sewing box and if you take out the top layer, the one with all the little compartments for spools, needles, and buttons, there is a large compartment underneath with room for balls of yarn, knitting needles, and a crochet hook. The dining-room furnishings are kept in dark glossy woodwork, and every mealtime she asks me to set the table with place mats kept in the same rose-patterned fabric as the armchairs. I light white candles and get the green plates, the pale-green linen napkins, and the heavy cutlery from the kitchen cupboard. The kitchen is so tiny that it fits only one person at a time. A narrow double bed in the bedroom is covered with a hand-sewn patchwork quilt. For my confirmation, Nanna has promised me a hand-sewn patchwork quilt just like this one. The finest patchwork quilts take years to make, she says. Every evening before we go to bed, she folds her quilt and places it in a drawer under the bookshelf. She would like me to sleep next to her in bed the way I did when I was little, but I'd rather sleep on the camp bed, which is usually folded and stored under Nanna's own bed. Nanna wants me to lie in the crook of her arm, but I don't want to. Her arm is thin and sinewy and it hurts to lie on it, and sometimes there are stains on the sheet. On the wall above the bed she has tacked a drawing I made several years earlier. It depicts a girl standing under a tree. In thick, grayish-black block letters, it says: NANNA AND THE TREE. The wall on one side of the bedroom is packed with books and there is just enough space for a small record player on the broadest shelf.

When Nanna has guests, I lie on the bed and read or listen to records—softly, so they won't hear anything in the next room. Sometimes one of Nanna's women friends will open the door and peek in. The guests have to pass through the bedroom to get to the bathroom. One woman friend has large spectacles and a big lipstick-red mouth. She will sneak past the bed as if to say: Don't mind me, I'm quiet as a mouse, look, I'm not bothering anyone, I'm nearly invisible, wave, wave, I wave back. Another woman friend is tall, skinny and gray like a birch tree in winter and speaks with a loud, throaty voice. I've heard her voice through the wall and recognize it. Nanna has told me that she smokes too many cigarettes and has lived a hard life. When she walks through the bedroom, she always makes a full stop mid-journey to have a look at me. I put down my book and make myself as small as I can there on the bed. She crosses her skinny arms and asks which grade I'm in and how I'm getting on in school. I answer that I'm in fourth grade and that I'm getting on all right. A third woman friend, a doll-like little lady with done-up hair, pretty and freshly ironed dresses, and a stomach-turning soapy-smelling perfume, will sit down on the edge of the bed and caress my hair. She doesn't say anything, nor do I. She'll just sit there for so long, and so quietly, that I'll begin to wonder whether she's forgotten that she has to go to the bathroom.

I can't live alone by myself, so when Mamma is away I stay with Nanna, or she stays with me. When Nanna doesn't have time (Nanna doesn't have time, Mamma cries and tosses her hair, Nanna doesn't have time, *hahaha*, does Nanna even know what *time* is, does Nanna have any idea of what it's like not to have time!), I live in Mamma's big flat with one of a number of nannies. Mamma calls them babysitters even though I'm no longer a baby. I'm ten years old and will be starting fifth grade. When one babysitter moves in, the other moves out.

Mrs. Berg plays the piano and makes delicious food and patters around in fluttery clothes and weeps because she thinks she is a lousy babysitter.

"All I want is for you to be happy," she sniffles, sitting on a kitchen chair with an untouched cup of tea in front of her. I stand next to her, pat her arm, and say that I am happy.

"It's just that I know . . ." she sobs, "I know you miss your mother, and you wish she was here instead of me."

I say that I don't miss my mother.

She wipes her nose and looks at me with a tear-stained face.

"Do you love me a little bit too?"

She gathers me in her arms. She has bad breath and smells of cabbage. I wish I knew how to hold my nose without using my hands. The only alternative is to stop breathing.

"I love you too."

I say it in such way that she'll know I'm lying. She *wants* to hear the words, even though she knows they're not true.

I draw maps, make tables, and write lists. I'm skinny and pale and take ballet classes and smile politely and don't want any more babysitters, I want the babysitters to get sick and die or be offered other babysitter jobs, for example in Australia, you can't get much farther away than that. I want Mamma to come home and hold me close and never leave again.

When Mrs. Berg quits, a new Mrs. Berg starts. The new Mrs. Berg is older and heavier than the old Mrs. Berg. A coarser grade of paper. She has whiskers on her chin that she tries to pluck out with tweezers, and her hands tremble. The tweezers are kept in her toothbrush glass in the bathroom. She knows it's me who steals the tweezers and yet she buys a new pair every time the old pair disappears. What I don't understand is why she keeps putting them in the toothbrush glass when she knows I'll find them there and steal them. She doesn't want me to see that her hands tremble, so she always lays one hand on top of the other on the table. In the evening we play cards. She lets me win.

If you want to torment a babysitter, you have to find her weak spot. Mrs. Berg's weak spot is Horst Tappert, the German actor famous for playing Chief Inspector Derrick every Friday night on TV. When Mrs. Berg, at the end of the workweek, finally sits down in the green sofa with a glass of sherry and a little bowl of peanuts, it is as if her whole body relaxes. Her hands guide the sherry glass to her mouth without a single tremor. Three Fridays in a row I sneak into the living room and pull out the plug. I wait until Chief Inspector Derrick appears on the screen. Then I wait a little longer. I wait until Chief Inspector Derrick turns

toward Mrs. Berg and looks at her with his big, doleful eyes.
All the misery in the world could fit into those eyes. And just
as Mrs. Berg guides the sherry glass to her mouth, just as that
good feeling begins to spread through her body, the TV screen
goes black and Mrs. Berg is left sitting alone in the dark. She has
no idea how to get the television going again, she knows I have
something to do with the blackout, but not exactly what. After
a month she writes to Mamma to tender her resignation. She
wants to quit and will be moving out with immediate effect. The
girl is not right in the head, she writes. And besides, she adds,
Mamma should think a little less about herself and her so-called
career and, instead, like a proper mother, start looking after her
daughter, before the ship goes down.

When Mamma is home we have the big flat in Erling Skjalgsson Street to ourselves. Mamma sleeps late in the morning and
makes fried eggs for dinner. Fried eggs are not dinner, so dinner
with Mamma always feels like a party—Mamma and I are the
mavericks of love and dinner. At night we sleep in the same bed.
We eat when we want. Not at four o'clock, not at five o'clock,
when people usually have dinner, but when it suits us. Mamma
can whip up a sumptuous stew based on a canned-food con-
coction called Spaghetti à la Capri. Mamma's stew consists of
tomato sauce, sausages, meat balls, a little bit of paprika, herbal
salt, and sugar. If we don't have eggs or Spaghetti à la Capri in
the cupboard, we take a taxi to the Chinese restaurant at Bis-
lett. I like the crunch of bamboo shoots and water chestnuts. I'm
allowed to order orange soda and ice cream for dessert. Three
scoops of ice cream, vanilla, strawberry, chocolate, served on
an oblong platter with parasols and a wafer. The trick is to save

the wafer for last and eat it in such a way that you can suck out
the sugary filling.

Every once in a while, Nanna will come out and eat with us.
Nanna puts on her best clothes when she goes out to a restaurant. A pretty dress and high-heeled shoes. Mamma wears a
long kaftan and is impatient. She is hungry. She wants a glass of
wine. She wants another glass of wine. Her nerves are frayed.
There isn't a single nerve left that can hold all the other nerves in
check. All the people who tug at her. I wonder what it looks like
inside Mamma's head. The waitress comes to take our order,
it is always the same lady who takes our order, Mamma lights
up with a big smile and asks how her husband is doing. *Better
now? Home again? Wonderful! It's not easy being alone with all
that responsibility.* She uses up her very last nerve to orchestrate
this conversation. Once the waitress is gone, Nanna tells us that
she has been back and forth to America forty-two times, and
that everyone knows her there.

"In America?" asks Mamma.

"Pardon . . . ?" Nanna looks confused.

"You said that everyone knows you there," says Mamma.
"Did you mean that everyone knows you in the United States?
I assume you mean the United States when you say America?"

"There are many people who know me, yes," says Nanna.
"You are forgetting that I have been back and forth forty-two
times."

"Many or everyone?" Mamma asks.

"Pardon . . . ?"

"Does *everyone* in the United States know you, or do *many*
people know you?"

"Let me tell you," says Nanna, and looks at me with what she herself would describe as a mischievous glance. She chooses to ignore Mamma.

"Let me tell you. When I landed at Kennedy Airport a few years ago, I was recognized by the immigration officer. Guess what he said?"

I shake my head and cast a worried glance at Mamma.

"He said . . ." says Nanna leaning forward, "He said: Well, if it isn't Mrs. Ullmann come to visit us again? Welcome back to New York!"

Mamma stares out the window.

"Why do you always have to exaggerate," she says quietly.

"I never exaggerate," says Nanna.

"You always exaggerate," says Mamma. "I'm so sick and tired of all your exaggerating."

I have many nicknames. Pappa calls me "My Little Chinese" because I'm well mannered and smile politely. I doubt if Pappa knows the slightest thing about China, apart from what he has read in the papers, he has never eaten Chinese food, or any dish containing fruit, vegetables, garlic, spices, and sauce, truth is that any food not prepared by Ingrid gives him a stomachache. The year is 1977, I am eleven years old. Any knowledge Pappa has about China has been gleaned from reading Chinese poetry. *The good rain knows when to fall.* I think Pappa calls me My Little Chinese because he has this idea that Chinese girls are always smiling and polite and not given to displays of emotion and I can be all of those things when I want to. Nanna has taught me pretty much all I need to know about good manners and polite behavior, among other things:

One gives up one's seat for old people on the tram.

One curtsies and says a proper hello and goodbye.

One says thank you and eats up all the food on one's plate.

One pays attention to one's grammar, one washes one's face, ears, neck, and hands every day, grooms one's nails, places the knife on the right side and the fork on the left, addresses adults by their last names (*in which back alley did we end up on a first-name basis, may I ask?*).

On escalators, one *stands* on the right and *walks* on the left.

When finding one's seat in a theater or cinema, one moves along the row facing the people already seated (*no one wants another person's bum in their face!*).

One keeps one's feelings to oneself and conducts oneself politely regardless of the situation.

Pappa doesn't like to travel, but now he has gone off to Germany and made his home in Munich, he has left Sweden for good, taking Ingrid with him. Mamma explains that he didn't want to go, but he had no choice. He has done nothing wrong, she adds.

"Your father has paid his taxes just like everyone else. Don't worry about what the newspapers say."

"What do the newspapers say?"

"They say that your father has cheated on his taxes, but he hasn't."

"Are you sure?"

Mamma sighs and looks up at the ceiling. Three nerves, two nerves, one nerve left to answer the question.

"Of course I'm sure."

———

If Mamma had known that Pappa calls me My Little Chinese, she would probably have protested. She does *not* think that I am always smiling and well mannered and good at keeping my feelings to myself. Mamma calls me Mouse. Mamma and Pappa don't know about each other's nicknames for me. Actually, I don't really mind that Pappa has moved to Germany. I don't think about him that much or where he is when he's not at Hammars. When Mamma is away I miss her all the time. I long for her from the moment she walks out the door until the moment she comes back. I miss her so much that I need an extra body: one body for me, one body for all the longing.

When I was almost two and soon to be christened, my father wrote in a letter: *I wish for you constant longing and hope, for without longing we cannot live.*

What did he mean by that? *Without longing we cannot live?* He couldn't have meant this madness. This hunger. This fear. I miss Mamma all the time. And now she's gone away again. To America this time. Next time I'll get to go with her, she says, but now she wants me to stay in Oslo and go to school. Nanna will look after me. Mamma will be gone for several months. I'm scared of losing her, scared that she won't come back, scared that she'll disappear. But fear is not what Pappa means by the words *constant longing.* Mamma and I talk on the phone and before we hang up we always agree on a time for her next call. Which is today. Which is now, soon. Half an hour before the agreed-upon time I feel sick, keeping vigil by the phone. It rings, it is three minutes before the agreed-upon time—but it isn't Mamma. It's a chipper lady who wants to speak to Nanna. Why isn't it Mamma? Why doesn't Mamma call three minutes before our agreed-upon time to save me from this fear? *Constant longing*. And why does the lady asking for Nanna have such a chipper voice? Doesn't she know that my mother is dead? Nanna takes the receiver, exchanges some words, but ends the call quickly. She tells the lady that we're expecting an overseas call from the United States. I sit on the straight-backed chair, squirming. Nanna hangs up the receiver and looks at me.

"If you sit there waiting for her to call, you'll only start to worry," she says.

"I'm not waiting on anyone."

"It's waiting *for* someone, not *on* someone."

"I'm not waiting for anyone."

Nanna looks at her watch. Why is she looking at her watch?

"Why are you looking at your watch?"

"I don't know, I'm just looking at it. No reason."

"Are you worried?"

"Absolutely not. There's no reason to be worried. Why should I be worried?"

"Because Mamma isn't calling."

"She'll call soon."

There are countless ways to die. Airplane crashes. Murder. Embolism. All the clocks in the flat have now passed the agreed-upon time. People vanish off the face of the Earth. Mamma is fleeting, not entirely part of this world, maybe she has fallen off a cliff. I imagine her falling and falling and falling. It's fifteen minutes past the agreed-upon time. Will Nanna and I sit hand in hand in the church when Mamma is buried? I begin to cry. *For without longing we cannot live*. What are the chances that Mamma would make me wait when she knows how scared I get? What are the chances that something has happened to her? It is now forty-five minutes past the agreed-upon time. I get up from the chair, I stand upright, I get up from the chair and stand upright, I get up, I get up, I stand upright, and then I begin to cry.

"She's . . . hysterical," whispers Nanna.

I stand on the floor crying. I walk across the floor crying. Nanna clutches the phone, follows me with her eyes, she has called a doctor.

Now it's one hour past the agreed-upon time, and I walk from room to room in Mamma's big flat. I don't want to stop walking, I don't want to stop crying. I have walked like this for a hundred thousand years and can walk for another hundred thousand. You don't need consonants to mourn. Only vowels. Only this one single sound. I'll pierce the sky with sound. There is magic in this, in walking and crying, but only as long as I don't stop. The flat is full of things. No one has as many things as Mamma. And then she leaves all her things and gets herself new things, and then she leaves those, and all across the world there are flats and houses and hotel rooms filled with Mamma's things. Vases, bowls, dolls, photographs, big sofas, coffee tables, chairs with silk slipcovers, even more photographs, vermilion curtains, silk flowers, footstools, dresses, bedcovers, paintings, writing desks, dressers, suitcases, rugs, plates . . . *we cannot live.*

Two hours have passed since the agreed-upon time and no one can tell me that Mamma is alive. No one can promise me that. Nanna begs me to stop.

She says: "Mamma has been held up. Anyone can be late. She'll call when she gets a chance and when she can find a telephone."

"Can you swear that nothing has happened to her?"

Nanna hesitates.

"I can't *swear* to anything, but I'm sure it hasn't."

Not good enough. I go back to crying and walking, and curse Nanna because she made me stop.

When the doorbell rings, it's the doctor, but I'm sure it's the minister coming to deliver the bad news. I've seen it in movies. It's either the minister or the police. God does not rescue. If I continue to walk from room to room in the big flat, crying, if I don't give in, if I can prove that I can walk like this from room to room without ever resting, then maybe I can bring her back. I will not stop. Nanna has called the doctor, I recognize her, it's the tall, skinny lady with the throaty voice, the one who's lived a hard life and who always stands with her arms crossed and asks me how I'm getting on at school. Now she's here, shaking her head, saying: "This isn't normal."

Arms crossed. I don't know what Nanna has told her. The doctor takes out her stethoscope and wants to listen to my heart and starts following me from room to room, but eventually gives up.

Can the doctor tell me when Mamma will call? Can the doctor tell me what God wants from me? Can the doctor tell me that Mamma is alive? The doctor puts the stethoscope back in her purse and tells Nanna that she sees no other alternative but to give me *something calming*.

"But pills are not the answer here," she sighs, throwing her arms up in the air.

When the doctor has left, Nanna positions herself in the kitchen. I walk from room to room and will not rest, the expedition starts in the hallway, then through the kitchen, the dining room, the library and the TV room and then all over again. Nanna stands quietly in the kitchen and whispers my name each time I pass by. She doesn't think Mamma is dead. Something must have come up, and she hasn't been able to get to a phone. These things happen. *But dammit*, she may be thinking. *You'd expect my daughter to call on time, knowing the kind of havoc it causes when she doesn't.*

"Come here, darling," says Nanna, "come, I want to tell you something. Give me your hand."

I give her my hand but carry on sobbing, albeit a little more softly. I'm exhausted from all the crying and walking.

Nanna pours a glass of water. She breaks the pill the doctor gave her in two and asks me to swallow one half. The other half she slips into her purse.

"We will eat supper now," she says, "and Mamma will call soon, I promise."

She looks at me to make sure I swallow the pill.

"Maybe she won't call this evening, but if not, she's bound to call tomorrow."

Nanna strokes my hair, her fingers running into knots and tangles.

"I think we'll have to trim your hair soon," she says, but at that I start howling again.

Nanna hushes me, holds me and hushes me, shhh, shhhh, shhhhh, the way you hush a baby. Gently, softly, repeatedly. We stand on the kitchen floor, her arms wrapped around me, until the crying subsides.

"There is a perfectly natural explanation for why she hasn't called," she whispers, and then she takes my hand in hers and squeezes four times.

Which means *Do you love me.*

And then I squeeze Nanna's hands three times, which means *Yes, I do.*

And then Nanna squeezes twice, which means *How much?*

And then I squeeze Nanna's hand so hard that it hurts, which means *THIS MUCH.*

"Ow," she says and pulls back her hand, but she's not angry. She prepares tiny little banana sandwiches and tells me to fetch the Asbjørnsen and Moe book of folktales. I sit down at one end of the table, she sits down at the other. The kitchen lamp is blue. It's long past bedtime.

"The sobs last longer than the tears," she says, and leans over the table and wipes away a few breadcrumbs from the corner of my mouth.

MAMMA BARGES INTO MY room in her long, fragrant silk nightgown, hair going every which way, black makeup smudges under her eyes. She has just watched a news report on TV about young girls and anorexia. She pulls the duvet off me and moans at the sight of my rib cage. In the letter Pappa wrote to me on the occasion of my christening, he said: *For the time being I suppose you are entwined with your mother in such a way that everything else, while interesting, is none of your concern.* It is not like that anymore. I'm not *entwined* with anyone, I yank the duvet from her hands and cover myself with it. *Go away. Get out.* It's not that Mamma worries *all* the time, days or months might pass between every time she worries about me. Worries of the *what-if-my-child-were-to-die* sort. But now that she's home, she worries all the time. Day and night and night and day and day and night. I think she wants to catch up on all the worrying she didn't do while she was away. It's hard to divide worry and spread it evenly over the days, the months, the years. Nothing is ever even. I'm growing up, but without any plan or direction. Am I ugly, am I pretty? Am I a real girl? My teeth and feet are too big, my wrists are too thin, my eyes are those of a child and I don't want to be a child. And what will I do if she dies? Next time she goes away, I want to slice open my stomach, move the dagger from right to left, let my blood and guts spill out of me, honorably in black and white—until, finally, I offer up my head so that someone can chop it off. I know how it's done. I've seen the film *Harakiri* together with Pappa at Dämba. Twice. I don't want to die, I want to live, but if she dies, there is no place for me in this world.

There are lots of photographs of Mamma and Nanna, they smile and pose for the camera, I, on the other hand, duck whenever someone wants to take a picture. My face is round and pale, I have chubby cheeks. My bangs are heavy and get in my eyes, my legs are too skinny. Mamma thinks I'm *a lot of work*. Twelve years old and impertinent. Rarely smiles. Pulls away. Impossible. More and more demanding. I've been given my first pair of pointe shoes and whirl round and round and round. Pink silk ribbons around my ankle, double crisscross, I'm good at tying my ballet shoes, less so at fixing my hair, making the perfect ballet bun, it's not tight enough. Dance, dance, dance. Lumps form on my head and strands of hair are sticking out and hanging down, I'm told that I have do something about the hair, I have to strengthen the back, accentuate the *pointe*, lift the head, extend the arms, fix the gaze, discipline the heart.

Mamma pulls back my duvet. *She can't just come into my room and pull back my duvet.* I don't want the whole world to see my body. My nightgown is torn and she fiddles with the ripped seam. She yells. Sometimes when she's home, I wish she was out traveling again. *You are too skinny, you're way too skinny, you have to eat more, you don't eat enough.*

I was born skinny, there's nothing to do about it. Heidi says that she was born skinny too. Heidi and I are friends. Everyone says we look alike, but I don't think so. Heidi is pretty. Thirteen and a half. Older than me. Shapely. Boys like her. We could have been sisters, that's how often we are together. She doesn't worry about her body. Or about her mother. Or about a lack of direction. She worries about what will happen to her if she walks alone through a big room full of people.

I have two pairs of jeans in my closet, two identical pairs of jeans. What if I were to put on both pairs at the same time, one pair on top of the other? Would that create the illusion that there is more of me, a little bit more body? I put on the two pairs of jeans, take them off again and put them back on. It feels clammy and too tight. Will this give me a shape? There are bulges in strange places. I walk with my legs apart, like a wading bird. Like a little kid who's just peed herself. The girls at school look at me strangely. The boys don't look at me. When I *have to* pee, I lock myself in the girls' bathroom and try to pull the two pairs of jeans down. It doesn't work, I can't get them off, one pair is stuck to the other, *I'm* stuck. I'm more jeans than girl. And now I have to pee so badly that either I'll actually *have to* pee myself, or else . . . or else I'll let out a scream that will blast time itself and this stupid, disobliging, childish little body into bits. There! Now I can pee.

Girls' voices and running footsteps. Knocking at the door to the bathroom stall.

"What's happening?"

"Why are you screaming?"

"It's nothing. Go away."

Figenschou, the physics teacher, comes into the girls' bathroom. She has recess supervision that day. I can't see her, I've locked the door to the stall and won't come out, but something happens to the air when Figenschou is nearby, it darkens, it thickens as if a jumbo jet were coming in to land right where you're standing. Loopy girls all chattering at the same time.

"She's in there."

"She's locked the door."

Three loud knocks.

"What's going on? Are you all right?"

"Yes."

"Then I want you to unlock the door right this minute!"

I pull up the one pair of jeans and fold the other into a little pile and hide it as best I can behind the toilet. I unlock the door and open it.

Figenschou is big and stocky and looks like a monkfish. Her husband, Tank, also teaches at the elementary school. He is tall and thin. I wonder if they fuck.

"Why were you screaming?"

She snarls when she speaks.

"Screaming?"

"Didn't you just lock yourself in the toilet and start screaming?"

"Nope," I said. "Not me."

Heidi says that some people are fat and some are skinny, that's just the way the world is. She says it was a stupid idea to wear two pairs of jeans at the same time, it doesn't make you look shapely, it makes you look as if you've put on two pairs of jeans, one on top of the other, and now everyone knows I was the one who screamed in the girls' bathroom and was sent to the school psychologist.

———

Heidi is the only girl who can fix broken cassette tapes. She doesn't give up until she has straightened out the tangles and carefully wound the tape back into place with the aid of a pencil. When a tape gets jammed in the cassette player or slips off the spools in some other way (it always happens very quickly, there's a low, hissing sound of the tape getting bunched up) it's as irreversible as being stung by a wasp. If *I* start fiddling with the cassette, the tape will snap and the cassette will be ruined forever. Heidi's hands are no more delicate than mine, not that we compare hands, comparing hands is bad luck, we're pale girls, no one notices us when we walk down the street, who is who, blond hair and small hands; what no one knows, is that Heidi's hands can undo knots and tangles in a way that mine can't, whether it's cassette tapes, shoelaces or girls' hair. My hair is tangled, and Heidi can undo the tangles without pulling and ripping out a bunch of extra hair.

At night we listen to our tapes. We are neighbors and can have sleepovers as often as we like, and if we don't get permission, we sneak out once her parents and my babysitters have fallen asleep. When Nanna is in charge, sneaking out is out of the question. Nanna stays awake all night long, pacing back and forth through the big flat. But as a rule, Heidi and I have sleepovers as often as we can, although perhaps I want to sleep over a little bit more often than she does. I'm the eager one. Sometimes Heidi says she doesn't feel like it, that she's made other plans.

Heidi's bedroom has yellow walls, mine are painted white. At night everything is swathed in half-darkness. Sometimes we tiptoe around the different rooms, I live in a flat, she lives

in a house, but we know each other's walls and floors and corners as though they were our own. Nothing has been moved
or rearranged, the furniture sits where it usually sits, but
everything is different when all are asleep, as if the rooms have
caught a fever.

The window in my room is hidden behind long, thick vermilion curtains. Mamma chose the fabric and took it to the
seamstress to have them sewn. My bedspread matches the curtains. I have a black cassette player the size of a shoebox. It has a
handle on one end, like a purse, I carry it with me when I sleep
over at Heidi's.

If Heidi hadn't really existed, I would have made her up.

Her father and my father are the same age. Old. Gray. In
winter, Heidi's father wears a green wool coat, my father most
likely wears one too. They sit immersed in their own thoughts,
one of them in Norway, the other in Germany, behind closed
doors. Heidi's father has nightmares. Sometimes we hear his
cries echoing through the rooms. The nightmares have to do
with the war, says Heidi, and when her father falls asleep, his
dreams run wild. There's nothing anyone can do. I feel sorry
for him.

"Can't you go inside and hold his hand or something?"

Heidi shakes her head.

The cries are like prayers, but not like any prayer I've ever
heard. I've heard Nanna say bedtime prayers, but that's entirely
different.

A grown man whose dreams run wild.

Does my father have dreams like that? Or my mother?

Apart from the nightmares, the nights are quiet. When
Heidi and I sleep over at each other's houses, our goal is to stay

up until dawn. To accomplish this, we place a bowl of cold water under the bed so that we can dip our faces if we feel ourselves falling asleep.

Summer is approaching and Mamma has come home. She is going to have a party. *I am going to have a party*, she says, all lovely and dewy and full of energy. Heidi will sleep over. We have decided to stay awake and spy on the grown-ups, and for a while we run around and pretend we're actual guests, but eventually we fall asleep side by side to the sounds of laughter and music and voices. We don't wake up until late the following morning. There is no one here now. The morning sun lights up all that the night left behind. Dirty glasses and wine bottles everywhere, greasy smudge marks on the windowpanes, as if all the guests had pressed their hands against them in an effort to get out. Heidi says we should open the windows to let in some air. When Mamma dances the way she did at the party, whirling around the living room, I'm scared she's going to topple over. For a while I follow her around, trying to clear away everything in her path, but I can't very well follow her around for the rest of my life. At some point you have to lie down and sleep.

Heidi and I get up together in the morning and lie down together in the evening, and sometimes I hold her so tight that she says I'm practically strangling her.

Girls faint in ballet class. First a thud. A crash. A collapse. It's not unlike a natural disaster. Utter chaos ensues. When a girl faints, everybody rushes over with water and napkins and towels and tutus and magazines and flapping notebooks—anything that can be used as a fan. Competent female hands lift, rescue, stroke foreheads, resurrect. Collapse and resurrection. It happens all the time. The city returns to itself after the earthquake. The girls come around, pull themselves shakily onto their long spindly legs, and life goes on.

Mamma has received an offer to sing and dance on Broadway. She who can neither sing nor dance.

"Would you like to move to the United States?" she asks.

"Again?"

"Yes."

"No! I really don't."

THE FIRST TIME MAMMA and I lived in the United States, I was five years old. We moved into a large house in Los Angeles and I was taught how to swim by a wiry female body with a long nose and a rubber swim cap. She never smiled, but gave me a popsicle after each completed swimming lesson. Mamma had a suitor who refused to use soap, "The Frenchman," she called him, he didn't want to cut his hair either, or brush his teeth with toothpaste, it was *political*, Mamma explained. When I sat on his lap, I could wrap his hair around my face. It was black and bristly and smelled like the ocean floor, and Mamma said he was the most brilliant man in the world. She had another suitor too. His name was Dick, I think, or John. I'm not sure. Names are difficult. Difficult to give, to have, to remember, to live with, to get rid of. Bob, maybe. He took Mamma and me along to what he called the world's biggest toy store, and said I could have anything I wanted. He wore wide shirts and bell-bottoms and told me that he loved me. I knew it didn't mean that he *actually* loved me, Mamma said that in Los Angeles everyone says *I love you* even if they don't mean it. Mamma tapped her big nose and said: *You have to learn how to sniff out the difference between what people say and what they mean and not let things go to your head.*

Dick (or Bob) turned to Mamma and me. His face was one big smile. He loved the toy store. I could see his mouth and both his ears, but not his eyes. They were hidden behind large sunglasses that he never took off.

We were just getting started.

"What about this?" he said, and showed us a kind of pan or pot made of aluminum foil.

"You put it on the stove, and a few minutes later, pop-pop-pop-pop, the pan expands into a pot full of popcorn."

Mamma and I looked at the pan.

"We want a couple of these, right?" His voice was impatient. He put six popcorn pans into the cart.

The toy-store suitor smoked nonstop. Cigarettes, cigarillos, pipes, glass tubes. In the toy store he smoked candy cigarettes that looked just like real cigarettes, but tasted sweet. Mamma and I each got one. It was hard keeping up with him. Mamma took my hand.

"What about this?" he cried out. We could hear him, but not see him.

One moment he's here, the next he's gone. Now he's holding a fair-haired doll in his hand. She has blue eyes and long black eyelashes like cat whiskers, chubby wrists, chubby thighs, and when you press her tummy she starts to cry.

The toy store is divided into long, narrow aisles with shelves from floor to ceiling. The lamps in the ceiling emit a green fluorescent light. We fill two carts with toys, mostly dolls and doll clothes, but also a big fish that I can play with in the bathtub. Mamma's suitor lifts me up into the shopping cart and runs as fast as he can down the aisle with tanks and popguns, it's like sailing underwater. Mamma is also running, following right behind us, laughing.

In the days of the beautiful Helen of Troy, lists were made of her suitors. One such list was compiled by Pseudo-Apollodorus (thirty-one suitors), one by Hesiod (eleven suitors), and one by Hyginus (thirty-six suitors).

Mamma says in her little-girl voice: "I can get anyone I want just by *looking* at them."

She often called men *them* and girls *us.*
They don't like us when our voices are shrill.
We shouldn't be too eager—it scares them away.

I have notebooks with stiff red covers, I don't keep a diary. I make lists. Among them lists of:

> The number of babysitters.
> The number of boyfriends (Mamma's).
> The number of times I've moved house.
> What I will buy once I have my own money.
> The prettiest girls in class.
> Books I've read.
> Films I've seen.
> The number of days until I'm thirteen.
> The number of days until I'm sixteen.
> The number of days until I'm eighteen.
> The number of times I've lived in the United States
> (lived for a period of time, as opposed to just visited).

The second time Mamma and I flew across the Atlantic to *live,* I was ten. We went for six months. Mamma's suitors brought gifts. "The Russian" gave me a big jar of Beluga caviar, which Mamma said he had smuggled out of the Soviet Union. It was left on top of the kitchen counter in a hotel suite in New York. The hotel suite was like an apartment, I had my own bedroom, but in the beginning Mamma let me sleep with her in her bed. The name of the hotel was Navarro. It sounds like a place I've made up, but I didn't make it up. Margot Fonteyn, the ballerina, would glide by in the long, dimly lit, thickly carpeted hotel corridors and was more beautiful even than Mamma and pat me on the head and say, *Very nice, dear, very nice.* The jar of caviar was blue and gold and all mine.

Often when Mamma talked, she said incoherent things that I pieced together into something even more incoherent. She talked a lot about the Iron Curtain. I already knew quite a bit about the Iron Curtain.

"I can see it from Pappa's house at Hammars," I said.

"No, you can't," said Mamma.

"Yes," I said.

"What you see is the *horizon*," she said, "not the Iron Curtain." She repeated the word several times.

"Horizon. Horizon. Horizon."

The art of following a train of thought. Mamma immediately went off-piste. The Russian's appearance in her life and his subsequent disappearance from it were a mystery. Mamma talked and talked. Her blue silk nightgown was as blue as the jar of caviar. Sometimes a bottle of vodka had been left on the kitchen counter as well. That's what Russians do—they fight their way through the Iron Curtain, bringing with them vodka for their girlfriends and caviar for their girlfriends' daughters. Mamma said that the Russian was afraid of the dark, and that this was why he always had to stay the night and why I couldn't sleep in her bed. But since the Russian was a grown man and *very proud*, he didn't want anyone to know that he was scared. I didn't answer. I walked out into the hotel corridor so I wouldn't have to listen to her, later I came back, and then I left again. Sometimes I took the elevator to another floor, which was like traveling to another country. The broad hotel corridors looked exactly alike, that wasn't it, they all had carpeted floors and heavy chandeliers hanging from the ceiling, and you could walk on endlessly past door after door after door. But each corridor had its own air. If it had been possible to weigh air, it would have weighed differently on each floor.

I ate all the Beluga, every single little fish egg, slathered it across big slices of bread that I lined up on the hotel kitchen counter. I chewed and swallowed. I liked the salty, sticky, musty taste of black.

WHEN MAMMA IS SLEEPING, you are not allowed to wake her. If Mamma falls asleep and someone wakes her, she can't go back to sleep again, and then the night is ruined, and not only that night, but the following day, and the next night after that, on and on.

I used to dream about her. It was always a variation of the same dream, which ended with us yelling at each other in such a way that she dissolved and disappeared. In the dream, I would start looking for her. A frantic search through shelves and cupboards, underneath sofas and in the bathtub, is she hiding behind the curtains, maybe, the vermilion ones, or in Nanna's sewing box, or among the forks and knives in the kitchen drawer?

Mamma is sitting in her bed reading *Madame Bovary*. She raises her eyes and looks at me and says that it is a novel by a French author.

"What's it about?"

"It's about a woman named Emma."

I stand in the open doorway and nod.

"Maybe you could go outside and play," she says, "or else find your own book and come up into bed with me and read as well."

I nod.

"But we have to be quiet," she adds. "We can't read if we're not quiet."

Her hair is down, and she's all black around the eyes. Her eye-makeup remover never removes all of her eye makeup. In the evenings and mornings, the area around her eyes is black and smudgy. Once I spat on my fingers and tried to rub it away. She didn't say *gross,* even though it was a little gross, she only said I shouldn't rub so hard.

Years later, when I read the novel myself and try to imagine what Emma looks like, I'm convinced that she too is all black around the eyes. I don't think Flaubert mentions anything about it, but he does write that "What was beautiful about her was her eyes: although they were brown, they seemed black because of the lashes," but not a word about the blackness that won't go away even if you rub and rub.

H<small>E WORE A WHITE</small> suit and was much older than her. She had just turned seventeen. Cousin Henry was known as a ladies' man and a charlatan, and Mamma has told me how her mother, my nanna, hovered by the open window, waiting for her to come home. Cousin Henry was well mannered and handsome to look at, but not to be trusted. What on earth possessed her daughter to go out with him? Why not someone else? Why him of all people?

It was a bitter cold evening. It was just before Christmas. They went to the movies. Maybe they had a bite to eat. Did they drink wine? When was the first time she realized how good it felt to drink? The sense of freedom? The lack of shame. *Finally, finally, finally. I'll tell no one, but I never want to stop doing this.*

They walked home through the park, and he suggested they sit down on a bench and talk, even though it had begun to snow and it was far too cold to do any such thing. He slipped his hand under her skirt, fiddled with her garter, stroked her thigh, his hand was clumsy and small and cold. When he grabbed her underpants to pull them off, she said no, but he pulled them off anyway and they had sex there on the bench. It was the first time. She remembers the cold. The cold bench. The cold hand.

When they walked home—he insisted on walking her home—he asked her what she would like for Christmas. The year was 1955, maybe they had danced to "Blue Suede Shoes," maybe she had pictured the shoes, those blue suede shoes, only she wanted red ones, she could feel the chill in her nose, in her throat, in her mouth, in her eyes, between her legs, and she was afraid she'd get sick and that her mother, who was hovering by the window, would get mad and hit her. I can't imagine Nanna hitting anyone, but she did, not me, but Mamma, whenever she got angry and couldn't control herself.

Mamma told Cousin Henry that she'd like a pair of red high-heeled shoes, and when he asked what size she wore, she lied and said 6. Mamma has always been embarrassed about her feet, she has big feet, 9.5, with a small purple protuberance on her right big toe, but she didn't want Cousin Henry to know that.

On Christmas Eve 1955, Mamma is presented with a pair of red high-heeled shoes, size 6. She squeezes her feet into them and walks around in them all evening even though it hurts. Cousin Henry is smiling at her and she doesn't want to appear ungrateful.

The red shoes are among the first presents to be unwrapped that Christmas Eve, and the evening is long. When she's finally alone in her room and can take them off, her feet are red and swollen and there is a hole in one of her stockings. When she gets out her sewing kit and starts sewing—does she do what Flaubert's Emma did? Does she keep pricking her fingers, raising them to her mouth to suck?

TELL MAMMA THAT IF she's serious about us moving to the Unites States again, it will only happen under certain conditions. I am twelve years old and attach conditions.

My conditions are: I want to go to a good ballet school, and I want a cat.

"You can have your bloody cat," says Mamma, "whatever you want, I'm sick and tired of everything. I'm so exhausted."

I T'S TOO EXPENSIVE TO call Heidi from the United States, but we can write letters, Mamma says. That's one thing. The other is that children must live near trees.

Mamma's rules for good parenting:

1. Children must drink milk.
2. Children must live near trees.

Mamma decides that I will live in a big, yellow house in a small town almost two hours' drive from New York City. The small town has many trees. I don't know what sort of trees they are. Big houses, tall trees, and dark green grass. It dawns on me that Mamma won't be living in the house with me, she will be commuting, she says. Sometimes she'll be in New York, sometimes in the small town. I'll be with the trees.

The owner of the house is a corpulent, bespectacled lady of about sixty with tiny feet crammed into even tinier high-heeled pumps. She will show us the house and offer practical advice before handing over the keys to Mamma. Following what turns out to be a tedious tour of the kitchen, the main living room, and the second-floor bedrooms, she takes us down again to the room she calls the *drawing room*. She opens the door to the veranda and garden and is about to say something. But Mamma cuts her off.

"A garden," she exclaims, letting out a little cry of joy, "a *garden* with *trees*!"

She takes my hand and wants to run outside, I can tell that she wants us to hold hands and run out into the garden and dance around in it and show the corpulent lady and the new neighbors how wonderful everything is. I pull back my hand, make myself stiff and heavy, turn myself into fifty layers of girl blubber. I hiss: "Don't touch me!"

I have one boob. You would think that when you finally got them, they'd both come at the same time. But no. On the right side you can see it, on the left side—nothing! One nipple glows violet and hurts when you touch it, as if a bumble bee had moved inside. The other is soft, pink and no bigger than a cat's nose. I'm thinner than a blade of grass. I hate America. I hate my mother.

Mamma runs outside and begins to dance in the garden. The sun gleams in her hair. She doesn't know how to dance. It's not as charming as she thinks. The corpulent lady purses her lips. She and I stand next to each other. I have blue sneakers. She has yellow pumps. It occurs to me that she probably likes yellow, since the house is yellow and the curtains in the living room are yellow and her shoes are yellow. She wants to say something, hesitates, but then pulls herself together and calls out to Mamma: "I don't encourage . . . please don't . . . I don't want anyone treading on the grass!"

Mamma stops dancing and gasps for breath. What did the corpulent lady say? Mamma tosses her beautiful hair and tiptoes exaggeratedly back to where we are standing, as though she wants to show us that she has mastered the art of walking and dancing on grass without touching it. She doesn't dare say that the garden is the reason she rented this house in the first place, doesn't dare say that it took her forever to find precisely *this* house and *this* garden, that everything was supposed to be perfect this time, doesn't dare say that while still in Oslo, she had sent for real estate brochures, twenty, maybe more, with photographs of houses and gardens and trees and rooms, yes, she had pored over them in bed, looked at all the different properties, and when she came to the photograph of the big yellow house surrounded by all that greenery she had said to herself: This is where we're going to live. She had a daughter, a child, trees would be climbed.

Mamma doesn't dare tell the lady any of this, she is intimidated by all that corpulence, doesn't want to initiate a conflict. Besides, the contract is already signed. *Does that mean tree-climbing is out of the question?* She doesn't dare ask. Everything was supposed to turn out well this time around. Children need peace, order, predictability. A nice house, a nice garden, a nice neighborhood. Trees, milk. She feels like she's losing her daughter. Something's slipping. They were so close. *But now she shies away. Answers back. She was so dear, so full of light. Sunshine in her hair. Now she looks at me and her eyes speak of a thousand accusations. Can't she just stay my little girl?*

The wallpaper in the drawing room has a brocade pattern, the sofa as well, children are not allowed to bring food into the drawing room, says the lady.

THE CAT COSTS A thousand dollars. It is a long-haired Persian with a complicated, finely spun silver-threaded coat and an equally complicated disposition.

"Most importantly you must remember to brush her coat every day," says the cat breeder.

The cat breeder looks like a Persian cat herself and has not only one cat living at her house, but over twenty. She has a tiny squashed-together face, a pink nose, small dainty ears, and dopey green eyes with a somewhat bewildered or dejected or offended look about them. Her body is gaunt. She has gathered her frizzy, waist-length hair into a high ponytail. For a while it looked as though Mamma was considering ditching the cat and taking the lady home with her instead.

I have decided that the new cat will be called Suzy Jolie, I decided it on the flight over, and now here we are, still jet-lagged from our trip, mother and daughter in the cat breeder's living room, seated on creaky chairs with pink floral covers. The table and the windowsills are adorned with various white and green cat-shaped porcelain sculptures, and we have been offered lukewarm Lipton tea in small black cups with the tea bags still floating on top. While the breeder is in the kitchen arranging crackers on a plate, Mamma discovers that she doesn't have a teaspoon. She coaxes the tea bag out of her cup with her pinkie, the bag drips on the tablecloth, and she glances desperately around, looking for a saucer to put it on, can't find a saucer and drops it back into the cup with a little plop. Mamma likes her tea weak, it has to be scalding hot and not made from a tea bag dunked straight into the cup but from tea leaves brewed in a pot, all this I know. One of the things I used to do when I was younger was to make tea for Mamma when she was tired and had a headache. She'd lie on the sofa and sip the tea while I massaged her brow. *You have good hands*, Mamma used to say. *Hands that soothe frayed nerves.*

The stench of cat pee hits us as Mamma parks the rental car outside the cat breeder's house. Mamma sticks her big nose in the air—a nose that paradoxically both spoils and emphasizes her beauty—sniffing and saying: "Nothing smells as bad as cat pee! Are you sure you want a cat?"

Talk. Tea. This will take time. On an overseas call between the United States and Norway, the cat lady had insisted on meeting the mother face-to-face. She doesn't sell cats to just anyone. You can be as much of a movie star as you like, her only concern is the well-being of her cats, and in order to ensure this, she has developed her own cat-owner-approval process. It is not a given that you will be allowed to take the cat home after the first interview, or ever, for that matter. She doesn't breed cats for the money, she repeats, once we're all seated around the table having tea and crackers.

"A *little bit* for the money," I mutter in Norwegian. Well, I know the cat costs a thousand dollars.

Mamma doesn't like that her girl has become so sarcastic. It's getting worse all the time. And rude. That's gotten worse too. Mamma says nice things to the cat breeder about her living room and all the cat sculptures, about her long, frizzy hair, which Mamma calls *wavy*, about the fat cat that has jumped up on Mamma's lap, curled itself into a ball, and gone to sleep. She says nothing about the stench or the lukewarm tea, or about the stained tablecloth. Mamma can bend an iron rod just by looking at it, making it feel seen and loved. I hold my tongue. I don't have the same effect on people as Mamma does. My teeth are much too big and my mouth is too full of braces to make it worth-while to say anything at all, and I completely lack the ability to make people feel seen and loved. Persians in assorted stages of cat lives lie sprawled in the overfurnished room—on the sofas strewn with cushions covered in the same cat-nose-pink fabric as the living-room chairs, on the fur-infested carpets beneath the sofas, on the windowsills, coiled round the largest porcelain figurines, under the giant radiator that breathes and pants and crackles and oozes heat. The breeder says to the mother that she is generally opposed to selling her cats to families with children. I shove the big cat away from Mamma's lap so I can sit there myself. Strictly speaking, I'm too old to sit on Mamma's lap, I know that, but I don't care.

"I want to leave," I mumble in Norwegian, "let's just go. She's weird."

Mamma's rage erupts without warning. She's still smiling at the cat breeder, but I can feel the anger by the goose bumps on her skin. *This child who has become so big and heavy, who has climbed onto my lap, who whines and puts on airs and makes every-thing so difficult.*

"It's not easy being a *woman*," my mother says, partly to herself and partly to the cat breeder. The cat breeder nods in agreement.

———

Every time Mamma utters the word *woman*, she speaks in italics. It is obvious to everyone, including me, that when Mamma
speaks about being a *woman*, she is talking about something
much more complicated than simply being female. I, for example, am nowhere near being a *woman*. I am the opposite of
woman. I am a girl, but not in italics. I remember learning about
distillation in school and thinking that if you boiled Mamma at a
thousand degrees you would be left with the distilled essence of
woman. I get up from her lap and walk into the kitchen. Maybe
I'll find the cat I'll be taking home with me? *My* cat. That was
the agreement. Mamma will make it happen. She usually keeps
her promises except when she has promised to call at a particular
agreed-upon time.

  Your mother is the most sincere liar in the world, Pappa says,
with a certain measure of admiration.

They are like prodigal sons, the two of them, the mother and
the father, each in their own way, each in their own world, the
beloved younger child who expects the fatted calf to be brought
hither and killed for him, who wants to eat and make merry and
be dead then alive again, to be lost then found, and who doesn't
want the fun and games to ever end.

And the agreement with Mamma was: I will leave Heidi and
move to the United States with you if you let me have a cat. I
don't want a fatted calf, I want a cat. I don't want to be a child,
either, but I have no choice but to be one for a few more years.

———

The kitchen floor crunches under my feet, there is cat litter everywhere, a big white cat is shitting in the litter box over by the door and kicking the litter over the edges, a half-eaten ham sandwich lies forgotten on a plate on the counter. Mamma and the strange woman are talking in the living room. I wander from room to room, and maybe it's the jet-lag, maybe it's the heat, maybe it's the smell of cat pee, but it feels like I'm wandering around inside an early morning nightmare—the glaring lights, the crawling surfaces.

A few years earlier Mamma finished her book, the one she had been struggling to write. I remember she spent every day in the basement of the house in Strømmen, writing and writing, seeing the pile of paper getting bigger and bigger. Her nerves were frayed. We got a color TV. I was seven. Then eight. She danced around and fell down and had to be helped into bed. She cried and said she couldn't take it anymore. *Men—over and out.* The telephone kept ringing. Everyone just tugged at her, and finally, the book was finished. When it was published in the United States, she took me with her to an elegant bookstore in New York, where I had to sit quietly behind a big table for several hours while people lined up to buy the book and get her autograph on the title page, some of the people, mostly women, patted me on the cheek, some wept, some took pictures. In chapter one, Mamma writes: "I want to write about love, about being human—about loneliness—about being a woman." All of which seem like excellent things to write about. She also writes: "It may be the lost kingdom of childhood I am in constant search for." Which I *don't* get. What loss? What kingdom? One day I'll be an adult, but that's still years away, unfortunately. I'm twelve. I don't like being a child. I don't like other children, I don't like the way they look at me, their whispering, their pretty hair, their secrets. I miss Heidi. She's a child, but in a way that I understand. I've been in the United States for three days and I already miss her more than I can bear. If only there was a way to make time pass more quickly.

I open the door to what must be the cat breeder's bedroom. Six kittens lie entangled on an unmade narrow bed, unaware of my presence until I stretch out my hand and try to pet them. The smallest kitten, no bigger than a lemming, sticks its head out of the huddle, hisses and clamps its teeth round my hand, I cry out, but there's no sound to be heard. I try to pull my hand away, but the cat digs its teeth in again and this time it gets a good grip. It hurts. It's like the time when Heidi jabbed my hand with a piece of glass from a broken Coca-Cola bottle. But that time I was supposed to bleed, we were both supposed to bleed, we were mingling blood so that we could become blood sisters. When I lift up my hand, the cat follows along and dangles in midair. The other cats move a tiny little bit, barely noticing that the cluster has lost one of its component parts. Heidi said that pain numbs pain. Maybe it's true. The cat consists of mostly fur and a few teeth, claws, heart and bone. I shake my hand until it lets go.

I make my way back through the smelly rooms and stop in the living-room doorway. Mamma and the cat breeder are sitting close together on the sofa, immersed in intimate conversation as though they'd been friends all their lives. Mamma looks up and sees me.

"One of the cats bit and scratched me," I say and splay my

fingers. A speck of blood seeps from the soft skin between my thumb and index finger.

"Then go and wash your hands," Mamma says.

"Maybe I'll get rabies," I say, "or tetanus. It bit really hard."

I move a few steps closer.

"See! There's blood everywhere!"

I make my eyes roll back in my head.

The cat breeder looks at me, then at Mamma. We're talking Norwegian, so she has no idea what we're saying. Mamma always tells me to speak English when we're in the United States. *Remember to speak English, sweetie, it's rude not to.* I look at the cat breeder's ugly green eyes. I don't think she's going to give us the cat even though Mamma is paying her a thousand dollars.

My behavior has jeopardized the approval process. Stupid girl!

"My daughter caught her hand in the door," Mamma says gently, smiling at the cat breeder.

Or maybe she can make it happen after all? Mamma can get clouds to change shape, hearts to beat faster.

Mamma gestures at me to come and sit on her lap. She kisses my fingers, she doesn't kiss where it hurts, but it's still nice.

Babysitters move in and out of the yellow house. Their job is to take care of the girl. Get her up in the morning, give her food, help her with her homework, take her to ballet class in New York, take her back to the little town, this *fucking wasteland*, get her into bed at night.

The mother thought it would be wise to hire *two* babysitters this time. If one of them jumps ship, the other can take over. The girl is impossible, unruly, simply no longer a *mouse*, and the mother must find out how best to take care of this cluster of bones and mouth and knees and braces and expenses, this pile of limbs that clings to her and rejects her and that is, and always will be, her sole responsibility. The girl's mother, long-haired and lovely, has so many things on her mind. So much to do. The year is 1978 and soon she will be forty. She stands in the middle of the floor wearing a long, sheer dress, and everyone comes tugging at her. Kissing her, patting her, poking her, bumping into her, shaking her, stroking her hair, rubbing her tummy, licking her, twisting her nose, lifting her up, setting her down, knocking, ringing, pecking, stinging, swarming, and it's not as if the girl's father ever *lifted a finger*. Not a single goddamned finger to help. Is anyone writing to *him* about the ship going down? Is anyone asking *him* where his child is, or where *he* is? Is anyone pulling and tugging at *him*? Is anyone taking the liberty of judging him—as a *father*? No. He's got enough on his plate already, coping with being a genius and all his bloody demons.

The mother rolls her eyes.

"You and I are on our own, Mouse," she tells her daughter, and hugs her tightly, "it's just us two."

The two babysitters come from Sweden, they are twenty-two and twenty-four and *devastatingly* beautiful. Mamma promises them lots of money to take care of the girl. There's no limit to what one must shell out to guard against the ship going down. A thousand dollars a month they are to be paid. Mamma meant to say a thousand *kroner*, she later confides to her daughter, but said a thousand dollars instead and didn't dare take it back, at least not once the Swedish girls had thrown their arms around her neck and showered her with kisses. Mamma doesn't want to disappoint people. *It's difficult, you know. I can't bear to disappoint people.* Sometimes the girl is the only one who listens and the only one who knows how to console. The mother's women friends tell the mother that she has to stop confiding in her daughter, one shouldn't try to be friends with one's child, one should be a *mother*, say the women friends, and in theory at least the mother agrees and adds this to her list of rules for good parenting:

1. Children must drink milk.
2. Children must live near trees.
3. Mothers should not try to be friends with their daughters, nor should they confide in them, mothers have to remember who is the mother and who is the daughter, who is the adult and who is the child.

In the stories the father told, the girls were always *devastatingly* beautiful, with emphasis on the word "devastatingly." This made the stories more interesting. When the phone rings (the telephone in the yellow house is also yellow, with push buttons and a long black cord and a chime so loud that it makes you start) and it's the father calling long distance from Munich, the daughter tells him that she has moved to a small town outside of New York and that she's living with two *devastatingly* beautiful girls from Sweden and that she's doing very well.

As time passes, Mamma comes home to the yellow house less and less often. Every morning I walk to the end of the street to wait for the school bus. I go to an all-girls school set in its own large, parklike grounds. The school uniform consists of a green pinafore dress, a white blouse, brown shoes, green knee socks, bony knees sticking out below the hem of the dress. I am put into a class of girls younger than me—demoted to a class of little kids, brats, eleven-year-olds. My English isn't good enough yet, explains the headmistress, a haggard and ravenous lady with pointy breasts.

"You would feel rather lost if I were to put you in a situation in which you were measured against girls of your own age," she says.

"*Lost?*" says Mamma meekly, and glances over at me. We're each sitting in a huge leather chair in the headmistress's office.

"Yes," says the headmistress.

I glare at her.

"Isn't that a bit extreme?" whispers Mamma. "I mean, she won't be *lost*."

"What matters most is that our students feel safe and secure," says the headmistress.

———

The classroom is large and bright with tall arching windows. All of the children politely greet the new student. The teacher's name is Miss French and her subject is English. She is so beautiful that I understand what Pappa means by *devastating*, not just a word to spice up a good story, but as a real thing, something palpable, something that certain God-chosen women exude. Miss French materializes in front of the blackboard in all her horrible beauty and so perfectly groomed and alluring that she crackles as she moves around the classroom. She speaks softly, almost in a whisper, and the children must lean forward to hear her every word. I sit in the back row and squeeze my eyes shut so I won't have to look at her.

Once and only once do I find myself alone with Miss French. It is my very first day at the new school. I barely survive it. Well, that's not entirely true. But I do catch a fever.

She takes me to a small windowless room where the uniforms are kept.

"They're not exactly the prettiest dresses in the world," she says softly and all girlfriend-to-girlfriend.

I'm standing in the middle of the floor in my underwear and tights and a white blouse that itches. I'm struggling to pull the green pinafore dress down over my head.

"But you'll get used to it in no time," she says, "and in any case, you won't have to worry about what to wear every morning."

She laughs a spine-chilling little laugh.

She hands me the knee socks. I sit on the floor and pull them over my tights.

"No, no," she whispers, "you can't wear knee socks over your tights. You have to take off your tights."

"But I don't want to take off my tights. It's freezing."

"Oh, but you're not allowed to wear tights under your knee socks." Silky soft voice, creamy smooth skin. Her silk stockings glisten, most likely they're the kind you attach to a garter belt. Her earrings sparkle, the silver brooch on her lapel flashes. I wonder whether Miss French hates girls. She is so lovely and we are so ugly. Especially me. There is a full-length mirror on the wall of the uniform room. I stand in front of it. Miss French sneaks up behind me like a milky-white frosty mist. The knee socks itch. She puts her hand on my shoulder. We stand there for a moment looking at ourselves in the mirror. My knees stick out from below the hem of my dress, big and blue like globes of the Earth.

Every day a new tailor-made dress more exquisite than the one before. Maybe she does it on purpose? Maybe she needs me, my ugliness, my scrawniness, as yet uninitiated, in order for her to shine?

My cat lives in a large walk-in closet with a window. I move my mattress into the closet and lie down. I feel hot and woozy. I say it's because I have to wear knee socks in the middle of winter. I forget to brush the cat's silky coat, and it gets tangled into knots that are impossible to undo. The Swedish babysitters make an attempt, one of them holds the cat firmly on her lap while the other wets her hairbrush and combs as gently as she can. But still she combs too hard, and big tufts of fur are pulled from the cat's body. When they're done, the cat is covered with sores and large hairless patches.

One of the two Swedish girls falls in love with a boy with bangs. He isn't really a boy, he's at least twenty-five, but the bangs make him look like a kid. He transforms the yellow house into a sweetly fragrant, smoky den with many rooms and voices and music. The smoke and the sweetness envelop us all. The neighbors don't like what's going on. In their opinion, neither Mamma nor the Swedish girls nor the scrawny little girl nor the neglected cat are right for the neighborhood.

Single mother with plunging neckline comes and goes.

Questionable Swedish girls come and go.

Scrawny little girl (who squeezes her eyes shut when you talk to her) comes and goes.

Every afternoon before dinner, the two Swedish girls prepare an odd spicy stew that no one wants to eat. I know *I* don't. Little white bones stick out of the grainy sauce. The stew is left simmering on the stovetop. One day we're invited over by one of the neighbors, Mrs. Lyndon, for tea. The next town over has boasted visitors such as Alice Cooper and Bette Davis, so what are two slutty Swedish babysitters and a Broadway star's scrawny daughter compared to that? Mrs. Lyndon has many children, her oldest daughter is my age and goes to the public school that I wish I went to.

"You're going to a party," Mamma says on the telephone.

"It's not a party," I say. "It's tea."

"Well, whatever . . . this is your chance to make new friends," she says.

I nod. She can't see that I'm nodding and gets annoyed when I don't answer. She says I have to remember to brush my hair and be on my best behavior.

I nod again.

"Can I talk to one of the girls?" says Mamma. "I want to tell them they have to remember to remind you to brush your hair."

"I can remember it myself."

"Okay."

"Do you still want to talk to them?"

"No, in that case I don't need to."

"Bye," I say, "I think we should hang up now."

I can hear Mamma breathing on the other end.

"I have homework to do, okay?"

"Mouse . . ." her voice wavers.

"Yes, what?"

"Please remember to be nice."

"I'm always nice."

Mamma hesitates. She wants to protest. She doesn't think *I'm always nice*, in fact, this is something she feels we should talk about before things . . . escalate . . . unravel . . . before there's another shipwreck . . . but she doesn't have time now, someone is waiting for her.

"You're nice when you *want* to be nice," she says, her uncertainty all but gone now, and then we say goodbye and hang up.

Mrs. Lyndon has set out cheese and crackers and juice and tea and coffee for the adults. Four squashy sofas are arranged

around a large coffee table. The sofas are pink. I reach out and
take a cracker. I hope no one notices, because Mrs. Lyndon
hasn't said help yourself yet. The sofas are spruced up with lots
of little cushions. You have to wrestle your way through them
and lunge forward if you want to get something from the tray
on the coffee table. The cracker is good. It's thin and crispy and
salty, like chips, but it's more like food than chips, maybe it's an
herb or some type of coarse flour that makes it so tasty. I take
another one and spread a little cheese on it. Mrs. Lyndon looks
at me and laughs and says: "Help yourself."

"Who would like tea," she says, "who would like coffee?"

The Swedish babysitters say they would like tea, I ask if I can
have a glass of water. The girl who is my age has been instructed
by Mrs. Lyndon to ask me about my home country.

"Do you have sidewalks in Norway?" the girl asks, glaring
at me and the Swedish babysitters. My mouth is full of crackers
and I can't answer.

The Swedish babysitters laugh and say that we have sidewalks and streets and buildings and cars and summers and win-
ters and cities and fields and birds and cinemas just like here.

"We're from Sweden," they say simultaneously, "and this
one's from Norway," they add, giving me a squeeze.

"Uh-huh," says the girl my age, turning her attention to an
invisible spot on the ceiling.

"That's very interesting," says Mrs. Lyndon, and looks like
she means it. "But the languages are different, aren't they? Yet
you understand one another?"

"Oh, yes," the Swedish babysitters say, and give me another
squeeze. "And this young lady speaks both Norwegian and
Swedish fluently, so it's no problem at all."

"Interesting," Mrs. Lyndon says again, smiling at me. "They're such beautiful countries, Norway and Sweden. I've always wanted to visit Scandinavia."

I take another cracker. The girl my age, whose name is Ashley, makes a face, signaling to her mother that she wants to go. She's due at practice (gymnastics? basketball? cheerleading? drama?) and someone or other (Lisa? Kimberley? Mary? Michelle?) is waiting for her, and now she's stuck around long enough. Mother and daughter don't think I notice, but I do. I take another cracker and an extra big dollop of cheese. I've decided that after this cracker I'm going to count to a thousand before taking another.

"How do you like being here, then . . . in the United States?" asks Mrs. Lyndon, and smiles at me.

When she smiles, her mouth becomes a necklace of little white teeth. I have crackers in my mouth and don't want to speak until I've swallowed everything, so I smile back and nod and point the way you do when you want to say *Just a moment, let me swallow this so I can answer your question*. To speed things up, I wash everything down with water and wipe the cracker crumbs from my lips. I have a linen napkin. Everyone has linen napkins. I don't know where to put mine once I'm finished with it. Sometimes my English sounds worse than it really is. Often when strangers ask me questions, I forget words and start to stutter. To get around this problem I look down at the floor and mumble. Or squeeze my eyes shut.

"Yes . . . thanks for asking . . . I'm sorry for my English . . . I like it very much."

"That's lovely," says Mrs. Lyndon. "Maybe you and Ashley could get together one day. Ashley does gymnastics, perhaps you would like to go with her?"

Ashley stares at her mother, horrified. Her eyes turn into two narrow slits. I can do exactly the same thing with my eyes.

"I don't think I have time to go to gymnastics," I say, now in fluent English, "I take ballet."

"She takes ballet lessons in New York," says one of the two Swedish babysitters, "three times a week we go back and forth on the train."

"Well, there you go," says Mrs. Lyndon, clapping her hands, "gymnastics with Ashley was not such a good idea then, was it?"

After that, not even Mrs. Lyndon knows what to say, and everything goes quiet around the coffee table.

I want another cracker. So far, I've counted to 234. I know I can wait till I reach 500. The crackers are salty and herby and emit a perfect *crunch* sound if you take care not to chew too hard or too soft.

We did eat before coming here, the Swedish babysitters made sandwiches for all three of us and we dressed up a little and they said it would be exciting to meet the neighbors and maybe I would make friends with the girl. It's the salt—475, 476, 477. No way am I waiting till 500, but this time I get up resolutely and kneel down next to the coffee table. I slather another cracker with cheese, but wait to eat it until I've sat back down on the sofa again.

"Are you hungry, dear?" says Mrs. Lyndon. She smiles and points at the tray. "I can go get a bit more."

Sometimes at night the boy with the bangs comes over, once in a while he brings a friend, usually he comes alone, he doesn't want the spicy stew on the stovetop, so the babysitters make something else for him. A green salad. A grilled cheese sandwich. He smokes nonstop. One evening he offers me a drag. I know it's pot.

"No, no," says one of the two Swedish babysitters, "put that away, John, don't do that."

"Relax," he says, "let her try it." He sits on the edge of the sofa and queries me about Godard's *Two or Three Things I Know About Her*. When I say that I haven't seen that one, only *Breathless*, we talk about *Harakiri* instead, because I've seen *Harakiri* twice, and he's never met a kid before who's seen *Harakiri*, he says.

Mamma lives in an apartment in the middle of Manhattan with a view of Central Park and is about to play the lead role in a Broadway musical about Mama, not my mamma, but *a* mama. The mama in the musical is also from Norway, she's the backbone of her family, *the Hansens*, who live on Steiner Street in San Francisco at the beginning of the last century. The papa has lost his job, money is tight, but thanks to the mama's quickwittedness there's nothing that can bring her or the papa or the children down. My mamma can neither sing nor dance, but she is a combination of endless variables and, when offered the part, she says yes right away. Why shouldn't she sing and dance on Broadway? One of the variables is terrible clumsiness, another is sweetness, a third is bravery teetering on the brink of hubris, a fourth is vulnerability, a fifth is irresistibility, a sixth is a longing so great that it has neither beginning nor end. She has numerous solos and can't hit a single note in a single song.

HAIR IN HER EYES, not pulled back tightly and gathered in a proper ballet bun, not a proper *turnout*, equally skinny as the talented ballet girls, but not as talented, skinny because she was born that way, not because she doesn't eat or throws up what she eats, the girl eats all the time, just not stews with bones poking through the sauce, she's always hungry, but remains skinny, skinny as a caterpillar—as skinny as the caterpillar in the book before it eats its way through the one red apple, the two pears, the three plums, the four strawberries, the five oranges, the chocolate cake, the ice-cream cone, a pickle, a slice of Swiss cheese, a slice of salami, a lollipop, a piece of cherry pie, a sausage, a cupcake, a slice of watermelon, and a green leaf, *but one day she turns into a fucking butterfly*, says the boy with the bangs who is sitting on the silk sofa in the yellow house smoking a joint and going on about Antonioni's *Blow-Up*. The two Swedish babysitters laugh. The boy nods at the girl.

"Have you seen it?"

She shakes her head.

"Antonioni is better than your father, you know."

"Okay."

"Cares more about the world."

"Okay."

"More interesting."

"Okay."

"How about you and I go to the city one day and see *Blow-Up*?"

"Okay."

But apart from him, no one says anything about the girl and butterflies, or invites her to go to the movies.

TWICE, THE FATHER STAGES productions of Gombrowicz's *Yvonne, Princess of Burgundy*, a play about a bored prince, who, out of sheer desperation (because he is so very bored), marries the mute and ugly princess of Burgundy. The prince's parents are shocked by this. The whole court is shocked. I don't know what is most shocking, that the princess is ugly, or that she never speaks. In the end they kill her. I don't think the girl's father was happy with the Munich production, the reviews were bad, he didn't quite pull it off, he had lost his touch, the critics wrote.

In *Diary*, Gombrowicz writes about the nature of beauty and how it manifests itself differently in women and men. A woman, he writes:

> *betrays herself all the time with her desire to please and so is not a queen, but a slave and instead of appearing like a goddess, worthy of desire, she appears as terrible clumsiness trying to conquer an inaccessible beauty.*

The mother appears as anything but terrible clumsiness. I would sooner say she appears as a goddess worthy of desire trying to *conceal* her terrible clumsiness.

Appearances mattered to the mother. How she appeared. How the world around her appeared. She existed by appearing.

The mother is no goddess, but her beauty is of the sort that belongs to everyone and no one—like a national park. When the girl pictures her, she sees many different faces, one after the other or one on top of the other. She wonders whether the mother has a separate beauty—a separate face—just for the girl. How does the mother look (the girl wonders) when she looks at me without anyone looking at her looking at me?

THE NOBEL LAUREATE SAYS he has started to doubt everything.

The mother and her new suitor are eating spaghetti with meat sauce in a little Italian restaurant in New York City. The mother is wearing a long, dark-red dress pulled tightly over her breasts. Maybe he thinks: Not long ago she was one of the most beautiful women in the world.

The Nobel Laureate feels a kinship with the girl's father in ways he can't quite explain. The mother has had many suitors, one of whom was the girl's father. The other suitors were usually curious about him, asking questions, feeling close to *him* when they were with *her*. The Nobel Laureate could have talked to the girl's father about music, he thinks, and starts telling the girl's mother about a childhood memory involving the conductor Fritz Reiner and Mozart's Symphony no. 40, and then he wants to tell her about his little sister's hands at the piano, but before he gets that far, the girl's mother exclaims: "Oh, I *love* Mozart!"

The Nobel Laureate stops talking, looks away, and changes the subject.

The mother is often called the father's *muse*. The father is never called the mother's muse. He was the man, she was the girl, he was older, she was young, he was searching, she was discov-

ered, he looked, she was looked at—to cut a long story short.
He created, she inspired. The father had nine children, but
none of these children, neither the boys nor the girls, were ever
called muses, children got in the way of work, or so, at least, the
children's mothers and father seemed to believe, although the
mothers would assume all responsibility for the children once
the father was out of the picture—to cut another long story
short. Almost all the mothers (there were five mothers with nine
children between them, in addition to the father's own mother,
making it six altogether) have been described as muses. Ingrid,
his last wife, was a practical woman and therefore he loved her
the most. And mourned her when she died. Mourned her so
deeply that he himself wanted to die. The father believed that a
condition for lasting love is that practical matters are taken care
of. One must never underestimate the importance of being practical. This rule applies to love, and also to work. The father did
not call the women in his life muses. I don't think he ever used
the word "muse." He called them Stradivariuses—violins—
instruments—but never muses.

In Norwegian, "muse" is a somewhat amusing word since you
can't help associating it with the similar word *musa* (which can
mean either "mouse" or "pussy"). In the early 1700s, the poet-
priest Petter Dass wrote a number of letters to the poetess and
hymnist Dorothe Engelbretsdatter, including the following lines:

> *Matron! How fare thee?*
> . . .
> *Howe'er be it fated*
> *With Lady Minervæ affairs?*
> *Her Joy all abdicated*
> *To foster Days of Tears?*

Is now Parnassus' Praise
Laid waste and lifeless bled?
The Muse vexed by Malaise?
Do all the Nymphs lie dead?
Has every Poet's friend, then
Her Writing Tools forsworn?
Are Paper, Ink and Quill Pen
Abandoned and forlorn?

Petter Dass waited in vain for a reply. He admired Dorothe immensely and never deemed to call her *his* muse, indeed, the rhyme makes it clear that he thought of her as his colleague, his equal, a true poet, and when she fails to answer his letter, he wonders whether *her* muse may be "vexed by malaise" and whether this might be the reason for her silence. Thus, by referring to a sick muse, he beat Baudelaire to the punch by 150 years. Baudelaire would famously write a poem about *his* ailing muse in 1857.

Unlike Dorothe, I would probably have answered Petter Dass's letter, had it been addressed to me. If for no other reason than the sheer pleasure of replying to a letter, or, what's more likely, an email in which the author didn't open with a silly "Hi" followed by my first name (*in which back alley did we end up on a first-name basis, may I ask?*) and, God forbid, a smiley, but rather greeted me with a lovely "Matron! How fare thee?" I wouldn't have thought twice about replying.

The father said that the mother was his Stradivarius. I have never heard her express displeasure at either the term "muse" or "Stradivarius."

But did she really want to be a *violin*?

King Pierus had nine daughters and believed they were so beautiful as to outshine the nine muses, but he was wrong; hubris is always punished, and the nine daughters were turned into magpies.

There are worse fates: a muse's raison d'être is to act as a mirror for the great artist. No artist, no muse. A magpie is no one's mirror, it is visible all on its own, what's more, the magpie actually recognizes its reflection in the mirror. Not many animals are capable of this, a few great apes, of course—the bonobo, for example—some dolphins and also a particular type of ant. In the case of the ant, it appears that it washes itself after having looked in a mirror and noticed a spot on its head, but refrains from doing so if there is no spot. Studies have also been carried out on elephants. Some elephants recognized themselves in the mirror, but not all. The studies with the elephants were complicated by the fact that the mirrors were not big enough.

Maybe she can be *my* muse as well as his, the Nobel Laureate thinks, and looks at the girl's mother. Several years later, waiting for a friend who happens to be late for dinner, he takes up his napkin, and quickly, almost nonchalantly, outlines a theory about the nature of memory based on years and years of research. At that point his affair with the mother has long since ended, so perhaps he didn't need a muse after all, or a magpie or a mirror, but only a tardy friend?

On the one hand, he wants the whole world to see that he can get a woman like her, on the other hand he has a sneaking sus-

picion that she isn't what he wants. She is forty. She makes a
fool of herself onstage (he doesn't find the singing and dancing
endearing, he finds it embarrassing). There is an arc spanning
from pride to shame, and the Nobel Laureate is always uncertain about where and at which end of the arc he finds himself.
This constant uncertainty is his greatest weakness.

He pictures his little sister's fingers hovering over the key-
board, those tiny little hands. He opens his mouth to tell her
about them, but restrains himself—*Oh, I love Mozart* still hangs
in the room like a bad smell.

The mother tells the girl that the Nobel Laureate is trying to
create a brain. One day the mother visits him at his laboratory.
Two things register with her that day. One, all the rats scuttling
around, and two, a palpable doubt about whether this relationship has any kind of future. She feels an overwhelming compas-
sion for the rats, but she also thinks they're disgusting.

The girl's mother calls it love, but only for the first few weeks,
many years later she will say that he was *simply not a very nice
man* as far as she was concerned.

As a young boy he too had played the piano. In order to have
some time to themselves, his parents used to install him and his
little sister in a box at Carnegie Hall. Brother and sister sat quiet
as mice as Fritz Reiner conducted Mozart. He could have told
the girl's mother about his sister's white dress, her long black
hair neatly drawn back into a braid and finished off with a bow,

her little hand in his, but he doesn't. Instead he raises his own hand and waves his index finger at her.

"We don't even know exactly what part of the brain makes my finger wave at you," he says.

The girl's mother notices the manicured nail, the delicate, smooth hand. His nails are better cared for than hers.

She lifts her own index finger and waves back.

They sit like this for a while, waving at each other with their index fingers.

"I know for certain that I am not you," he says, a bit abruptly, perhaps, and the mother is taken aback. She dreams of a love in which two people are so wrapped up in each other that they no longer know which of them is which. But the Nobel Laureate is not talking about love, he is talking about the difficulty of understanding precisely what inside the brain steers our motor functions, and that we are the sum of our movements.

"Nothing is static. Nothing is determined. Everything is movement."

"Hmm," says the mother, and wonders how long they have to sit like this and wave at each other.

He pulls back his hand.

He drinks a little wine. She is silent. And then he says: "Picture the cerebral cortex . . ."

She pictures the blue portrait of her father in his officer's uniform, all the different shades of blue. She doesn't want to interrupt, doesn't want to say anything stupid, sometimes she feels stupid, but she has a special way of looking at men that makes them feel like geniuses. Even geniuses feel like geniuses when the mother looks at them.

"The complexity of little things," he says.

"The complexity of little things," the mother repeats, and

feels a headache coming on. It's not a migraine, she doesn't get migraines. Her headache is like an itch, a discomfort more than a pain, like something sifting through her. Living brains are cotton-candy pink, not gray. It occurs to her to say that living brains are cotton-candy pink, not gray, but that he, who has seen so many brains, has probably only seen gray brain matter— since it turns gray when it dies—and he can't very well cut into a living brain. But then it occurs to her that she shouldn't say any of this, that it probably doesn't have anything to do with what he's talking about. There is a constant sifting inside her head when she feels like this. Frayed nerves. She drinks more wine, it usually helps, calms things down.

She wants to say that she likes it best when everything is very, very quiet.

Her red dress is tight and scratchy. She worries that he will notice the sweat under her arms.

When the Nobel Laureate visits the yellow house, he spends most of his time squirming on the silk sofa in the living room, whispering to the mother that he wants to leave.

On one occasion, he tells the girl to go to the kitchen, find a glass and some sugar, pour the sugar into the glass and then calculate the number of molecules in a glass of sugar. Once she's figured *that* out, she can come back in to the living room and tell him the answer. The complexity of little things. Possibly, also, the prospect of a reward, I don't remember. The girl dashes off to the kitchen, can't find the sugar, calls to her mother, *Mamma, Mamma, where's the sugar?*, the mother sighs and comes into the kitchen—she certainly doesn't know where the sugar is—and starts opening and closing cupboard doors. The two Swedish babysitters have the day off. *They* probably know where the sugar is, but are never around when you need them, and on top of that, they're overpaid. The Nobel Laureate starts calling for the mother. He wants her in the living room with him. The whole point of this molecular game is to keep the bastard (which is what he calls the girl when he thinks she isn't listening) occupied, so he can be alone with her mother. He has a wife and children and a big house and a Nobel Prize and a career and a *limited amount of time* to spend with his mistress. The bastard isn't part of the plan. And now the whole thing is going down the drain. The girl finds a glass, but no sugar, the mother flutters between the yellow rooms complaining about the babysitters. The Nobel Laureate looks at his watch.

I eavesdrop on Mamma's phone calls, sometimes she knows about it and then we talk about it afterward, how dumb some people are. The Nobel Laureate, for example. More and more it's Mamma and me against him. There is a particular way of picking up the receiver when you want to listen in on the other end, you have to do it slowly and carefully and it mustn't say click, if it says click, you're caught.

"You are my woman!" says the Nobel Laureate on the phone.

He is very convincing. His voice is dark and hoarse. Mamma is the chosen one, the most beloved, she is seen by him and exists for him, and it all makes sense even when he behaves like an idiot.

I was unable to calculate the number of molecules in a glass of sugar, Mamma and I couldn't even find the sugar, but what I *was* able to calculate, or figure out, was that I was still a little girl, and that I could not, with any measure of credibility, be called someone's *woman*.

TOOK TO MY BED and refused to get up. I told everyone I was sick. The first time I stayed in bed for three days. The second time I stayed there for seven days. The third time I stayed there for ten days. For ten days I stayed in bed hugging the scabby cat.

"Why is she always running a temperature?" Mamma asks on the phone.

"We're not sure," whispers one of the two Swedish babysitters. "She says she's freezing cold because she has to wear that uniform for school. It's minus ten degrees outside, so no wonder?"

They come with tea and blankets and pat me on the cheek.

I never again want to set foot in a classroom ruled by Miss French. I can't take any more of her beauty. *Be careful what you wish for.* And finally, after three bouts of fever, I transfer to the local public school, where the students are allowed to wear their regular clothes. This is where I get to know a boy my age named Adam. He wears a blue wool sweater with a white pattern just like the one I have. *Marius sweaters*, they're called back home. In Norway everyone wears them; here, no one does, except for Adam and me. He comes over to the yellow house after school and plays Monopoly and listens to the Village People and Supertramp. Adam has a hint of a mustache. A little downy black mustache that partially conceals the childish cleft between his nose and mouth. I like it. I think it's interesting. Manly, even. When we kiss, it tickles my upper lip. He strokes the outside of my sweater, barely touching my boobs, even though I don't have proper boobs yet, as in plural, just that one, aching nipple.

For a while Adam is my only friend, but then I meet Violet, the girl next door with the long dark hair. Violet says that the ugliest thing in the world is little boys with mustaches. Disgusting. The mustache exposes Adam to be the stupid little idiot he truly is—he's obviously not even close to being able to shave or to grow a real mustache like, say, Violet's big brother Jeff.

Adam is small. Everything about him is small and delicate. Narrow shoulders, small hands that tremble when he tells me that he likes to read. Right now the whole class is reading *To Kill a Mockingbird*, I'll help you, he says, we can read it together and discuss it, he tells me I shouldn't worry that I can't keep up with the reading assignments since I'm from another country and speak a different language. It takes me days, weeks, months to finish *To Kill a Mockingbird*.

I spend more and more time with Violet. One day I tell Adam that I don't want him to come over anymore, I don't want to play Monopoly or read books or listen to the Village People and Supertramp.

Violet's favorite song is Led Zeppelin's "Stairway to Heaven," and that's my favorite song too.

Adam sits on the yellow sofa in the yellow living room where the Nobel Laureate usually sits when he comes to the house. I tell him I've made up my mind, it's finished, it's over, and when he begins to cry, I think he's disgusting, that the things we've done together are disgusting. Adam is not a terrible clumsiness, like Gombrowicz wrote about, just a small disgusting clumsiness sitting there on the yellow sofa sniveling and crying like a baby.

"CATHERINE IS HEARTBROKEN," Mamma says. "Remember that! *Heartbroken*. And from now on Catherine will be at the helm," she adds. "And God help you if she quits as a babysitter. Then I don't know what I'll do."

Mamma's arrangement hasn't gone according to plan. It rarely does. The arrangement with the Swedish babysitters was that if one girl jumped ship, the other could take over. That was the whole point of hiring two rather than one. But now both want to quit. They want to *see America*, they say, they're only young once—and the boy with the bangs is going too. The three of them have split the cost of a car, and now they want to *live life*—all of this they tell Mamma—*you just have to live and life will give you pictures*, they trumpet, both talking at the same time. The thing about life giving you pictures they got from the boy with the bangs who got it from Henri Cartier-Bresson.

Mamma tells me that Catherine once dreamed of becoming a nun and even lived in a convent for a few years, but then she fell in love with a man and, well, she couldn't really be a nun after that. She chose *earthly love*, says Mamma. Yes, and then she abandoned the convent and her vows and everything she believed in to be with the man.

Mamma has completely forgotten the advice from her women friends not to confide in me.

And not long after Catherine abandoned the convent, the man abandoned Catherine.

"*Heartbroken*," Mamma repeats. "So you have to be really, really, really nice to her and do exactly as she says."

Mamma is going away on yet another long trip, with a final stop-over in Munich. This is Pappa's city. This is where Pappa lives. She is not going to Munich specifically to see Pappa, she tells me, but she is bound to run into him once she's there. And then she sighs. Everyone's tugging at her. Everyone wants something. If only she could shut herself away somewhere and just sleep.

I'll be thirteen soon. I've made a birthday wish list on which I've written: lip gloss, mascara, rouge, eyeliner.

"I've invited Catherine to come and visit before she moves in," Mamma says, "She's coming on your birthday."

"Why?"

"As I said, I think you should get a chance to say hello."

"I don't get it."

"What don't you get? I've invited her to come to the house so that the two of you can get to know each other before she moves in."

"Yes, but why is she coming on my birthday?"

"Because of all the days in the year," says Mamma, "your birthday is the one day on which it wouldn't occur to you to be rude."

———

Pappa and Mamma are going to meet, Mamma doesn't think I'm paying attention, I don't usually pay attention when she's talking, but when she talks about where she's going and how long she'll be away, I pay very close attention.

We *are bound to run into each other*, she says, and it's happening in Munich. I don't know anything about Munich, except that Pappa lives there.

The big question is: How will *I* get to Munich?

I'm not allowed to fly on my own without permission. I am a heap of knuckles and bones. A foolish child dependent on adults and their money to get from one place to another, at least if getting from one place to another involves a journey across the Atlantic. A heap, a ruin. Ruins are beautiful. I am *not* beautiful. Venus de Milo is more beautiful without arms than with them. You wonder what happened to her arms. She is a mystery. I'll be thirteen soon, a mishmash of skinny limbs and a big mouth. I'm *not* a mystery.

If I can get myself to Munich and into a room with both my mother and father present, I will ask someone to take a picture of us.

I would like to own a picture of the three of us together.

I want to be there when my day and my night meet.

I raise my head and look at Catherine. She doesn't say a word. Neither do I. Catherine promises Mamma to take *complete and full* responsibility for the girl, but she doesn't know that this particular child can neither fall asleep in the evening nor wake up in the morning. It's always either the middle of the day or the middle of the night where this girl's concerned. Mamma will be going away soon. Catherine doesn't know the meaning of panic.

"If the ship capsizes," Mamma says, and smiles nervously, "you can call Mr. P. His number is in the kitchen drawer."

I take her travel itinerary with me everywhere. It's a type-written sheet of paper with stains on it, smudged dates and places, cities, hotels. I know most of it by heart, even some of the telephone numbers. Under no circumstances, though, am I allowed to dial any of them, because of the expense involved in calling overseas.

During the day, I carry the sheet of paper with me in my school bag, inside my math book, at night I keep it on the bedside table underneath my cup of cocoa.

Catherine (who came to the yellow house with a small suit-case and her oboe) makes hot cocoa with honey every evening and lets me drink it in bed. She says it will calm me. Before I go to sleep, I have to make sure my radio cassette player, my notebook, my mother's travel itinerary, and my cup of cocoa are arranged in exactly the right order on the bedside table. There is a symmetry to this. Compulsion as discipline. Compulsion as choreography.

Actually, it is strictly forbidden to set cups and glasses down on tables in the yellow house. The corpulent lady was very spe-cific about this. When Mamma and I lived in the house together, we had to remind each other about it all the time. If Mamma forgot to put a coaster under her wineglass, she had to pay *me* a dollar, if I forgot to put a coaster under my cup, I had to pay *her* a dollar. When Mamma started staying over in the city, and eventually, for all intents and purposes, moved to the apartment in New York, she told me I could take the train to Grand Cen-tral Station and visit her whenever I wanted. This wasn't quite true. Not whenever I wanted, which was all the time, but some-times, when I didn't have school the next day, for instance. In Mamma's New York apartment, it didn't really matter if you got marks on the tables. We ate Chinese takeout in her large king-size bed, and I drank Coke or ginger ale from a can that I could put down anywhere. The more marks I left in the apartment, the better, said Mamma, and kissed me and rubbed her nose into the nape of my neck, "Mouse, I love you so much and miss you so much when you're not with me," even though both she and I knew that I was too old to be called *Mouse*. Now and then we'd watch three or four films in a row on TV, and often I was the one who fell asleep first.

But now Mamma has gone off on her long trip abroad and I take out her travel itinerary and put it on my bedside table, and then I place the cup of hot cocoa on top of it.

Eventually the sheet of paper is covered with cocoa rings. The longer Mamma is gone, the more rings on the sheet of paper, like the growth rings inside a tree. The cocoa rings are small, just smudges on a piece of paper, while the rings inside a tree are large, yet both are evidence of time passing slowly. Each new ring is a new day, a new week, a new month, or in the case of the tree, a new year.

I know exactly when she is in Leningrad or Moscow or Belgrade or London—and there is still a way to go until Munich. Right now, she is in Moscow, behind the Iron Curtain, Hotel National on Mokhovaya Street, and it's difficult for her to call, she's prepared me for this, she said that when you find yourself behind the Iron Curtain, it's really hard to put in a call anywhere and that I shouldn't start worrying. If I don't hear from her, it's because of the *overall world situation*, she tells me, the Cold War, communism, and *not* because she doesn't love me.

———

Catherine has been instructed to avoid all situations in which I start waiting for Mamma to call me. If I start waiting, things are liable to go off course. I'm incapable of waiting for Mamma's phone calls. I overreact, I'm frightened, I get hysterical, things get out of hand. Catherine has to find ways of diverting my attention to prevent these unfortunate episodes. So, if there's a crisis and it's impossible to get hold of Mamma, Catherine may (as already mentioned) call Mr. P, whose number is in the kitchen drawer.

One evening, Mamma calls and shouts, *I love you, my darling*, but there is so much crackling on the line that I can't bring myself to answer, I just stand there in the kitchen clutching the receiver and nodding, I love her too, I do, she knows that, I love her so much that I burst into tears

"Go on, say something," whispers Catherine, "say something!"

She stands in front of me, nervously shifting from one foot to the other. I don't know which one of us is more relieved that Mamma has finally called.

"She can't see that you're nodding," whispers Catherine, and gesticulates, "she can only hear you crying. Don't cry. Why are you crying? You have to *say* something so she can hear your voice and doesn't think you're just going around being sad all the time."

I remember what the Swedish babysitters looked like and what their names were, I remember their bodies, I remember their faces and their scent, but when it comes to the woman whose name may have been Catherine, I remember nothing. What I mean is that I remember nothing about what she looked like, her body, her face, but I can recall the atmosphere that surrounded her, dark, deep, blue, sad. If I were to compare her to a berry, I'd say blackcurrant. She played the oboe and practiced early every morning before I even got out of bed, her playing usually woke me up. It was nice, but a little tiresome too, the same passage over and over again. Once she said: "I'm grateful if I'm allowed to work in the garden, play my oboe, or just take a walk in the forest, I hope that I'll always be able to abide by what the apostle Paul tells us: *Rejoice evermore, pray without ceasing, in every thing give thanks.*"

Apart from that one time, she never spoke of her faith. She laid her hand on my shoulder and pressed me down onto a chair, she wanted me to stop crying, *rejoice evermore, pray without ceasing, in every thing give thanks,* I could tell that it came from the Bible, Pappa would sometimes quote from the Bible, Nanna too, but not with this kind of insistence. I didn't get it. *Rejoice evermore.* Catherine was the saddest person I had ever met.

Before Mamma left for Europe, Catherine said to her: "Your daughter needs new clothes. Something other than that blue-and-white wool sweater she's always wearing. If it's okay with you, I would like to take her shopping. She feels like she doesn't fit in anywhere."

Catherine cooks dinner every day. She always puts coasters under glasses and bottles. She helps me with the essay I have to write about *To Kill a Mockingbird.* She picks me up at the dentist's office when I have my braces removed. Afterward she takes my face between her hands and tells me that I look pretty. She combs the cat every day and untangles the knots without ever pulling out tufts of fur.

———

The air is still warm, even though it's late autumn, and on week-end nights I climb out the window to meet Violet and her brother and their friends on the beach down by the yellow house. We listen to music and drink either beer or concoctions poured from the bottles in Violet's parents' liquor cabinet. Her parents have marked the liquor bottles so they know how much should still be inside, but Violet gets a funnel from the kitchen drawer and replaces the missing liquor with water. It's important to be accurate, she says, and puts the funnel back in place.

We sit in a circle around the bonfire. I have borrowed a blouse from Violet and a pair of pants. Violet is older than me and has nicer clothes. I turn around and there is Catherine. She is standing down by the water's edge, a little way off. The sun is fat and pushy, glaring at us as it sets on the horizon. Jeff has turned up the music. He picks the tapes, it's his boom box. Catherine's hair blows in the wind. She is wearing a black dress. She is shouting to me. Shouting my name. Not with a loud voice—*shouting* is the wrong word. She never calls me anything other than my name. I turn back to the others, the fire is crackling, I pretend not to see her. Catherine continues shouting or not shouting or whatever it is she's doing. Eventually, I turn to Violet and tell her I have to go, I'm being fetched, I say, and we roll our eyes. Everyone turns to look at Catherine. She doesn't come any closer. The sun is fading, there is a chilly breeze blowing off the sea. I shrug. I'm the one who has to leave. I feel nauseous, but finish my drink. I don't rush. Catherine will never let go of me. I dreamt that she said that. *I will never let go of you.* I gather my things and my shoes and walk barefoot across the sand. She takes my hand, but I pull away. She came to the house the day I turned thirteen. She came with her sadness and her prayers and her abandonment.

I say: "I'm not surprised your boyfriend doesn't want you. You're ugly. I don't want you either. I hate you."

N THE END, I am the one who calls Mr. P. The telephone number is written on a piece of paper in the kitchen drawer, to be used in the case of an emergency. This is an emergency. Mr. P has a secretary, and the secretary says that Mr. P is in a meeting. I tell her that I must speak with him immediately, could she please go and get him. It's urgent.

My English is good. I speak directly into the receiver. Clearly. Standing up straight.

"Good afternoon," says Mr. P. He calls me *Miss*, but mostly to tease me. "How may I help you?"

I say that he needs to withdraw some money and buy me a plane ticket, "I'm going to Munich."

"Hmm," says Mr. P.

I say that these are *my parents' specific instructions*. The word "parents" is surprisingly compelling.

"Hmm," he says again.

I say that it's not possible to get hold of them just now.

"May I please talk to the lady who takes care of you?" says Mr. P.

"Catherine is not here."

"Does she know about this . . . that you're calling me . . . that you intend to go to Munich?"

Mr. P is hesitating. That's good. He's not sure what to say next. He's wavering.

"Of course, she knows! Mamma has talked to her."

I have to fight the urge to say that I'm not a child who needs anyone's permission.

It is important that he does as I ask, a plane ticket to Munich, it doesn't have to be round-trip, but it would be nice if he could arrange for a car to pick me up and take me to the airport.

"Hmm," he says a third time.

Mamma is in Moscow, I tell him, behind the Iron Curtain, it's not possible to call her at the moment, Mr. P is quite aware of that, and Pappa, I add, is a man who under no circumstances should be *disturbed*, I don't even have his telephone number, he is, so to speak, his own iron curtain, all of this I tell him. I have a plan. I have written it down. I am not improvising. And I don't tell Catherine anything, not until the car that will take me to the airport pulls up outside the yellow house.

I walk into the kitchen, lugging my suitcase behind me.

Catherine is making lunch. It's Saturday afternoon.

"I'm leaving now, okay."

She raises her head and looks at me.

"Excuse me?"

I take hold of my suitcase, unable to lift it, I'll have to lug it along all the way.

"I said, I'm leaving now."

"Where are you going?"

I take a deep breath and say as clearly as I can: "I'm going to Munich."

THE NOBEL LAUREATE WAS no longer in the picture, and Catherine quit when I ran off to Germany. Eventually Mamma and I moved back to Oslo, resettling in the big flat on Erling Skjalgsson Street.

Mamma has come to a point in her life, she says, that she wants to do something for other people.

She wants to be useful.

She looks around at the world and wants to make it a better place.

She will not (like Elisabet Vogler) go silent.

If you need me, she said.

If you miss me.

If you want me to come.

If you want to talk.

If you want me to be with you.

Mamma left for London. I don't know why, I no longer sat by the phone waiting for her to call. But I was still terrified of losing her. Sometimes I forced myself to walk a hundred times quickly around the block, or run up and down the stairs until I wept from exhaustion, once I poured salt into a glass of water and forced myself to drink it. *Do it, or she'll die!* I knew it was just my thoughts forcing me to do these things, that the thoughts were mine and no one else's, I knew I should ignore them and go about my day. I needed one body for life and one body for all the thoughts. I skipped ballet class. It didn't matter. I quit ballet. That didn't matter either. I was fourteen now. Heidi and

I had sleepovers and prepared ourselves for a life with men. She already knew about smooth skin, ways of moving, the looks she elicited when she walked through a room or down the street. She had overcome her old fears and replaced them with new ones. I hovered somewhere between the old and the new.

In London, Mamma was profiled by Yugoslav television. Bogdan, a name that would have suited him, is Slavic and means God-given. Dressed in a white linen suit, he interviewed my mother and fell so deeply in love with her that he packed his suitcase and followed her to Oslo. I picture him landing at Fornebu Airport. I picture him taking the bus, not a taxi, and getting off at Olav Kyrres Square, then walking, suitcase in tow, the 150 meters to the tall, white turn-of-the-century apartment building where Mamma and I lived on the third floor behind heavy vermilion curtains. He stands there in the ice-cold Oslo air with autumn leaves swirling around him, with his suitcase and his books (in a large leather bag slung over his shoulder) and his deep voice and his broken English, asking if he can move in.

"I have left everything," he says.

And then he spreads his arms as if he had wings and were about to fly. Mamma has run down the stairs to open the main door, and when he spreads his arms, she thinks he wants to embrace her, but he only wants to show her how big *everything* is. It starts to rain. He takes a step toward her, says: "I have come here to live with you."

Mamma was forty-two. He was a year older. In the first part of the Yugoslav television interview, her hair is pulled back in a tight ponytail, in the second part it hangs loose. It wasn't he who loosened her hair, she is in the midst of shooting a film and the interview is recorded between takes. In one of the film scenes she wears her hair pulled back, in another she wears it down. Halfway through the interview he thanks her for making the time to see him.

The interview, which was later aired in its entirety in Yugoslavia, starts with him sitting on a sofa saying a few words to the TV viewers, then he turns his attention to Mamma, who is also sitting on the sofa. Now the camera is fixed solely on her. I don't know whether she is thinking about the camera's gaze or his gaze or both. He asks questions, she answers them. He quotes Beckett. She's impressed. She does this thing with her eyes, it's a trick, it drives men crazy; she looks at them, stares, her eyes bore into them, and I imagine they feel seen in a way they've never been seen before, I've tried doing it myself, in front of the mirror, but when I do it, it just looks like I'm squinting. He asks her if her beauty is a burden and she gives a little laugh and doesn't know what to say, and then he asks her if she can remember the first words she heard as a child. And in her little girl voice Mamma whispers that it is a lullaby her mother used to sing . . . and then she starts to sing.

She sings very softly, as if singing for him alone and not for the whole of Yugoslavia, as if she wants to sing herself and him to sleep:

> *Sleep sweetly little child*
> *rest quietly and mild,*
> *angels watching at your feet,*
> *sleep in peace, my darling sweet.*

To me she said that he had defected, which apparently meant that he couldn't go back home. He *had* to stay with us, it wasn't as if we had a choice, he had nowhere else to go.

This was not the first time love and the Iron Curtain had somehow crossed paths. It was difficult to explain, she said. I didn't care. I'd stopped listening. It annoyed her that I never listened. That I rolled my eyes. That I couldn't be bothered to answer when spoken to. As for Bogdan, when he imagined what it would be like to leave everything behind to be with my mother, he'd forgotten to imagine me. I wasn't part of his plan, he wasn't part of mine. He had his own children in Belgrade, but had abandoned them to live with us. Or not *us* precisely. Her. To live with her. *Be careful what you wish for.* He and I made a pact. A pact of silence. He let me bum cigarettes, I left him alone. Mamma came and went. Spring arrived. Neither of us looked up when she walked into the room. Winter arrived.

Mamma said: "All day and no light."

Bogdan blew smoke rings through all the rooms in the big flat.

Spring arrived.

Summer arrived, and one night he knocked on my bedroom door and told me I had to come right away. It was the middle of the night, I wasn't myself, I wasn't the girl, I wasn't my name. I was sleep. I was heavy and light at the same time and impossible to reach, to stir, to wake, lying there under the warm duvet, but he said I had to wake up now, I heard his voice, as in a dream, first softly and then a bit louder. "I don't know what to do," he said, "I . . . she . . ."

He had never said so many words before. At least, not to me.

When we spoke to each other, we spoke English. His was broken and handsome, like old woodwork.

"She is in there."

He pointed at the door to Mamma's bedroom. It stood slightly ajar.

"She says that she has . . . I think she just wants to frighten me . . ." he didn't finish his sentences, "but then she says that she *hasn't*."

He hesitated, looking at me.

"Can you talk to her?"

I went into Mamma's room and lay down next to her in the bed with the golden bedposts. The stench of clammy, stuffy sleep and liquor. White wallpaper with a pale red border. When I was little, Mamma and I used to lie in bed and trace the border with our fingers, and Mamma would hum a lullaby to which she didn't know the words.

Mamma whispered something.

She wanted to sleep. She wanted me to leave. She wanted to be left alone.

I nestled up close to her, gently: "Mamma, did you take pills?"

"No, no . . . but maybe a little too much to drink."

A pill bottle was standing on the bedside table. I picked it up and laid it between us.

"Mamma . . . ?"

"Not because I took . . . it was already empty."

Her body was still the warmest place. I lifted her arm and draped it around me, and then she sighed, not resigned, but like a child who has woken up at night and been comforted and who finally dares to fall asleep again, I closed my eyes, her sleep was so vast it had room for the both of us, a breeze blew in from the open window and Mamma stirred, it was hard to tell who was asleep and who was keeping watch, but then she started to cry and everything became clear.

"I didn't mean to do it," she wept, almost inaudibly.

And then she whispered: "I don't know what to do."

Bogdan sat in a chair in the dark in the living room and smoked. If you ever happened to wonder where he was, you could follow the thin swirl of white smoke curling its way through the flat.

When the paramedics came stomping up the stairs and into the flat, I spoke to her softly.

"Mamma?"

She turned away and moaned.

"Look," she cried, "look what you've done now."

She was lifted from the bed onto a stretcher, and the paramedic said: "Perhaps the two of you should take your own car to the hospital."

I translated for Bogdan. The paramedic said: "We're going to take her with us now, and you can both follow in your own car. Okay?"

And then he looked at me and repeated: "We have to go now. And you'll follow in your own car."

I nodded.

I was still wearing my nightgown when Bogdan and I got into the taxi to go to the hospital.

"Do you think," he said, "do you think that your mother has ever been happy with a man?"

"I don't know that," I said. "How should I know?"

"But why did she do it?"

"I don't know."

"She's done it once before."

He lowered his voice and added, "I'm only wondering whether it's possible for her to be happy with a man."

I turned and looked at him.

"I don't know, Bogdan."

The taxi driver looked at us in the mirror. He didn't like us. My nightgown was grubby. Bogdan smelled of cigarettes. If I threw up in the car, the taxi driver would probably kick us out.

"You have to stop asking me stuff! I feel sick!"

Bogdan took my hand and squeezed it.

The car seats were black and shiny, I imagined throwing up all over the blackness and shininess; there was a faint smell of windshield wiper fluid in the air.

The doctor laid her hand on my shoulder. I didn't want it there, tried to shrug it off, but it stayed where it was, big and moist and sluggish like a jellyfish.

"Has your mother been very sad lately?"

Bogdan came and stood next to me, took the doctor's hand, and removed it from my shoulder. He said something to her in English, but she didn't speak English or pretended that she didn't; she wouldn't look at him, tried to catch my eye instead.

"Has your mother been very sad lately?"

The doctor had braids, she was younger than Mamma. I thought she should lose the braids. She looked like a little girl.

"Maybe," I said, looking away, "or maybe she would just rather live in New York. I have no idea."

THE PARTY IS HELD in a *chambre séparée*, It means *separate room*, says Mamma, it's French, Okay, I say, even though we're in Germany, Yes, she says, this is one of Munich's finest restaurants. The maître d' takes our coats and points at a long, sweeping staircase. Mamma takes hold of her dress and starts running up the stairs, she runs and runs and runs, we mustn't be late, she says, and turns in the middle of a leap, the hem of her silk dress weaving its way up.

She points to a closed, gilded door and says: "That's where we're going."

I stand next to her—voices and laughter on the other side of the door. I turn toward Mamma.

"Is Pappa in there now?"

"Yes, Pappa and a few other people."

"Are we going in?"

"I just have to catch my breath."

"Does Pappa know I'm here?"

She lets out a small giggle.

"Does he know that you ran away from home and came here without anyone's permission . . . Yes, he knows."

"But I wasn't at home."

"What?"

"I wasn't at *home*, so you can't say that I ran away from home."

"No."

"Catherine is not my mother."

"Catherine is just sad, she probably feels that you *ran away* and now she doesn't want to be our babysitter anymore."

"Are you mad?"

"No."

"Is Pappa mad?"

"No."

I take her hand. "Well, are we going in?"

Mamma looks at me, her cheeks blazing. Her silk dress is so long and sheer, it looks like a nightgown.

"Do I look nice?" she asks.

"Yes," I say.

"All right, in we go," she says, and is about to open the door.

I squeeze her hand, I want her to wait a little.

"What about me? Do *I* look nice?"

Mamma smiles at me. She lets go of my hand, takes hold of my shoulders, and looks at me. I'm wearing a blue dress.

"You're beautiful," she says.

IV

HAVE MERCY
ON ME

...

He is forced to coin words himself, and, taking
his pain in one hand, and a lump of pure sound in the
other (as perhaps the people of Babel did in the
beginning), so to crush them together that a brand
new word in the end drops out.

—VIRGINIA WOOLF, *"On Being Ill"*

SHE   Did you and your father ever speak about God?

HE   Father and I?

SHE   You've told me so many stories about your mother and your grandmother, I feel as if I know them even though they died before I was born, but I know very little about your father. He was a minister.

HE   Yes, but he was quite aloof, he was silent and aloof. One didn't have deep conversations with Father.

SHE   Never?

HE   No. He had to follow certain rules, and even if you were thankful for the rules, it was always *rules, rules* . . . Fuck! When's lunch? Isn't it time?

SHE   Yes, soon. We will finish up in a moment.

HE   (*hesitates*) No . . .

SHE   Yes, we've gone into overtime, but tomorrow is Saturday and we will meet at eleven o'clock as usual. Should we write it down in the book?

HE   Yes.

SHE   And Sunday is free.

HE   Ah, I see.

He avoids looking at her.

SHE   Should we write it down in the book?

HE   That we're free tomorrow?

SHE   No, tomorrow we're working, Sunday is free. Should we write it down in the book?

HE   Yes, I suppose you can do that.

She gets up and walks over to the calendar, which lies on his desk.

I know that she does this because her voice is far away from the microphone. His voice is close. This creates a new dissonance between the two voices.

SHE   (*from a distance*) I'm wondering whether . . . when we meet tomorrow . . . I'm wondering whether it's okay if I ask you a few questions about your father?

HE   (*up-close, as though he's bending over and speaking directly into the microphone*) No.

SHE   It's not okay?

HE   Not very okay, no.

SHE   Why not?

HE   Because there's been a lot of *okay* today. I'm going to feel exhausted, and I don't want another day like this tomorrow.

SHE   Would you rather not work tomorrow?

HE   No.

SHE   But let's just agree then, that we won't meet tomorrow.

HE   Is that okay?

SHE   Do you want to work the day after tomorrow then? On Sunday?

HE   No.

SHE   Do you want a break from the project on Saturday and Sunday?

HE   Yes.

SHE   Do you want to work on Monday?

HE   Yes, let's do that.

SHE   Should we write it down in the book?

HE   We can do that.

SHE   Then I'll write it down. Monday at eleven o'clock . . . okay?

HE   Okay.

BEFORE HE GOT SICK, he would write on his nightstand whenever he couldn't sleep. Not on a piece of paper on the nightstand, but on the table itself. He had a black marker. The table was white.

He wrote on the walls too, for example: *Turn out the lights!* And on the tables in his study and in the living room. A name, a telephone number, a time and a date he mustn't forget, maybe a concert on the radio.

But the nightstand was reserved for the night and is covered in closely written words, sentences, notes, dreams. From a distance, the tabletop looks like a map of the moon.

One place it says, like a three-line poem:

> *The true nightmare*
> *SARABAND*
> *The bloody cataract is spreading*

He once said that he envisioned the Sarabande of Bach's fifth cello suite as a painful dance for two.

HE   I am no longer able to do my work! It's over.

SHE   No . . . it isn't over.

HE   Yes, it is.

SHE   You and I have been talking for a whole week . . . and there's nothing to indicate that it's *over*.

HE   Really? . . . You think so? . . . (*eagerly*) Sometimes it feels as if my creativity, the desire to write, returns like a godsend, settles on my shoulder and speaks to me. And when that happens, I get such a bloody urge to sit down at my desk with my yellow sheets of paper. They're still lying in the drawer over there . . . I'm talking about when writing is *fun* . . . when writing is snazzy-pazzy . . . what happens is, I get an urge . . . and then . . . the next day . . . uh, you know, all that . . . the next day the urge is gone.

SHE   Yes, but you've told me that all it takes is discipline.

HE   Yes, but that was before.

SHE   Before, but not now? Why not now?

HE   I don't know. It's . . . before I felt like a child at play.

Long silence.

HE   Oh never mind, forget everything I just said, it's bullshit.

SHE   Forget what?

HE   All that stuff about being a child at play.

SHE   That was bullshit?

HE   Yes, I say: it was a game I played ... and that I thought was essential, and then it vanished.

SHE   Are you saying that work and play were the same thing to you?

HE   No. Or yes. On the one hand, you see, I am very precise, very meticulous ... as you've probably heard from my colleagues.

SHE   Yes, but more than that, I've heard it from you.

HE   Yes.

SHE   Well, you never liked to improvise.

HE   No, I certainly did not.

He laughs.

SHE   No!

HE   (*continues to laugh*) No. Improvising is not my thing. When I made *The Magic Flute*, I was like a child at play, it was a game, every day Mozart's music in the wings, but, mind you, all of it was very precisely thought out. Precision. Precision. Precision, my heart.

D R. N IS AN elderly man, slight and distinguished-looking in a brown tweed jacket and a bow tie, small fingers, small teeth, long eyelashes. He conducts home visits like physicians did in the old days, only it isn't the old days, it's now, or not now, it's seven years ago, so you might still be able to call it the present. One of the six women who cares for Pappa serves Dr. N a cup of coffee in the kitchen. Afterward he is shown into the living room, where Pappa is waiting for him in his wheelchair. I am sitting on the sofa. When Dr. N has greeted us both—the whole thing is so well-mannered you'd think we were hosting a soirée—I get up and leave. I say something like, *Now I will leave you gentlemen to your own devices*. I haven't even had a chance to close the door behind me when I hear Pappa tell Dr. N that he is surrounded by strangers.

He lowers his voice: "I believe she is a relative, but I'm not sure."

"She's your daughter," says the doctor, and laughs, a little embarrassed. "The youngest one, I believe."

"Really?" says Pappa.

They remain sitting for a while in silence.

And then Pappa says: "How old is she?"

"Uh, hmm, well, I don't know," says Dr. N, and mumbles something about how a wise man should never try to guess a woman's age.

"Maybe seventy," says Pappa.

"No, no," says Dr. N.

"No?" says Pappa.

"Perhaps you're exaggerating a little," says Dr. N. "My guess would be that she is somewhere around forty."

"Aha," says Pappa, "you might very well be right about that."

SHE   Can you tell me about Ingrid? Look, here is a picture
       of her. Do you see her? Can you see the picture?

*A photograph of Ingrid as a young woman hangs on the bedroom
wall. She takes it down and shows it to him. Ingrid's thick, dark
hair is drawn into a braid descending down her back. He studies the
picture. When she holds it in front of him, as if it were a mirror,
Ingrid looks straight at him. There is a hint of a smile in her eyes.*

HE   (*almost inaudibly*) For her, life was a straight, wide,
       open road on which we could travel together in safety.
SHE   Safety for both? Or just for you? Did she also feel
       safe?
HE   Yes. That's how it was.
SHE   Do you still talk to Ingrid?
HE   Yes, I do, she is always nearby.
SHE   Do you believe that you will see Ingrid again when
       you die?
HE   I'm utterly convinced of that.
SHE   Do you believe that you will see others beside Ingrid?
HE   I don't know, but I know I will see Ingrid. I am abso-
       lutely certain of it. Is your loudspeaker still on?

He says *loudspeaker*, but means *microphone*.

SHE   Yes. Is that okay? We'll finish up soon.
HE   It is finished.

SHE   Are you tired?

HE   Yes, I am.

SHE   Would you like to rest a bit before lunch?

HE   I don't know. When is lunch?

SHE   Lunch is in forty-five . . . or, no (*she looks at her watch*) . . . in forty minutes.

HE   Lunch?

SHE   Yes, in forty minutes.

HE   Twelve o'clock?

SHE   It is twelve twenty now. Lunch is at one. It is forty minutes till lunch.

HE   What . . . I don't know.

SHE   Yes, but I know. You are having lunch at one o'clock.

HE   I am having lunch at one o'clock?

SHE   Yes. Omelet at one.

HE   Omelet at one.

SHE   So, just over half an hour from now.

HE   Are you sure about that?

SHE   Yes, I am. Dead sure.

HE   Dead sure?

SHE   In Norwegian we say *skråsikker*, from *skrá*, meaning parchment.

HE   What was that?

SHE   *Skråsikker*. So sure it might as well be written on skin.

Long pause.

HE   Yes, well, I think that we should finish today's exercises.

SHE   Then let me turn this off. Listen, did I upset you when I asked about Ingrid?

HE   Yes.

SHE   I'm sorry.

HE   No, you couldn't have known that it would hurt, but it did. Damn!

SHE   We'll finish up now.

HE   Yes.

SHE   But listen . . . Should I get the book so we can write down the time for tomorrow?

HE   Yes, but you see, that will be very complicated.

SHE   Why is that?

HE   Because then one of the women who works here will have to come all the way in here and help us . . . and we can't drag them here at all hours.

SHE   But can't we just get the book ourselves and write whatever we want in it without the help of other people?

HE   No, that's not possible.

SHE   I see . . . but should we just agree to meet tomorrow at eleven?

Endlessly long pause.

HE   Yes.

SHE   You sound doubtful?

HE   Well, yes, you know, I am a very busy man.

SHE   Yes, of course.

HE   A busy man has the right to doubt.

SHE   That's true.

HE   If you don't mind, I would like to suggest that we
       meet at one o'clock.

SHE   No, that's when you have lunch.

HE   Well, then you and I will have lunch together! I think
       they're serving eggs, probably an omelet, and maybe
       we'll even have a glass of wine. I believe we have a
       plan, no?

HE SAT QUIETLY POKING at the omelet in front of him, his smooth heavy head bent. He raised his head and glanced at me, lowered his head and took a bite, raised his head again. Finally, he opened his mouth, not to eat, but to say something.

We had been sitting there forever, so when something was finally about to be said, I was relieved and leaned forward. He had shriveled up, faded away, his eyes involuntarily mild, but his cheeks a rosy red.

Anne Carson has written: "Why do we blush before death?"

He pointed at the ketchup bottle between us on the table. It too was red. And ugly next to the little glass vase with wildflowers that someone had taken the time to pick. The kitchen table was comfortably familiar, pine, the wildflowers too, but the ketchup bottle was all wrong, a big, ugly, red wrong in my father's house.

After a long silence, Pappa asked whether I had ever tasted ketchup. I realized he was trying to make small talk. If this were a party, he was the host and I was the guest. He said that if I hadn't tasted ketchup, I was in danger of missing out on one of life's great joys. I wasn't sure how to respond to that. Should I say something about ketchup?

———

I have arranged parties since I was sixteen, always with a feeling that something terrible was going to happen.

Some days he would recognize me, other days he wouldn't. Every morning I hoped that he would be in the one state and not in the other. After a while I discovered a third state, more perplexing than the one or the other. He often knew who I was, but doubted whether what he knew was in fact true.

It took time to die, it was an ongoing task, and if anyone had asked me that summer: What is he doing now? I would have answered that he lay dying although, of course, that wouldn't have been entirely correct, because even if he was mostly *lying* on his back, he would also *sit* or *double up*, now and then he was *lifted* into his wheelchair by meddlesome or well-meaning female hands and *wheeled* into the kitchen to be served an omelet.

I was afraid that his head would grow too heavy for his body, that he would rip, rupture, unravel like a rag doll. He weighed no more than a bag of apples.

The bedroom windows were kept shut to prevent flies and insects from getting in, but still there were butterflies on the walls, on the ceiling (sitting? standing? clinging?), there was something leaden about them, something winterlike, flecks of black on smooth white surfaces. If I lay on his bed and stared at the ceiling, squeezing my eyes shut so that everything became a blur, the butterflies started to look like other things. They looked like blood spatter, maybe because I had just read an article about blood-spatter analysis, how the spatter can uncover what happened at the crime scene. They looked like gravel in the snow, his bedroom was warm and stuffy, it was warm outside and warm inside and I longed for snow. I lay on the bed next to my father and longed for snow, or at least a chilly breeze, sometimes I spoke to him, sometimes I sang, it occurred to me that he may not have wanted me there next to him in bed, talking, singing, maybe he wanted to be left in peace, die in peace, but was too weak to tell me.

The butterflies were a type of presence that can't be called corporeal or even physical, I counted one, two, three, four. One butterfly is lovely, it strays into your room, perhaps you ascribe meaning to it, you admire its beauty, you are thankful that something so exquisite reveals itself to you, but many butterflies all at once—inside a dark, warm room—is something else. It is what it is, they are what they are. They want nothing from you, they don't even want to flee. I got up from the bed, drew the curtains, and opened the window wide.

"No, not that," Pappa mumbled when the light fell on his face.

One would think that the butterflies would have appreciated the chance to escape, that they would have spread their large wings and fluttered into the light, but no, I stood there tottering and waving and whispering *shoo, shoo*, but they remained stuck to the walls.

The house was an extension of him. You were not allowed to move around in it as you liked, there were rules for everything, I would never, for example, have taken a glass of water from the kitchen into the living room. No one ever told me. No one said: You are not allowed to take a glass of water into the living room. It was something I knew. I knew it so well (and had known it for so long) that I didn't have to think about it. The long narrow house, lying stretched out with a view of the stony beach and the Baltic Sea, maintained a chaste order whereby everyone who lived inside it, children and adults, saw to their work, watched the time, and avoided emotional hurly-burly. A small world sketched out and planned in advance.

In Ingrid's day, butterflies wouldn't have gotten inside. I went to fetch the long-handled broom from the cupboard in the hallway between the foyer, the kitchen, and the living room. Had King Solomon come to the house at Hammars, he would not only have said that there is a *time* for everything, but also that there is a *place*.

Every morning, Ingrid went through the house with a carpet beater to beat the pillows on the armchairs, the sofa, the beds, and if you sat on the sofa after she had beaten the pillows, the whole sofa would collapse and become all squashed and sloppy. Although Ingrid died many years before Pappa, it sometimes felt as if she still went from room to room beating pillows.

WHEN HE SAT IN his wheelchair, it was hard not to notice his spindly legs, ballerina legs, his feet wrapped in large sheepskin slippers. On one of the slippers he had written the letter *L*, on the other the letter *R*. He had used his regular black marker. It was several years since he had written *L* and *R* on his slippers. Now he wouldn't have been able to write anything at all.

His striped nightshirt flapped around his knees, several sizes too big, as if it belonged to another and much heftier man than he, a heftier man who was now walking around looking for his nightshirt because the one he himself was wearing was too small and too tight. When Pappa was wheeled from his bedroom to the kitchen, he hollered NO!, and then he would double up and try to make himself small, as if he wanted to vanish into the wheelchair, *become* the wheelchair, he took time to die and it wasn't as if he simply lay down and died or sat and died or doubled up and died or hollered NO! and died, he mumbled and hollered and whispered and rattled and one day I lay next to him in bed and sang a lullaby, the same lullaby I've sung for my children, the blackout curtains were drawn as usual, so even though it was the middle of the day and the sun was blazing outside, the room was dark. He always said that all his nightmares and thoughts of death played out in bright sunlight, and he would protest whenever I tried opening the curtains, heavy, yellow-beige curtains that dragged along the floor and lapped up dust. To me everything in here felt dark and stuffy, and I didn't like having to keep a constant eye on the butterflies, but I lay there in the dark and sang for him, the same song that my children loved so much. I couldn't see him clearly, and he couldn't see me, we

were two shadows lying side by side, one shadow singing, the
other shadow quiet, he hadn't said anything for a long time,
and, then, right in the middle of the song, I wondered whether
he had died, I hoped that he had, that he had *passed quietly away
in his sleep*, as the expression goes. The lullaby had many verses,
that is why my children loved it, it takes time to get through it,
and they wanted it to take as much time as possible from when
I started singing until I said good night and turned out the light
and closed the door. Eva is afraid of the night, she dreads the
moment she has to go to sleep, always tries to put it off, asks for
a slice of bread with jam, asks for a glass of water, asks for a kiss,
asks us to sing the long song with all the verses, and when I lay
there next to my father on the bed—in the middle of the third or
fourth verse—I thought: Maybe he is dead now?

But then, after a few more verses, a thin rasp: "Very
beautiful."

His voice was perfectly clear, as if from an earlier time. This
was a new time.

We were always courteous with each other. I said: "Do
you think so?" without getting an answer. And then I asked:
"Would you like me to sing it one more time?" and he said:
"No, thank you."

Courtesy was important, I am grateful for the courtesy, we
made an effort until the end.

SHE   But you have always portrayed characters who rumi-
      nate about death—death is all over the place, in your
      films, in your plays, in your writing.

HE   Oh, is that so?

SHE   Do you disagree? Haven't you been more than just a
      little preoccupied with death?

HE   Well, maybe, in a way, but not too much, my preoc-
      cupation with death has been quite modest, actually.

SHE   I'm surprised you should say that.

HE   Death as lore, death as fantasy, yes, but I've never
      taken death seriously. That, of course, is what I have
      to do now.

SHE   What do you mean?

HE   Ah, what's with all the questions!

SHE   Does my asking make you angry?

HE   No, no, no.

SHE   Tell me if you'd like to stop.

HE   No, no.

SHE   What do you mean when you say that you have to
      take something seriously?

HE   To take something seriously means to be *concrete*.

SHE   To be concrete?

HE   Having to be concrete frightens me.

SHE   Why?

HE   Don't you see: because it is real. It can't be altered, it is
      tangible, it is something you have got to get through.
      No fuss. The truth of the matter is that I have never
      taken anything seriously.

Silence.

SHE   Is that the kind of person you are: someone who never takes anything seriously?

HE   Sometimes I think so, yes. And no—I am also the opposite.

SHE   Someone who takes everything seriously?

HE   Yes . . . I don't know who I should rather be.

THE WOMEN WHO CARED for him during his last year worked in shifts. They came and went and did a lot more than open and close the bedroom curtains. One woman listened to the radio in the evening, the second woman ironed laundry in the living room, the third woman tried on dresses in the kitchen, the fourth woman sang, the fifth woman said, *He says I remind him of his mother*, the sixth woman walked around jingling with a big chain of keys, and little by little the house changed. Everything in this house had happened in compliance with certain rules, in designated rooms and at specific times, no one had listened to the radio in the evenings, except for Pappa, no one had ironed laundry in the living room, or tried on dresses in the kitchen.

If I try to picture the women's faces, everything becomes a blur. When I think about them, I think about their hands.

He had made arrangements for dying. *I will lie in my own bed, in my own house, looking across the stony shore, the gnarled pines, the sea, and the ever-shifting light.* "Everyone must bear his own universe," Henry Adams wrote, "and most persons are moderately interested in learning how their neighbors have managed to carry theirs."

The women who cared for him had tended children and old people before, these were experienced hands, weathered hands, yet I would hesitate to call them caring hands. But it was all part of his plan. *I don't want to go to some fucking retirement home. I want to die in my own house. I will not be left helpless and at the mercy of my children. I will not be subjected to displays of emotional brouhaha.*

The women, most of whom were in their sixties, and whom my father tended to refer to as the women or girls who work here, did what they had always done, at least since becoming adults. I can't even picture them as ever having been young girls. That summer everything was about dying, the work of dying, death leaning into life, life leaning into death, he would wake up in the morning and fall asleep at night, but died every day nonetheless. The heart was still beating, but the absence was overwhelming. The women from the island, doing what they had always done, cared for him as they knew how—they wheeled and lifted and fed and washed and patted and dried and sometimes they caressed his brow or held his hand.

I fetched the long-handled broom and walked back to Pappa's room. When I was little, I would count the steps from Pappa and Ingrid's room at one end of the house to Daniel's and my rooms at the other.

Back then it was Ingrid who washed, vacuumed, and ironed, who mended socks and typed his manuscripts, who hung up sheets and linens in the drying closet and mangled them in the wringer and made up the beds so nothing would bulge or wrinkle, who shopped and prepared meals, who cleaned as she went, who archived and did the accounting and responded to letters.

Standing on tiptoe, I carefully nudged one of the butterflies with the broomstick, I was afraid of nudging it too hard, I didn't want to kill it, I would have killed a fly no problem, but not a butterfly, I don't know why, these weren't even pretty, and they wouldn't budge, not even when I gave them a poke. They kept sitting there on the wall, one, two, three, four, and a fifth that I hadn't spotted earlier, they sat there with their wings, not going anywhere, not wanting anything, I gave up, placed the broom in a corner, and lay back down on the bed next to Pappa.

It isn't true that he weighed less than a bag of apples, I could just as well have written that he weighed more than a large tree. I can't say whether he was heavy or light.

I was unable to lift him from a lying to a sitting position. I meant to give him some water. He must have weighed a ton— how much does a large tree weigh? An elm, for example? He ended up half lying, half sitting in bed in an uncomfortable and entirely unsuitable position for drinking water while I balanced on the edge of the bed, also half sitting, half lying, with one arm draped around his shoulders and the other fumbling for the glass on the nightstand, both of us deadlocked in this position, an unfinished sculpture of indeterminable origin. Once I had finally gotten hold of the glass and brought it to his lips, I managed to coax us into place. We were no longer deadlocked, we could move, but Pappa wasn't able to open his mouth and drink. I gently nudged the glass against his lips. I don't know where I got the idea that he was thirsty and wanted to drink, he had not said: I am thirsty. He had not pointed at the glass. He had not spoken in several days. Perhaps he had decided not to drink any more water.

Later it occurred to me that I should simply have moistened his lips. I had never before been present at someone's deathbed, but I've read lots of books and should have known that this is what you do. You moisten their lips. *Have mercy on me and send Lazarus, that he may dip the tip of his finger in water, and cool my tongue.* The rich man in the verse doesn't ask for a glass of water. He asks that the poor man dip his fingertips in water and moisten his lips.

I blew it. I blew it because of my clumsiness, my terrible clumsiness. The women in my family—on my mother's, not my father's side—are all beset by this terrible clumsiness. I trip on the street, walk straight into trees, spill wine on the floor. This time I spilled water on my father, it ran, it ran down his neck and under his collar, down his chest and all over the sheets. He gasped as the water hit him, it was the coldest thing ever to hit his skin, or what do I know about his skin and its experiences with hot and cold, all I know is that it was a long time since he had been touched in the places he was being touched now— water spilling down his neck, along his collarbone, his chest— and I believe this is why he opened his mouth to speak, although he didn't exactly speak, but mumbled what would be his very last words to me.

"Fucking bitch," he said.

I said: "I'm sorry, Pappa."

And he said: "Fucking cold . . . fucking bitch."

GROWING OLD IS WORK. To convince your body to obey your brain, and eventually convince your brain to obey itself, to ask God for mercy. His entire life, Pappa zigzagged between faith, doubt, and disbelief. Once he said: "On the one hand I believe I will see Ingrid again, on the other hand I believe dying is like blowing out a candle."

He said: "Get out of bed, shower, put on socks and shoes, fresh clothes, eat breakfast, ride your bicycle, go to work."

For instance: Think about the work that goes into tying your shoelaces. It calls for physical exertion, dexterity, and cleverness, any child between the ages of six and nine years old knows it, early in life it is a serious matter, the bow the greatest mystery, the fingers, the hands, the laces, altogether an apparently unsolvable riddle. But once you have mastered it, you forget how complicated it is, the years pass until one day—having put your socks on—you look down at your feet, unsure of how to proceed.

At night, before he was confined to a wheelchair, he would seek refuge in the smallest room in the house, sit down on a bunk and surrender himself to thinking about other people. Regarding this ritual, he once said: "I see her before me, her lips, her gaze, her form, I say her name out loud, I hear myself say her name, I see her turn toward me, there may be something awkward about her movements, maybe she is laughing, and then I think about her laughter, or something she says . . . look, it doesn't have to be a woman, it could be a man, or a child . . . I think about others, the living and the dead, and then I light a candle."

He asks her to open the curtains. She gets up, walks to the window and draws them apart.

HE   To let some more light in.

She remains standing by the window.

SHE   Now we can see the ocean.
HE   I can't.
SHE   Should I open them some more?
HE   No.
SHE   Are you cold?
HE   No.
SHE   Would you like another blanket?
HE   No.
SHE   Fine, then, I'll come sit down next to you.
HE   When someone asks me where I live, they always reply before I've had a chance to say anything . . . they tell me I live at Hammars.
SHE   But this is where you live.
HE   Yes.
SHE   Do you miss Stockholm?
HE   Yes.
SHE   Do you miss the theater?
HE   Yes.

WHEN I WAS IN my twenties, he wanted me to read Agnes von Krusenstjerna's *The Misses von Pahlen*, a novel in seven parts. I started on the first part, but got bored after only a few pages and put the book back on the bookshelf. When he noticed that I wasn't reading it, he couldn't hide his disappointment and irritation. Some years later I told him that I had read Hedvig Charlotta Nordenflycht's poem "The Duty of Women to Use Their Wit" from 1741, although this didn't appreciably make up for the fact that I never read *The Misses von Pahlen*. Many years later he built his library—based on his own sketches and assembled from pine, light, and glass—and the house at Hammars grew even longer. In the library, I found a collection of poetry by Hedvig Charlotta Nordenflycht. *The Sorrowing Turtledove* was written when the poet's second husband, Jacob Fabricius, a priest, died, leaving her a widow after only nine months of marriage. Its full title is: *The Sorrowing Turtledove, or Numerous Wretched Songs, set to beautiful MELODIES and collected by a compassionate Listener.*

He had thousands of books, he was always reading and underlining passages he thought were important.

Around the time Ingrid lay dying, he read Ulla Isaksson's *The Book About E*, which recounts the story of a woman, the author herself, who loses her husband to Alzheimer's. Pappa lost Ingrid to cancer. He asked me to read it. He himself had read it with his black felt-tip pen in hand. Notes in the margins. Underlined sentences. To read a book that he had read and scribbled in was like talking to him without being afraid of saying the wrong thing.

Some weeks after Ingrid's funeral we spent an entire night sitting on the living room sofa looking out over the pines, the shore and the ocean. Hand in hand, nearly blinded by the red sun ascending slowly and furiously from the septic depths of the Baltic Sea.

"By the Shores of this lonesome Place," wrote Hedvig Charlotta Nordenflycht, "she beholds the Waves."

He kept telling me to go back to Oslo, he didn't want me around. And then he took my hand and wouldn't let go. Our knuckles turned pale to the point of blue during the night.

"I am a seventy-four-year-old man," he said, "and only now does God decide to kick me out of the nursery."

In *The Book About E*, Ulla Isaksson quotes the Swedish poet Elin Wägner: "Even in hell you have to arrange the furniture." Here, my father had added an exclamation point in the margin.

When I was seven, he told me not to use exclamation points. I had just written a story about three little kittens. Its title was "Three Little Kittens!"

As he got older, his handwriting became increasingly difficult to read. His hand began to tremble, his one eye gave out— the letters of the alphabet blurred into one.

Pappa's exclamation point in the margin bore the mark of all this. A short vertical line and a dot. A burning candle. A broken twig. Mainland and island.

HE   And now and then I walk into the living room and say: I want us to do something about that picture on the wall. There is a man standing in the room, I turn to face him, it is an anonymous person, and I say: That picture was already here when I arrived, and the anonymous person replies: There was nothing here then, you are the one who hung the picture, drew, built, and furnished all the rooms, all of this is yours . . . And that line—*all of this is yours*—is played back in continuously new variations . . . I dreamed that I was on my way to the Royal Palace, and along came a man, an utterly anonymous person, and said: So where do you come from? To which I replied: I come from Hammars, on Fårö, and then he said: Indeed, it is about time we learned who lived there, and I say, with a shade of doubt, that, yes, I believe I am the one who lives there.

V

YOUR BROTHER
IN THE NIGHT

...

The only thing we knew for sure about Henry Porter
is that his name wasn't Henry Porter.

—BOB DYLAN/SAM SHEPARD

I N ORDER TO WRITE about real people—parents, children, lovers, friends, enemies, brothers, uncles, or the occasional passerby—it is necessary to make them fictional. I believe this is the only way of breathing life into them. *To remember* is to look around, again and again, equally astonished every time.

"Autobiography begins with a sense of being alone," writes John Berger.

I wanted to see what would happen if I allowed us to emerge in a book as though we didn't belong anywhere else. For me it was like this: I remembered nothing, but then I came across a photograph of Georgia O'Keeffe that reminded me of my father. I began to remember. I wrote: "I remember," and felt unnerved by how much I had forgotten. I have some letters, some photographs, some scattered scraps of paper, but I can't say why I kept precisely those scraps rather than others, I have six recorded conversations with my father, but by the time we did the interviews he was so old that he had forgotten most of his own and our shared history. I remember what happened, I *think* I remember what happened, but some things I have probably made up, I recall stories that were told over and over again and stories that were told only once, sometimes I listened, other times I listened with only half an ear, I lay out all the pieces next to each other, lay them on top of each other, let them bump up against each other, trying to find a direction.

———

For the past several years I've been lying awake at night, for a while I took sleeping pills just to get away, I was never able to put my sleeplessness to good use, all I did was lie in bed and stare at the ceiling.

Not long ago my husband found the tape recorder in the attic. I pressed Play, and there we were. Pappa and me. Our voices faraway. The recordings had been gone for so long that I had started to believe I had dreamed them.

When my father couldn't sleep, he wrote on his nightstand. I took a picture of the table after he died, the picture is on my cell phone, I can zoom in on different places on the tabletop:

TEN YEARS

I look frantically
for Ingrid
DREAD
DREAD
DREAD
DREAD
DREAD
Made a rather gray and
boring film; wanted to
depict the spirit of our time
Ingrid also frightened

A hideous fiasco
And malicious reviews
SHITTY NIGHT

The bed he was lying in when he wrote this is now properly made
up, and has been for many years. A white crocheted blanket is
spread over the pillows and duvet. The last summer he was alive,
someone had written on the bedroom wall as well, the wall has
since been scrubbed clean. He wasn't the one who wrote on the
bedroom wall, he got one of the women who cared for him to do it.
In big capital letters and with the same thick, black marker he himself always used, she had written his name followed by the place
names *Hammars, Fårö, Sweden, Europe, The World, The Universe.*
   His room was an envelope—a child's stationery pad.

Everything is left precisely the way it was when he was alive.
The house at Hammars is *preserved for posterity*, as the expression
goes. Strangers wander from room to room. Some take pictures.
Some sit down on the chairs or on the sofa and put their things
on the tables and turn on and off the light switches and gingerly
lie down on his bed to check out the mattress.

One evening I turn on the TV here in Oslo and see a renowned
middle-aged film director sitting in the green armchair in the
room we used to call the video library. There were two green
chairs in there, one for Ingrid, one for my father. The middle-
aged film director is sitting in Ingrid's chair, speaking directly
into the camera.

———————

The video library—synopsis of a room: When Daniel and I had outgrown our children's rooms, Pappa converted them into one big TV room. He had a large collection of VHS cassettes, all of which were catalogued and placed in alphabetical order on custom-built shelves. Between eleven and three in the afternoon, you were allowed to come to the house to borrow cassettes.

Every time you borrowed a cassette, you registered the film's title, the date, and your signature, and, upon returning it, you made a note of the time and date of return. On a little table, a pen and a yellow notepad were provided to write down all this information.

Sometimes he comes in to the room while you are looking for a film.

"How about *Claire's Knee*?"

"No, I don't think so, not tonight, Pappa, I've seen it lots of times."

"It's Rohmer."

"Yes, I know."

He shuffles around, browsing the shelves.

"What about *A Heart in Winter* then?"

You notice that he has written a big *L* on one of his slippers and a big *R* on the other. You are about to say: When did you start writing on your slippers?, but instead you mumble something like: Yes, well . . . Sautet is a wonderful director.

What you actually want is for him to go away and leave you alone and since that's not likely to happen, you might end up

taking *A Heart in Winter* just to get him off your back, and come
back later to borrow another film.

Or you say something like this: "I've seen *A Heart in Winter*
many times, so tonight I was thinking Woody Allen."

Pappa stares at the ceiling. His eyeglasses are thick, at times
his mouth is so thin and long and tightly strung that it can
stretch from one end of the house to the other.

"Well, of course. One makes a suggestion, but she appears
to have seen every film ever made. By all means, Woody Allen
is first-rate. *Crimes and Misdemeanors* is a masterpiece, but I see
you've chosen *Manhattan*. Good enough. You do as you please."

And then, many years later I turn on the TV here in Oslo and
the renowned middle-aged film director is telling the camera
that he feels a kinship with the *master*.

He is sitting in Ingrid's green chair, surrounded by video-
cassettes, saying he feels a kinship. He has long dark eyelashes
and a mop of curly dark hair. A glass of water sits on the table.
It's the same table on which the yellow notepad and pen used
to lie. Now and then he takes a sip of water. He doesn't sit up
straight, but leans back and gesticulates.

*You're not allowed to bring water in here, you idiot, the glass will
leave rings on the table.*

The film director says he can feel the master's presence in
the room and produces a stopwatch from his inner pocket.
He says that the stopwatch is a magic pendulum and goes on
to explain that if the pendulum starts to move, it will prove
beyond doubt that the master is present. *Ah, yes*, he says,
breathing softly, swinging the watch back and forth, *it moves,
see, it moves, he is here.*

All the rooms—the study, the living room, the kitchen with the two pinewood tables, the video library, the library, even the bedroom—are intact.

Death commenced when he arrived seventeen minutes late. Seven, no, eight years later I try to account for them. The minutes. What should I call them? An archivist asks: What should be preserved, what should be discarded, what should be sorted under what?

All of his belongings were sold at auction. That's what he had decided. He left a will with precise instructions: I want to be buried in my brown corduroy trousers, the red-checkered shirt and the reddish-brown knitted vest. Displays of emotional brouhaha shall not, under any circumstances, be tolerated.

The will stated that his eight surviving children could each take one item valued at 5,000 kroner or less, "as a memento of their father."

Everything else should be sold to the highest bidder, "preferably at auction."

I picture a procession of objects making their way from Hammars to the auction house in Stockholm, the straight-backed chairs, the tables, the rust-red sofa, the green armchairs, the bed, the bedside tables, the desk, the pictures, as if drifting down a river, one after the other.

As a memento of their father.

I chose a portrait of the dancer and choreographer Pina Bausch— a signed and framed poster from her first production of *Café Müller*. After Ingrid's death, when I went to Hammars to try to

console him, or at least to keep him company, he had no interest
in seeing films at the cinema at Dämba. After a few days, though,
he did want to watch either opera or dance on the big TV in the
video library, which had a wide selection of dance and opera cassettes. For days on end we looked at Pina Bausch. *Café Müller*
is dream and night, oblivion and memory. The choreographer's
parents owned a small café in Wuppertal that she re-created for
the stage—chairs, tables, and sleepwalkers. A man rushes around
the stage, moving all the chairs out of the way so the sleepwalkers
won't trip and fall. Pina Bausch herself is tall and thin, pale as
water, every time I come down the stairs in my house in Oslo,
she's there, hanging on the wall, wearing her loose-fitting, white,
almost transparent nightgown. In the photograph she stands half-
hidden behind a door or a partition, her eyes closed. She is thin
and fragile and strong, not old and not young, her nightgown is
so loosely arranged around her limbs that it almost reveals her
left breast. Every time I walk past her, I'm afraid her dress will
dissolve if I so much as brush against her.

Next to the poster of Pina Bausch hangs a framed photograph of my mother and father. My son gave it to me. They are
sitting side by side, they are no longer lovers, but friends, colleagues. He looks directly into the camera, she looks at him and
makes a funny face—squints and pouts. They sit very close.
Ola said that he found the picture on the Internet and wanted
to give it to me because they looked so happy and free and sort
of goofy.

"They look like they're having fun," he said.

When my father's parents died and he himself had begun to
grow old, he started writing about them.

In one of his three novels about his family he writes:

I look at the photographs and feel myself powerfully drawn to these two people, who in nearly every way are so unlike the half-averted, mythical, larger-than-life creatures that dominated my childhood and youth.

I look at the photographs of *my* parents and wonder who they are and who they were, do I carry them with me, did they get answers to any of the things they wondered about, did they feel that time slipped away from them the way it is slipping away from me?

The man who bought my father's house also bought all of my father's things. He decided that every single piece should be returned and put back in its original place. The heavier pieces of furniture had not been gone long enough for the dents in the wall-to-wall carpets to disappear. A small group of competent professionals, armed with tape measures and documentation (photographs and descriptions of how all the rooms had looked before they were cleared out), oversaw the process of moving everything back, taking care not to put the straight-backed pine chairs by the wrong table in the wrong room in the wrong house, and that the grandfather clock at the one end of the living room was still perfectly aligned with the old linen cupboard at the other end, you should be able to draw a straight line between the little door of the grandfather clock and the heavy door of the linen cupboard. Both were heirlooms, the clock came from his father's side, the linen cupboard from his mother's, or maybe it was the other way around. And here they stood, back in the house at opposite ends of the room, scowling at each other. The clock ticked, the cupboard creaked. All the other furniture was purchased when the house was being built, lots of pine, lots of green and rust-red upholstery bleached by sunlight, two battered armchairs and two footrests, once black, now brown, one pair in the study and one pair in the library. When my mother and I came to live in the house in 1967, everything was ready.

After his death, all his belongings drifted off to Stockholm, and then they drifted back home again to Hammars. I walked through the house alone. Everything was as it should be. Not a single piece of furniture stood in the wrong place. Every room was the spitting image of its former self. I found myself wishing that the two small tables in the living room had switched places, or that the third, and much bigger table had somehow mistakenly been put down in front of the sofa rather than between the two bulky armchairs. I wished for something to be wrong, but everything was right and everything was quiet. I opened the windows and sat down on the floor. A speck of ash flickered in the fireplace. No one lived here now. All his things had lost their thingness. What was it Rilke wrote: *O night without objects.*

The butterflies wake me up. Or no, of course they don't. That was a long time ago. They were on the wall and on the ceiling. I can't stop thinking about him. If I get up now, I can make coffee. I can walk down the stairs, go to the kitchen, and make

myself coffee. Maybe sit down and write. I can hear my husband
breathing. Our daughter breathing. All three of us are sleeping
in the same bed. The dog breathing. If I listen, I can hear cars
out on the road, it's still nighttime, or early morning, it depends
on who you are, how you were raised, what experiences you
bring to the different times of day, it's three forty-five now, do
you call that morning or night, I call it morning, but too early
to get up, I check the time on my cell phone and then I check
my messages, I sit up and lie down, a few cars drive past right
outside my window, *there and there and there*, and farther off a
gentler stream, cars driving past at night sound different from
cars driving past in the daytime. Today is the first of December.

Virginia Woolf writes that the ways in which we read differ
greatly depending on whether we are in good health or struck
by illness. When we are sick and no longer soldiers in the "army
of the upright," bedridden, or, if we are lucky, sitting in a chair
in the shade with a blanket over our feet, we tend to be far more
audacious and reckless in our reading than before we became
"deserters." Ideas strewn across the page evoke, when collected,
"a state of mind which neither words can express nor the reason explain," she writes, "incomprehensibility has an enormous
power over us in illness, more legitimately perhaps than the
upright will allow," not unlike the middle of a sleepless night,
or early morning, when your heart is pounding and everything
has come undone.

The world looks different when you're standing and walking
than when you're lying down. When you lie recumbent and

stare at the ceiling, like I am doing right now, for example, or like Beckett's nameless old man does in *Company*, or the nameless patient (the reader, the narrator) does in Woolf's essay on illness, you start noticing other things. The stains, the flies, the flecks of paint, the edge of the wallpaper, the window, the sky, the constantly shifting clouds. Like a "gigantic cinema playing perpetually to an empty house," writes Woolf.

———

Our house is quiet at night, I seem to be hearing dog paws on the stairs, but the dog lies sprawled asleep on the floor next to the bed. Maybe I'm hearing the dog we had before the one we have now? I don't think people linger on after death, but I wonder whether dogs do. And that we can hear them scuffling about for many years after they're gone.

I've started getting up instead of taking sleeping pills. I get up and walk down the stairs. It's almost four a.m. I go into the living room and sit down on the sofa, looking in on the open kitchen. The coffee machine blinks. The laptops glow. The refrigerator hums. The house has three floors. The rooms are small. Often (during the day, when everyone is awake) there is a crash from one of the floors. There are four of us living here now. We used to be six, but the two oldest children have moved out. Four people and a dog. One of us is always dropping things, or bumping into something, or tripping and falling. And every time that happens, the other three stop whatever they're doing and shout: Hey, what's going on? Is everything all right?

Are you okay? And more often than not things are okay and the
reply comes quickly: Yeah sure, everything's okay.

—————

On August 17, 1969, my father wrote a letter to my mother and
instead of signing his name, he signed it "Your brother in the
night." He wrote letters to her when they were newly in love,
and again when things between them had ended.

I have copies of all the letters they wrote to each other.

This is the story of the copies: When my father died, my
mother gave all the letters he had ever written to her to an
archive, a foundation dedicated to his legacy, consisting of private papers, notebooks, handwritten manuscripts and photographs. The archive was set up during his lifetime and on his
initiative, and on that occasion, he instructed two of his daughters (my older sister and me) to join the foundation's board of
trustees and watch over everything on his behalf. The board
meetings were held in the main building of the Swedish Film
Institute in Stockholm, on the third floor. The archive itself—
steadily growing and claiming to hold his life's work—was
located in the basement. And then he died. The trustees continued to hold their meetings on the third floor, while the archive
remained in the basement. It was like keeping watch over a large
and formless animal. I never went down there.

Before my mother donated her collection to the archive, my
husband's father, a university librarian, offered to sort and make
copies of all the letters so she could still take them out and read

them whenever she wanted. I don't know what my mother and father-in-law said to each other when she entrusted the letters to him, at the time I didn't care about the letters or what was written in them, all I cared about was that she donate them to the archive as quickly as possible. In the weeks and months following my father's death, I turned into a person who insisted that everything be handled *properly*, frequently resorting to expressions such as *by unanimous agreement* and *nonreversible consensus* and *as stated in the minutes*. If I were to—and I do this reluctantly—summon an image of who I was during that time, I see a twitchy woman who talks too loud and walks too fast and whom no one wants anything to do with. I certainly wouldn't have wanted anything to do with her. Her voice is shrill and the emails she sends are too long. Every morning she sits up in bed and talks incessantly about her father's house, all the houses— *and what is going to happen to his houses*, she cries—before her husband has even had a chance to open his eyes and wake up.

Once my father-in-law had sorted and copied the letters, he put the copies into two large brown folders, each with a black, stiff spine finished off with a black silk ribbon and boasting the logo of the university library's manuscript collection on its cover. Several years later, when he too had died, my mother found the folders in a cupboard in the big flat in Erling Skjalgsson Street (where she and I and Nanna and several babysitters and Bogdan had once lived) and brought them to my house for me to look at.

"I know you are writing a book about Pappa," she said. Sometimes when she says *Pappa*, it's not entirely clear to me whether she means her father or my father, or whether she means that my father is her father too. In which case we would be sisters. *Things* are easier to relate to. A grandfather clock. A poster with a photograph of Pina Bausch. A bed. A window. A kitchen table. Chairs. A sheet of wallpaper with flowers that yawn at night.

Y*our brother in the night*. One day I sat down and read all the letters he had written her, it took many hours, my husband had to help me because I still found his handwriting almost impossible to make out.

When, in 1969, my mother left my father, she took the child with her. It was spring and the girl would turn three in the summer. My father remained at Hammars.

In order to administer their breakup, they compiled a register. I write *register* because I think they intended to set up a system, or a catalogue of rules, to help them navigate the chaos in which they now found themselves and the new chaos that awaited them. The register consists of scattered, handwritten notes and lists—viewed as an actual catalogue it isn't very impressive— but I'm moved by the sincerity that has gone into it: "What can I expect of you, now that we won't be living together any longer? Who are you then? What stories will we tell about each other and ourselves?"

I picture them sitting side by side and writing, perhaps at his desk at Hammars. They're having a *sitting*. The child has been placed in the care of Siri or Rosa or some other babysitter. I imagine he has offered up one of his yellow notebook pads for the occasion, the sheets of paper will in the course of the day be covered in her handwriting. They speak two different languages, Norwegian and Swedish, and they have very different ways of talking and writing. They themselves claim that the reason they couldn't stay together was that they were so alike. But to me they are night and day. When I find myself wondering about who I am and why I am like this and not like that, I can hear a voice whispering: *You are like this because of her; you are like that because of him.*

In their separation register (my expression, not theirs) my mother has written: "There is no such thing as a pure life—a faithful life—we can never give each other that. But as long as you hold my hand and I hold yours and we don't let go—never mind if your hand is 100,000 kilometers away or next to me in bed—then it's up to each of us how we live our lives, including our secret, lonely lives."

Here, as she writes the word *lonely*, I imagine she gives the pen to him. Now it is his turn to write. But then he hands the pen back to her. Perhaps he says something about her handwriting being more legible than his. (In the black folder, I found a letter in which he wonders whether she actually *reads* his letters, or just pretends to; another letter is written entirely in block capitals, as if he wants to make sure she will read every single word.) I wonder whether they laugh a little while they're busy with their task, this planning of the rest of their lives now that their breakup is a fact. I don't think they called it a breakup, I associate the word "breakup" with my own life, not theirs, I

think they used the word "separation." I also think it was my
mother who decided what to include in their catalogue and how
to word it.

1. Be considerate. Do not make decisions that
   impact on the other person without hearing what
   he or she has to say.
2. Do not live a double life.
3. Honesty in difficult situations.

The list is not numbered. They wrote on yellow scraps of paper
that are not at all systemized as I am giving the impression they
are. They sat next to each other and wrote down a few thoughts
of how they wanted things to be now that they were no longer
going to live together. I am the one doing the systemizing and
numbering, the cataloguing and registering. In this way, I'm
taking part in their conversation, talking to them.

The year is 1969, I'm almost three, my parents are separating.
We are at Hammars, it is spring, the decision has been made, it
is final, but for the time being they both act as though the status
quo continues to apply, that leaving each other is not the same as
being left, that a life apart is almost the same as a life together.
*But as long as you hold my hand and I hold yours and we don't let
go—never mind if your hand is 100,000 kilometers away or next to
me in bed.* I still have my room, my cot, the dog that lets me pull
its ears, it's a small dog, smaller than me, and right outside my
bedroom window there are a couple of pine trees, the wind in the

trees is the first sound I hear waking up in the morning and the last sound I hear falling asleep at night, I tell myself that I can remember the sounds from when I was two, the sound of the waves, the sound of gravel scraping against a shoe, the sound of the refrigerator in the kitchen, the sound of the grandfather clock in the living room, the sound of the flies in the window panes because Mamma always left the windows open, the sound of the sleepy flowers in my flowery wallpaper, *the flowers in the wallpaper yawn at night when it's time to go to sleep*, was it Mamma or Pappa who said that, the sound of the newly laundered bed linen when I turn from one side to the other, the sound of night and everyone's sleep, and of Mamma's and Pappa's footsteps through the house, their voices, I'm lying in bed and I hear them moving from room to room, the house is long and narrow, like a fortress. When the day of our departure finally arrives, the weather is mild and Mamma leaves behind my knitted sweater and some of the long-sleeved jerseys and doesn't pack all of her own clothes either, doesn't want it to be final, although she knows it is. When Mamma takes my hand to help me into the backseat of the taxi, Pappa stands in the doorway, scowling. Back then, there was only one taxi for the whole of Northern Gotland, and Mamma greets the taxi driver in an overly friendly manner so he won't be upset with her or think she's stuck-up. The dog is running around. It doesn't like being outside in bad weather, but this day is blessed with blue skies. It is because of the dog's particular sensitivity to weather that my mother remembers the day as bright, warm, and quiet; had there been even a hint of rain or thunder or strong winds—the winds at Hammars can be quite brutal—the dog wouldn't have been running around outside. It was a dachshund. It stayed behind with Pappa.

And then comes an item I read as an accusation disguised as an admonition disguised as a prayer:

4. Do not tear down her homemade safety, but add a pinch.

It is a peculiar sentence. First of all, I'm puzzled by the phrase *homemade safety*. I have never heard my mother or father use that expression. One knows one's parents by their words and phrases. Things they used to say. Mamma always said, *My nerves are frayed*, Pappa always said *I'm angry as a poisonous liver sausage*. But I've never heard the words *homemade safety*. Homemade— as opposed to what? *Canned safety?* Neither of them knew how to cook; perhaps one of the reasons they couldn't live together was that they had no idea how to prepare a meal, I am probably overstating this, I realize that, but neither of them knew how to iron clothes or clean a floor, they didn't know how to care for a child, I'm not talking about love, they had love, I'm talking about the work, I'm talking about what it takes once you've set up a home and a family. They were children of the bourgeoisie, and yet they were incapable of living a modern, Scandinavian middle-class life. Nor did they want to. They yearned to be free. They yearned to be children. They talked about freedom and art, but came running back to safety whenever the unknown proved to be too much. They were children of the little world. My mother and father both wanted to be the prodigal son, and when the fun and games were over, they wanted to go home. Or go away. Or go home. Or go away. The lost son is the most beloved. He is always well received, his father runs out into the field to greet him, slaughters the fatted calf for him, and dismisses the dutiful older son with crumbs. *My child! Thou art ever with me, and all that I have is thine. But it is fitting that we should celebrate and be glad: for this thy brother was dead, and is alive again; and was lost, and is found.*

Maybe what Mamma and Pappa both needed was a *father*. Someone who would love them and greet them and care for them every time they lost their way and yearned for home.

Or they needed a *wife*. Artists need wives. And when she or they try to define the word "safety," they resort to a word epitomizing food and shelter. *Homemade.* And then Mamma writes: "but add a pinch." My father must not tear down the homemade safety she had managed to build, but rather add a pinch, like salt to chicken soup.

They didn't talk all that much about the girl, not in the letters the father wrote to the mother, and not in the separation register. Each of them has played a significant role in her life, and I believe she has played a role in theirs, although not in their shared life. It was never the three of them. The mother and the father talked all the time and continued to work together, but I don't think they talked about their daughter. *So, what did she do today? Well, let me tell you.* That sort of thing.

They had so much of their own thing going on, their own childish games, their own secret language. In several of his letters, my father writes about a black puma that I am guessing means *danger*, and now and then the word *piiiiiitsjjjhhhh* surfaces—its meaning not at all clear to me. They had their secret signs, their secret references, their secret places on the island. And they had their work. Their child—I, she—was not a part of all that. They were children themselves who, as children do, sit down together and in great earnestness make rules for the games they are about to play.

Albeit—one item is devoted to their roles as parents:

> 5. No more than one month (30 days) away from the child.

Punctuality is important. *When* things will happen, and *how long* they will last. We begin here and end there. We do not come late. We do not come early. When I was a child, Pappa explained to me that being late was only just a *little bit* more unforgivable than being early. There is no such thing as improvising.

But what does item number five mean? Does it mean that neither of them should be away from me for more than a month, or that *Mamma* shouldn't be away from me for more than a month? The child is not mentioned by name. Even though I wasn't christened yet, they did call me by a name, so it occurs to me that this rule may not be about me at all, perhaps it just means that they shouldn't be away from *each other* for more than a month? Yet another reassurance that their separation is not really a separation, that what is final is not final, and that what is in fact over will continue on as before.

———

I carefully open the door to Pappa's study, everything looks like it usually does, the battered black armchair and footrest by the large paned window facing the sea, the stones and a few scattered pine trees, twisted, wind-swept; under the window a narrow built-in bench upholstered in sheepskin and with a folded gray wool blanket at its foot. When I was a baby, my mother sat on the bench with me in her lap. That probably happened only once. He didn't want us anywhere near his study while he was working. Usually the bench would be covered with piles of books and records, so that every afternoon, after finishing up at his desk, he could sit in the battered armchair, resting his legs on the footrest, and either read or listen to music. He comes to Hammars at the end of April and leaves at the end of September. When he glances up and out the window, he will see the pines, the stony shore, and the sky and know exactly what day and time it is, the light doesn't lie, but then, of course, he knows what day and time it is, light or no light, there are clocks everywhere in this house, and if the clocks weren't enough, he has the book (also called the calendar), in which he writes brief summaries of each day as well as reminders of future tasks. The book lies on his desk, which is positioned right in the center of the room.

At the time of his death the walls of his study are bare, as they always have been, no pictures, no drawings, except for two yellow Post-it notes behind the door, fastened with Scotch tape.

I open the door all the way, and there they are, my mother and father at his desk. They sit close together, facing the opposite wall, giggling, whispering, writing, kissing, and then, slowly, Mamma turns around and looks at me. I stand in the doorway, Mamma's sitting at the desk, and now she's no longer laughing, she looks worried, or is it just the light that keeps changing, it's that kind of day today, a typical Nordic spring day, sunshine one moment, dark clouds the next, the spring of 1969 is mild, but with icy drafts. She has a face that captures every nuance of light and she is young enough to be my daughter. She looks at me. I am forty-eight, Mamma is thirty-one. I think she worries what will become of us. My father could let the camera dwell on her face forever.

6. Six weeks on Fårö every summer as a family.

That's not how it went. Not her. Not us. Not family. But I went to Hammars every summer and stayed for several weeks, not six exactly, but more than a couple, and for a long time I knew nothing about the great and upheaving love that had brought me there.

———

On the tape recording dated May 2007, he flailed and stuttered and struggled with his sentences, the way an infant struggles to lift its head from the floor. When I was a little girl, we looked at each other with a kind of alarmed curiosity.

In order for a relationship to work, he once said, you have to make sure you're able to take turns at being the adult and the child. You can't be the child all the time, even if that's what you want to do.

———

When Pappa died, I couldn't bring myself to listen to the tapes: the floundering, the slowness, the searching for words. And my voice like an overeager recorder player in the middle of the requiem.

———

I can remember what happened often and what happened rarely. The ordinary and the extraordinary. It is not always clear to me which category a particular memory belongs to. Am I remembering this because it happened all the time, or because it happened only once?

I remember Pappa reading to me in the evenings, I have written about it many times, remember him opening the door to my room, sitting down on the edge of my bed, unfolding a yellow piece of paper or opening the book on the bedside table, how he smiled at me and said NOW!, and that there was so much anticipation in the room that the wallpaper flowers opened up and shouted YES! YES! YES! It is curious to think of all the things that live and can crawl out of wallpaper patterns.

> *That stars tore themselves asunder*
> *I listen my heart*
> *my heart is*

I forget names, faces, words, dates, places, conversations, events, boyfriends, books I've read, songs I've heard, films I've seen, I even forget articles I myself have written, once I forgot the title

of one of my own novels, a man asked me about the name of
my latest book and for a moment I drew a blank. I went to the
doctor and asked her whether she thought there was anything
wrong with me, she said there wasn't, but that I was probably
tired, exhausted, and possibly depressed. I have always envied
people with photographic memory, I have the opposite of photographic memory—what would you call that?—that's why I
avoid quizzes, I loathe quizzes of any kind, the only time I ever
participated in a quiz, I witnessed my husband falling for another
woman, I witnessed the fall, but didn't realize it until later, we
were a group of people sitting around a table, and the question
had to do with a Bible quote, the dark-haired woman with slender wrists—younger than me, obviously—knew the answer
right away and whispered it out, I don't remember whether it
was the quote itself she whispered, or whether the quote was
included in the question, I don't even remember the question,
only that it had to do with a specific quote from the Bible, and
that my husband later that evening said: Did you notice how she
whispered out the answer? and I said, no, I didn't notice that,
and he said, yes, everyone was so loud and no one listened, they
were all talking on top of each other, but she just sat there and
knew exactly what the answer was. I should have realized it then.
But she was probably shy, he continued, or so flustered by all the
talking, that all she could do was whisper.

———

The Bible quote was: *You hurled me into the depths, into the very
heart of the seas, and the currents swirled about me; all your waves
and breakers swept over me.*

———

The year was 1981. He was an American photographer, and I met him in an elevator in a building on West Fifty-Seventh Street in New York. He told me to cut my hair even shorter. I was fifteen. I remember we sat face-to-face with a table between us, there was food on the table, we were at a Chinese restaurant and I remember that his face was lit up by a big, red lamp and that he kept hitting his wineglass with a chopstick.

Listen to this, he said, and put on a Jimi Hendrix record. We were in his studio. You know who this is, right? Yes, I said, because I had seen *Apocalypse Now!* a few years earlier together with Pappa and recognized the song. What's it called, he said. I don't know, I said. It's surprising that you don't know more about music, he said, and put on a new song, what about this one, *surprising*, considering who your old man is, as far as I know your father actually cares about music. I should have known more, remembered more, listened more, who gives a shit, I said, that's what I always said when someone started talking about my parents. I was no one's daughter, I was fifteen and no one's child.

For a while, I did everything the photographer said, I wore the white summer dress he liked so much and bought *Are You Experienced*, which, of course, I wasn't (and was that intended as a question from Jimi Hendrix to me?), I listened to the album over and over again, and then I went to his studio after school and sat on the black leather sofa in the corner, the one with the clothes and purses and hats, rhinestone jewelry and lighters scattered all over it, and drank cola while he smoked and photographed girls and talked incessantly. One evening he took me to the Chinese restaurant down at the corner, it was just the two of us, I don't know why he wanted *me* along, but I was flattered, and he kept hitting the glass with his chopstick and said, It's my birthday today, forty-four years old, I'm so bloody old, I could be your father, your grandfather, theoretically, I'm so old that I remember the moon landing, do *you* remember the moon landing, and then he laughed and said: Fuck . . . He had watched it on TV and never gotten over it, had played with the idea of going to Ohio to photograph Neil Armstrong, buy him a beer, get him talking, do something real for once, and not all this fucking nonsense he had going on in New York and Paris, nothing worked like it used to, not the booze, not the drugs, not the sex, not his old friends, who used to be interesting, nor his new friends, who were never interesting, not a single fucking trip, models came and went, half-naked, young, willing, replaceable, in and out of his studio, like the tin soldiers he'd played with as a child, but, he said, if an ordinary woman runs up the stairs and her skirt slides up and I get a glimpse of her knee or a bit of thigh, I can go around thinking about it all day, *that* woman, you know.

He was a burned-out yet sought-after fashion photographer, a convulsive insomniac, always high or low or strung out on some new or old drug, and it wouldn't have hurt him to take a walk in the forest and pick mushrooms, not magic mushrooms, obviously, but ordinary chanterelles, give Hendrix a rest and listen to Cage's "4'33"," although I doubt he would have had the patience to listen to *nothing* for four minutes and thirty-three seconds, all of this is me thinking now, not then, at fifteen, I didn't know who John Cage was, the photographer was right when he said I didn't know all that much about music, so we discussed films instead, Godard, Chabrol, *they're like ten thousand times more interesting than your father's stuff*, he said, and then, lighting a cigarette, he suggested we go to the movies, he is almost eighty years old now, I Googled him and was surprised that he was still alive, I mean, when I think about all the people who are dead, who died even though they were too young to die, who died unexpectedly and suddenly, or old and tired and sick, hungry or much too full, died in one of the many wars between then and now, in fires, avalanches, waters, died because they wanted to die, or because they had no choice, died because they drove themselves too hard, died of loneliness, when I think about all of them, all of us, it seems strange to me that *he* should still be alive, I thought about writing him an email, *Do you remember me*, or something like that, *the girl with the short hair?* He was prone to tenderness and violent rage, in the beginning he said we should be friends, he was an adult, I was a child, why shouldn't an adult and a child be friends, we didn't touch each other, the thought of touching him never occurred to me, he was so old, I had slept with boys, two boys, but mostly to have done it, I was eager to cross every threshold into adult life as quickly as possible. He saw something beautiful in my face that no one else had seen, least of all myself, the girl in the mirror and the girl in the photographs were two completely different girls, maybe he had discovered a new way of looking at my face, a secret angle, I don't know, I think that both he and I fell a little bit in love with the pictures he took of me, the other girl, as we called her, a little older than me and with a serenity to her glance that didn't match my own, there was nothing serene about me, nothing in my face had settled quite where it was supposed to. He was tall, with long hair, his skin reminiscent of something a saddle maker would keep in the back of his store, aged, tan, cracked, and soon he would take me to Paris on assignment for a French magazine, he would take pictures of me and I'd have even shorter hair and almost no makeup, it was going to be great, maybe the best thing he'd done in a long time. He called my mother and told her he wanted to take me to Paris, and she said, No, she's only fifteen, I can't possibly let her go to Paris, and I begged her and she said no, and he called her again to explain what kind of picture he wanted to take and how great it was going to be and how highly he regarded her as an actress in my father's films, the muse of an amazing artist, he said to my mother, and she said no, I'm saying no, she said.

Bogdan's cigarette smoke drifted through the rooms in the spacious, dark apartment on West Eighty-First Street where we all lived, Mamma, Bogdan, and I, drifted through the rooms accompanied by Bach's fifth cello suite, which he played over and over again on the record player, it took the same amount of time for Bogdan to smoke a cigarette, he once said, as it did for Casals to play the Gavotte. I'm so alone, I heard Mamma say, she looked for him but couldn't find him in any of the rooms, there was smoke, there was music, a record was playing on the turntable, Did you know that the cello is the musical instrument that most closely resembles the human voice, he also said, Mamma didn't know that, and now she couldn't find him, I'm so alone, she said, maybe he had dissolved, curled into his own cigarette smoke, I'm so alone, can't you please answer me . . . Mamma didn't want me to go to Paris, she agreed to let me go, but under duress, she didn't want me to go, she kept repeating this over and over again, wandering from room to room, I'm so alone, and I don't want her to go to Paris, wandering from room to room, as if hoping to garner support from the walls, the rugs, the chairs, the lamps, the cigarette smoke that coiled along the walls like an infinite strip of gray wallpaper border, she always had to make these decisions on her own, never anyone to consult with, the girl's father didn't care, Bogdan didn't care, where *was* Bogdan, when had she actually seen him last, heard his voice, seen his face, not just the damned cigarette smoke drifting through the rooms, the scratching sound of a cello, there are still so many beautiful things that can be said in C major, Bogdan once said, he had a habit of volunteering quotes, Mamma would have liked them to discuss their relationship, she was forty-three, a single parent and sole breadwinner, supporting both her child and her boyfriend, and she had no idea what to do, there was no one to help her with decisions, finances, meals, letters from the girl's school informing her that her daughter had an unusually high absentee rate and disappointingly low grades, now he was simply nowhere to be found, and she repeated that she had agreed to let her go, but meant to say no, she had been pressured, and who was this photographer anyway?

The day before I left for Paris, Mamma took me to Macy's.

"We have to go shopping, you need new clothes for your trip," she said.

But you don't want me to go, no, I don't want you to go.

A nice skirt. A warm sweater. Two tops. Tights. A suitcase. I wanted high-heeled boots.

"Not until you're seventeen."

Mamma had just cut her hair and decided on bangs, I'm not exactly sure what I was going for, she said, and touched her hair and burst into tears, we were surrounded by mannequins and dresses and hats and belts and skinny saleswomen who came and went, and shelves and hangers and mirrors, and Mamma cried and said that she missed her long hair and that there were so many other things on her mind that she couldn't explain just now, and then she took my hand and squeezed it hard. I don't know when her hands began to tremble, but that time at Macy's was when I first noticed it. We remained standing like this for a while, on one of the eleven floors, I don't remember which, surrounded by our shopping bags and the new suitcase. My hand in her hand.

Gradually, the trembling became more noticeable. This is why Mamma can't send text messages or write on a computer, she can't hit the right keys, and when she drinks tea, the china rattles.

When Mamma was done crying, we found a place that served banana splits, they have everything at Macy's, bananas are solace, Mamma used to say. When I was little, she showed me how you could put a banana and a piece of chocolate on a plate and leave it out in the sun or stick it under a lamp, and when the chocolate had begun to melt and the banana was squishy and warm, you would take a fork and stir carefully, it was important that the chocolate didn't melt completely and that you didn't stir too hard.

   Later that day she bought me a blazer, and then she decided to buy one for herself as well, we got the saleswoman to put our old wool cardigans into a shopping bag so that we could wear our new purchases right away. The blazers were brown and a little too tight, with pockets on the sides, prominent lapels and shoulder pads the size of turtles. They were woven from some kind of dense fabric that immediately felt clammy. The escalators at Macy's weren't working and we kept walking upward and upward without feeling we were getting anywhere, like treading air, Mamma's face was all flushed, *I don't think we'll get any further up or down today*, and, *Oh my, this jacket is making me feel warm*, and then I caught a glimpse of us in one of the large department-store mirrors, there were mirrors everywhere, and we looked like two overgrown boys, brothers, perhaps, in ill-fitting prom suits.

When I arrived in Paris, I lost my sense of direction. I had always been able to orient myself and draw up a map of where I was, but in Paris I immediately lost my way, I didn't speak French, and after asking a young couple for directions and not understanding a word they said except the young man's impatient *Elle est stupide*, I burst into tears right there, in front of them, in the light of dusk, it was dusk all week the way I remember it, dusk or night, and the young couple turned and walked down the broad avenue whose name I didn't know, and after that I stuck with the photographer, who knew the city like the back of his hand and spoke fluent French. The first time we slept together, I threw up afterward. Was it *he* who made me feel sick, or his body or my body, or the touch itself, the pleasure, the way he stroked, kissed, licked, jabbed? I wanted him to keep doing it and said so, I want you to keep doing it, and when I came, it surprised me, how sudden and violent it was, like shame, like betrayal, and it surprised him too, and he laughed a little, not to make fun, but because he hadn't expected it, I was still small and skinny, and the fact that I came made him want it even more and even harder, and his hair, which was so much longer than mine, spread across my face like a thousand threads, and when it was over and he kissed me on the lips, I put my arms around his neck and hugged him the way little girls hug. And then I started feeling sick and ran to the bathroom and threw up. I felt dizzy being with him and just as dizzy throwing him up, I didn't know it could be like that. I wanted him, I wanted him to want me, I let him, I threw him up, it didn't stop. Once he asked me what I was doing, locked in the bathroom for so long, and I said I was putting on makeup. I have often wondered whether he heard me throwing up and whether he was curious why. On the fourth day he took the pictures of me he had promised to take.

———

To see, to comprehend. It all depends on where you stand. Once there was a Renaissance astronomer and Jesuit priest called Giovanni Battista Riccioli. He is known for naming the lunar seas, craters and formations: *Mare Tranquillitatis*—Sea of Tranquility—owes its name to him.

The lunar maps—with all the new names—were drawn by Riccioli's younger colleague, Francesco Maria Grimaldi. *Their life was to give name.* I try to picture the two of them, who they were, how they went about their work.

I imagine that they were friends, I imagine they were very learned—Grimaldi gave up a professorship in philosophy in favor of a professorship in mathematics because philosophy became too much of a strain on his health—I imagine they worked day and night, writing and calculating and experimenting and building and making use of advanced instruments.

Grimaldi, for example, built an instrument that could measure the height of clouds.

But sometimes they probably just stood straight up and down on their feet, peering at the moon. They had known each other for years, both lived in the university town of Bologna, they probably installed themselves someplace in the city, or maybe they ventured outside, found a deserted field where they could observe in peace. Did they stand in silence, did they have a rule to be quiet during work, or did they talk, and if so, did they talk about what they saw in the sky or about other things, everyday things such as—well, such as what? How exactly would an everyday conversation unfold between two Jesuit astronomers in the seventeenth century?

Much of their work must have taken place at night, and it occurs to me that conversations between friends, brothers, colleagues, fathers and sons—I don't know how the two astronomers would have defined their relationship—unfold differently at night than during the day.

A copy of Grimaldi's lunar map adorns the entrance to the National Air and Space Museum in Washington, which I visited together with Ola when he was still little, but we didn't stop to look at the map, I can't even remember noticing it, we were freezing cold and hungry, it was raining in Washington that day, and our only thought was to find a place where we could warm ourselves and have a bite to eat.

I wonder whether the men and women who dedicate their lives to map, classify, and give names—regardless of whether their eyes are trained on the sky or on the earth, or whether what they are looking at is nearby or far away—sooner or later become overwhelmed by their task.

———

When Eva was still in preschool, my father-in-law would take his daily walks in the neighborhood—the school lies in a park known for its three thousand trees—and occasionally he would stop and rest for a while under an oak hoping to catch a glimpse of the little girl running about. He kept his distance, he was a tall, broad-shouldered man with a full head of white hair and a cane, a man who, because of his towering presence, didn't easily blend in with the crowd, but who disliked the idea of inconveniencing anyone or getting in anyone's way.

Once, on one of these daily outings, Eva looked up and saw him, and called to the other children: "Look! There's grandpa standing under the tree!"

Eva started fussing about getting her ears pierced when she was six, we had told her she would have to wait until her tenth birthday, but then her paternal grandmother died and we told her she could have it done, even though she was only eight. My father died when Eva was three, my father-in-law died when she was five, and my mother-in-law died when she was eight, and this time the matter took on a sense of urgency, I don't know why the word *urgent* comes to mind, but in the days following her grandmother's death, it became a matter of utmost importance to Eva that she'd get her ears pierced, preferably before the funeral.

We called a neighborhood salon and spoke to a lady named Liv, I told Liv that Eva's grandmother had died and would be laid to rest in a week, and on hearing this, Liv said she would squeeze Eva in before that, as though there was an obvious connection between these two rites of passage—an old woman's death and funeral, and a little girl getting her ears pierced. Eva and I went shopping and bought a new top and a new skirt for her to wear, funerals more often than not involve the purchase of clothes, even the greatest sorrow resolves itself into a question of trying on dresses, wrote Proust. When my father died, one of my sisters and I went to a department store in Stockholm to find something to wear for his funeral, I bought an expensive, black velvet dress that I somewhat sentimentally thought Pappa would have liked. I can't remember what my sister bought, she likes cashmere and silk, soft things, but I do remember that we tried on many different dresses and that we were in high spirits. I have never worn the velvet dress since, it doesn't look very good on me, more than once, I've pulled it out of the closet, tried it on and then quickly taken it off again. The day before her grandmother's funeral, I went with Eva to Liv's salon, we had rubbed her earlobes with anesthetic cream, something that had to be done at least half an hour before the actual piercing. A girl from Eva's school had just gotten her ears pierced *without* anesthetic cream, Eva told me, and it had hurt so terribly that the girl had held her ears and cried for days on end, after which things had become infected, one ear had swelled up and grown twice as big as the other ear, I remarked that the story probably was exaggerated.

When Eva and I were nearly at the salon, she stopped in the wind. We had to cross a large public square to get there, and all of a sudden she stopped cold. It was autumn and the leaves were falling and she stood there in the middle of that large public square all wrapped up in autumn and wind and whirling leaves, as if inhabiting her own snowstorm, and that's when she said: "I've changed my mind. I'm scared. I don't want to do it."

When she wakes up in the morning, we'll spend some time in front of the bathroom mirror getting ready. I'll brush her hair, it's difficult to pull the brush all the way through, *Ouch*, she cries, *Mamma, stop that*, her hair is fine and tangled, long, thin, strawy shoots that splinter only to get snarled up again. When she's been at the public pool, her hair takes on a greenish tinge. I gather the shoots and pull tight, sometimes I lean down to look at our faces in the mirror and ask her if she wants to wear her hair up, it looks nice, I say, and she shakes her head and says, no, she wants to wear it down. Her hair dries out now that the cold weather and the snow are coming. Autumn has been warm this year, last year was warm too, warm and dark, every morning a great, pivoting darkness. I hope it will begin to snow soon, the roses in the garden blossomed for the third time in early November, the flies came to life in the windowsills, they thought they were dead and then they woke up; flies on the windowsills, in the sink, they had lain down to die, but now they are ascending through the plumbing, a lone fly buzzes sluggishly through the rooms just before the first advent candle is lit; had the flies been able to sing, they might have sung about how cold it is to wake up from what they thought was death. We are living in the Anthropocene, I tell the flies, there is no prestige in having an epoch named after you, roses blossoming in November, insects coming to life in December. I look at Eva in the mirror, we look at each other, lots of people tell us that we look alike, I tell her it may be time to trim her hair, and she tells me she *just* trimmed it, and then she says: "Mamma, it's a *myth* that you have to cut your hair to make it grow faster."

"I think you're probably right," I say.

Sometimes she comes right up to me and stands very close, trying to catch my eye or wrapping her arms around my waist, but then she pulls away, sensing that I'm *busy*, or whatever it is I say, *Just a minute*, I tell her, *not right now, okay*, or else I pretend that I'm listening while I'm actually thinking about something else. At night her neck is damp, and more likely than not she has kicked off her duvets. Her father and I have two duvets each, so she wanted two duvets too, two duvets even though she gets hot and kicks them off. The dog lies on the floor, breathing almost inaudibly. Sometimes, when he is dreaming, he whimpers so noisily that I have to shout his name into the room to make him stop, and every so often he takes a deep breath and releases a sobbing sound reminiscent of that made by an infant after a bout of tears. The dog sleeps on a sheepskin rug on the floor by my side of the bed, he is in the middle of life and might live for another six or seven years. He has never figured out what it means to be a dog, he is always guessing. My husband and I are the same, we have no idea how to be us, it's a perpetual guessing game. Often, the dog will remind us of other animals, a seal, a small black horse, a sheep—maybe because he ran freely among the sheep at Hammars during his first year of life. My husband once commented that the dog resembles an Australian platypus. When he curls up on the sofa, he looks like a giant snail, his muzzle is too large for his head, he likes it when I run my fingers gently along it. When he eats, he does so by placing a considerable distance between himself and the bowl, and then, when he thinks no one is watching, he quickly snatches one morsel at a time, as if the act of eating is a secret he is keeping from us. His ears are luxuriously soft and shiny, like precious fabric, they remind me of my black funeral dress, the one my father would have liked. I think it's because it accentuated my figure while at the same time being seemly, he himself might have used the word *classic*. Long before he died, almost thirty years earlier, when I was still a girl, I flew to Munich to see my mother and father together in the same room, Mamma was wearing a low-cut silk dress, it was long and blue, her hair, too, was long and blue, or that's how I remember her—blue—as if someone had installed a blue lightbulb in the ceiling and placed her directly under it, and when Pappa opened the door, he pointed at her plunging neckline and said in a kind of whisper, "Good God, I wish you would have chosen another dress."

He didn't like dogs, they scared him, at least that's what he said, but my mother and father had a dachshund while they lived together. When they separated, my mother kept me and my father kept the dachshund. He said he didn't like animals, but then he would go on and on about the animals at Hammars, the rabbits, the birds.

When she wakes up, Eva never forgets to say good morning to the dog, she gets up, walks around the bed, lies down on the floor, and wraps her arms around him. It's the first thing she does every morning, and then, like a sleepwalker, she continues into the bathroom, into the shower, turns on the water, and rests her head against the tiled wall, motionless, unapproachable, the water from the shower gushing down, she doesn't raise her head even when I call her name, doesn't open her eyes, sleeps standing up, like a foal. I say: "You have to open your eyes now, grab the soap, time to get a move on," and a little bit later, "it's time for you to stop showering, come downstairs and have your breakfast."

I will exercise caution in describing her. She will want to do that herself. Every once in a while she baffles me with a look so infinitely her, an *other* altogether, right in the midst of her childhood, relentless in its grip, and even though she will soon abandon it, or it will abandon her, it will follow her for the rest of her life.

―――――――

The book Pappa and I were supposed to write together had come to a halt. I recorded six long conversations on tape, at times clear, at times a blur, and then he lost his mind (is "lose" the right word?) to such a degree that it seemed inappropriate to continue taping, and then he died and I couldn't bear listening to the tapes for more than five minutes at the most, and then I misplaced the tape recorder, I'm ashamed of having misplaced it, of not being able to hold on to things, I'll write another book, I thought, about that last summer, about him and me, about a father and a daughter, about fathers and daughters, about an old man, about a place, I sometimes think I mourned the place more than the man—the things, the stones, the shadows under the gnarled pine trees.

When he was alive, there would never have been butterflies in his bedroom. But he *was* alive. And there were butterflies. He was alive when he lay in bed, staring at the ceiling. I don't know whether he noticed them, but he was alive.

Exactly when that summer did I begin thinking about him in the past tense?

The rule was: no insects inside. He used to be so strict about the windows. They had to be kept closed. When I was little and had my own room at Hammars, I would run all the way from my room to his and curl up between him and Ingrid. Same room, same bed, same pale yellow bed linen, same window, same trees, same stones, same sea.

The butterflies sat, stood, clung on the walls. I lay on the bed, next to him, and stared at the ceiling.

Sometimes he would tell me about where he was. We didn't talk that much, but sometimes he spoke a few words. I had long since stopped recording things on tape. The butterflies reminded me of snow. Blots of snow. Filthy snow. Snow that won't melt. Snow that stays by the wayside when all the other snow is gone, April snow, May snow, snow that refuses to disappear, piles and mounds of snow, snow that is as much dirt and gravel and exhaust fumes as it is snow, snow on which people have stepped and animals have defecated. I don't even know whether what I was staring at actually could be called butterflies, they were black and ugly, maybe some type of moth, but heavier, more compact, with large wings, patternless.

———————

Give it time, said a friend who had also lost her father. It was like being pregnant, you see other pregnant women everywhere you go, you look for them, you quietly greet them, a kind of sister-

hood, and then you become fatherless and you start looking for
other people who are also fatherless, you read books and articles
written by authors who have lost their fathers, or their mothers,
although offhand I can name more authors who have written
about their dead fathers than about their dead mothers. I didn't
know how to mourn my father, I thought I might be doing it
wrong, not only when he died, but in the years that followed
his death, and so I read countless books written by authors who
had lost their fathers or their mothers or both parents, and then
I read books by authors who had lost their spouses, I couldn't
get enough of books about loss and different forms of mourning.

When little Ivan, also called Vanya, also called Vanechka, died
of scarlet fever in 1895, his mother didn't write in her diary for
two years.

But before that, she wrote about unquiet nights, watching
over her sick son and about the feeling of joy and relief when
the boy shows signs of recovery. Then there are a few entries
of everyday activities and everyday worries before his illness
abruptly returns and he dies.

The mother's name was Sophia Tolstaya. The father was Leo
Tolstoy. There is no time lapse in Tolstoy's diary, instead there
is the bicycle. He is sixty-seven years old and had never before
ridden, let alone owned, a bicycle. Now he writes about his new
bicycle all the time, his diary is full of entries on the subject,
listing compelling moral reasons why he should treat himself to
such a vehicle, referring, among other things, to L. K. Popov's
Scientific Notes on the Action of the Velocipede as Physical Exercise.

When Chekhov visited Tolstoy at his beloved estate Yasnaya Polyana, Tolstoy suggested they go swimming together in the river, something Chekhov was reluctant to do. Although he admired Tolstoy greatly, he didn't necessarily want to go *swimming* with him, which is understandable.

There is a photograph of Tolstoy posing next to his new bicycle. Sophia is also in the picture, wearing a black dress and an impenetrable expression on her face. Grieving the loss of her son? Sick and tired of her husband? Absolutely determined to compose herself and play her part. I think about the time lapse in her diary. Two years of silence. Two years of nothing. Tolstoy is dressed in white, sporting a loose-fitting white linen shirt or tunic and a small white visor cap and that full, white beard. He has a slightly resentful look about him. He holds on to his bicycle with a hard and determined grip, and maybe with some apprehension.

The photograph of Tolstoy and the bicycle reminds me of my father. You see one thing and think of another.

Tolstoy doesn't look like my father, apart from that old-man-like quality they both radiated in the final years of their lives. My father didn't have a beard, at least not one as full and white as Tolstoy, and even though he went swimming naked every morning in his ice-cold swimming pool, he preferred to swim alone.

When I look at the picture, it is the bicycle, more than anything else, that makes me think of my father.

My father on his big, red ladies' bicycle.

————

Some days before Tolstoy died, in 1910, he fled his home and left the following note for his wife, Sophia: "I am doing what old men of my age usually do: leaving this worldly life in order to live out my last days in solitude and quiet."

Pappa never left a note like that, although he too wished to live out his last days in solitude and quiet. But things didn't work out exactly as he had planned. Worldly life intruded until the end, but in slightly different ways than for Tolstoy. One hopes that death will be peaceful, one puts one's house in order and makes the necessary arrangements, but then everything turns out otherwise. After he died, I found two handwritten yellow Post-it notes on the wall of his study. They were hidden behind the door. They had been there for a good while. I peeled them off. The pinewood was paler underneath.

The note to the left read:

> *It is a fearful thing to fall into the hands of the living God. But only then can man find atonement.*

The note to the right read:

> *Maybe that's what we look for all our lives, the worst possible grief, to make us truly ourselves before we die.*
> — CÉLINE.

December 24, 1998. It was snowing when I woke up, snowing into the near-empty rooms of the flat in Sorgenfri Street, where I lived at the time, it was snowing when I ran to catch the bus to the airport, snowing as the plane took off from Oslo to Stockholm.

Pappa and I were going to celebrate Christmas Eve together, and he had outlined the following plan for our evening:

3:00 P.M.:	You arrive at the flat at Karlaplan.
3:30 P.M.:	We walk to Hedvig Eleonora Church at Östermalmstorg where your grandfather Erik Bergman was a minister for thirty years.
4:00 P.M.:	Christmas Mass.
6:00 P.M.:	Dinner. Meatballs. You can have wine, if you like.
6:30–10:30 P.M.:	*Sitting*.
10:30 P.M.:	End.

I was thirty-two and divorced. My son was celebrating Christmas with his father, I was celebrating Christmas alone. I had never done that before. Maybe I could take a sleeping pill and sleep through the whole thing? Or go to church? But there wouldn't have been enough services to get me through the night. My father was eighty years old and a widower. It had been his idea, not to write a book—that came several years later—but to celebrate Christmas together. Writing a book came under the category *work*, and the very word itself lent it legitimacy. Celebrating Christmas together fell into an entirely different category.

To stand by the window, dressed in your Sunday best, food ready, tree lit, and be able to say to the person standing next to you: *Look. There comes my little family.*

A week earlier, Pappa and I had spoken on the phone and in the course of the conversation stumbled upon each other's loneliness. Or—that's how I've always thought about it. I've thought that we were there for each other on that Christmas Eve. But there's something not quite right with this line of reasoning. When Ingrid was alive, he didn't want to take part in any sort of Christmas celebration. I believe she celebrated the evening with her children and grandchildren—not with him. And after she died, he continued to spend the evening in solitude. So perhaps we didn't stumble upon each other's loneliness, as I've thought. He didn't need me. I was the one who needed him. And he said: Come to Stockholm.

This is my very first Christmas memory: It was Christmas Eve, 1967, I was eighteen months old, so it's a lie to call it a memory, someone must have told me, someone must have said: Your father didn't want to celebrate Christmas, he had shut the door on Christmas parties, Christmas gifts, Christmas cookies, Christmas trees, Christmas decorations, and Christmas candles. To your mother's despair. It was their first Christmas together as parents. She was very young and lived with him at Hammars, far away from the rest of the world. It was snowing and it was dark, and he was the one who called the shots. But she wanted to celebrate Christmas. She didn't just want to pretend Christmas Eve was a day like any other. They had a child together. At the very least, they owed it to their daughter to make an effort. The fact that the girl wasn't old enough to understand the difference between Christmas Eve and any other day of the year was a different story altogether. He demanded absolute silence in the house while he was working and because of this he never noticed that she took the baby and the car and went to the store to buy candles. The store was a fair way off. The ferry between Fårö and Fårösund left only once every hour. At the store, she bought an entire shopping cart full of candles, maybe even two carts, in any case, a lot of candles. Thick, white candles inside beautiful glass cylinders. She also bought canned Sauerkraut, a frozen ham (which she didn't realize was frozen), and mustard. Then she drove back. He was still busy at work, the door to his study was closed, and she flitted quietly from room to room, placing the candles on windowsills and tabletops, in the living room and in the kitchen and outside in the snow, where the sky was already pitch-dark, but where the snowfall brightened things up a bit, and when she had all the candles in place, it looked to her like something out of a fairy tale. What she didn't know, and what he may or may not have told her that evening, was that the candles she had bought were grave candles. She had chosen the prettiest candles in the store. She didn't know they were intended for the dead. And when he finally emerged from his study, ready to have dinner, but not to celebrate Christmas, he was met by the flickering of grave candles in every room and outside in the snow.

And a frozen, dripping ham in the middle of the kitchen table, the size of a man's head.

———

When I arrived at his flat at Karlaplan, we were both so nervous that we waddled about like hens in the narrow hallway. I took off my coat, he hung it up on the coat rack, I sat down on a chair and began pulling off my boots, and he said: "But we have to go soon, to church, I mean, maybe you didn't have to take off your coat," and I said: "Yes, you're probably right," pulling my boots back on, standing up and fetching my coat from the coat-rack, but then he said: "But we don't have to leave for another twenty minutes, so maybe you should take off your coat and come inside and sit down for a bit."

It had stopped snowing, but when twenty minutes later we found ourselves in the hallway to put on our coats—for real this time—heavy snow came flurrying down once again.

"It's snowing," I said, pointing at the windows.

"Yes, it's been snowing all day."

He opened the hallway closet and took out a green wool coat and a green wooly hat. I put on a pair of wooly tights, my coat, and a hat. Then we sat down on identical stiff-backed chairs and started pulling on our shoes and boots. We had never sat together like this, putting on shoes. At Hammars, in the summer, one simply slipped off one's shoes before going inside. I had high-heeled boots that I had to wriggle into. By the time he had put on both his shoes *and* galoshes, I had only managed to pull on my right boot. He stayed seated in his chair, looking on as I continued to struggle with my left one. After a while, he said: "Why, for heaven sakes, would you wear high heels in this weather?"

Once we were ready to leave, we took the elevator down and walked out into the snow. It was beginning to turn dark, but the street lamps had come on and light shone from all the win-

dows. I could glimpse the decorated Christmas trees and all
the people getting ready for the evening, and it struck me, as
I glanced into one window after the other, that the Christmas
trees in Stockholm were much bigger than the Christmas trees
in Oslo, or maybe it just seemed that way because we were outside and everyone else was inside. I walked along these broad,
dark streets surrounded by the city's large old apartment buildings and it snowed on my father, who was walking here beside
me. We kept the same pace, with equal strides, he didn't have
to wait for me, I didn't have to wait for him, I wore high heels
and he used a cane, but we walked quickly, quietly, as the snow
settled on his wool coat and hat and turned green into white.
When we were almost there, he gently stroked my cheek as if
to carefully wake me, pointing at something and speaking, and
there it was, the church, large and yellow, with snow swirling
around its mighty dome.

"Hedvig Eleonora has three bells," he said, "Little Bell,
Middle Bell, and Big Bell, which weighs nearly five tons and
was cast in Hamlet's hometown."

"In Helsingør."

"Yes, Helsingør, for Kronborg Castle in 1639."

And then he fell silent. I wondered whether he would say
something about his father, the former minister, or about himself?
About the boy called Pu? No, not now. What he said, was: "The
service starts in ten minutes, we have enough time to take off our
coats and let our eyes adjust to the light."

I turned toward him, brushing a few snowflakes from his
shoulder. By now it was almost dark outside. He knew these
streets and this place and this church and this snow. To me,
everything was new. We had never walked along these streets
together, I had never seen my father in snow.

When we returned home, we had meatballs with boiled potatoes and a green salad. A woman named M worked for my father a few days a week. She cooked and cleaned and shopped and did the washing and ironing. They got along well, my father and M, she was ten years his junior, her food tasted good, and she was unsentimental and punctual. How would he have managed without her? M had let herself in to prepare dinner while we were in church. She had set the kitchen table and put out wine for me. When she saw that everything was as it should be and that we were seated at the table, she said, goodbye and Merry Christmas, and we said, Merry Christmas, and she said that she looked forward to celebrating with her children and grandchildren, and Pappa said, Seems like it was Christmas only yesterday, but here we are, here we are, and she told us that it was just a short walk from Pappa's flat to her daughter's flat, but now she had to hurry, and we said Merry Christmas once again and Pappa said, Put on some warm clothes, it's snowing outside, make sure you don't catch a cold.

Snow continued to fall throughout the evening. The grandfather clock in the living room struck twice every hour. I remember telling him that for me Christmas was all about one's children and how I missed my kid. He said that for him it was all about memories. So there we were, wishing we were somewhere else, wishing we could go back home, wishing we could go back in time. Later it occurred to me that it was stupid of me to sit there wishing I were somewhere else, considering it was the only time we'd celebrate Christmas together. And ever since then, before he lost his memory and forgot everything, we would laugh at ourselves and how uneasy we had been and how the hours had dragged by. The taxi was pre-ordered for ten thirty, but neither of us had the nerve, at seven or eight or nine o'clock, to even think about scrapping the plan and saying out loud, "Well, how about calling it a night?"

I remember thinking that I was lonely, that he was lonely, filled with longing, but not for each other's company. I don't think much about that now. Instead I find myself going back to when we walked together in the snow and my father stroked my cheek and pointed at the mighty church dome enswirled in white and said: "Look, my heart, we're nearly there."

———

HE   I feel so uncertain . . . I have to ask . . . I have to ask . . . there's a woman who comes and goes, what's the name of the one working here today?

SHE   Ann Marie.

HE   Yes, Ann Marie. I like her. She has a beautiful voice . . . She was an opera singer, did you know that?

SHE   Yes, I know.

HE   But in any case, I have to ask Ann Marie to come in and check my . . . what the hell is it called . . . ?

SHE   Your book? Your calendar? Is that what you mean? You want Ann Marie to come in here and help you check your calendar? The one right there on your desk?

HE   Yes . . . I wrote in it . . . You wrote in it . . . You wrote your name and I wrote my name and we wrote down the times . . . well . . . despite the fact that I'm sitting here . . . on time . . . waiting for you to come, I find myself in a situation where I have to ask ... what's her name?

SHE   Ann Marie.

He takes hold of the armrests and tries to push himself out of his wheelchair. He groans and sits back down again.

HE   I can't do this. I can't get away from here.

He tries pushing the wheels.

HE   I haven't had a chance to actually learn how to do this ... What a miserable wretch I am.

SHE   No, Pappa, don't say that.

HE   I can't walk. I can't see.

He drops his hands in his lap and doesn't speak for a long time.

HE   It's so frightfully uncomfortable, so unsettling, it's shameful, you see? I find myself surrounded by props ... I walk and I walk and then I find myself surrounded by props or caught in the same damned camera angle ... always the same props, always these dreams ... I can see it the instant it starts happening ... you see? ... But by then it's too late to get out ... I don't want to do this anymore.

SHE   When I was a little girl, you'd ask me about my dreams and then you'd sit me down and tell me what they meant. If you were to stand outside yourself for a moment, what would you tell yourself about these dreams that haunt you?

HE   But you're not listening to me! My heart! You and I
have completely different ways of looking at things,
completely different ways of looking at . . . you have
your mother's . . . you have my . . . I have . . . I don't
know what this is . . .

He looks at the turntable but does not put on a record.

HE   I have become so *tangled up* in a dream system that I
cannot escape, it's no fun anymore, I don't enjoy my
dreams, not a single fucking enjoyable dream. This . . .
these dreams don't have anything to do with reality.

SHE   Well, then, what *is* real to you these days?

HE   *You* are.

SHE   That's true, I'm real.

HE   Before you came, I sat here for twenty minutes and
was all ready to get to work, but then I started to
worry that I had somehow accidentally called you
and canceled, that you weren't coming after all . . .
and then I had to call for . . . ?

SHE   Ann Marie.

HE   Yes, Ann Marie . . . she had to help me over to the
desk so I could look at my calendar. I was so goddamn happy. Something I thought was a dream, or
something that seemed uncertain, was actually quite
clear . . . And then I heard your voice outside. Thank
God. You are here, I am here. Yes, that's how it goes.

He takes her hand.

SHE   My hand is cold.

He rubs it, leaning forward and placing his forehead against hers.

HE   I have a cold nose.
SHE   Yes, it's cold, that's a good sign.

He leans back again.

HE   Is it?
SHE   Yes, at least for dogs and cats.

Puts her hand on his forehead.

SHE   Your forehead isn't warm, but it's not cold either, you
        don't have a fever.
HE   No, I believe I'm in excellent health and ready to start
        working now.

––––––

It's started snowing here too. I look out the window, there is so much snow that when I wake Eva up in two hours, it will be easy to get her out of bed, all I have to do is whisper: Time to wake up, it's snowing, and she'll jump up to see the newly fallen snow with her own eyes.

I walk up the stairs and lie down next to them.

"Where have you been?" my husband whispers from his side of the bed.

Eva is lying between us, taking up most of the space, even though she's the little one.

"Downstairs. Listening to the tapes."

"It's started snowing."

"I know."

Eva moves.

"I want to sleep," she says, "Mamma, it's not morning yet, you have to be quiet."

"But I'm whispering," I whisper.

Her breathing is quicker than ours, softer, not so strained, when I stroke her head, her warmth streams into me, her hair is wiry and tangled and stickily soft at the same time, like drawing your fingers through powdered sugar, she wants to grow it long, it can't ever be long enough, she says.

I stroke her hair away from her face and kiss her cheek.

Eva has curled up like a little shell.

VI

GIGUE

. . .

It will be very tiresome
to have to leave it all.

—AMONG THE LAST WORDS
SPOKEN BY SWANN

THE PALLBEARERS HAVE LIVED their whole lives on the island. They are *Fårögubber* — Swedish for *Fårö oldsters*. My father also wanted to be a Fårö oldster. He visits the men, one by one, and asks them: When I am dead, will you carry my coffin to the grave?

HE KEPT COMING BACK to what he called the epilogue, but whether by *epilogue* he meant the last years of self-imposed exile at Hammars while still in good health and riding around in his jeep at breakneck speed, or the final six months, the sickbed, the wheelchair, the blind eye, or the work of dying itself, the aftermath, the funeral—I don't know. As far as the funeral was concerned, it was planned as meticulously as everything else, the final chapter, the final gig. He wrote and revised his will. He searched for and found a gravesite. He walked around the churchyard on Fårö, alone and with the sexton, discussing the benefits and drawbacks of lying buried under a tree or by a stone wall, surrounded by others or off in a corner by himself. Once dead, he wanted to lie next to Ingrid and began the process of obtaining permits for her grave to be moved from a different location in Sweden. He had conversations with the minister—who often adorned her hair with a single red flower—about what to say and not to say during the officiation. He was adamant that she stick to her sermon and not *set up shop*, an expression he used when actors strayed from his direction and started improvising during a performance. There are many reasons why one might want to set up shop, go out on one's own, so to say—one might want to elicit laughter from the audience, or tears, or love, or just get a little more applause; he once canceled a production of Molière because his critically acclaimed Alceste decided to set up shop, and now, here he was, faced with a situation where the option of canceling the festivities was limited to say the least.

———

My father knew several local carpenters and woodworkers, and the house at Hammars was extended until the very end, expanding horizontally rather than vertically, a library at one end, a quiet room at the other. I'm the one who calls it the *quiet room*, he called it the *meditation room*. This particular room, the last one he had decided to build, was the smallest room in the house, almost like a wooden box, with a window facing the sea, sparsely equipped with a cot, a candle, and a radio. Before he became wheelchair-bound, he would come here at night when he couldn't sleep, and light a candle.

He is eighty-four years old when he moves to Hammars for good. He will not be making any more films. He is not planning another play. He is selling the flat in Stockholm, the one at Karlaplan. He will live in the house at Hammars now, he will live here until his last day, he will listen to records and keep track of the seasons. That's the plan. He and the house have an agreement. *When you are done with your assignments, come here, come as you are, come alone and shut yourself away inside of me.* Winter is the island's true garb. In winter everything is dark and still. All that is red blushes when faced with its own redness, blushes until it wanes and erodes, the poppies are gone, the blistering sunrises, even the red jeep and the red bicycle wane in the silvery light of winter. The jeep is parked under the tall pine tree at the front of the house, the bicycle is in the bike shed. In the morning, the jeep and the bicycle are shrouded in rime and frost—and snow, if snow has fallen. When he opens the door and steps outside, everything is white.

H E NO LONGER SEES films every day, and when he's not seeing films, he might spend the afternoon catching the ferry over to Fårösund to buy newspapers. Sometimes when he's out driving, there's time to spare before the ferry leaves, so he takes a right by the church, past the old store, toward Sudersand rather than a left toward the ferry dock. Many years ago he bought a house not far from Sudersand, at Karlberga, probably the most beautiful of all his houses, a white limestone farmhouse with a lush garden and a big barn. Not long after Ingrid's death, it was sold. Now he might be thinking that he will drive to Karlberga and have a look at that house.

The barn at Karlberga was dark. And big. With a lofty ceiling. And full of things, mostly film props, stacked from top to bottom. Sofas on top of tables, chairs on top of sofas, rugs on top of chairs on top of beds. Once, a long time ago, Ingrid took me there with her. She left the barn door open and blazing sunlight poured across everything inside. All around me things were breathing and steaming, as if the abandoned pieces of furniture, like restless captive animals, had begun to stir. Ingrid was looking for a nightstand lamp and found it strangely wedged between a table and a mattress, a brass lamp with a long, thin neck and a yellow porcelain lampshade of indeterminable age. A dozen bees, having found a dwelling place inside the lampshade, now swarmed toward the open door. Ingrid pulled back as the lamp fell from her hands. "Oh dear," she cried, although she hadn't been stung. And then she gathered her hair in a knot, bent down, and picked up the broken shards.

Along the way, he passes the primary school and kindergarten. The school will soon be shut down, every year the island becomes a little more depopulated, but the kindergarten will survive a while longer—and every afternoon the children gather round the windows, waiting to be picked up by their parents. He can vaguely glimpse them in the light of dusk, their faces in the windows, three in one, two in another. The school is housed in a long, squat limestone building. It is just past three o'clock. The children are disappointed. His was not the car they were waiting for, they knew it the moment they heard the hum of the engine, they can distinguish the different sounds the cars make even from inside with the windows closed, they knew it before they saw the jeep speed past, *that* wasn't the car they were waiting for, that wasn't the sound. And the old man with the bat-eye sunglasses doesn't wave. He never waves. Not to them. He looks straight ahead at the road. The lambs stand silent out on the moors, they don't raise their heads to look. They don't bleat. They don't move. They look as if they've been standing there for a thousand years and will continue to stand there for another thousand. Only the dumbest visitors assume that the name of the island is Fårö because of its many sheep (*får* = sheep). Originally, the island was called *Farøø*, derived from *far* as in *to fare*. And right now, he who was my father and wanted to be a Fårö oldster is faring along the main road, wondering whether he has enough time to reach Karlberga and return to the ferry dock before half past three, he glances at the clock on the dashboard, it's ten past three, no, he won't make it, he hits the brakes, backs up, turns around, and races back, now in the opposite direction, past the kindergarten once again, the pale faces in the windows, past the church, the old store, the moor, the windmill, and all the way to where the road ends. Here, at the ferry dock, he is met by a large yellow signpost with thick black lettering: *Drivers of vehicles transporting dangerous goods must contact the vessel commander before boarding*. He doesn't know that when I was a child, lying in bed in my flower-wallpapered bedroom making lists and hierarchies of men who ruled the world, my father came high up on the list, but *the vessel commander* came highest.

He arrives on time, at three twenty-eight, exactly two minutes before the ferry leaves. He slows down. The barrier goes up and Pappa lets the jeep roll over the gangway. Up on the bridge, the ferryman in sou'wester and oilskins raises his hand and waves.

N APRIL 2005, HE sits alone in front of the big television set in the video library, watching the funeral of Pope John Paul II.

The Bible passages being read he knows by heart.

Truly, truly, I say to you, when you were young, you used to dress yourself and walk wherever you wanted, but when you are old, you will stretch out your hands, and another will dress you and carry you where you do not want to go.

Pappa has grown so thin that he takes a rope and ties it around himself just to prevent his trousers from falling off. A life in solitude. He eats next to nothing. A slice of toast and a cup of tea for breakfast, yogurt for lunch, and a piece of meat or fish (no spices, no vegetables) in the evening. Every day, a woman comes and prepares his dinner and tidies up and washes and irons his clothes. Gradually, the number of women increases. Cecilia, who is in charge of hiring extra help, comes to the house several times a week. Pappa doesn't care all that much about food. He never did. Food is the root of all mischief and stomachaches. Wine too. Maybe a glass of beer with dinner. The windows must be kept closed, food (the kind that causes stomachaches) must be avoided, wine does not taste good and causes headaches, no excesses of any kind, a strict daily schedule will be observed.

"I have to use a rope to tie it around myself so my trousers won't fall off," he says on the phone, "but at least I dress myself."

The pope's funeral is a magnificent performance. Grand

processions. Opulent tapestries, scarlet robes, white headgear, the colors remind him of a film he once made, the one with the red room and the women dressed in white. "Every now and then," he wrote in one of his notebooks, "images return unbidden without making it clear what they want from me. Then they disappear and return and present themselves in exactly the same way. Four women dressed in white, a red room. The women move about and whisper to each other and are utterly secretive." He returns to the television screen. When the pope is laid to rest, everyone knows precisely what to do. Nothing is improvised. The choreography is symmetrical and elegant. He thinks of the last plays he directed for the stage. *The Misanthrope. The Winter's Tale.* He misses the theater. The actors. He misses getting up in the morning and lying down at night, and in between the two, going to work. That's a lot more fun than this. He is eighty-six years old, turning eighty-seven this summer, and sometimes he wonders whether solitude is overrated. Maybe he should move back to Stockholm, renounce his self-imposed exile, write a script, direct a play, or at least go to concerts, be among musicians. My father stares at the pope's coffin, a simple wooden box amidst all the pomp and circumstance. *I want one just like that,* he says to himself. A few days later he climbs into his jeep and goes to see a carpenter in Slite, an old friend. I use the word "friend" in the broadest sense here, acquaintance is a better word, my father now surrounds himself with what Strindberg called *an impersonal circle of acquaintances.* People you recognize and nod at when walking or driving by, people who, like yourself, prefer to avoid any intimacies. This is what he wants. This is the plan. He wants to be left in peace. He wants to walk from room to room in his house and not say anything to anyone. But then, in the milder days of spring following the pope's funeral, he feels exhilarated and restless. He visits the carpenter in Slite and shows him newspaper clippings and photographs, and starts explaining. The carpenter takes a sip of coffee—Bible black, no sugar. He doesn't say much, allows the old man to present his business. My father doesn't want coffee. He wants mineral water, which is put in front of him. The carpenter leans over to look at the photographs. *The pope's coffin*. A simple wooden box, says Pappa. No ornaments. The carpenter lets out an almost inaudible sigh. Well, let's see, he says. He finishes his coffee, stands up, pulls out a notepad and a pencil, sits back down, outlines and sketches, we don't have cypress in this part of the world, he mumbles without waiting for a response, ordinary pine or spruce will have to do, and then he shoves the notepad across the table for Pappa to take a look. Pappa leans over and studies the sketch, nods.

"Yes," he says, shoving the notepad back across the table. "I want one exactly like that."

THERE WERE NO STAIRCASES in the house at Hammars, and toward the end there were no doorsills either. When my father became dependent on a wheelchair, Cecilia removed all the doorsills so that he, at least in theory, could move freely from one room to the other.

He didn't like the wheelchair, couldn't figure out how to maneuver it.

He missed putting on his chalk-white sneakers and taking walks on the beach or bicycling through the forest.

He missed the red jeep and the sound it made when you stepped on the gas and sped along the narrow roads, for example from Hammars to Dämba to see a film, or from Hammars to the church to light a candle for Ingrid, or from Hammars to the ferry dock to buy newspapers in Fårösund.

Toward the end, he no longer had a word for *loss*, he no longer said *I miss this* or *I long for that*, the assumption that he missed his jeep, his bicycle, his sneakers, is mine. When I say *toward the end*, I mean the last weeks of summer before he died. Some of his children were at Hammars during this period, we spoke with him, one at a time, but I no longer recorded our conversations on tape. He didn't have a word for *tape*, either. Or work. Or children.

On the next to last recording we made—it was in the spring— he wonders whether he should go find his sneakers and his jeep and go on a journey. His whole life he has longed for Hammars. Just to be able to be there. Not having to pack his bags every autumn and return to Stockholm or Munich. To be. But now that he finally *is* here, he thinks it might be time to go. Maybe to the city. To Stockholm.

He didn't like to travel, it gave him stomachaches, he hated the thought of moving from one place to another. The thought of unfamiliar streets, unfamiliar rooms, unfamiliar faces, unfamiliar voices filled him with dread. Travel stole time from meticulously planned and deeply ingrained routines, and not least from what he proudly called the *exercise of his profession*.

Many people like to travel, but for those who don't, the experience is roughly like this: A trip is not only the trip itself, it's all the time you spend *thinking* about it before you leave and after you come back home. I don't know whether *thinking* is the right word here. You may very well manage not to *think* about it, but you can't avoid feeling permeated by it in some way, the trip has taken up residence inside you, and you have to live with it for some time before embarking on it and for some time after it has come to an end—in this way, it's a lot like the flu.

I have long runways for takeoff and landing, he used to say.

Despite all this—at the end of his life, while still able to remember the word *longing*, he longed to travel. Away from the island and back to the city.

HE   Yes, I long for a little three-room flat somewhere, near Hedvig Eleonora Church ... *Storgatan, Jungfrugatan, Sibyllegatan* ... I miss going to the theatre, going to concerts. I find it difficult to let go of all of that.

He places his hands on the wheels of the wheelchair to show her that they remain motionless, regardless of how he moves his arms.

HE   I can see myself living in that little flat ... do you remember the one on Grev Turegatan? It was the ideal place for me. That's where I would have wanted to live now in the autumn of my life. But that's not likely to happen, is it?

He lets out an exaggerated sigh.

SHE   I don't know ... maybe?
HE   Maybe?
SHE   Yes, why not?
HE   I don't know ... to be present at an orchestra rehearsal, I don't know if you can picture it, there is nothing like it. You open the door and walk into a gigantic concert hall ...

———

Seven years later I'm lying on the sofa in the living room at home in Oslo. My husband and our daughter are asleep upstairs. It's night or early morning and many hours until dawn. I'm listening to the tapes. It's four a.m. I'm lying with the Mac in my lap, writing down every word we said, and while I'm transcribing, I'm also translating from Swedish to Norwegian. The act of translating is liberating—perhaps because it gives me ownership of the voices. I've borrowed Eva's big blue headphones. On the tape, my father says that he would like to go back to Stockholm, move into a small three-room flat near Hedvig Eleonora Church, he has two months left to live, and even though I don't remember this conversation, I can tell by my voice that I'm deliberating whether to contradict him (yes, but, Pappa, you can't move now, this, *here*, is where you wanted to be) or to humor him (of course you should go back to Stockholm and live in the city), it turns into a kind of compromise. *I don't know*, I say, *maybe?* And then I say: *Yes, why not?* We do not talk all that much about death, he has more than enough grappling with the life he is living now. The forgetfulness. The dreams that come and go. The women that come and go. All the windows that are thrown wide open. The women don't know that the windows must be kept closed. Cecilia hasn't told them. It's spring and the sun is shining. The fly buzzes on the windowsill. He talks a lot about his eye. He worries about the surgery scheduled for June 18 at three p.m. at Visby Infirmary. Worries about the drive there. The procedure. Having to check himself into the infirmary. It takes about an hour and a half to travel from Hammars to Visby. He used to say that no Fårö oldster would voluntarily check himself into Visby Infirmary.

Check yourself into Visby Infirmary and you'll never get out alive. Better to die at your post than at Visby Infirmary.

Charting the heart's early development:

The nascent heart tube begins to elongate in the middle of the fifth week of gestation, initially taking the shape of the letter C and developing into a compressed S.

When I was pregnant with Eva, long before I knew she would be called Eva, I woke up one night with cramps and bleeding. Two pregnancies had gone wrong over the past years. One at week twelve. One at week ten. When I woke up that night, with ominous symptoms, I was in my eleventh week.

It was the summer of 2003, and we (my husband, my son, and my husband's two children) had been on the island for a few days, staying at Ängen. We had brought the dog, not the one we have now, but the one we had before, called Brando, after Marlon. He was a large dog and I hadn't worked up the courage to tell my father that we had brought him with us, so every night when the old man dropped by for what he called *evening sittings*, we locked the dog into one of the upstairs bedrooms and hoped he wouldn't bark or whimper. I didn't want my father to get angry, to start going on about how we had to *lose* the dog, or *leave* the island, or choose between *him and the dog* because he didn't want a fucking mongrel running around. I was nauseous all the time, and most days I couldn't get out of bed. I didn't play with the children. I didn't write. I didn't go to afternoon screenings at Dämba. I imagined myself throwing up in the middle of the movie and being banished for all eternity. My sister Ingmarie had been nauseous too, she said, when she was pregnant. It runs in the family, she added. I liked that she said *runs in the family*.

My father called on the telephone and said in his most gentle voice: "Why don't you come today? You can have a blanket for your tummy. That will help calm the nausea. We're seeing the one with Gregory Peck."

"Which one?"

"You know the one. One of the two . . . the one with Gregory Peck."

When I woke up that night, frightened that I might be losing the baby, my husband roused the two eldest children and told them that we had to go to the hospital, and that they must look after their little sister, make sure she had some breakfast, and that they mustn't forget to walk the dog, but not down by Hammars where the old man could see them, instead they should walk into the forest and down toward the moor. And then we took the car and drove to the hospital in Visby. In the car, I said: "Better to die at your post than at Visby Infirmary."

To which my husband replied: "Sometimes you attach too much importance to what your father says."

The ferrymen had already been informed, they knew where we were headed and why. On that morning the ferry waited for us rather than the other way around.

The hospital corridors were quiet, the midwife was quiet. She whispered—that's how I remember it—that I needed to see the doctor and have an ultrasound. She helped me gather my things and sent us even farther down the corridor.

———

I remember lying on the doctor's examining table in a dark cubicle, only the ultrasound machine emitting light.

I remember covering my face with my hands.

After a while, the doctor touched my arm.

"Look," he said.

My husband took my hand in his.

The doctor pointed at the screen and moved his finger carefully around the sonogram, as though showing us a rare map, and then, because we couldn't quite believe what we were seeing and what he was telling us, he turned up the sound so we could hear the steady beating of the heart.

———

On the next to last recording, my father says he would like to live in a three-room flat, then he says he would like to live in a one-room flat, then he opens the door and walks into a concert hall of such impressive proportions that birds fly around inside it.

HE   And I open the door and there are one hundred and fifty musicians and I know that a great and unanalyz-able . . . non-analyzable . . . indescribable experience awaits me now. A Beethoven symphony. Or the *St. Matthew Passion* with full choir and orchestra. It is overwhelming. Impossible to describe. This is the best life has to offer.

SHE   Is that the best life has to offer?

HE   That's it. Yes. It's the best there is.

DÄMBA IS MADE UP of a main house, an annex, a cinema, and an old windmill that has been turned into a small apartment with a kitchenette on the first floor, a narrow flight of stairs, and a bedroom with an enormous bed on the top floor. When my siblings and I were younger, bringing our girl- and boyfriends to Fårö for the summer, the windmill was reserved for the newly-in-love.

"With some determined fucking," my father said, pointing at the four windmill blades that had remained motionless for the last hundred years, "the blades will start spinning again."

Inside the cinema, four sloping steps lead to the projection room. A steep narrow staircase, not unlike a ladder, leads from the projection room to Cecilia's office, which for a while also served as an editing room.

If you walk a straight line from the cinema, across the moor, past the lilac hedge, and through the garden, you'll end up at the foot of a modest wooden staircase with a blue banister. The staircase will lead you to the main house entrance. When you enter the main house, you are met by a dizzying flight of stairs.

The annex was originally built with an external staircase, so to get from the first to the second floor, you had to go outside and

up and inside again. Since then, the annex has been renovated
and the stairs relocated inside the building.

During his forty years on the island, my father worked with
local architects, carpenters, and woodworkers. He never tired
of renovating and expanding the houses. I read somewhere that
the coffin maker from Slite had worked on building many of the
staircases.

My husband, our daughter, our new dog, and I moved to the
island in late summer 2008 and lived there for a year. Now
that my father was dead, the houses (Hammars, Ängen, the
Writing Lodge, and Dämba) had to be looked after until their
fate had been resolved. During the first autumn and winter,
we lived at Ängen, when spring arrived we moved to Dämba.
Eva went to the local kindergarten. I told my husband and
Eva that we were *islanders* now, and they didn't object, but the
islanders themselves didn't seem to agree. We were outsiders.
We didn't belong.

That first autumn, having just moved from Oslo to Fårö, Eva
received a letter from my father-in-law, the university librarian. Eva was almost five years old, and the letter was met with
much ado, since this was the first time she had ever received
mail addressed to her. The envelope contained a postcard—a
glossy picture of a gray-brown kitten inside a blue velvet purse.
    The back of the card said:

Dear, dearest Eva,

*Here comes a kitty cat all the way from Norway to Sweden
to say hello to you! Can you see that it has white paws?
Grandpa and Grandma can't wait to see you again. Today I
walked past your old school in the park, but all the children
were hiding inside, so I only heard their voices.*

When, after a long winter at Ängen, we moved to Dämba, my
father-in-law had died. The summer, too, was long. And quiet
and very hot and clammy. Every night we carried mattresses
and sheets down to the room with the two grand pianos. Käbi
used to play on both of them, practicing on one and giving her
recitals on the other. Now they were covered with dark blankets, like horses in winter.

The room with the two pianos was the coolest one in the
house, and we all sprawled out on the floor.

One late morning in August, my husband took the car and
headed for Oslo, it would take him two days with an overnight
stay in Örebro, where he would meet the woman with the slender wrists. He had been planning it for months, but I didn't know
that then. He started the car and drove away quickly. I remember noticing how fast he was going, much too fast on these narrow dirt roads, but, then again, he had two ferries to catch. We
were moving back home to Oslo. He had the dog with him and
most of our things. Eva and I and the older children were flying
back a few days later. When I could no longer see or hear the

car, I walked across the moor and over to the bench outside the cinema and sat down. I had the key to the cinema in my pocket. That whole year, I carried all the keys to all the houses around with me, and sometimes I would wander through all the rooms at Hammars, sit in the chairs, lie down in the beds, rummage through the kitchen drawers, drink wine in the study, and open all the windows.

The houses had been put up for sale, and I thought to myself that all of this—abandoned rooms, abandoned houses—would soon come to an end.

I unlocked the rust-red door to the cinema. I walked past a large tapestry depicting the characters from *The Magic Flute*, Sarastro, Monostatos, Pamina, Tamino, Papagena, Papageno, Queen of the Night, and up the sloping steps to the projection room and further up to Cecilia's old office. After my father died, Cecilia left the island for good. *My work here is done*, she said. The office was left in turmoil. Papers and binders that nobody had managed to sort through. We have to get together soon, I thought (as I did every time I came in here), and put everything in order. I found a vacuum cleaner and took it downstairs and vacuumed the green armchairs and the green carpet. There were dead flies everywhere. Then I carried the vacuum cleaner back up to the office, switched off the lights, walked out, locked the door, and sat down again on the bench.

It was then that I noticed a young man on a bicycle coming my way. He was struggling to cross a cattle guard and I could see right away that he wasn't from the island.

The bicycle was white, he had dark hair and wore brown shorts and a large black T-shirt. He pedaled all the way to where I was sitting and rode around in a loop, as if to show me that he was here, that he had arrived.

"Hello," he said in English, but with an accent.

"Hello," I said, and looked away.

He came to a stop right in front of me. Had I stretched out my arm, I could have touched him, or better still, knocked him off his bicycle.

"Is this the cinema?" he said.

"Yes," I said. "Actually, though, it's a barn."

"The master's personal cinema," he said with rehearsed reverence.

I didn't reply.

"I have come all the way from Germany," he said.

"On a bicycle?" I said.

He gave a long and loud laugh. And then he stopped just as abruptly as he had begun.

"No, I rented the bicycle in Fårösund. But I've come all the way from Germany . . . to meet *the master*."

"Where in Germany?"

"Hamburg."

"Well, I'm sorry to say, the man you've come to see is dead," I said. "He died two years ago."

"I know that," he said, lowering his voice, "but I can feel his presence everywhere. This is a kind of pilgrimage for me, you see."

He got off his bicycle, let it keel over on the grass, and seated himself next to me on the bench.

"I saw you come out of there just now," he said. "You have keys. Could you let me come inside and have a look?"

"No," I said.

He was dumbfounded. And took some pleasure in showing it. As if instead of saying "no" I had said, *Show me what you look like when you are dumbfounded.*

"No?!" he said.

"No," I said.

He stared at me.

I got up from the bench, stuck my hands in my dress pockets, glancing at the bicycle he had tossed down on the grass. I took my hands out of my pockets, pulled the bicycle up onto its wheels and leaned it against the limestone wall.

"But I just saw you come out," he said. "You have keys."

"That's true," I said, "but now I don't want to go inside again. It was a bit strange . . ." I cut myself off, didn't feel that I should have to explain myself.

He stood up.

"You don't want to?" he said, raising his voice. "You don't want to give up five minutes of your so-called valuable time to show me his cinema?"

"No," I said.

"No?"

He sat down and got up again and said almost pleadingly: "But I've come such a long way."

"Well, I'm sorry."

He walked over to his bicycle, climbed onto it, and started pedaling. A moment later, he stopped and turned.

"You are not a very nice person," he cried. "I meet people all the time, and they are nice, but you are not nice."

He cycled across the clearing and out onto the road.

"Wait," I called.

His legs were pale, jutting out from his brown shorts.

"Wait," I repeated, and started running after him.

He stopped and turned, putting his feet to the ground. I ran out onto the road. We stood on either side of the cattle guard. He couldn't have been much older than twenty.

"Come back," I said, aiming for a calm voice. "I'll open the door and show you the cinema."

"No," he said, crossing his arms.

"It's okay," I said and moved a little closer. "It was just so strange when you showed up. I was all alone, and then you suddenly appeared and then . . . but come back and I'll show you around."

"No," he said. "It's too late now. I don't want to."

He turned around, put his feet to the pedals and rode off. As I watched him disappear down the road, he turned around one last time, shouting: "I don't want to! You ruined it for me!"

Sometimes that summer I would run up and down the stairs in the main house just to see how many rounds I could do without stopping to catch my breath. I told Eva about the ghost in the lilac hedge. My father, her grandfather, whom she almost couldn't remember, used to say that if you didn't want the ghost to visit, you had to lay out forks and knives on all the steps, Eva thought we should do the same thing, but when night fell, she asked me why I had told her that stupid story about the forks and knives, because now she was scared of falling asleep.

Teach them the beauty of forgetfulness, sings Lou Reed in the song about all the things you have to remember to teach the children. I remember almost nothing of my father's funeral. I remember that the minister wore a rose in her long, flowing hair, and that she sang a lullaby from Gotland, its lyrics incomprehensible because of the local dialect. I remember that the cellist performed the Sarabande from Bach's fifth cello suite. I remember that he who once played Hamlet broke down and cried so hard that he started sobbing. I remember the red flowers on the coffin. I remember the endless processions, in and out of cars, in and out of the church, and then, finally, the long walk through the church cemetery and to the grave waiting to receive him.

TOWARD THE END OF the sixth and final day of recording, my father and I made a plan. We were, if not well under way, at least making progress with the work—the project—the book—and when you are making progress with something, the question of *how to proceed* inevitably arises. It is May 10, 2007, and I have to go back to Oslo for a few weeks.

"But," I say.

"But?" he says.

"But," I say, "I'll be back soon, and then we can pick up where we left off."

This was the new plan. I will leave, but I will come back. We will pick up where we left off.

But when I came back, he was so frail that it was impossible to continue, to meet at agreed-upon times, to record conversations on tape. He had forgotten everything. The project. The tapes. Me.

The work we had done so far could be described as follows: After every meeting, we close with a ritual. First, we repeatedly agree that it's time to finish. Then we talk a little bit about what we'll have for lunch, and finally I wheel him over to his desk. This is where the calendar is kept, also called the book, or the diary. I leaf through its pages and find the date for our next meeting and write down the agreed-upon time. Every now and then we discuss whether to meet at a different time than eleven, only to conclude that there is no better time than eleven. And then, as though to seal the agreement, we write our names on the page of the calendar. I write his name and he writes mine. This ritual lasts for about twenty minutes. He takes his time writing. My name consists of four letters. He sits in his wheel-chair, I stand next to him and he takes his time writing my name in the calendar. His hand is shaking. I have to bury my own hands in my dress pockets to keep myself from yanking the pen away from him and finishing the task myself, *one* n, *and then another* n, *there, we're done.*

He needs assistance—or help—or care—around the clock. Six women take turns caring for him, with Cecilia making all the decisions. Cecilia who operated the projectors when he still went to the cinema at Dämba, Cecilia who found him in the ditch when he had driven off the road, Cecilia who removed the bullets from his rifle when Ingrid died.

The plan was to meet every day. But that is not how it turned out. We didn't meet every day, not even every other day. In the course of those final months, even before I left to go to Oslo for two weeks, he took a rapid turn for the worse. I don't know whether *rapid turn* is the right expression here. The choreography of aging is complex. An intricate combination of quick and slow. There are no breaks. Not during the day, not at night. Sometimes we just listened to music. Once, I asked him if he wanted to put on a blues record for a change, or jazz, or maybe gospel? What about Mahalia Jackson? But he said, *Ssshh*. Or he said *Bach*. And then he shook his head.

When the cellist Pablo Casals was asked why he still practiced six hours a day, even after he had turned ninety, he replied, "because I think I'm making progress."

Sometimes he wasn't able to get up in the morning, and then I would just sit by his bedside. Other times, one of the women who cared for him called me on the phone and said: He's too tired today. Or: Today is not a good day. Or: He doesn't want you to come today. I didn't know who made these day-to-day decisions. Was it him or one of the women or Cecilia? I didn't know whether he knew who I was when I wasn't there. Days and faces and voices blurred into one. A fog spread over Hammars and everyone who came and went.

Cecilia with the long, dark hair and the beautiful face wrote a note and put it on the kitchen table: *He wants to be left in peace! Don't come here tomorrow!*

Cecilia had her own plan and her own arrangement that did not coincide with mine.

———

My father had the rare ability to make others feel as though they were the *one and only*. That they were seen, heard, chosen. He would take you by the hand and say, *Come with me*, and for a brief or a long moment you might think you were the first person he has ever said this to. That it was you and him against the world. Even when he was very old and one-eyed and frail and forgetful and the abscess in his mouth had grown so big that it obstructed his tongue, when he was no more than a heap of skin and bones stuck in a wheelchair behind seven closed doors, even then he had this ability. *Stay with me. Don't abandon me. You are the only one I let come close.*

Perhaps he said: We are so alike, you and I. Prodigal children. Brothers in the night.

You are loved, you are not loved, you could have been loved, you were loved, you are the most beloved. If Pappa had been a song, it would have been—thinking of all the women, all the breakups, all the regrets and all the words—a song with more than a little dash of country and blues, two genres of music he himself didn't care much for, or know much about.

I'm trying to understand something about love here, and about my parents, and why solitude played such a significant role in their lives, and why they, more than anything in the whole world, were so afraid of being abandoned.

Here is from a love letter written in 1958, addressed to Käbi, the fourth of the five wives:

Today I received four most enchanting letters from a
HIGHLY BELOVED PERSON. In one of these let-
ters she asks why I love her so much, and why "her in
particular."
Should I attempt to answer, or should I dodge the question
with a haze of beautiful words that easily flow from the pen.
The thing about LOVE is that it is such a peculiar and mis-
used and sad word besides, so I don't want to love you.
But maybe I shall nonetheless attempt to say something
about all that fills me and rises and falls inside me like so
many waters.

When he moved to Hammars for good, Cecilia made him a
promise. He had never been like a father to her, I don't believe
they thought about things that way, not a suitor, either, nor a
brother, nor a friend. So, what were they? I know they conducted regular morning meetings. I know they wrote messages
to each other on yellow notepad paper, void of emotion but full
of abbreviations—FYI, ASAP, e.g., etc., i.e. Short messages
about practical things: the house, the cinema, bills, repairs. My
father was not a practical man, he could never, like my father-
in-law, have gone into the forest, found a piece of wood, and
carved himself a knife or ax handle, but he understood the
value of being practical. A proper piece of workmanship. Doing
things right.

"You have to be practical, my heart. Always. In love as well
as in work. *Especially* in love. Impractical love is doomed. You
can't—how do I say this?—you can't build a house with a fistful
of sand and a million beautiful words. Are you listening to me?"

———

Throughout his life, my father elicited promises from women, the first was his mother, dark-eyed Karin, the last was Cecilia.

What will become of me when I'm too old to take care of myself?

The question haunts him long before there are any noticeable signs.

He is brimming with energy, the flat in Stockholm has been sold. Finally he can live at Hammars all year-round. He is eighty-four years old, it's springtime, windflowers everywhere. He is looking forward to his new life as a Fårö oldster. So why is he asking this question now?

A girl is standing at the railing, face averted, she is staring down into the water as though planning to jump. He is on his way to Fårösund, to buy newspapers. The rain pours down. The girl stands perfectly still. He would like her to turn around and look at him. She is young, he can tell by her slender back. The ferry throbs. The rain pours down, and he switches on . . . what's that word? It all comes to a halt. Around him, everything continues, but inside him something comes to a halt. The girl doesn't turn. It rains, the girl stares down into the water, leaning far across the edge and he wonders whether she wants to jump and he switches on . . . well, what do you call them . . . ? The things you switch on in the car when it rains and they move back and forth and go swish-swish-swish?

He is sitting in his jeep, rain pouring down, and he can't think of the word "windshield wipers," and what the hell will things come to when I can no longer articulate myself? Once my hip and my eye fail me, once my language disappears?

All his life, he wrestled with language, with writing. The yellow notepads and the pens. The strict rules he would like to break, but doesn't quite have the nerve to break, not in his writing, only on the film set, surrounded by actors and coworkers—people who know how to do their jobs. His colleagues. It's a beautiful word—*colleagues*—but when he sits down to write, he's on his own. No one around but ghosts. And the occasional bloody critic (*I despise you and hate you and hope that evil will befall you, and more than anything I hope that at least once in your life you will come face-to-face with your own spineless self*). The silence in his study is not entirely benign. The words do not come easily, or they come in the wrong order. The sentences become entangled and have neither beginning nor end. "The limits of my language mean the limits of my world," Wittgenstein said, but what happens now, asks the old man, what happens now that I am about to lose my language? Soon nothing left but shards.

He sat up in bed and thought of Strindberg. *How the hell did you do it?* And Strindberg replied: *I live in a confusion of tongues.*

What can be said about the task of writing can also be said about the task of growing old. Once again, invoking Strindberg: "This disparity between myself and my landscape strains my nerves to such a degree that I am about to go to pieces and flee." And yet . . . every now and then it's actually fun to write. It's easy. Every now and then, I can write about anything any-where, I can stand on my head and write. The world expands. The world is new. In situations like these, he could have said, one might dare utter the word "grace." When the day and the light and the writing appear easy.

But growing old is nothing like that.

I think that growing old is hard, grueling, unglamorous work with very long hours.

Strindberg glances disapprovingly at him from the wall every time he leaves his desk and walks through the silent rooms of his house, like a dance hall with a thousand windows, he thinks.

"So many things become crucial when you attempt to examine an event in retrospect and have the blueprint in front of you," my father wrote in one of his three autobiographical novels about his parents, "an event that, moreover, consists of only a few aimlessly floating shards. You have to add common sense and a good deal of imagination. At times, I can hear their voices, but only faintly. They encourage me, or they reproach me, saying 'that's not *at all* how it was. That's *not* what really happened.' "

One day he summoned Cecilia to a meeting. Listen here, Cecilia, I trust you. I don't have many years left. I've started forgetting things. Words. "Windshield wipers," for instance. For heaven's sake, it's nothing to worry about. It happens with age. I'm not complaining, I'm eighty-four years old, I'm not whining, but I am a bit astonished: Well, well—I'm turning into an old fogey. It all seems somewhat comical to me, my body that won't cooperate, the ailments, there are many forms of astonishment, and this is one of them. Astonishment keeps me company. But . . . (he places his large hand on top of her long, slender one) . . . you must promise to do what I ask of you, and not leave before it's over, and what I am asking is this:

I do not want to go to some damned old people's home. I want to die in my own house, in my own bed. I will not be left helpless and at the mercy of my children. I will not be subjected to displays of emotional brouhaha. I want peace and order around me. May my death be gentle.

THE FIRST TIME HE said he wanted to visit his mother at his family house, Våroms, in Duvnäs in Dalarna, I said: But your mother is dead, Pappa, she died forty years ago. This made him angry and he refused to speak to me and asked Cecilia to call for a taxi. I don't know whether the taxi was meant for him or for me. Cecilia shrugged and continued what she was doing, and after a little while he had forgotten the whole thing. The second time he said he wanted to visit his mother at Våroms, I replied: But I'm not sure how we'll get there, or if she's even at home. He looked at me for a long time, *What on earth is she talking about?*, and then he asked Cecilia to call for a taxi. The third time he mentioned visiting his mother, I didn't want him to involve Cecilia and I didn't want any more talk of a taxi, so I told him that, yes, I would like to go with him to Våroms.

P ERHAPS I COULD LIE here, he said, or words to that effect. Yes, but wait, said the church sexton. As a rule, the next of kin chooses the gravesite, but the sexton refrained from pointing this out to my father. Who has sovereignty over the body, the living or the dead? *Are* we our dead body? If so, we *aren't* for very long. The body turns to dust and then it hardly matters to it where it is buried—as long as it is buried. Or cremated. Or lost at sea, like so many here on the island throughout the centuries. Two paintings adorn the church walls, a larger one from 1618 and a smaller one from 1767, both depicting seal hunters adrift at sea. I imagine that the sexton was thinking about those men who, hundreds of years ago, huddled together on the ice floe in the freezing cold. Now it's spring, the sun is shining on the two elderly gentlemen, the sexton and my father, but neither of them takes off his jacket, blessed is the earth that receives us again and again since the dawn of man. My father gazes out across the graveyard with its tall trees and scattered headstones. The two men do not speak much. Come, says the sexton, if we walk a bit further I will show you an even nicer spot.

When you walk across the graveyard, the way they did that day in 2005 or 2006, you come to a stone wall, and behind it there is a field where the lambs graze in the summer.

Here, in a corner, against the stone wall?

My father and the sexton stood there for a while. A mild wind fluttered through the crowns of the ash trees. Neither of them spoke. How long did they stand there? Long enough for my father, or so the story goes, to make up his mind.

EVERY SUMMER, A YELLOW welcome note lay on the kitchen table—at Ängen or Dämba or Karlberga.

MONDAY, 7 P.M.
Beloved
Youngest Daughter!
Warm
Welcome Wishes
From
YOUR OLD FATHER

Come see me tomorrow at around eleven
—but only if you feel like it.

WHEN I WAS NINETEEN he traveled to Greece, he called it time travel—back to antiquity. He defied his dizzying fear of travel—the fear of freedom, the fear of the unknown, the fear of losing his footing—and flew from Stockholm to Athens, where he was received at the airport by a procession of distinguished-looking individuals with ribbons of honor across their chests, suits and ties and dresses, TV cameras and microphones, flashes and clicks and a throaty female voice shouting louder than all the other voices: *Welcome, Maestro!* He was scheduled to direct Euripides's *The Bacchae* at the Royal Dramatic Theatre in Stockholm in six months' time, and traveled to Greece with his very own troupe of assistants, technicians, a choreographer, and a literary adviser. They came to learn, they came to see, they came to visit the Oracle of Delphi and to climb around the Great Theatre of Epidaurus.

Ingrid came along too, but mostly to hold his hand. I'm not sure why he brought me. Pappa and I had not spoken much during the last few years, I lived in New York, he lived in Stockholm, I was a teenager, he was *your old father*, which is what he called himself the few times a year he telephoned me. There was (as he had already pointed out when I was little) a vast age difference between us, not always easy to know what to talk about, but then, one time, he suggested—I imagine baffling both of us—that I should come along with him to Greece. Fly to Stockholm and join him and Ingrid on their trip to Athens. I was studying literature at university and could conceivably contribute to discussions about Euripides. *Well, well, look at this, she's at university now, studying literature and putting on airs. Next thing you know, I'll have to stand idly by and watch her become a critic. I will not have it! I will cut her out of my will. Two things, my heart: I don't want you to become a critic and I don't want you to talk disparagingly about the royal family. Queen Silvia of Sweden is an admirable queen. Just look at how beautifully she carries herself.*

It would be a trip back to the age of great theatre, he said, a pilgrimage.

In the car on the way to the airport, Ingrid was upset because I was wearing ripped jeans.

To Pappa: "Doesn't she have proper traveling clothes?"

To me: "Don't you have proper traveling clothes? Couldn't you at least have chosen a pair of jeans without holes in them?"

Pappa was dreading the trip and had taken Valium. His voice was remarkably calm, but not in a calming way. It was as if he had left himself behind and sent someone else in his place, equipped with his clothes, his limbs, his distinct features and an eerie pre-recorded voice. He said he agreed with Ingrid, but didn't she realize that young girls nowadays bought jeans with ready-made rips in them, that my jeans weren't actually old, but quite to the contrary *brand-new*, and that the holes and rips and tears on my thighs and knees and down my calves weren't a sign of slovenliness, but rather proof that I had attempted to dress up for our little trip.

He turned and looked at me, smiling proudly.

We flew first class. Ingrid and Pappa sat in the second row, I sat in the first. Next to me sat an Englishman who took up all of his and most of my seats. He drank whiskey, read the *Financial Times*, and glared disapprovingly at my ripped jeans, my knees were cold, my arms were cold.

The seats were spacious, but I squeezed up against the window, wishing I could crawl out of it and vanish. I looked at the clouds below and listened to Pappa's anxious breathing behind me. The businessman opened his paper and spread himself out even more. Now I had his newspaper right in my face and his elbow poking my side. Perhaps he hadn't even noticed that I was sitting there in the seat next to him? Perhaps he hadn't seen my ripped jeans and bare knees after all? Maybe I was invisible? What was worse? To be glared at or be treated as if you weren't even there? Visible or invisible? Whatever I was, I had his newspaper in my face and his elbow poking my side, all of which my father must have observed through the crack between our seats, because now he stood up, leaned over and extended his arms as if he were a golden eagle ready to swoop down and attack, addressing the businessman in his peculiar American-German-Swedish accent: "Get your fucking arm away from her seat. And your newspaper too. That is my daughter sitting there beside you! My daughter!"

The businessman turned bright red. Unable to come up with a reply, he folded his newspaper and removed his elbow. All this while my father hovered.

I almost felt sorry for the businessman and blushed when he said: "I apologize, miss."

My father made a sound, a combination of a snort and a neigh, after which he sat back down and refrained from speaking another word for the remainder of the flight.

———

In 340 BCE, the architect Polykleitos the Younger built a large amphitheater in the small town of Epidaurus, birthplace of Asclepius, the god of healing and medicine. The theater was the most important venue for all who were sick and wanted to be healed, large enough to accommodate more than 13,000 spectators. The acoustics at the theater are such that you can hear what the actors are saying, no matter where you are sitting. Previously, it was believed that the wind carried the sound, or that the actors' masks doubled as amplifiers. Later it was found that the steps serve as acoustic traps that filter out noise such as wind. This is due to the phenomenon of "virtual pitch" whereby the listeners themselves, even those far in the back, fill in the missing tones.

The evening before we left Athens for Epidaurus, we had dinner at a restaurant. Pappa and I had not had dinner with strangers or been to a restaurant together since that one time when I was a child and Mamma and I showed up at a swanky restaurant in Munich and he refused to hug me because I sneezed. I sneezed, not because I had a cold, like he thought, but because I hadn't seen him for almost a year and my nose started tickling the moment he laid eyes on me. *Would he notice that my braces were gone? Would he think I was pretty?* But now, here we were at a restaurant in Athens, surrounded by Swedish and Greek scholars and theatre people, I was nineteen and no longer little, and Pappa sat there in his plaid flannel shirt, saying "yes, please" to wine even though he didn't like wine, and "yes, please" to bread before dinner, even though he didn't eat bread before dinner, and I noticed that he had combed his hair in an offbeat fashion, over the top of his head in a kind of *comb-over*, and that his

English pronunciation bordered on the comical, and I wondered whether the others around the table thought so too, and whether it was true, what he used to say about himself, that in many situations he felt as though he were his own cousin.

He raised his wineglass, pointed at the bread, and, in a voice that sounded like it was borrowed from some actor about to play a flâneur strolling down the boulevards of the world, he said, "I would like to make a toast to the fantastic invention that is *this* wine and *this* bread."

Everyone joined him in the toast, after which he somewhat lost his zest. When the food arrived, he quietly asked the waiter if he might have a glass of beer.

It had been a long day of guided tours and lectures when my father and I climbed all the way up to the top row of seats at the Theatre of Epidaurus, finally sitting down. Far below, on the stage, people were walking around and talking. We could hear their voices, hear what they were saying, but didn't grasp all the words. Some spoke Swedish, some English, some Greek. Standing by herself, some way from the others, I noticed a girl. I couldn't see her face, she was young, maybe a few years older than me. She stood perfectly still, wearing a large wide-brimmed black hat and black sunglasses, looking up at the sky. The sun had begun to set, the light was warm and gray and red all at the same time.

"We can't re-create light like this onstage no matter what tricks we might have up our sleeves," Pappa said, pointing.

I looked from the girl to the green cypresses and the ochre mountain peaks beyond them. A wind blew up. The girl's sun hat tore off her head and scurried along the ground.

The voices below died down and everyone turned in unison toward the mountains, as if deliberating where the wind came from.

"I can see why . . ." my father said, and put his arm around my shoulders. He fell silent.

"What?"

"No. I don't know. Being here makes you think."

"About what?"

"About how thousands of years ago people would sit right here, just like you and I are sitting now. . . I mean, this is one hell of a concert hall."

His arm still lay heavily around my shoulder. I moved a little closer.

"What I was going to say," he said, "is that I can see why they thought the gods were right nearby."

W<small>E ARE SITTING BY</small> the brown-stained bench at Hammars, looking out across the gravel drive. The jeep. The bicycle. The pine trees. He is sitting in his wheelchair, I'm sitting in a folding chair. He asks me to go get his shoes.

"Which shoes, Pappa?"

"*My* shoes, the ones in the bedroom closet."

"Your sneakers?"

"The white ones."

"But you're already wearing them."

"Good. Because we have to leave now."

"Where are we going?"

"To see Mother, at Våroms."

"Can I come with you?"

"Of course you're coming with me. I was thinking we might take the train, but I've decided to take the jeep."

"But Pappa, I don't have a driver's license. I don't know how to drive."

He is irritated and squirms in his wheelchair.

"You aren't the one who's driving!"

"Oh, okay, that's good."

"I'm driving!"

"Of course!"

"We will leave soon. And go to Våroms. Have you ever been to Våroms?"

"No, never."

"Have you been to Dalarna?"

"No."

"My heart . . . where have you actually been?"

"I've never been to Dalarna."

"Well, then I want you to listen up. First you go get my shoes, then we take the jeep—*I'm* driving. What do you think—should we stop by the church? I don't think so. It's not Saturday today, and they won't be ringing in the weekend. No bells today. One time I sat there, waiting for the bells to ring, but the bell ringer never showed up, it was six o'clock, five past six, ten past six, and I sat there waiting like an idiot . . . I wanted to light a candle for Ingrid . . . I wanted to light a candle. . . and when it was quarter past six, I took my cane and marched up the stairs to the tower and rang the goddamn bells myself. The minister found me on my way down and said that I wasn't allowed up in the tower and that there was a problem with a blown fuse. *This*, apparently, was the reason why the bells didn't ring. A blown fuse! And *I* said, well if that's the case, you might have heard about something called a *rope*. Punctuality, my heart, punctuality. And now we mustn't sit here and chitchat, you will get my shoes and we will catch the ferry. We shall take two ferries. First the little one and then the big one. Would you mind if we made a side trip to Uppsala? It's a detour, I know, but I would like to show you where I lived when I was a boy. Have you been to Uppsala?"

"No."

"No, well okay. It can't be helped. And then we will have lunch. I know of a place on the way where we can stop and rest. They have overnight accommodation and a beautiful view of the lake and good food, but under no circumstances do I want to spend the night there, we have to be at Våroms before dark. We can sit outside for a while and enjoy the beautiful weather, and you can have a glass of wine, if you like. I want mineral water. Did you know that mineral water can cause dehydration?

Something to do with the bubbles. The carbon dioxide. The salt. The doctor said I shouldn't drink mineral water. I should drink still water instead. He said I was dehydrated! Now, where were we . . . For me, the bubbles were company."

"Yes, but you can drink mineral water when we're on the road. That's okay. I won't tell anyone."

"Where are we?"

"We are on our way to Våroms."

"We are driving north."

"North?"

"North for a long stretch. Duvnäs isn't far from Borlänge, if that means anything to you? In Dalarna."

"I haven't been to Dalarna."

"No, you haven't. And here . . . ?"

"In Duvnäs?"

"In Duvnäs, yes . . . in Duvnäs . . . a little ways up the hill, just above the train tracks, you will find Våroms. I think Mother is standing at the window looking for us. It is late now. She is looking out at the road. The large birch tree casts shadows, the freight train switches tracks and the river runs black, even on the brightest days."

CECILIA TURNS TO ME and shouts: "You keep stomping in here at all hours of the day, disturbing him. It makes him restless. Don't you get that?"

She asks me to return the house key. It is her responsibility to see to it that he gets peace and quiet. That was how he wanted it. I can't just come and go as I please.

"But he asked me to come," I say.

Cecilia shrugs.

"He asked *someone* to come. I don't think he meant you."

I T WAS CHILLY THE summer he died. I have a few pictures of him and me from those last weeks. We are sitting by the brown-stained bench. We are wearing wool cardigans. He has a blanket over his legs. I have a somewhat odd-looking hat on my head, he is wearing his favorite green wooly hat.

Käbi still spends her summers at Dämba. Two of her musician friends have come to visit and they invite my husband and me over for dinner. This is when we plan the last recital.

We have allied ourselves with one of the six women; someone who would also like Pappa to hear Käbi play the piano one last time. He almost never says a word now, most of the time he just lies in bed and stares at the ceiling. At night he babbles. The woman, I will call her Anna, tells me he believes he's working on a major translation. It never ends, he tells her. She thinks it'll be good for him to get out of the house. We can't say anything to Cecilia, though, who runs the house and has planned his days according to a precisely worked-out schedule, most likely concocted together with him a long time ago: get out of bed, get dressed, eat breakfast, sit in study, sit outside on brown-stained bench, eat lunch, eat dinner, listen to radio, go to bed, and then everything all over again the next day. Things he is no longer able to do (for example, *get out of bed*), she effectively crosses off the list. The only thing she doesn't cross off the list is the omelet. Eggs have protein. Eggs are good for you. Cecilia believes in doing things the same way every day. No sudden whims. No improvisations. And now, just a few weeks before he dies, we are planning an improvisation of dizzying proportions. And then comes the day we carry him off, smuggle him out, wheelchair and all. We are strong in numbers. We take two cars. Like robbers, like thieves. We steal my father and drive from Hammars to Dämba and arrive a little before two. We help one another get him out of the car and into the wheelchair. Anna, who has brought along a number of supplies that a very old and sick man might need on an outing, all of them packed in a big black bag that I carry, wheels him across the moor. Pappa is first in line, Anna is number two, pushing the wheelchair, I am number three, carrying the bag. Walking behind me is my husband, and behind him Käbi's two musician friends. We walk and walk. At the top of the stairs with the blue banister, far in the distance, Käbi is waiting for us. She is well over eighty. She has put up her hair. She smiles. A woman's beauty lies in how she stands and how she moves. My father turns in his wheelchair and asks Anna where we are and where we are going.

"We're at Dämba," I say, running out of the line and up beside him. "We're going to see Käbi, who has promised to play for us."

We have walked and walked, never before has the moor and the garden seemed so vast. We are a small procession on a very long march. We are here at Dämba, headed for the room with the two pianos, headed for the world's smallest concert hall, and Käbi has promised to play.

Once we arrive, there is a moment of confusion. Standing at the foot of the stairs, we wonder how to get the old man up and inside.

"Come on," says one of the two musician friends, "we can do this."

The procession shifts. Anna goes to the back of the line, I stand next to her, the men position themselves around the wheelchair, and then, on *one, two, three*, they take hold of the chair with my father in it, carry it up the stairs, one step at a time, and wheel him into the living room.

When everyone has settled, Käbi sits down at the piano, raises one hand, and begins with a mazurka by Chopin. While she is playing, I look at my father, his profile, I don't know if this is where he wants to be, I don't know if he wants to be anywhere right now, he is all alone, off on an ice floe far, far out at sea, and Käbi plays her Chopin and the sunlight falls through the windows, it's two o 'clock, and then it's five past two, she plays like she has done a thousand times before, for him and for many others, and she has more to offer, the recital has been planned in detail, but when the mazurka is over and, resting her hands in her lap, she turns toward her small audience to speak, perhaps to introduce the next piece, he who was my father raises his head and looks out the window.

"I want to thank you all for this lovely evening together," he says. He speaks to everyone and no one, to day and night, to the bright afternoon sunlight rippling across the wide wooden floorboards reminiscent of piano keys.

We hold our breath, we have not heard him say this much and speak so clearly for a long time. And then he says: "It's late and the old man wants to go home."

EVERYTHING WAS READY. There was nothing left to be done. The hour had been set. The guests were on their way. The minister had written her sermon, rehearsed her song, and picked a rose for her hair. The funeral programs had been printed. The organist knew which pieces to play, the cellist too. The pallbearers had put on their Sunday best. And the next of kin were preparing to say goodbye for the last time.

Ingmarie, the eldest among us siblings, had called every single florist in Visby making sure the family's wishes were clear: red flowers *only* on and around the casket. If someone expressed an interest in sending yellow or pink or purple flowers, this should be politely discouraged by the florist in charge.

Ingmarie's mother, Else, was the first wife of the deceased. She was dead. Ellen, the second wife of the deceased and mother to four of his children, was also dead. In their day, Else and Ellen had both been celebrated dancers and choreographers. Gunvor, the third wife of the deceased and mother to my brother the airline pilot, had taught Slavic languages and worked as a translator of Yugoslav and Russian literature. Notably, she had translated Tolstoy's *Theory of Everything*. She, too, was dead. The fourth wife of the deceased, Käbi, pianist and mother to Daniel, would attend the funeral in person. As would my mother.

My mother and father were never married, she came between wife number four and wife number five, but they were good friends and colleagues, and once, when she was very young, he said to her that they were painfully connected.

His fifth and last wife, Ingrid, the mother of my sister Maria, would be exhumed from her original gravesite and soon lie next to him here in the graveyard at Fårö.

The deceased had requested a modest funeral with only the closest family in attendance, his closest friends, his colleagues, and his island-acquaintances: the women who had cared for him when he was old and sick, and the men who had built and renovated his houses.

He had given instructions regarding the guest list and specifically asked that his actors be included, not all, but a few, he missed them very much when he left the theater and moved to Hammars. And the actors came—one by one and two by two. Mr. and Mrs. Vogler and little Miss Åkerblom came. Alma and Elisabet came. Uncle Carl came. The suicides, the knights, the cuckolds, the crybabies, the musicians, and the clowns came. The bourgeoisie came. The kings and queens came and at least one prince. When the coffin was lowered into the ground, the prince sobbed so violently that he had to be supported by the *devastatingly* beautiful woman who had accompanied him and who was herself moved to tears.

The journalists and the photographers came too, but not past the stone wall. They were not allowed into the church or the churchyard. To ensure peace and quiet during the ceremony, the family had hired three guards who by no means took their task lightly, carrying it out with such bravado that you would think they were donning black suits of armor and helmets to guard the gates of fire and water. The journalists regretted bitterly having put on their best shoes, the grass around the stone wall had grown tall and they couldn't help stepping in sheep muck wherever they went. When the mourners began to arrive on foot and by car, most of them with plenty of time before it was all set to begin, the lambs hardly raised an eye.

True to tradition, the guests entered the church first and sat down, and only in the very end did the next of kin arrive, a little procession in itself, to take their seats in the front pews.

———

A few days earlier I called my mother. We hadn't really talked for a while, maybe just exchanged a few words in passing. I meant to tell her about the plans for the funeral, the program, practical things—time and place and so on. What I didn't tell her was that Pappa, as he lay dying, babbled every night, and that eventually the babbling turned into cries and rattles. I didn't tell her that Anna, who looked after him most nights, leaned over to ask what he was trying to say, and that he told her he was working on a major translation.

When I was with him during those last days, I never heard him utter the word "translation," I imagine he had forgotten the word "translation." But if what Anna said was true, it was a precise word with which to end things. To find a new language for the old, an old language for the new. Growing old, very old, as he did, was itself a work of translation—from what had been to what was to come.

———

In one of the novels about his parents, he wrote:

> *I can't claim that I have always been overly meticulous with regard to the truthfulness of my story. I have spliced, added, subtracted and discarded, but as is often the case with these kinds of games, playful as they are, the game most likely has become clearer than reality.*

———

Swedish funeral customs include a particular dress code for men that only applies to next of kin: all the men must wear white ties. I'm not a hundred percent sure, but as far as I know, Sweden is the only country where this is practiced. Funerals are the theatre of death, I believe it was Proust who wrote.

This time we traveled by plane. First from Oslo to Stockholm. Then from Stockholm to Visby. Our dresses and suits were packed in suitcases. Dresses in one suitcase and suits in the other. There were six of us: my husband, me, and the children. Three-year-old Eva was the youngest. We don't expect the youngest children to wear black, so for her we had packed a white denim skirt that she liked and a pink T-shirt.

When we arrived at the airport in Stockholm, the men's suitcase was nowhere to be found, it wasn't in Oslo, it wasn't in Stockholm, it had disappeared and could not be tracked. Our only option, if we all wanted to be properly dressed for the funeral, was to take the airport bus to Stockholm and buy new suits. The last plane to Visby left at eight so we had just a

few hours to get it done. This, then, would be my second visit
that month to the elegant Stockholm department store near the
Royal Dramatic Theatre. The first time I went with my sister to
buy funeral dresses. This time I went with my husband and our
children to buy funeral suits.

At the men's clothing department, we were greeted by a
woman with eyelashes so long and false and heavy and black
that it was all her skinny little body could do to keep them in
place. I told her we needed suits, three of them.

"Pardon?"

I repeated that we needed suits. I spoke Norwegian, not
Swedish. My voice is shrill when I speak Swedish, and I was
shrill enough as it was.

"Pardon?" said the woman again. She blinked. My son
stared at the eyelashes, turned to his stepbrother, and asked him
if he thought they hurt.

"Pardon?" said the young woman a third time. "I don't
understand . . . you're looking for a lady's suit? This is the *men's
department.*"

"Men's suits," my husband shouted in Swedish. He took a
deep breath and repeated, a little more calmly, but only a little: "We want to buy three men's suits! We're on our way to
a funeral. We have a plane to catch. We're in a hurry. Do you
understand what I'm saying?"

An elderly gentleman with a silk kerchief in his lapel pocket
and large, sensitive nostrils overheard the entire exchange and
came dashing over. He laid his hand on the young woman's arm
and nodded her away. He had measuring tape around his neck,
a pincushion in his pocket and a voice I wanted to crawl inside
of and be warmed by.

"A funeral," he began. "My condolences. My condolences."
He looked at the six of us and nodded reassuringly. "As you will
see, we have an excellent selection of men's suits. Hugo Boss.
Armani. Kenzo. We have other suits as well, not quite as expensive. I always say: one should not have to spend a fortune on a
good suit. Everything will be fine. Did I hear you say that you
have a plane to catch? Are you members of the family? Next of
kin? May I ask about the deceased? Who was he . . . a father,
a father-in-law, a grandfather? In that case, you must all wear
white ties. Let me see now, up on this stepstool here, one by one,
so I can take your measurements."

———

We were late. It's my father's funeral, and I am late. *Punctuality,
my heart, punctuality.* And all because of the white ties. Eva and
I are waiting in the car, dressed and ready, my fourteen-year-
old stepdaughter is walking back and forth outside on the moor,
she, too, is dressed and ready. It takes ten minutes to drive from
Dämba to the church, we have to be there at a quarter to twelve
and now it's eleven thirty. My plan was to arrive early, park at
the old store, and sit in the car for a while, but now we are at
the point where we *have* to leave if we want to be on time. I dig
out my cell phone and call my husband, who is still inside with
the boys.

"Are you coming?" I snap.

"We're coming," he says. "We're having a bit of a problem
tying the ties."

"Problem doing what?"

I start to yell.

Not because my father is dead, but because no one knows how to tie a tie and because we're going to be late.

"I've tied mine," says my husband, "and now I'm helping the boys with theirs. It's fine."

"It's not fine," I shout. "It's not fine. It's not fine. It's not fine. Don't ever say that it's fine."

"We'll be out soon," my husband says. "I promise. We won't be late. We have plenty of time."

"It's not fine," I cry.

I hang up and turn around and look at Eva in the backseat. Her eyes are bright blue. She is strapped in a child's seat that we had to pay extra for when we rented the car in Visby. The child's seat is also bright blue, and a little too big. Eva looks at me. I run my fingers through my hair and try to think of something to say. *I'm sorry. Don't worry. Mamma didn't mean to raise her voice.* I don't want to yell and quarrel and make a spectacle in front of my children, but I keep forgetting myself. I don't say anything to Eva. I turn away and look out the window. It's a sunny day, my father liked rain.

"Mamma," Eva says. I turn around and look at her. She picks away a crumb from her white denim skirt, fixing me with her eyes.

"Mamma," she repeats. "It's fine."

And there, across the moor, three men in black suits come running toward me, or rather, one man and two boys. They run, but their progress is infinitely slow, the wind is blowing, and they run, and three white silk ties hover like taut gull wings in the air, and when they finally arrive, my husband takes his seat behind the wheel, the boys and my stepdaughter squeeze together in the back, and we drive at full speed along the narrow roads to the church to bury him who was old and who now had died.

SHE   We have talked for a long time now.

HE   But we could keep going a bit longer . . . I've got nothing else to do.

SHE   Well then, I want to ask you about your work at the theater.

HE   Yes, go right ahead. The theater is, so to say, my thing.

SHE   Your thing?

HE   Yes.

He laughs out loud.

HE   Really. In every way. Demonstrably. Theatre . . . and film . . . and Ingrid. And everyone I hold dear. But there is no ranking or hierarchy when it comes to love. It just is.

SHE   Weren't you ever worried that devoting yourself to the little world of the theatre was somehow inconsequential . . . I mean, when the real world is the way it is?

HE   No, never inconsequential. It's like a heart that beats and goes on beating. Everything is set into motion. And if it isn't, then to hell with it.

SHE   I don't know . . .

HE   Grace is . . . it can manifest itself in the most peculiar ways. It's the same for you and me.

SHE   What do you mean, it's the same for you and me?

HE   Oh, my darling girl. You keep asking me these

questions. You know what I mean. Come, let's go eat.

SHE   Yes, we'll finish soon.

HE   Shall we have lunch?

SHE   Lunch is in forty-five minutes.

HE   Forty-five minutes?

SHE   Yes, in forty-five minutes. And Pappa, listen, there's something I have to tell you. I'm taking a little trip to Oslo, so I won't be back here until the end of the month.

HE   Where are you going?

SHE   I'm going to Oslo, where I live. And then I'll be back in two weeks. Once I'm back, we can continue working on our book. I think we should get the calendar and write down our next meeting.

HE   No.

SHE   Yes, let's do that.

She wheels him over to the desk. Leafs through the calendar. Pointing.

SHE   I'll be back here. And once I'm back, we'll start working right away. On Monday, May twenty-eighth, see, that's when we'll start working again.

HE   I don't know.

SHE   Let me just find a pen so we can write it down.

HE   But there's a problem . . . I'm having an operation on my eye.

SHE   Yes, you are, but that's on June eighth. I'll be back long before that.

HE   Yes.

She leafs through the calendar and points.

SHE   Your eye surgery is *here*. And we'll be meeting *here*.

HE   The twenty-eighth of May?

SHE   Yes. Should I write first?

HE   Yes.

SHE   See. The twenty-eighth of May. Eleven o'clock.

HE   Is that when we will meet?

SHE   Yes.

HE   Should I write your name here?

SHE   Yes.

Long silence while he is writing.

SHE   And then I'll write your name here.

HE   Yes.

SHE   It's a date.

HE   Are we done now?

F ROM A DISTANCE IT appears as if they had been summoned to a dance. First the pallbearers with the coffin between them, followed by the minister, then the family, then the actors, then the friends, neighbors, and acquaintances from the island, and finally the three men from the funeral home with their arms full of big red roses. A little girl in a white denim skirt leaps forward between the ranks toward the open grave and the stone wall and the photographers and the lambs on the other side. A woman runs after her, lifts her up, and carries her back. We must walk with the others now, she whispers. The procession emerges black and white and red in the bright sunlight. Down the road, between the church and the sea, cars motor past, but not so many, the tourist season is winding down and these are mostly islanders on their way to or from the ferry dock. Some of them slow down by the old store to cast a quick glance at the church and the graveyard above. It looks as if the mourners are holding one another by the hand, each helping the other forward in a long, long succession. No one speaks, no one says a word, and yet there are a thousand sounds here. The church bells ring, the cameras click, a gust of wind takes hold of skirt hems and trouser legs, silk scarves, suit lapels, men's ties and the minister's ivory robe. The little girl spins around in the wind, laughing.

ACKNOWLEDGMENTS

This novel's transit into English has involved many people to whom I am extremely grateful.

Thank you:

Thilo Reinhard, my brilliant translator.

Sean Kinsella and Ingvild Burkey for offering their expertise and insight on various translation queries; Becky Crook, for her stimulating input on a partial draft translation; Barbara J. Haveland for her beautiful first sample translation.

Geir Gulliksen, Ingeri Engelstad, Cathrine Narum, Ellen Hogsnes and everyone at Forlaget Oktober.

The good people at NORLA.

Jill Bialosky.

Andrew Wylie and everyone at the Wylie Agency, especially Charles Buchan, for his tireless, always intelligent and thoughtful guidance.

Simon Prosser and everyone at Hamish Hamilton.

Niels, always.

THE FOLLOWING WORKS
ARE CITED IN *UNQUIET*:

HENRY ADAMS, *The Education of Henry Adams: An Autobiography*, Modern Library, 1996.

SAMUEL BECKETT, "Ill Seen Ill Said," in *Nohow On: Company, Ill Seen Ill Said, Worstward Ho. Three Novels by Samuel Beckett*, Grove Press, 1980.

The Letters of Samuel Beckett, Volume III: 1957–1965, Cambridge University Press, 2014.

JOHN BERGER, "Mother," *in Selected Essays*, Vintage, 2003.

ELLEN HOLLENDER BERGMAN / LINA IKSE BERGMAN, *Tre frågor*, Leopard Förlag, 2006.

INGMAR BERGMAN, *Bilder*, Norstedts, 1990.

———, *Den goda viljan*, Norstedts, 1991.

———, *Söndagsbarn*, Norstedts, 1993.

GUNNAR BJÖRLING, *Skrifter, band IV*, Eriksson förlag, 1995.

ANNE CARSON, *Glass, Irony and God*, New Directions, 1995.

———, *NOX*, New Directions, 2010.

JOHN CHEEVER, "The Swimmer," *Collected Stories*, Vintage Classics, 2010.

JEAN COCTEAU, *The Art of Cinema*, Marion Boyars Publishers Ltd., 2000.

NIELS FREDRIK DAHL, *Norsholmen*, Flamme Forlag, 2010.

PETTER DASS, *Samlede verker*, Gyldendal Norsk Forlag, 1980.

BOB DYLAN AND SAM SHEPARD, "Brownsville Girl," from the album *Knocked Out Loaded*, 1986.

GUSTAVE FLAUBERT, *Madame Bovary*, translated by Lydia Davis, Penguin Classics, 2010.

WITOLD GOMBROWICZ, *Diary* (The Margellos World Republic of Letters), Yale University Press, 2012.

KÄBI LARETEI, *Vart tog all denna kärlek vägen?*, Norstedts, 2009.

BIRGIT LINTON-MALMFORS, *Karin—åldrandets tid. Karin Bergmans dagböcker 1952–1966*, Carlsson Bokförlag, 1996.

WILLIAM NICKELL, *The Death of Tolstoy*, Cornell University Press, 2010.

NORSK HELSEINFORMATIKK, "Hjertets utvikling" (Development of the heart), nhi.no.

FERNANDO PESSOA, *The Book of Disquiet*, translated by Richard Zenith, Penguin Modern Classics, 2002.

PLUTARCH, *Advice to the Bride and Groom*, edited by Sarah B. Pomeroy, Oxford University Press, 1999.

MARCEL PROUST, *The Guermantes Way* and *Sodom and Gomorrah*, *In Search of Lost Time*, translated by Terence Kilmartin, revised by D. J. Enright, Vintage, 1996.

RAINER MARIA RILKE, *Duineser Elegien*, Suhrkamp Verlag, 1975.

———, *The Notebooks of Malte Laurids Brigge*, translated by Michael Hulse, Penguin Classics, 2009.

ALBERT SCHWEITZER, *J. S. Bach*, translated by Ernest Newman, Dover Publications, 1967.

AUGUST STRINDBERG, *Days of Loneliness*, translated from the Swedish by Arvid Paulson, Phaedra Inc. Publishers, 1971.

MIKAEL TIMM, *Lusten och dämonerna*, Norstedts, 2008.

LIV ULLMANN, *Changing*, translated from the Norwegian by Liv Ullmann in collaboration with Gerry Bothmer and Erik Friis, Random House, 1977.

JEAN ELIZABETH WARD, *Du Fu: An Homage to*, Lulu Pr, 2008.

VIRGINIA WOOLF, *On Being Ill*, Paris Press, 2002.